Brand of Malice

The Cleric's Curse

TRAVIS KOWLESSAR

This book is dedicated to the friends and family who reached down into that deep, dark abyss and pulled me back up to the surface.

The love, patience, and kindness you have shared with me required a special kind of bravery, as my demons leave nary a soul un- scathed.

Not a day goes by that I don't quietly reflect on how blessed I am to have you all in my life - a life that I owe to you.

It is a debt that can never be repaid, except by ensuring that it is a life well lived, with dreams that come true. It is because of you that this book exists. It is because of you that I exist.

Thank you.

CONTENTS

CHAPTER ONE
Obscurity Fades

Ever in silence, the hillcrest village peaked from the mists which eternally drowned the moorlands below. A namesake for the loch hidden at its base, the humble hilltop village was known as 'Lakhdorian', and it was home to a meager, fragile, and broken flock. Long had the last generation of its founders passed, yet the harrowing impetus rousing this defensive perch still lived on. It was a legacy carried forth merely through hushed fireside stories and threats from tired mothers, yet it still sent fear into the hearts of all those who heard it.

The intricacies of his small village's dark history meant little to William. To him, it felt like he was at the end of the world, far away from any of the woes that the city folk moaned of. He knew merely of his own peaceful lifestyle, nestled in an obscurity that only a truly mundane existence could maintain.

"Are ye finished son?" asked his father, raising an eyebrow as he watched William daydreaming.

"Aye father, almost there!" replied William, snapping back to reality and hurriedly scooping the remaining dung onto his pitchfork before tossing it into his muck bucket. His father was an intimidating man. The six foot-five bearded giant was generally regarded as the strongest man in the village. Nobody dared cross him, including William. He was quiet, reserved, and well known for being an incredibly hard worker. He did his best to instill this same work ethic in his children through strict discipline. Sometimes William grew tired of the jokes about how he couldn't possibly be the man's son, considering his diminished frame and flighty nature. Despite not inheriting his father's stature however, he had certainly inherited his work ethic at the very least.

William's mother entered the stables carrying some warm bread for his father, who accepted it enthusiastically. She ran her fingers through his hair lovingly and inspected the bridle that he was working on.

"How goes it?" she asked curiously.

"Aye," responded her husband gruffly.

"Will ye have it finished in time?" she asked, glancing over her shoulder nervously towards the town's entrance.

"I will if you'd stop pestering me about it…" he answered in annoyance. She rolled her eyes as she continued to silently observe his progress. Today was the day that the town's one and only celebrity would be returning home for an extremely rare respite from his duties. He was a cleric of Bethmael, not that William entirely understood or cared what that was. All he knew was that they were in some way responsible for keeping the gateway to the other world closed. Due to their duties keeping everybody safe, there wasn't a corner of the kingdom where they weren't known and appreciated. The fact that such a high-profile individual could've come from their village made him the pride of Lakhdorian. This would be the first time that the cleric had returned home in his life, and as such, the whole village was abuzz with excitement.

Just as William was finishing up mucking out the stable, he heard the telltale sound of Annemarie's front door closing. He tried to hide his sudden excitement from his parents as he awkwardly shifted his way towards the front of the stables. He sidled his way into eyeshot of the road where he could see her as she passed by. As soon as he caught sight of her, his heart skipped a beat.

"Annemarie!" he shouted, waving enthusiastically as she came into view. She was carrying two buckets of milk hanging from a rod she had over her shoulders.

"Good morning, William!" she replied merrily.

"That's a lot of milk! Where are you taking it?" he asked, looking at the hefty load she was carrying.

"Up to your uncle Wilton's cottage, he's making green cheese for Father Marcus's feast!" she replied excitedly.

"Oh, that's… great!" said William, allowing an awkward silence to form.

"Well… I'll be off then!" she finished before continuing on her journey. William waved goodbye heartily as he watched her leave. His parents both shook their heads at their boy's dismal courtship skills.

"Ye should've offered to help her carry those buckets," said his father without looking up from the bridle he was working on.

"Oh no, Annemarie's really strong! She doesn't need my help," replied William, missing the point. William's mother let out a sigh before kissing her husband on the top of his head and leaving the stables. William stared blankly after her as she left.

"Why don't you take that manure up to your uncle's house now then?" asked his father, nodding towards William's muck bucket

"Aye father!" replied William, perhaps over enthusiastically. It was a little premature to be bringing the manure to Wilton's farm, but it would give him an excuse to catch up with Annemarie. He quickly picked up the bucket and headed for the stable door.

"Don't forget to bring back fresh wood shavings this time," said his father gruffly as he was leaving.

"Aye father," replied William dejectedly. As he left the stable, he walked past his mother who was now in conversation with one of their neighbors. Perhaps if he just walked by casually, they wouldn't notice him and pull him into some dreary conversation about village life. He ducked his head down and quickened his pace as he passed the two.

"Willy!" his mother called out as soon as he was in eyeshot. He let out a quiet sigh.

"Aye, mother?" he asked after giving a polite smile and nod to their neighbor.

"Are ye going up to Wilton's cottage already?" she asked, looking at his not-yet-full muck bucket and raising an eyebrow.

"Aye," he replied flatly.

"Alright, well bring ye sister with ye," she commanded.

"But mother..." began William, wanting to protest with more vigor, but being afraid of doing so in front of the neighbor lady.

"I won't hear any of your moaning boy! You'll bring ye sister! I'm sick of havin' her hanging around in the house, always reading those moldy old books!" yelled his mother. Her conversation partner nodded her head approvingly.

"Aye..." replied William despondently, before walking over to the window of their house and rapping on it forcefully.

"Sasha, you're coming with me to Uncle Wilton's, hurry now!" yelled William impatiently.

"I dinnae want ta!" yelled his sister from inside the house.

"Mother says you have ta, now get out here!" yelled back William angrily, slapping the window for emphasis. After a loud moan of frustration and the sound of a book being slammed down, there was a moment of silence before the front door of their house opened, revealing his younger sister Sasha. She squinted her eyes as they met the sunlight.

"Hurry up!" commanded William immediately.

"Aye, shut up!" yelled Sasha in response, putting on her boots as quickly as she could. She gave her mother and the neighbor lady a polite smile and nod as she passed them, and with that, she and William set off on their short journey.

***

"Slow down brother," said Sasha in annoyance at the lightning pace William was setting.

"No! You need to learn to keep up. Yer not always going to be treated like a little princess you know," replied William wryly.

"Dad makes me do more work than any of the other girls in the village and you know it!" defended Sasha, hurt by his accusations. William rolled his eyes as he kept up his pace. After a few minutes of quiet walking, they had already reached the outskirts of their small village.

"So, what were ye reading today anyway?" asked William, beginning to feel a little guilty for snapping at her.

"A book about the knight's college and the clerics of Bethmael of course," replied Sasha, as though this should've been obvious.

"Oh? So, what about them? What makes 'em so special?" asked William.

"Yer fourteen Will, shouldn't you know this already?" asked Sasha incredulously.

"Well fine, don't tell me then you little runt!" he replied angrily.

"Sorry Will…" apologized Sasha earnestly. She had the privilege of attending their village's humble school a few days per week. The rotation of books that were loaned to them from the Mistfall townhall kept her well informed. This was a privilege Will hadn't had since his sixth birthday when his father had begun putting him to work around the stables.

"Well, when they managed to close the gateway, they couldn't keep it closed forever," explained Sasha. William listened on quietly.

"The clerics of Bethmael needed to keep working away at it," she continued.

"Ay? For how long?" asked William, confused.

"Forever," she replied with a nod.

"What? Even right now, they're still going?!" asked William, his interest piqued.

"Aye. Apparently, it's horrible work too. The monsters still want to get through. The book said that the clerics see all sorts of dark visions and hear horrible voices in their heads all day. Some of them have died from exhaustion because they nigh get a minute of rest," explained Sasha. William cast a worried glance at her.

"Are you sure these books don't have any of the forbidden knowledge in them?" asked William.

"Course not!" she defended vehemently, despite a little worry being evident on her face. William looked down at his little sister and let out a sigh.

"Are you sure ye should even be reading about this stuff? Yer a bit young aren't ye? Don't be giving yourself nightmares now," said William, genuinely concerned about her.

"I'm twelve years old William," she replied, rolling her eyes. William smiled lovingly down at his little sister.

"Aye, you are. So, tell me more about these clerics then. Does yer book say anything about Father Marcus?" asked William.

"Aye it does!" replied Sasha excitedly.

"It even said that he's from a rural mountain village!" she added enthusiastically.

"Huh? It didn't even say our name?" asked William, raising an eyebrow.

"Nay, it did not..." she replied with a sigh. Just at that moment the two of them caught sight of Annemarie up the road some way.

"There's Annemarie! Let's catch up with her!" suggested William.

"Aye!" agreed Sasha, joining him in hurrying their pace to reach her. Finally having caught up, the trio set off cheerfully towards Wilton's farm together, babbling excitedly about the feast that was to be held in the village center this evening.

***

Before long they had made it to their destination, immediately getting stuck into their respective tasks. As soon as they'd arrived Sasha had been taken off by their aunt Genevieve, leaving William alone in the compost area to do his work. From here he could see through the cottage window to where Annemarie was talking excitedly with Wilton about his cheese making process.

"Aye, this is lovely and fresh! Make sure to thank ye family for me!" said Wilton, tasting some of the milk that Annemarie had brought with her.

"I will! Father will be happy to see our milk being used for such lovely cheese!" answered Annemarie as she watched Wilton already beginning to prepare his station.

"Well, let's just hope that Father Marcus is a cheese lover..." replied Wilton as he chopped some lemons.

"Even if he aren't, none of your cheese will go to waste. I'll eat it all myself!" said Annemarie jokingly. Wilton laughed heartily in response.

"Why girl, you're so small I can hardly imagine you eating more than a morsel! Either way, you'd better be careful not to eat too much cheese, or you'll end up looking like me!" said Wilton in response, patting his belly. Annemarie laughed and shook her head.

"Aye girl, of course I'm only joking. You can eat as much as you'd like deary, you'll always be a beauty. I've seen the way the lads in the village look at you, especially young William…" said Wilton, raising an eyebrow. William blushed and hurried his shoveling.

"What?! Me? No, surely not!" replied Annemarie modestly.

"Aye girl. Next time you see my nephew, you let him know I said hello, won't you?" asked Wilton, mixing his ingredients together.

"He's here right now!" replied Annemarie, looking out the window to search for William and immediately making eye contact with him. He'd been caught staring. He stood in stunned silence for a moment before hurriedly trying to finish his job. Wilton poked his head around the corner of the window and waved to William, who waved back awkwardly.

"Why don't you go out and see how he's going?" asked Wilton.

"Aye! I will!" replied Annemarie happily. William took a deep breath to steady his nerves as he anticipated her arrival.

"Wow, you're already finished, that was fast!" said Annemarie looking at his bucket full of wood shavings. Apparently not wanting to be labeled as an eavesdropper was a good motivator for fast work.

"Oh my…" said Annemarie before William could respond, looking over his shoulder and walking behind the cottage.

"What is it?" asked William, following her curiously. As they rounded the back of the cottage and left the cover of Wilton's fruit trees, the view of the mists below the midday sun could be seen from their hillside perch.

"It's so beautiful!" said Annemarie joyously, clasping her hands together. As William walked forward to join her in front of the incredible vista he had to agree, she really was. She suddenly turned to face him, blushing slightly as she caught his eyes. He felt like his heart had jumped into his throat as he took in the romantic setting that he'd suddenly been dropped into.

"Did you hear what yer uncle said to me?" she asked, her blushing intensifying. William stammered nervously. He quickly tried to wipe the sweat from his brow, spreading dirt over his forehead in the process.

"Uh, no I wasn't listening…" lied William distractedly as he tried to wipe his forehead clean.

"Oh…" she murmured, before reaching over and grabbing him by the hand that was rubbing his forehead.

"Wow, look how many callouses you have!" she said, analyzing his palm in detail. William felt his heartbeat racing. He hadn't had this much physical contact with Annemarie since they were kids.

"Aye… I do a lot of work…" he replied, cursing himself and his rough hands. There was a long moment of silence as Annemarie began to stare up into his eyes expectantly. He could feel the heartbeat in his chest intensifying. He wasn't sure what she was expecting from him, but he had to say something, anything at all. She was staring into his eyes with such anticipation.

"Did you know that the clerics of Bethmael sometimes die from exhaustion?" he spurted out suddenly. Annemarie had a change of expression into pure confusion.

"What?" she asked, taken aback by this random outburst.

"Yeah, the monsters from the gateway haunt their nightmares and won't let them go to sleep, so sometimes they die from exhaustion," finished Will, unsure even himself why this piece of horrible trivia was the first thing that came out of his mouth. Annemarie suddenly released her grip on his hand and took a step back.

"I'm sorry William. I thought... yer uncle told me something earlier, but he was wrong," she said, shaking her head again and beginning to shine bright red.

"Oh don't worry, he's wrong about all sorts of stuff!" said William hastily, unwittingly making the situation even worse.

"I'd better get back home. I need to help set up for the feast..." said Annemarie, beginning to walk backwards towards the cottage.

"Oh, yeah of course. I'll..." William almost said he'd come with her before he thought about it some more. She was the prettiest girl in the village, and he was a sweaty, callous-handed dung-tosser who was spouting out creepy nonsense about the gateway. She didn't want him to walk her home, there was no way. He had to use his brain for once.

"I'll go and check on Sasha," finished William. She gave him one last wry smile before turning and beginning her trek back to town. When she was out of sight, William turned around to face the view once more.

"What is wrong with me?!" he desperately wanted to scream, but instead released his woeful question as a dull groan. He paced around for a while, kicking stones and cursing himself before he caught his breath. He stared at the vista before him in silent reflection. It was time. Tonight, he would do it. At the feast, he'd tell her how he really felt about her. That'd make up for all of his awkwardness this afternoon. He nodded with conviction at his plan. As much as it pained him to imagine such a thing, he swore an oath to himself. He would follow through on this, no matter what happened. It didn't matter if she thought he was a creep for saying it; it was finally time that he showed some courage for once in his life.

CHAPTER TWO

The Feast of Bethmael

"And then, she taught me about breaking rhythm!" said Sasha excitedly, jumping up onto a low wall and miming the striking of an imaginary foe with a sword.

"Rhythm? Are you sure she isn't teaching you how to dance?" William scoffed. Rather than taking the bait of his coaxing quip, Sasha stopped and considered it for a moment.

"I suppose you're right; it is an awful lot like dancing," she thought aloud. William rolled his eyes. He desperately wanted to pretend that his sister was learning some kind of useless, second rate, women's fighting techniques from their aunt. In reality he knew that Genevieve had learned her fighting techniques in the military. They were the real deal. The best he could do to mend his wounded ego over his little sister knowing more about battle than he did was to release the occasional wry comment. History books told of a time before the great catastrophe when women were excluded from learning such art forms, however times had changed. Upon facing the literal end of the world, it was quickly decided that leaving any section of society unable to defend themselves was an unwise cultural standard.

As their house came into view Sasha ran towards their mother who was sweeping the front porch.

"Mother! Mother! You'll never believe what Aunt Genevieve taught me today!" she yelled gleefully, running up to her mother and regaling her with excited chatter about her self-defense lesson. Rather than glee, William was returning from this trip still feeling rather glum after his unfortunate and confusing exchange with Annemarie behind the cottage. Arriving back at home only amplified his unease due to his proximity to her. Their two families shared one large house which had been split down the middle, with a thin wall constructed between its two halves. William's family had the left half of the building, including the stables. Annemarie's family had the right half of the building and a nearby field housing their cattle. The reality was that Annemarie's bedroom was separated from Will's by naught but that single, thin dividing wall. At any moment she could be mere inches away from him. It was hard to get her out of his head at the best of times, but with the feast taking place tonight he was beginning to feel dizzy from thinking about her so much.

"Wonderful! And how about you Willy?" asked his mother, raising a questioning eyebrow.

"Aye," replied William flatly. His mother and sister shared a curious glance with one another before both turning to assess him with excruciating focus.

"Is he upset about somethin'?" asked his mother.

"Aye," responded Sasha with a knowing nod.

"What are ye upset about darlin'?" asked his mother.

"I'm not upset," responded Will angrily.

"See? He's definitely upset," confirmed Sasha.

"Poor boy, you haven't gotten yourself all worked up over the neighbor girl have ye?" asked his mother coaxingly.

"Okay, now yer just tryin' to annoy me!" yelled William.

He was just about to evacuate into the stables when he suddenly heard a ruckus erupting from the village's entrance. As soon as he looked over to investigate, he immediately spotted what was causing the commotion. It was the fanciest brigade he'd ever seen make the trek up into their unremarkable village. Three knights wearing intricate sigils on their gear led at the front of the pack. Behind them was a lavish caravan towed by two horses with a squire controlling them. Sitting by his side, was the man that they'd all been waiting for, the hero of Lakhdorian; Father Marcus, Cleric of Bethmael. As soon as the villagers caught sight of him, they erupted into a round of appreciative applause. William still wasn't entirely sure why they were applauding but joined in anyway so as to not stand out. It was only once the man drew closer that people let their applause dull and began murmuring with each other in concern. Rather than the mighty hero cleric they had been expecting to see, the man on the passenger seat of the caravan looked positively sickly. He was wearing black hooded robes which stood out in stark contrast to the shiny pieces of armor his knightly compatriots were wearing. One look at the man was all William needed to see that he was clearly not healthy enough to support wearing a suit of armor. He suddenly felt his father's hand on his shoulder and immediately knew something was wrong. He watched on nervously as the diminished robe clad man approached. On closer inspection as his face came into view, William was again filled with a sense of unease. His skin was as pale as porcelain, and he had giant black bags under his bloodshot eyes. His long black hair fell over his face messily and he seemed to be muttering something to himself.

"Is that him father?" asked William quietly. His father simply nodded and tightened his grip on William's shoulder to implore him to stay quiet. It was as though the cleric had a dark cloud lingering over him. The closer he drew to Will, the more he felt the grip of his heavy atmosphere tighten around his throat like a noose. It made him feel cold, lonely and afraid. It gave him a sense of despair and misery in his heart that he'd never felt before in his entire life. His father's warm hand on his shoulder was about the only thing keeping him from quivering in his boots from the disturbing aura cast off by the cleric as he slowly rode past. As the pilgrimage trotted deeper into the village, William felt relief flood through his chest.

"Is he sick father?" asked William quietly, still not sure if his father was okay with him asking questions. His father continued staring after the brigade intensely without replying. His mother had been watching from the doorstep of their house and walked over to join them.

"He's really back," she said quietly.

"Aye," agreed his father, wrapping an arm around her shoulders. At this moment William noticed Annemarie and her family also standing out the front of their house. They looked to be discussing the situation in a similar manner.

"Well, it can only be expected," Sasha suddenly piped up, catching all of them off guard.

"What do you mean?" asked their mother.

"Most of 'em hang 'emselves," she finished flatly. Their father let out a dry chuckle at his young daughter's blunt outburst.

"Aye," he said with an amused smile. William wasn't convinced. Was the man's anguish really so intense that they could all physically feel it? Just from being near the gateway, did all the clerics have an aura of despair like that? If that were the case, then why would anybody want to become a cleric of Bethmael? His mother and father began to head back inside to continue their respective duties.

"William, after ye bring in the horses get ready for the feast. You're finishing early today," called out his father without looking back.

"Aye!" replied Will excitedly. He suddenly caught sight of Annemarie who had been staring at him. She blushed and turned away when they locked eyes, walking back into her house hurriedly. Will let out a sigh. What had gotten into her?

As he took the horses back into the stable, he peered over at his father who was adding the final touches to the saddle he was making. He looked incredibly unsure of himself, so William decided to say something to bring his spirits up.

"It came out really well. He'll love it!" said Will supportively. His father let out a sigh.

"I don't know if that man could love anything I made for him…" he thought aloud. William realized now that his father wasn't merely worried about whether he'd done a good enough job. He clearly had deeper feelings about the situation than William could comprehend.

He patted his father on his back before leaving the stables. It was time for him to get ready for the feast. As he retired into his home, his stomach was filled with a mixture of raw excitement and anxiety. Would he really be able to follow through on his goals with Annemarie, or was he just going to hide in a dark corner of the party like he always did?

***

When their family approached the village center, the excitement in the air was palpable. This was the least subdued William had ever

seen his fellow villagers. Children danced about with colorful rib-
bons on sticks, playing happily all around the village. Everybody
was wearing their finest Lakhdorian festive outfits with beautiful
braiding in their hair, and polished boots. Many had even gone as
far as to clean their teeth. Sweet smells of herbs and flowers ema-
nated from the pockets of everybody around them, and although
Lakhdorians weren't the musical type, a traveler from Mistfall was
even playing celebratory songs on a lute.

"Wow! This is fantastic!" declared Sasha, not knowing where to
look first. It was immediately obvious that this was nothing like one
of their boring old solstice festivals. It was as though they were celebrating something good happening, rather than just having a routine get together.

"Sasha! Over here!" shouted some of the local children her age
who were playing with marbles out the front of the school building.
After looking to her mother and getting the nod of approval, Sasha
ran over to join them. William looked up at his father who was
holding his fancy saddle and bridle awkwardly. He smiled when he
beheld the giant man looking so stiff and out of place. He was perhaps the only other person here who looked as unsuited to these
surroundings as William felt.

"Oh, look over there!" said William's mother pointing to a table
covered in gifts, before grabbing her reticent husband under his arm
and pulling him into the fray. Before he realized it, William was left
standing awkwardly on his own. He put his hands in his pockets
and sidled up to the town well. Since being put to work at a young
age, he hadn't formed the strong bonds of friendship like the other
village kids had. He'd also never developed the ability to just blend
in with a crowd and approach people he wasn't close to. He suddenly felt a rough punch to his shoulder, pulling him from his

thoughts. He jumped up, ready to defend himself before he noticed who it was.

"Eric?!" he exclaimed.

"Well don't be too surprised now, I'm a Lakhdorian too you know!" replied his old friend. Eric was a few heads taller than Will and had twice his girth. The boy's large size had been a focal point of bullying when they'd been in school together but looking at the giant lad standing before him, William doubted anybody would have the gall to pick on him now. William greeted him with the old hand shake they made up as kids.

"Of course you are! I'm so glad you came brother!" said William, letting go of him and beaming with joy. It was like Eric was an angel sent to save him from awkwardly standing on his own in a dark corner of the party.

"Do ye really think my father would miss an opportunity for free booze?" asked Eric, nodding over towards the keg stands where his father was already guzzling down a goblet of port. William hadn't seen either of them in years, and although Eric had grown quite a lot, his father had changed even more. Between his bloated gut, dark bags under his bloodshot eyes, his big nose and his dry skin, years of alcoholism had totally changed his appearance.

"Wow, yer pa really likes a drink huh?" replied Will. Eric's expression darkened and he shook his head in disappointment. Immediately realizing that he needed to change the subject, William slapped Eric on his shoulder again and smiled merrily.

"So, how's things down at yer farm? There's so much mist down there I can hardly see the moorlands sometimes!" said William.

"Aye it's going well. Of course, with all that land we can keep far more pigs than we ever could've up here. Plus, we're on a trading route, so merchants from the city buy livestock and meat from us sometimes," explained Eric.

"Did ye see this lot coming through?" asked William, nodding towards Father Marcus and his cohort who were drinking together with the village mayor.

"Aye..." said Eric, scratching his chin and adorning an expression of deep thought.

"I remember that look..." said William with a knowing grin. Eric chuckled abashedly.

"Go on, what are ye thinking?" asked Will, looking over at Father Marcus too.

"It's nothing really. It's just... my great grandfather's journal described this feeling is all," explained Eric. His great grandfather had fought against the monsters which had spilled out from the gateway a century ago. He'd been a knight in the old world, and as such, he'd been on the frontlines when the great catastrophe had occurred. He'd kept a detailed journal and records throughout the great war which Eric had inherited, and due to his studious nature, fawned over for years.

"I bet your granda met the clerics of Bethmael a bunch of times," replied William, nodding.

"No but that's the thing Will, that weren't when he wrote about it. He wrote about this feeling when he were on the battlefield," Eric explained, again scratching his chin deep in thought. William was shocked.

"Ey? What are ye saying? Does it look like we're on a battlefield?" asked William, gesturing around at the happy townsfolk. Eric chuckled and shook his head.

"No brother, what I'm saying is that I think he might be on a battlefield of his own. Even right now," finished Eric cryptically, narrowing his eyes as he stared at the cleric. William inspected Father Marcus in more detail. What had seemed like him mumbling to himself earlier, on closer inspection actually looked more like an argument. His whole body was shaking, and he would occasionally bite his lips which were torn up from having done this constantly. Every inch of his skin was covered in self-inflicted wounds, some of which he was inflicting right now by scratching his long nails deep into his arms, enough to draw blood.

"Aye. I see what you mean," replied William, a chill running down his spine as he beheld the battle this man was facing before his very eyes.

"He hasn't touched his drink," said Eric with a nod. As William watched him more closely, he realized that the cleric wasn't actually speaking a word to anybody but himself. He turned back to Eric, who was still staring intently at the cleric. If there was ever something that Eric didn't understand, or something he wanted to know, he'd stop at nothing to find out all he could about it. He hadn't changed since they were kids. It was just in his nature. William smiled to himself. What if he went out on a limb for his old friend here?

"What say before the feast starts, we take some seats close to them?" asked William. Eric cast a surprised glance at his friend.

"Are ye serious? I thought you'd want to be as far away from him as possible!" he laughed.

"What are ye trying to say?!" asked William defensively. Eric raised his hands apologetically.

"Sorry, I didn't mean anything by that! Sure, you're on! Let's go find a seat near him now then," said Eric, raising his eyebrow as if daring William to agree to it.

"Aye, let's go!" said William, gesturing towards the man.

"You lead the way, tough guy!" replied Eric, pushing his shoulder playfully. William laughed, shoving him back before shaking his head as he began to lead the way. He swallowed nervously. The moment that he'd turned away from Eric and started walking closer to Father Marcus, his merry mood began to decline as though all the joy in his body were being sucked out of him. He took a shaky breath and tried to steady his nerves. Was he just scared, or was there something more to this? He'd never felt dread like this before in his life, and the closer he drew the worse it became. With Eric in tow, he was going to have to suck it up and act tough, but despite his manly façade, he couldn't ignore the feeling swelling in his chest. It felt like they were making a huge mistake.

CHAPTER THREE

An Insidious Proposal

As an introvert, walking towards the spotlight was daunting enough on its own. Throw in the fact that the man literally seemed to be emitting an aura of despair, and you had a recipe for making William's legs quake. He stopped on the spot for a moment as he drew nearer and the choking atmosphere around him threatened to send him into a panic attack. Eric put a supportive hand on William's shoulder, filling him with some much-needed relief.

"We don't have to do this, you know," said Eric calmly. Will turned around to look at him. He didn't look half as scared as William felt. How was he so brave?

"Do you not feel it at all?" asked William bluntly. He had to throw his ego aside; he wanted to know why he was feeling like such a coward.

"Aye. I feel it..." began Eric, deep in thought.

"But this is the closest I've ever been to knights or clerics. Don't you want to know what knights talk about?" asked Eric, raising an eyebrow. William smiled at his friend. Even if only for Eric's sake, he wanted to continue onwards. He could see how piqued his curiosity was, and it was about time that Will started trying to get out of his comfort zone anyway. He turned back towards Father Marcus and immediately felt that despair begin to claw at his throat again. He didn't have time to worry about it however, as out of the corner of his eye he suddenly noticed Annemarie. She was with a group of other teenagers their age, but she was completely fixated on William. He didn't let himself react at all. He didn't want her to know that he'd seen her looking; but knowing that she was watching him filled him with the determination he needed.

He took one last deep breath, before leading the way over towards the cleric's cohort and sitting down at the table at some empty seats nearby them. He left a couple of seats as padding between himself and them, as he was far too anxious to sit directly beside any of them. The truth was that nobody else in the village had the gall to take those seats either, not even the adults. At first William was so focused on Father Marcus that he hadn't even looked at the knights sitting next to him yet, but as soon as he and Eric had sat down the knights stopped their conversation and assessed them curiously.

"Good evening…" said one of the knights with a smirk, looking at the two of them down the table. William suddenly realized that he was being talked to directly by a knight. He snapped his head around to look at them. She was a redhead, probably in her late twenties or early thirties. When William had seen them all on their horses earlier, he hadn't even thought to look at them in any detail, as he'd been so preoccupied with Father Marcus.

"Uh... Good... Um…" stammered Will. He had no idea how he was supposed to address a knight. He didn't know the first thing about high society. He was a stable boy, not an aristocrat. What in the world was he even doing here? Just as panic was truly beginning to grip his heart, Eric suddenly piped up.

"Good evening, Dame Azalea," he replied expertly, bowing his head politely. The knights exchanged some surprised looks, as did William.

"You know us by name?" asked one of the other two knights in surprise. He had a ponytail and a goatee, and up until this moment he had looked very bored.

"But of course, Sir Ivar. Good evening to you, and to Sir August and Father Marcus," continued Eric, politely bowing his head to each of them in turn. Ivar and August smirked to each other in amusement before nodding their heads in greeting. Will followed suit and bowed his head politely to each of them, deciding to keep his mouth shut.

"How is it that you have come to know of us?" asked Ivar, taking a sip from his goblet.

"Word spreads fast around these parts! It's not every day we have three first class knights and a cleric of Bethmael in town!" explained Eric, laughing awkwardly.

"Ah…" said August, giving a knowing nod. It was only now that William was up close that he realized how intimidatingly large Sir August was.

"I also purchased a college knight's ledger from a traveling merchant that told me a little about each of you," explained Eric.

"I hope it's not one of those awful, illustrated ones… is my nose really that big?!" asked Sir Ivar, looking between Will and Eric searchingly. The two of them shook their heads vigorously. William knew there was no way Eric could've afforded an illustrated ledger.

"No sir, I recognized you from your crest!" explained Eric, gesturing at the badge on Sir Ivar's chest that featured some kind of dragon, the meaning of which was lost on William.

"What interest does a boy like you have with a knight's ledger anyway?" asked Azalea, clearly surprised that a commoner would spend some of what little copper they have on what to them would simply be a useless trivia piece.

"Oh, I just think it's important to keep up with what's going on in Oxgate. Plus, what boy doesn't dream of becoming a knight?" asked Eric with a smile. August raised his eyebrows and nodded his head in approval.

"You're also accompanying the hero of our village!" explained Eric, gesturing to Father Marcus who didn't seem to have been listening to the conversation and was still simply muttering to himself. William stared at Eric blankly. Was William supposed to have known their names and recognized their crests too? How was he supposed to take part in a conversation like this? He'd thought that they'd ignore them, and that he and Eric would just sit here and talk about horse dung. He was in way over his head. A hand suddenly appeared on William's shoulder, accompanied by one on Eric's too.

"I am so terribly sorry about these two! They are lost and confused! Come now boys, leave these seats for the adults," said the voice of the town's mayor who had swooped in to do some damage control upon seeing two farm boys interacting with the knights. William immediately shot up out of his chair, seizing the opportunity to leave the terrifying situation he'd somehow managed to get himself into.

"Come now, please do stay!" implored Sir August, raising his hands in protest. William shared a confused glance with the mayor. Neither of them wanted William to stay here, but neither of them were going to go against the wishes of a knight.

"I must tell you my lord, these two are but lowly stable boys..." explained the mayor.

"Nonsense. You're all commoners. There's no difference," said Sir Ivar distractedly, swirling the wine in his goblet. The mayor clearly wanted to protest but caught himself.

"Take a look at them. This one's big, that one's small, this one talks, that one doesn't. They're a funny pair! I like them! Leave them be!" said Sir August, laughing merrily. The mayor hesitated for a moment before removing his hands from the boy's shoulders.

"Of course, as you wish. How about some more refreshments? The meal will begin shortly, but you can never have enough of our delicious Lakhdorian green cheese!" said the mayor, trying to pivot this awkward exchange into an opportunity to do some more schmoozing.

"We know where everything is," said Dame Azalea with a polite smile. Again, the mayor lingered for a moment.

"Very well then, don't hesitate to ask if you need anything!" he finished, bowing politely before reluctantly backing away and re-joining a nearby group of townsfolk. The three knights again turned their attention back to the boys. At the very least, they seemed entertained.

"So, this won't do," announced Sir August suddenly, gesturing at them. William gulped nervously, unsure of what he was referring to.

"How can you know our names without us knowing yours?" he asked, looking at Will and Eric expectantly.

"My apologies, I should've introduced us sooner. I am Eric Lakhdorian of house Rothmane," answered Eric boldly. There was a moment of silence as the knights shared surprised looks.

"Rothmane?!" asked Azalea. Eric nodded.

"As in, Sir Heinrich Rothmane?" clarified Ivar. Again, Eric nodded. The knights shared astonished looks.

"He was my great grandfather," confirmed Eric.

"I didn't know there were any Rothmanes left!" exclaimed August, dumbfounded.

"Yes… well, after the war my great grandfather was the last of our family line. He married a Lakhdorian woman and settled in the moors," explained Eric. William was still in silent shock that this was actually happening. He'd heard Eric talk about his great grandfather since they were children, but never did he imagine in a million years he'd have been noteworthy enough that even now, modern day knights knew his name. The idea of it sent a chill down his spine. He had an overwhelming sense of pride in Eric at being able to talk with these knights so well, but at the same time, how was he supposed to follow that?! His fears were suddenly amplified when Sir August turned his attention to William.

"Well? Do you talk?" asked Sir August. William stammered awkwardly as his mouth tried to find words to say.

"Aye!" he spurted out finally. Azalea and August both let out a chuckle.

"Aye?!" asked Ivar incredulously.

"They only say 'yes' in Oxgate," said Eric quietly.

"Oh… yes!" corrected William, shining bright red with embarrassment. Again, the knights chuckled.

"So, how about you? Are you from some famous old house that we thought had disappeared? Are you perhaps Lord William of house Ashdawn?!" asked Ivar, smirking at his own joke.

"Uh… no sir, I'm just William Lakhdorian," answered Will with a polite nod, missing the joke.

"Aww, I like him," said Azalea with a warm smile. At this moment suddenly someone brushed against William's right shoulder. When he turned to see who it was, he felt a jolt run through his body. There stood Annemarie, shining bright red with embarrassment. As terrified as she looked, she also wore an expression of determination. She curtseyed politely to the three knights and Father Marcus before taking the empty seat next to William.

"Another one?" asked Ivar, intrigued.

"Good… Good evening," stammered Annemarie, trying to sound confident and refined, despite her anxiety being evident. Azalea tilted her head, giving Annemarie a warm smile.

"What's your name sweetheart?" she asked, leaning her head on her hands as she looked at the three of them, enamored.

"Is it perhaps Lady Victoria of house Bellamour?" asked Ivar, again chuckling at his own quip.

"N-no my lord, it's Annemarie Lakhdorian," she stammered, missing the joke just as Will had. Of all the people in this village that would have the courage to come and join them here, he never imagined that it would be Annemarie. He smiled adoringly at her, his love for her swelling in his chest.

"No!" exclaimed Marcus suddenly, slamming his fist on the table, causing everybody to jump. The knights shared a concerned glance with one another. Will wasn't sure what to do. The man's outburst ended as quickly as it started, with him returning to mumbling under his breath and scratching at his arms. Will and Annemarie shared terrified looks with one another. When he turned to look at Eric, his friend simply shook his head and shrugged. There was an awkward moment of silence as nobody knew how to recover the conversation which had at this point been completely lost. At that very moment, a parade of the village's best cooks suddenly emerged from the crowd, beginning to bring their various platters of food to the giant series of dining tables that had been erected down the village center. A number of the townsfolk released a dull

applause as the food was uncovered, and everybody began mean-
dering their way towards the tables to claim a seat. Amid the chaos,
William noticed the knights leaning towards each other and having
a hushed conversation. They kept glancing over towards Marcus
and gesturing towards him in subtle ways.

"Do you see it?" whispered Eric suddenly in William's ear. He
turned to look at his friend searchingly. Eric subtly pointed his attention at Father Marcus' leg which they could see poking out from
the corner of the table from their vantage point. He'd taken the
knife from his belt and dug it solidly into his own thigh. He was
twisting it back and forth in the wound. If it weren't for his dark
robes, the blood running down his leg would've been obvious for
all to see. William felt goosebumps run down his arms. He'd never
seen anything like this in his life.

"Why would he do that?" whispered William shakily, terrified of
what he was seeing. Eric shook his head in response, a look of concern covering his face.

"Hey…" said Azalea suddenly, pulling William's attention back
to the knights. Despite the cleric's leg being out of her line of sight,
she'd clearly noticed how uncomfortable the two of them were becoming.

"What's the best thing to eat here?" she asked with a smile. She
was obviously trying to distract them. It hadn't worked particularly
well on William or Eric who weren't sure whether to keep looking
at Father Marcus butchering his own leg or at Azalea. Fortunately,
Annemarie piped up to answer.

"Definitely the pork belly!" she replied enthusiastically. William
smiled adoringly at her once again. She was too modest to mention
her family's contributions to the feast, but he wasn't.

"Annemarie's family has prepared delicious steaks, and the cheese was made with milk from their cows too!" added William, too proud of her to hold back. She blushed with embarrassment. Azalea raised a curious eyebrow.

"Is that so?" she asked, looking between the two of them. Suddenly the mayor burst back out of the crowd behind William once more.

"Esteemed guests! Please, don't trouble yourselves to fill your own plates, allow me to supply you with the finest selection of the delicacies our village has to offer!" he announced with a slight bow.

"We want the steak," said August bluntly.

"Of course, my Lord!" replied the mayor, surprised by his immediate choice.

"And the pork belly!" added Azalea with a nod to Annemarie.

"What did your families prepare?" asked Sir Ivar, looking at Will and Eric with a raised eyebrow.

"The pork was actually raised on my farm," replied Eric with a smile. The attention suddenly fell back on William once more.

"My... my family? Well... my father made the saddle and bridle over on the table of gifts..." replied William with a shy nod.

"Oh, that?" asked Ivar with a raised eyebrow, tilting his head to look over at it. William wasn't sure whether Ivar was impressed, or simply amused by his father's work. His instinct to defend his father suddenly kicked in.

"It bears the sigil of Lakhdorian, so that Father Marcus knows that we're always thinking of him!" proclaimed William passionately.

"Okay, okay!" replied Ivar with a chuckle, raising his hands defensively.

"Just give me whatever you think is best then," finished Ivar, turning his attention back to his drink.

"Very well! And for you sir, which of our village's fine delicacies do you desire?" asked the mayor, swallowing nervously as he turned to face Father Marcus. The cleric shook slightly upon being addressed, his hand which had been gripping the handle of his knife releasing. It was almost like he was fighting a losing battle against his own body's movements. His left arm slowly rose up, his hand taking the shape of a pointing finger. His right arm suddenly jolted out and grabbed onto his left robe sleeve, seeming to feebly attempt to pull it back down. Unfortunately, he failed, and as his arm finally found its resting point extending out in front of him, a shock ran through William's entire body. Marcus was pointing directly at Annemarie. There was a moment of complete silence as a shocked realization washed over the entire group. Even the babbling mayor wasn't sure of what to say. Annemarie grabbed onto William's knee for support under the table. She must've been absolutely terrified by what was unfolding. As anxious as he felt, at this moment William knew he had to be there for her. He placed his hand supportively over hers. This was like a nightmare.

"You want... the girl?!" asked the mayor in confusion. Father Marcus's head jolted left and right awkwardly for a moment before slowly dropping into a confirming nod. There was another chilling silence as realization ran over everybody.

"Wife..." he croaked awkwardly, before suddenly biting down on his tongue violently and causing himself to wince. Annemarie's grip on William's knee tightened. In Lakhdorian culture, usually marriages were arranged by parents. A bold proposal of this nature was extremely rare, but not entirely unheard of. Before anybody could respond, Annemarie suddenly got up to her feet.

"I'm sorry, I have to eat with my family," she announced, giving a polite curtsey, and then scurrying off into the crowd. William turned back to the knights who were all looking as surprised as William felt. He looked to Eric who widened his eyes and nodded in her direction, implying that Will should chase after her.

"Aye!" spurted out William impolitely, bursting up from his chair. He bowed awkwardly at the knights and then ran after Annemarie as quickly as he could. How had such a festive and joyful night taken such a dark turn so suddenly? William felt utterly sick. The horror which gripped his stomach threatened to make him gag. Surely this couldn't be happening. Surely Annemarie wouldn't really be wed to this dark and terrifying man. William had to find her. He had to help her. He couldn't imagine how she was feeling right now. As he pushed his way through the crowd searching for Annemarie, he swore to himself that no matter what, he wouldn't let this happen.

***

William searched for Annemarie everywhere that he could. She'd said that she needed to be with her family, but when he'd found them eating merrily at the feast she was nowhere to be seen. As panic was beginning to set in, a thought suddenly struck him. When they were children, whenever Annemarie was upset, she'd hide out behind the schoolhouse.

He took off towards the schoolhouse, running straight past and around the side of the building. A feeling of relief flooded through his chest as soon as he spotted the dark outline of Annemarie sitting on a large rock. He took a deep breath and approached her slowly.

"Annemarie…" he said softly. At first, she inhaled sharply in surprise, but as he drew closer she stood to see him.

"William?!" she asked, hurriedly trying to wipe tears away from her eyes. After a moment of silence, she ran over to him and caught him in a hug, bursting into tears and crying into his chest. For a brief moment William wasn't sure whether it would be okay to hug her back, but then his instincts kicked in. He hugged her warmly and rubbed her back soothingly. This was one of the rare circumstances where the silence formed by his inability to find the right words to say would be beneficial.

"I was so scared!" she cried into his chest.

"Aye..." agreed Will, continuing to simply hold her gently.

"I didn't know what to do!" she wept.

"Aye," said Will simply once more. There were a few moments of silence while William quietly consoled her. She pulled back and looked up into his eyes.

"Were you not scared of him, William?" she asked. He knew exactly how she felt. He'd felt the same way when he'd seen Eric's stoic face when they'd first drawn near to Father Marcus.

"I was petrified!" admitted William. A small, relieved smile appeared on Annemarie's face.

"Why would he want me to be his wife?!" she asked earnestly. Here it was. William felt his heart skip a beat as he noticed his queue. This was the moment he'd been waiting for.

"Because you're beautiful," he replied honestly. Annemarie was taken aback. She looked up into his eyes to see if he was being serious.

"Any man would be lucky to have you as his wife," he admitted, realizing that he might be overstepping the mark a little now. Annemarie began to blush and buried her face in his chest again. At first William thought she was sobbing as he felt her body under his hand, but then he realized she was giggling.

"I thought you hated me!" she said, pulling away from his chest again and looking up at his face. William was relieved to see her panic-stricken expression now replaced by a cute smile.

"Hated you?! Why would I hate you?!" he asked in surprise. He had no idea how he'd given her that idea.

"Well maybe not hated but… never mind…" she said, giggling again. There was a quiet moment as the two smiled and pulled apart slightly as they suddenly noticed how close they were. William blushed and averted his gaze. His heart was pounding in his chest, but the fear and worry that he was feeling mere minutes ago was now replaced by a warm giddy feeling that made his whole-body tingle.

"Are you going to eat with your family now?" asked William. Annemarie's face darkened slightly, and she shook her head.

"I don't want to talk to them…" she said with a frown.

"Why not? I just saw them; they're having a great time!" said William. Annemarie let out a sigh, sitting back down on the rock she'd been perched on before.

"What do you think they'll say?" she asked quietly. Will stared back at her blankly.

"About what?" he asked, so enraptured with her that he'd almost forgotten how they ended up here.

"He's our village's hero Will…" she said despondently. Suddenly it dawned on him what she meant. Arranged marriages were the standard in Lakhdorian culture. If her parents decided to accept his proposal on her behalf, it would be an extremely long and arduous battle for her to fight against it. They'd all seen it happen before, but it was always a messy and highly emotional affair which rarely if ever ended in the daughter's favor.

"Nobody is going to take his proposal seriously! He's a fruit-cake!" exclaimed Will, realizing that he was woefully unequipped to be having such a deep and important conversation.

"It don't matter," she replied pessimistically.

"It do!" insisted Will, trying to be convincing.

"It don't!" she yelled passionately, tears beginning to fall from her eyes again. William stood in stunned silence for a moment, not sure of what to say. He was clearly not going to be able to convince her to think more optimistically about this with his words. A minute ago, he'd managed to put a smile on her face with his actions. Could he pull it off again?

"Okay… wait here!" said William, beginning to back away towards the feast.

"What?!" she yelped in surprise as she watched Will's sudden withdrawal.

"Where are ye going?!" she called out.

"Just wait there! I'll be back, I promise!" replied Will, breaking into a run. He pushed his way back to the dining table, grabbing two plates and filling them with all of Annemarie's favorite foods. The pork belly from Eric's farm, the steak from her cows, even the roasted carrots he remembered her saying she liked several solstices ago. Once both plates were full, he snatched up a lantern and ran back to her. He smiled as he saw her silhouette still patiently waiting on the rock behind the school. As soon as she caught sight of him her face turned from sorrow to surprise.

"Come over here!" he said, putting both plates down on the grass beside the lantern and sitting down.

"William…" said Annemarie, walking over and sitting down beside him.

"Come on, we can't let all this delicious food go to waste!" said William, taking a huge bite of pork.

"Oh my! Are those Mrs. Geraldine's carrots?! How did you know I loved those?!" she asked in surprise. William blushed as he thought about how to explain that he remembered every little thing she'd ever said to him.

"Thank you, William," she said earnestly, with a grateful smile. For a moment, William was lost in her eyes before he snapped back to reality.

"Come on then, dig in!" he said with a laugh.

So, there it was, sitting in the dim candlelight behind the village's school that William and Annemarie ate their feast. As they ate, talked and laughed together, under the moonlight of a peaceful night, their worries were forgotten. At least for now.

CHAPTER FOUR
Three Knocks

As William wandered through the crowd, still feeling giddy from his romantic dinner, he noticed Eric's father passed out on the ground in the corner of the drinker's grotto. This suddenly reminded him that he'd left his best friend stranded alone with Father Marcus. Just as William spun around to look for Eric, he found himself staring directly at him. Eric was standing behind him with his arms crossed and an eyebrow raised.

"Eric!" exclaimed William in surprise, relieved to see him still in one piece.

"Sorry I never came back..." he finished guiltily. Eric shook his head.

"We should talk," he said seriously.

"Aye," agreed William with a sigh. As much as it pained him, chatting with Eric about what had happened might help. If anybody could make sense of the situation it would be Eric. Ever since they were kids, he had always seemed to know the right thing to do. Will nodded towards an empty table expectantly. Eric agreed before suddenly catching himself.

"Hold on, I'll be there in a moment," said Eric, turning around and walking over to where the gents were drinking and being merry.

Once Will had taken his seat he realized why Eric had done this, as he came back carrying two tankards of ale. William let out a laugh.

"Thank ye brother, but it isn't for me. I still can't stand the taste of the stuff," said Will, shaking his head.

"Ye won't be drinkin' it for the taste…" replied Eric, pushing the tankard of ale towards Will. He begrudgingly accepted it after he realized what Eric meant. Eric raised his tankard, and Will reciprocated, clinking them together before they both began to drink. There were a few moments of silence as the two boys drank and quietly processed the situation.

"So, how was Annemarie?" asked Eric. Will took a deep breath and released a sigh.

"You know her. She's strong. I think all things considered, she's doing alright," said Will. Eric nodded understandingly and took another sip of his ale.

"Do ye still love 'er?" asked Eric, catching William off guard. He blushed bright red as he tried to find the right words to respond.

"Do I… do I what?!" asked Will, knowing full well what Eric had asked. He stammered nervously for a moment before realizing that there was no real reason to be so coy with Eric. He let out a sigh.

"Aye. I do," he replied quietly. Again, Eric nodded understandingly. There was a quiet moment while Eric seemed to be sizing Will up.

"What are ye looking at me like that for?" asked William defensively. Eric took a deep breath.

"Will, I'm just going to talk about this bluntly with ye, okay?" asked Eric, making Will feel even more worried about the difficult conversation they were about to have. William nodded and furrowed his brow incredulously, as though it should be obvious that he's tough enough to handle such a difficult conversation.

"William, after you'd left, they kept on talking. He really did mean it you know… he means to make Annemarie his wife," said Eric somberly. William's heart sank. Annemarie had been right. Marcus' proposal was being taken seriously after all.

"But it were barely even a proposal, all he said was 'wife'! If I looked at a horse and said 'food', would they serve it up to me?!" rationalized Will. Eric smirked at his quip but shook his head.

"The mayor said he'll be discussing it with her parents in the morning. I thought you ought to know," said Eric seriously.

"What is there to discuss?! She don't want it!" growled Will angrily. The entire situation was completely devoid of justice.

"It's complicated Will-" began Eric.

"It ain't!" interjected William. Eric closed his eyes and nodded understandingly.

"It ain't complicated! If she don't want it, then it shouldn't happen!" said William. Eric continued to nod in agreement.

"Aye, I agree with you William. So, listen to me, we have to make a very important decision…" began Eric. William inhaled nervously as he anticipated where Eric was going with this.

"Do we want to get involved in this?" he asked firmly. William stared back at him blankly.

"What do ye mean?!" asked William.

"Do you think that you, and I, should try to help Annemarie?" reiterated Eric. William took a long swig from his tankard as he considered Eric's question sincerely. Was it really their place? This was between Annemarie and her parents. It wasn't any of his business. For him and Eric to try to get involved would not only complicate the situation for everybody, but it would also tarnish the names of each of their own families too. Stepping in and fighting against somebody else's marriage was as taboo as it got. You would be seen as meddling in affairs that weren't your own and disrespecting the sanctity of marriage itself. What made this situation especially dire was that they wouldn't be fighting against just anybody's marriage, but against the marriage of Father Marcus. A cleric of Bethmael. The hero of their village. What hope did the two of them have of making any kind of difference here? The more Will thought about it, the more helpless the whole thing seemed. He closed his eyes, finally accepting the situation for what it was.

"Aye. I want to help her," he said firmly. Eric assessed his expression. After a moment he released a small smile.

"I was hoping you'd say that," he said. William stared back at his friend. He wondered whether Eric would've been disappointed in him if he'd said no. Either way, he appreciated the candid way he'd approached the conversation. Eric was just as reliable as he'd always been.

"So... what can we do?" asked William, the hopelessness of the situation now lingering incredibly clearly before both of them. Eric took a final swig from his tankard, finishing it off before sitting back in his chair and assuming the same familiar expression that he'd worn when he'd first been looking at Father Marcus and the knights. Seeing this look on Eric's face restored some hope in Will's heart. This expression meant that Eric was thinking about a situation deeply, and if anybody could find a solution it would be him.

"Okay. So..." began Eric.

"From what I know, the clerics do not take wives," he said flatly. Will stared back at him blankly.

"Wait... what?!" asked Will, dumbfounded.

"If they aren't allowed to take a wife, then surely he can't marry Annemarie!" reasoned William excitedly.

"No, that's not what I said," replied Eric, holding a finger up to quell William's premature excitement.

"I said that they don't take wives; I never said that it was forbidden," reiterated Eric.

"I don't get it," replied William, confused.

"I don't fully understand the situation either. All I know is that in a book that I was reading which mentioned the clerics, it explained that part of their oath is that of celibacy," explained Eric. As William fathomed what Eric was saying, he felt sick to his stomach. He hadn't dared even let himself think about how sex factors into all of this yet. Although at first it made William feel sick, he suddenly felt a sparkle of hope form in his chest again.

"Wait... so can they take a wife or not?" asked William. Eric pondered the question for a moment.

"I suppose... technically... they could perhaps take a wife, but simply not consummate the marriage?" he finished with a shrug. William felt a little relief flood over him. He picked up his tankard and swallowed down what was left to steady himself.

"Well, that's a good start, right?" asked William, unsure of where they could take this train of thought, but feeling that they'd somehow already begun lifting a corner on the whole affair. Eric nodded reticently.

"Listen, the man is a mess. I don't know how much longer he even has in this world. You've seen him. He's covered in wounds, he can barely hold himself up, he talks to himself all day long... there's always the option of..." Eric trailed off, somberly. William stared back at him blankly.

"We could always just… you know… wait it out," finished Eric. William felt a chill run down his spine at the mere thought of it.

"No! You said we'd figure out a way to get Annemarie out of it! We don't even know how long it would take; it could be years that she'd need to be married to that creep!" yelled William passionately.

"I know, but if all else fails… there will still be hope," explained Eric. William took a breath to steady his nerves as Eric's words sank in.

"Keep going. What's another solution then?" asked William, wanting to change the subject. Before Eric could respond, there was suddenly a commotion from the drinker's grotto. The boys looked over and immediately realized what the cause was, when they saw Eric's father stumbling hopelessly into a keg stand, toppling it over and falling to the ground, spraying ale everywhere.

"Hey! Hey! What do ye think yer doing?!" cried out the men who had been drinking beside him.

"Oh, shut up!" slurred Eric's father, rolling on the floor in the puddle of ale and feebly attempting to get to his feet. Once vaguely upright, he spat in their general direction before collapsing face first back down into the ground with a groan. Eric let out a frustrated sigh. He hurried over to his father as quickly as he could.

"Get off me!" slurred his father when Eric tried to help him up.

"It's me father, let's get you somewhere more comfortable, ey?" asked Eric soothingly.

"Get off of me ya fat pig!" shouted his father drunkenly, swinging his fist at Eric's face and connecting hard. Eric winced in pain but didn't back off.

"Up ya get father," said Eric, lifting his father up to his knees.

"Piggy, piggy, piggy, here piggy! Sooie!" shouted his father drunkenly, cackling and slapping his son's belly. The scene was very difficult for William to watch. If it were anybody else speaking to his friend like that he'd jump to his defense, but in this case all he could find in himself to do was sit and helplessly watch as Eric was publicly humiliated.

Eric managed to get his father to his feet and began walking him away from the drinking grotto, his father protesting all the way. As he approached Will, he stopped for a moment.

"William, I'll keep thinking about our problem. Let's talk again in the morning," said Eric, struggling to keep his father upright. William nodded soberly.

"What are ye looking at? You want a go?!" yelled Eric's father, swinging an arm loosely at Will.

"Come on father, let's go..." said Eric, leading his father away and off into the night. As he watched their silhouettes disappear, Will let out a deep sigh. There was nothing more that he'd be able to do tonight. He looked around the party. Many of the townsfolk were still out celebrating, but he couldn't see Annemarie anywhere. With Annemarie and Eric both gone, he questioned whether there was any reason left for him to stay. He certainly didn't have the spirits to go and try to be merry with the rest of the townsfolk. The last thing he felt like doing right now was celebrating. As he began to walk around aimlessly, he suddenly caught sight of his mother, laughing heartily with a group of other village women. As soon as he saw her, a warm feeling spread in his belly. All he wanted to do was hug her and ask for her guidance, but when he saw how happy she looked, he realized that the last thing he should do is dump his worries on her.

"Ma! Ma!" a voice suddenly called out. Sasha and her friend burst out from the crowd and ran up to his mother.

"Yes sweetie?" asked his mother.

"Can I stay over at Isabel's house tonight?!" asked Sasha passionately, grabbing onto Isabel's hand and squeezing it tight. Her mother feigned struggling to make up her mind.

"Hmm…" she said, tapping her chin as though mulling it over deeply.

"Oh, do please say yes mother!" pleaded Sasha desperately.

"Okay then!" confirmed their mother finally. Sasha and Isabel started dancing around excitedly together.

William smiled at the wholesome scene before he began making his quiet retreat back home. He hadn't had a chance to ease up his nerves until now and being among the warmth of his family finally gave him the opportunity to relax a little. It had led him to realize how drained the night's happenings had left him. He turned around, disappearing into the night, his mind aflame with burdensome thoughts. Was he really going to be able to do anything for Annemarie, or was he going to have to watch as she was married to that dark and terrifying man?

***

As he opened his front door, a strange feeling washed over him. Being the only one home was very unusual for Will. The entire house had a cold and foreign feeling to it without his family inside. He splashed his face with water from the barrel outside on his way in, heading straight for his room and changing out of his fancy tunic. He collapsed face first down on his bed and let out a deep sigh. His small room was ordinarily shared with Sasha, but without her here he'd be sleeping in the room alone. It was another cold and unusual feeling for him to not have her candlelight flickering in the corner while she read her books well past his bedtime.

Tap, tap tap.

Will opened his eyes and flipped over onto his back. Had he imagined that sound? He waited completely still and silent for a moment.

Tap, tap tap.

He heard it again. Suddenly he was hit by a cannonball of nostalgia and excitement as memories came flooding back into his mind. When they were children, he and Annemarie would both climb inside their wardrobes and talk to each other through the wall every night. This knocking on her wardrobe's back wall was how she used to get his attention. He shot out of bed and almost fell over in his hurry to get into his wardrobe. Climbing inside the tiny wardrobe was far more difficult as a teenager, but somehow he managed to squeeze himself inside and crouch down with his ear against the wall. After a moment of waiting, he finally remembered that it was his turn to knock.

Tap, tap tap. He knocked back on the wall.

"William?" asked Annemarie's voice. Immediately his heart started racing.

"Aye! I'm here!" answered Will enthusiastically.

"I saw you walking past my window… and I just wanted to say…" she began, trailing off for a moment.

"Huh?" asked William, struggling to hear her through the wall.

"I just wanted to say… thank ye for the dinner," said Annemarie. William felt his stomach filling with warmth. His love for this girl was somehow still growing. How could she be thinking about him at a time like this?

"It were nothing… thank you for eating with me…" he replied awkwardly, blushing in the darkness. There was another moment of silence from her side.

"Will, do ye know why I came and joined ye?" she asked. He thought back to that moment. It had taken all of the courage they'd had to approach those knights and take those seats. It must've been just as daunting for her, if not more, considering that she had been alone.

"No?" asked William, only now honestly putting himself in her shoes.

"I was jealous," she said.

"What?! Jealous of who?!" asked Will, completely dumbfounded.

"I saw you talking with that lady knight and... I don't know... I guess I've never really seen you talking with any other girls before..." she said quietly before giggling.

"Hey! I talk to plenty of girls!" shouted William defensively, before chuckling himself when he realized that she was right.

"Hold on a minute... you were jealous of Dame Azalea?!" blurted Will in shock when he honestly processed what Annemarie was saying.

"Of course I was..." said Annemarie, not elaborating any further. There was an awkward moment of silence as neither of the two knew what to say next.

"Well... I'm sorry too..." said William honestly.

"What?! What do you have to be sorry about?" asked Annemarie.

"When you were in Wilton's cottage... I was listening to your conversation," admitted Will. Now was as good a time as any to admit to his eavesdropping. There was a moment of silence from her side.

"So, was your uncle right?" she asked quietly. William wracked his brain to remember that conversation which now felt like it had happened so long ago. Then it finally clicked in his mind. His uncle had told her that Will fancied her. He took a deep breath. Here it was. It was now or never.

"Aye. He was," said Will, his head spinning with anxiety. There was a long moment of silence from Annemarie which only accentuated Will's panic. Had he said the wrong thing? Had he made her uncomfortable again?

"I thought you were gonna kiss me," said Annemarie suddenly, only making Will's heart beat even faster.

"Huh?!" exclaimed Will in surprise.

"Up at the cottage, I thought you were gonna kiss me..." admitted Annemarie coyly. William could feel so much nervous energy building up in his chest that he could barely contain himself.

"I'm sorry, I didn't mean to make you uncomfortable..." said William, cursing himself for his own stupidity. Her next words hit him like an arrow through his heart.

"I wanted you to. I wanted you to kiss me, William," she clarified. The overwhelming joy he felt coursing through his body was making him feel giddy. Before he could respond, they both heard the front door of her house slam shut.

"My father's home, I have to go," said Annemarie suddenly.

"Annemarie, I..." William caught himself. He didn't want to put his foot in his mouth and say something overly sappy. He'd done enough by confirming that he fancied her.

"Goodnight," he ended simply, placing his palm up against the back of his wardrobe, longing to feel her touch.

"Goodnight William," she whispered back. And with that, all of the anxiety and fear that had been filling William's head was gone. His house no longer felt cold and empty. He no longer felt alone. He made his way over to his bed, sinking back into his pillow and closing his eyes. Maybe tonight wasn't so bad after all.

CHAPTER FIVE

The Shadow of Matrimony

William was woken by a loud commotion that made him jump upright in his bed. He soon realized that the sound was coming through the wall from Annemarie's house. She was arguing loudly with her father about something. At first William tried wrapping his pillow around his ears so as not to listen in and to get some more sleep, but then all of the events of the previous night came rushing back. He let out a groan and lay flat on his back. Should he listen in to their argument or not? It could be about Father Marcus. Either way it wasn't any of his business… but after the conversation he'd had with Eric last night, he wouldn't be doing his due diligence if he didn't at least try to listen in, right?

He quietly crept up to the wall and placed his ear against it. He was barely able to make out any of the words that they were saying. They were clearly not in Annemarie's room, but he could hear that things were getting rather heated. Both Annemarie and her father could be heard yelling loudly at one another.

"I hate you!" he heard Annemarie scream before stomping footsteps could be heard growing closer. Her bedroom door slammed shut, making Will jump back from the wall and rub his ear. Anxiety began tying a knot in his stomach as he guessed what this conversation was likely about. Eric had said that the mayor would be going to their house to talk about the proposal in the morning. He could only guess that he'd overslept and missed the whole affair. As he began to hear Annemarie's mournful sobbing, his heart ached for her. He turned around and sat on the floor, leaning against the wall. He wanted dearly to hug her and tell her that it was going to be okay, but right now all he could do was sit here, eavesdropping on her and being there for her in spirit at least.

He distantly heard an intense conversation between Annemarie's mother and father before hearing their front door slam shut too. Their whole family seemed to be in disarray. He shook his head. He felt utterly useless. He'd told Eric that they'd meet up and discuss things more today, but what was he honestly bringing to the table? He had no ideas. He was pulled from his self-defamatory thoughts when Annemarie's mother knocked lightly on her door and entered. He took a deep breath. If he wanted to hear this conversation clearly, he was going to have to really strain himself. He pressed his right ear up against the wall again and covered his left, listening intently.

"Go away!" yelled Annemarie, still crying.

"Sweetheart, let me talk to ye," implored her mother.

"There's naught to talk about! I won't do it!" asserted Annemarie. There were a few moments of silence as William heard the faint sounds of movement.

"Ye know… when I first met your father, I didn't want to marry him either," said her mother. Annemarie didn't respond, continuing to quietly sob. William's heart sank. So, Eric had been right. The mayor really had already visited and discussed the affair.

"He's big, and smelly, and hairy! Do ye really think I wanted him?!" asked her mother jokingly. Annemarie let out a slight giggle.

"I used to tell me ma, 'ma if you make me marry that animal, I'll never talk to ye again!'" recalled her mother. Annemarie sniffled some more.

"Really?" she asked, fascinated by her mother's story.

"Aye. It's the truth. But you see, all my family had were a few goats. His family had a whole herd of cows! Twelve of 'em!" exclaimed her mother. Annemarie silently listened on.

"My father offered his field as a dowry to marry me. He knew that marrying me into a good family like ye father's would keep me safe and secure for the rest of me life," explained her mother. Annemarie quietly processed her words for a moment.

"Yeah well, he might be fat and hairy, but at least he isn't a creep like Father Marcus!" said Annemarie, re-igniting her tears as she recalled how scary the man was. There were a few moments of quiet as William could hear her mother gently soothing her.

"Ye know... when I was your age... there was one man in the village that every girl dreamed of marrying," began her mother.

"Who was it?" asked Annemarie.

"It were Marcus," replied her mother seriously.

"Yer jokin' me!" exclaimed Annemarie.

"I'm totally serious! Every single girl was after that man. No matter how much we swooned though, he never proposed to any of us," explained her mother.

"You know, one reason I was so angry that my parents arranged my marriage with your father is because I was wantin' to save myself for Marcus," explained her mother.

"What?!" squeaked Annemarie at her mother incredulously.

"It's true! I thought, one day he'll come back from that gateway, and by then he'll be wanting a wife. I thought it would be romantic if I waited. I thought I was going to sweep him off his feet!" said her mother with a chuckle. Annemarie giggled lovingly at her mother's naivety.

"He were so handsome, you know? Long black hair, and big muscles from chopping wood all day. Even when I was a young girl, I remember seeing him when he was your age. He was a real sweetheart too. He weren't like any man I'd ever seen. He loved animals, so I would always see him talking to my goats and pattin' them on the head on his way home," recalled her mother.

"Are ye sure you're talking about Father Marcus?!" asked Annemarie in disbelief.

"Aye! He'd always be helping out around the village too!" recalled her mother fondly.

"Don't go falling in love again, ma..." warned Annemarie jokingly. Her mother giggled.

"Aye. I just might! He was such a good man. Not just handsome; he helped others when they were in need. He stood up for the other kids when they were bullied, he even saved animals when they were sick. They don't make em' like that anymore. They never really did. I suppose that's why they let him become one of them clerics," thought her mother aloud.

"What do ye mean?" asked Annemarie.

"Well, they don't let just anybody become a cleric of Bethmael! Why do you think we're all so proud of him? Why do you think he has three knights traveling with him?" asked her mother.

"To keep him safe?" guessed Annemarie.

"No darling, it's not just that. It's to show how much the King respects him. They are showing the world; look at this man! He is a cleric of Bethmael! He is the best of all of us!" proclaimed her mother passionately, again making Annemarie giggle.

"Ma... he really scares me," said Annemarie earnestly.

"I know sweetheart. He scares us all, but there was something my grandma told me about the great war. She said when her father returned to Lakhdorian after fighting, he were scary too. He weren't the same man anymore. Dealing with those monsters... it changes people," said her mother seriously. There were a few moments of silence.

"Listen, deep down, he's still that kind-hearted, special boy that we all remember. I know he is. You can't take all of that away from a man. It's what made him who he is," explained her mother ardently.

"But I don't love him ma. He terrifies me," reiterated Annemarie.

"I know he does sweetheart but try to put yourself in your father's shoes. How do you think it'll look if he denies a proposal from a cleric of Bethmael, to his daughter, a Lakhdorian milkmaid?" asked her mother.

"I don't care how it looks," replied Annemarie.

"Have ye forgotten what I told ye already? This is a man who travels with a group of three of the kingdom's glorious knights. Ye father wouldn't only be denying Father Marcus, he'd be spitting in the face of the King. He'd be saying that a man who has the King's approval don't have his own. Do you know how that would look?" she asked seriously. Annemarie stayed silent as she pondered the reality of the situation.

"Would they hurt him?" asked Annemarie after a short moment. Her mother sighed.

"I don't know sweetheart. But you should know, your father would let himself be executed if it meant making you happy. It wouldn't matter though. Even if he was dead, the proposal wouldn't go away," explained her mother solemnly. William slumped his shoulders in defeat as the chilling reality set in for him too. No wonder Eric made such a big deal about them accepting the risk of fighting against this marriage. Had Eric already thought about all of this? William was once again in awe of his intelligence.

"Sweetie, how about this: just meet with the man. Try talking with him and see if that sweet boy I remember is still in there," asked her mother quietly.

"No! Mother, he is so, so, so, so scary!" said Annemarie, her voice quivering. William shivered as he too remembered how it felt sitting close to the man.

"I know he is, but don't forget what he's been dealing with at that gateway over the years. Give him some time. I promise sweetheart, he's a good man deep down. I think you might be able to bring that out of him," explained her mother. There was a short silence.

"Don't do it for ye self, do it for ye father," said her mother. William cringed, deciding to stop listening at this point. He was beginning to feel sick from what he was hearing. The more the situation crystallized, the more hopeless it became. As he leant forward and hugged his knees, his emotions began threatening to get the best of him. As soon as he noticed tears beginning to form in his eyes, he quickly stood up and started beating his chest to quell them. He wasn't going to just sit here and cry. His father hadn't raised him that way. When the going got tough, his father had always told him that a real man should buckle down and work harder. So that's exactly what he was going to do. As he made his way out to the stables, he made a decision with complete conviction. He would save Annemarie, no matter what it took. He wasn't going to let this happen without a fight.

***

Eric lay with his eyes closed, straining his brain. Perhaps, just perhaps, there was a hint. A clue. A corner of this carpet for him to pull at. As soon as he had but a single thread that he could pull, maybe he could unravel this whole situation. He was yanked from his thoughts when his father rolled over in his sleep, kicking the side of Eric's head roughly. He let out a sigh. He needed to get out of this cramped little wagon.

The second he hopped out of the back of the wagon, he realized just how close to the knight's caravan they were situated. The majority of those who had traveled up from the surrounding areas had spent the night camped out in this same small part of town. Lakhdorian was a small place, but Eric had for some reason imagined some kind of lavish living situation set up for the knights and Father Marcus. Instead, there they were, practically mixed in with the commoners aside from their considerably larger and fancier caravan. Last night there had been somebody making a terrible racket. There was screaming, moaning, and crying. Eric had assumed it was some drunken domestic argument and fallen back asleep, however now that he realized where the knight's caravan was, he began to question whether that's where he'd heard the commotion from. Azalea and August were sitting out on tree stumps eating bowls of porridge. Ivar was pacing back and forth with his arms crossed muttering to himself. He did not look happy. As soon as he caught sight of Eric, his attention immediately focused on him.

"You there!" shouted Sir Ivar, stopping his pacing and pointing directly at him. Eric swallowed nervously, looking over his shoulder to see if perhaps there was somebody more noteworthy standing behind him.

"I'm talking to you, Rothmane!" confirmed Ivar, beginning to stomp his way forward. Eric scratched his head and smiled meekly.

What had he done to garner the ire of a knight? He hoped that William hadn't done anything stupid last night after he'd left.

"I was told that there were natural hot springs here. I haven't bathed in three days!" exclaimed Ivar, staring at Eric expectantly. Eric stared blankly back at him.

"Nobody told you not to wash yourself," piped up Azalea from her stump. Sir Ivar swiped his hand in Azalea's direction to dispel her meddling.

"Well?!" continued Ivar, raising his arms in the air.

"Leave the poor boy alone!" said Azalea.

"No, don't! Keep going!" added August, entertained. Eric glanced between them anxiously.

"Well... Lakhdorian does have a hot spring, but the fumes are deadly sir," explained Eric with an apologetic shrug, unsure of who had fed the knight his bad information. As soon as he'd said this, Ivar began shining red.

"This is an outrage!" he shouted angrily, as August erupted into haughty laughter in the background.

"Did the mayor not provide you with an ewer?" asked Eric, shocked at his mayor's negligence.

"Of course I have a bloody ewer! But I was promised a hot spring!" he yelled.

"The nearest safe hot spring is at the base of Mistfall Mountain sir. It's a day's journey northwest from here," explained Eric. Ivar's eyes lit up.

"A day's journey?!" he asked, spinning around to look at his fellow knights. He scurried over and stood before them.

"We must make the journey post haste!" he declared. Azalea and August exchanged an uneasy glance with one another.

"We're here to accompany the cleric to his hometown..." began August. Ivar continued to simply stare back at him expectantly.

"Is this 'Mistfall Mountain' his hometown?" asked August, raising his eyebrows to accentuate his point. Ivar let out a sigh. He looked over his shoulder to see who was listening in. Luckily for him, the majority of the villagers were too intimidated by the knights to make eye contact, let alone be close enough to eavesdrop. Eric began slowly making his exit from the awkward situation.

"Hey! Don't you go anywhere!" commanded Ivar, pointing a finger at Eric. He gave a timid nod and stopped where he was.

"Listen..." said Ivar to his knightly compatriots quietly.

"Does he even know that he's in his hometown?" he asked. Azalea and August gave each other an uncomfortable glance.

"Does it matter? Our job is to accompany him to Lakhdorian..." reaffirmed Azalea.

"And we've done that!" exclaimed Ivar, raising his arms theatrically.

"Look around!" he said, stretching his arms out and gesturing at the general area. The three knights looked around at the hung-over commoners lumbering about in the muddy camp area. Eric could see the reality of how out of place the three of them were beginning to dawn on them.

"Listen Ivar, do you really think I don't want to relax in a hot spring? The feeling of that hot, bubbly water relaxing my sore muscles?" began August, his eyes starting to glass over as he thought about it.

"The stress of this entire pointless journey, the anger at being appointed such a waste of time, washed away as a group of comely maidens scrub my back and massage me? The dirt and grime of travel disappearing and being replaced by a feeling of pure, unadulterated, bliss…" he trailed off for a moment before his idyllic vision was interrupted by a peasant vomiting loudly in the mud.

"Comely maidens aside…" began Azalea raising an eyebrow.

"We have a job to do. We're not here for leisure," she verified. The three knights shared a glum sigh.

"Listen, what if we bring the cleric with us?" asked Ivar expectantly.

"Wait, this whole time you were imagining a scenario where we leave him behind?!" questioned Azalea, flabbergasted. Ivar cleared his throat nervously.

"No… I… of course not!" he lied.

"What if we asked the cleric whether he wants to go there?" asked August, now seemingly onboard with Ivar's plan. The three of them shared a moment of silent accord.

"I mean… if he wanted to go there… who are we to stop him?" asked Azalea, now also seemingly on board with the plan. The two of them looked up at Ivar expectantly. He seemed confused about why, until it dawned on him.

"No!" he defended categorically.

"Look, Ivar, it's your idea. If you want to go there, you're going to have to ask him yourself," said August seriously.

"B…But…" Ivar looked between the two of them before seeming to have an idea. He slowly turned around to face Eric.

"Absolutely not!" yelled Azalea as if reading his mind. Ivar drooped his shoulders in disappointment.

"Fine!" he said.

"I'll do it!" he continued, taking a step towards the caravan before standing perfectly still.

"Well?" asked August after a few moments.

"Shut up! I'm thinking," said Ivar.

"Aw, he's scared!" giggled Azalea.

"I am not!" exclaimed Ivar, still not moving.

"If you're so brave, why don't you do it then?" asked Ivar, raising an eyebrow at Azalea. She raised her hands defensively. Eric was surprised to see that even these three brave knights were just as uncomfortable around Father Marcus as the rest of their village was. This was a grim reality that hadn't dawned on him until now. He'd held knights in such high esteem that in his mind they were somehow immune to the fear that had crept into the rest of their hearts upon facing the man.

"Okay fine! Here I go!" said Ivar, courageously entering the caravan. Eric stared blankly at Azalea and August, unsure of whether he was allowed to move yet. The two of them stared back at him, amused. Both were clearly aware of his current predicament but neither wanted to help him out of it.

"Um..." said Eric, nervously.

"So can I... go?" he continued, pointing towards the village. August raised his eyebrow.

"Hmm... well Ivar did tell him not to go anywhere, did he not?" asked August to Azalea.

"Hmm... he wouldn't want to go directly against what Ivar asked of him now, would he?" asked Azalea. Eric let out a sigh. Both knights chuckled. Before they could elaborate on their ruse however, they were interrupted by the squire that had accompanied their group into Lakhdorian. He came hurrying back into the encampment from town, huffing and puffing from running.

"The mayor says that the hot spring is unsafe!" cried the squire, still gasping for breath.

"Oh, yeah, the kid told us already," said August pointing his spoonful of porridge at Eric. The squire turned his head and looked at Eric dejectedly.

"Oh," he said simply, before sitting down on the empty stump to catch his breath. At this moment Ivar came back out of the caravan looking unsettled.

"Well?" asked August, hopefully.

"Hmm well... yes..." said Ivar, shooing the squire off his stump before taking a seat. The squire let out a disappointed sigh as he found a patch of dry dirt to sit down on.

"I don't really know," explained Ivar honestly.

"Well, what did he say?" asked Azalea, confused.

"I asked him if he'd like to go to the Mistfall mountain hot springs, and he said 'take me away, please!'" explained Ivar.

"Well, that's great! Let's go!" said August enthusiastically.

"But..." started up Ivar again.

"Then he started saying 'No, wife!'..." finished Ivar. There was a silence over the group.

"And that was it? You just left?" asked Azalea incredulously.

"Well, he just started mumbling to himself again and he wouldn't respond to me anymore," said Ivar.

"So... does he want to go or not?" asked August. Ivar stared back at him vacantly and shrugged.

"Maybe at first he wanted to go, but then remembered that he proposed to that Lakhdorian girl, so he wants to stay now?" guessed Azalea looking around at her compatriots. August and Ivar's shoulders slumped as they considered this possibility.

"Perhaps he was saying, 'Yes, I want to go to the hot springs, but not with my wife! No wife!'. You know how women can be!" theorized Ivar. Azalea rolled her eyes.

"No, I don't know how women can be. Plus, they aren't even married yet," she replied flatly, scowling at him. Ivar shrugged in reluctant agreement.

"But what if..." August's face suddenly lit up.

"Hold on, what if he is saying 'yes, take me away to the hot springs, I want to spend time with my new wife there'?!" he theorized excitedly. Ivar raised his eyebrows as though considering this a very valid option.

"That's a bit of a stretch, no?" asked Azalea.

"I mean, what if we just bring her with us? Where's the harm in that?!" asked Ivar excitedly.

"No!" exclaimed Eric suddenly. He immediately regretted it when all attention was suddenly turned on him.

"I mean... oh... no! I've... got to get to the privy!" stammered Eric awkwardly, beginning to make his escape. He needed to find William and discuss this new development.

"Rothmane!" he heard Ivar calling after him. He stopped in his tracks. He couldn't just turn his back on a knight when they'd called his name. He took a breath and turned back around.

"Yes sir?" he asked politely.

"You'll be our guide to these hot springs, yes?" proposed Ivar. Panic shot through Eric's body. This was an absurdly fortuitous opportunity for him. Being offered to do a job for a group of knights and a cleric of Bethmael was a rare prospect which was unheard of for a random farm boy from the Mistfall moors. He looked over at the cart with his father sleeping in it. What would his father say if he shot down doing a job for a group of knights? Even though he felt like in a way he was betraying William if he accepted, at least this way he could keep an eye on Annemarie.

"Aye. I mean… yes. Yes of course I will, my lords," answered Eric firmly with a bow.

"Excellent!" exclaimed Ivar, clapping his hands together excitedly.

"It's settled then! We'll bring the girl and head out to these Mistfall Mountain hot springs immediately! Squire, fetch the girl!" commanded Ivar enthusiastically, pointing a finger in the air commandingly as he began to pack up some of his belongings. The squire let out an exasperated sigh before getting back up onto his feet. Eric gave one last polite nod before turning tail and breaking into a sprint. He had to get to William and tell him what was happening. They needed to come up with a plan, and fast.

CHAPTER SIX

Father Knows Best

When William had lazily wandered into the stables after his sleep in, he'd immediately been riddled with guilt for being late. It appeared three of their horses were already rented out, with the one remaining in the process of being rented out to a festival goer. Once the deal had been made and he was out of sight, William's father let out a sigh.

"Looks to have been a big morning, pa," said William, hoping to gauge his father's mood based on his response.

"Aye..." he responded distractedly. His father seemed a little despondent, and Will couldn't help but feel like perhaps it was due to his own absence from being in the stables at the crack of dawn this morning. He guiltily got to work, beginning his usual morning routine.

"You'll need to be doing a full muck out today," said his father, sitting down and writing down some notes pertaining to the deals which had been made this morning. William stopped what he was doing and wiped his brow.

"Aye father," he responded obediently. The truth was that he was a little thankful for the distraction that work would give him.

"Pa..." began William, continuing his shoveling. His father didn't respond.

"Did you know Father Marcus when you were young?" asked William. Although he didn't respond, he'd clearly caught his father's attention, as he dropped what he was doing and looked up at Will. Before he could respond however, suddenly Eric came bursting around the door of the stables.

"William!" yelled Eric, completely breathless from running. As soon as he noticed William's father sitting in the corner, he adorned an expression of recognition.

"My apologies sir!" said Eric, bowing politely to his father before grabbing ahold of a stable post and doubling over to catch his breath. William's father simply gave a nod of greeting.

"Are ye okay Eric?" asked William, concerned about what could've spurred such a big lad to run so hard. Eric tried to respond but couldn't, due to his exhaustion. He held up his hand and continued to catch his breath for a moment. William's father let out a chuckle.

"How's old Barty holding up today?" he asked. Upon being addressed by William's father, Eric decided to respond to him first.

"He's... doing... well sir.... still... recovering from... last night," responded Eric between huffed breaths. William's father gave a wry smile before returning to his paperwork.

"William, we need to talk," said Eric, turning to William but glancing nervously at his father out of the corner of his eye.

"Aye, what is it?" asked William. Eric signaled to William that he couldn't talk about it in front of his father by nodding in his direction. William thought about it for a moment before letting out a sigh. He needed to work. It wasn't fair on his father if he stopped and ran off to have a secret talk with his friend.

"What is it?" asked William again, continuing to shovel while he talked. Eric looked at him exasperatedly before accepting the situation.

"Look, there's not much time. The squire will be here any minute to pick up Annemarie. They're taking her to Mistfall," explained Eric hurriedly.

"What?!" exclaimed William.

"Why in the world would they be going to Mistfall?!" he asked. Eric blushed as he remembered that it was he who had told them about the hot springs there.

"They're going to the hot springs, but it don't matter Will. All that matters is that they're taking Annemarie with them," said Eric speedily.

"What are you talking about?" piped up William's father suddenly. The two boys looked at each other in a panic.

"Why would they be taking the neighbor girl with them?" he asked, confused about the entire situation.

"We... well you see... last night Father Marcus he... he..." William couldn't get the words out of his mouth. Even now, there was a part of him which refused to accept what had happened.

"Father Marcus proposed to Annemarie last night," explained Eric flatly. William's father looked surprised, before confusion set in on his face.

"Well, what's that got to do with you two?" he asked suspiciously. The two boys looked guiltily between each other. Realization suddenly dawned on his father's face as he looked at William.

"William. This is absolutely none of your business," he decreed categorically.

"But father, she don't want it!" implored William desperately. There was no time for him to explain the whole situation to his father.

"I don't care!" he yelled, standing from his chair as the severity of the situation was suddenly dawning on him.

"Do you two boys have any idea what kind of powers you're playing with here?!" he asked, concern and anger plastering his face. William averted his gaze nervously. There was no way his father would ever understand what he was going through.

"Aye we do sir but... if I may..." began Eric, testing the waters. William pleaded with his eyes for Eric to shut up, but Eric raised his hand to subdue William's silent protest. Panic began to set in as William realized that Eric didn't understand how scary of a man his father could be.

"Sir... you must've seen him. You must've felt it. Surely you understand that we can't just let him take our friend away..." reasoned Eric. Surprisingly, William's father's rage seemed to subside slightly. He took a deep breath before responding.

"Aye. I felt it. But let me tell you boys, you don't know the first thing about that man. Not the first thing," he said assuredly, looking between the two of them sternly.

"William..." he began, turning to address William directly.

"I forbid you from involving yourself in his affairs. Do you understand me?" asked his father sternly.

"But..." began Will.

"I'll not hear it!" yelled his father, taking a few threatening steps towards William. He pointed his finger directly in William's face.

"You'll stay out of that man's affairs. Now I want to hear yes sir!" demanded his father, looming over him threateningly. William quelled the tears of frustration and desperation which he could feel brimming. His respect for his father was far too great to go against his will.

"Yes sir," replied William, looking down at the floor. His father suddenly turned to Eric.

"Eric..." he began. Eric straightened up, preparing for what was to come.

"I'm glad to see that you're looking well," said his father unexpectedly. Eric was taken aback by the sudden compliment.

"Aye, thank you sir!" responded Eric politely.

"I've always liked you," he continued. Eric nodded his head nervously.

"You've always been a good friend for William," he added, closing his eyes and nodding. William anxiously watched on, hoping that his father was going easy on his oldest friend.

"But... I must say... I'm very disappointed that you'd entertain this stupidity!" said his father, his eye twitching slightly.

"Him?!" he said, pointing at William without looking.

"He's not bright enough to understand, but you!" he said, moving his arm around to point at Eric.

"You should know better. And you know it too," he finished coldly. William was taken aback by how heartfelt his father was being. Eric looked at the ground silently. He seemed to be considering William's father's words deeply.

"Aye," he replied simply, surprising Will.

"I just..." he started, looking up at Will.

"I didn't want my friend to get hurt," finished Eric sincerely. William felt his fists clench. Did Eric not want to save Annemarie? Did he not care about her at all? Was he really doing this just because he felt pity for William? Did William really seem that weak and pathetic to him?

"If you really didn't want him to get hurt, you'd have told him how stupid it was to get involved in this in the first place," said William's father, walking back over to the workbench and sitting back down.

"William," his father suddenly said.

"Aye father?" he asked, seething with a confusing cocktail of emotions but remaining obedient.

"Finish your work later. Go and talk with Eric," said his father, returning to his paperwork.

"No, I think I'm good," said William coldly, staring at Eric as he returned to his work.

"Hey!" shouted his father, banging his fist on the bench. William snapped his head around in surprise.

"Don't make me tell you again boy!" he yelled furiously. William nodded his head obediently and put his pitchfork down before reluctantly leaving the stables with Eric.

***

The two boys walked in silence back towards Eric's wagon. There was awkwardness in the air, but mostly hopelessness. It was like a dark cloud had been cast over them.

"William…" began Eric.

"Just tell me this," interrupted William.

"Did you ever really want to help Annemarie?" he asked seriously.

"Of course I did!" defended Eric, clearly annoyed at the implication that he didn't. Will let out a sigh. Even if he had said no, he's not the one in love with her. He was just trying to be a good friend. William's resentment was ill placed, and he knew it, but he still didn't quite understand things from Eric's perspective.

"Did ye ever think we'd actually be able to stop it?" asked William, looking at Eric searchingly. Eric slowly shook his head.

"Your father was right. It wasn't just you that I was being dishonest with Will; I wasn't being honest with myself. It's time that I started facing reality. Against a cleric of Bethmael, what are we to do?" asked Eric. Will shook his head in dismay. Before he could respond, he suddenly caught eye of the squire who had finally made his way into town. He was muttering to himself angrily as he walked. When he saw Eric he scowled at him.

"If you were in town anyway, don't you think you could've gotten the girl?" asked the squire as he passed them by. Will looked between the two in confusion. Eric decided to keep his mouth shut and just keep walking.

"Hey! I'm talking to you! You can't ignore me you know, I'm practically a knight!" shouted the squire. Eric and William raised their eyebrows and looked at one another. The squire couldn't have been more than a year or two older than them.

"My apologies sir," said Eric politely, bowing his head slightly. The squire looked a little uncomfortable at being addressed in this formal manner but nodded.

"Good... good..." he said, as he kept walking. Although he had initially appeared satisfied, he suddenly stopped just after he'd passed the boys. He turned back around to face them.

"Hey, look uh... don't tell Sir August that I said that I was practically a knight..." pleaded the squire abashedly. Will and Eric smirked at each other, amused by the squire's antics.

"Aye," said Eric with a nod before they continued in their opposite directions. There was a moment of silence between the boys as they kept walking.

"What did he mean? Why would you have gone to get Annemarie?" asked Will, feeling oddly suspicious of his old friend.

"The truth is Will… they offered me a job. I'm to guide them to Mistfall…" admitted Eric ashamedly.

"What?!" exclaimed William, stopping suddenly. Eric rubbed the back of his head anxiously.

"Aye…" he said. William stared at him for a moment.

"Eric… that's amazing!" said William happily. Eric looked back at him in confusion.

"It is?" he asked, perplexed.

"Aye! That means you can keep an eye on Annemarie!" said William.

"Well… yeah! It does! That was one of the reasons I accepted the job!" replied Eric honestly.

"Oh, so the glory and coin of working for knights had nothing to do with it eh?" asked William coaxingly. Eric laughed.

"Aye, I suppose that had something to do with it too," he replied with a smile. As the two boys neared the campgrounds, they slowed their pace until they stopped and turned to face one another.

"Eric, please try to keep her safe," said Will seriously, holding out his hand expectantly. Eric nodded sincerely, before grabbing Will's hand and reciprocating their signature handshake.

"I don't know how long the job is going to last, but I probably won't see you again for a while," said Eric.

"Aye, it's been good seeing you brother. Thanks for putting up with all my shite," said William earnestly. Eric laughed heartily, patting Will on the back. He began to walk away before suddenly turning back to face Will.

"Hey, once this has all blown over… are ye going to marry her?" he asked. William smiled happily as he envisioned his future with Annemarie.

"Aye," he replied with a nod. Eric smiled approvingly before turning around and continuing his way towards the campground.

"Eric!" shouted Will suddenly, remembering one last thing. Eric turned around curiously.

"Congratulations on the job," said Will, only now registering what it meant for a country boy like him to work directly for a band of knights. His drama with Annemarie had almost made him forget to commend his friend.

"Thanks Will," replied Eric earnestly before continuing on his journey.

After watching him leave, William turned around and began his short walk back home. It didn't take long before he saw Annemarie and her parents walking in his direction accompanied by the squire. He held his breath anxiously as he passed, trying to stop his nervous breathing from showing. When he made eye contact with Annemarie as they drew closer, she looked surprised to see him, before averting her eyes abashedly. William understood the situation better than she knew, but in this fleeting moment there was nothing he could say to her. He wanted to say goodbye, or to tell her that he understood, but as he walked past all he could do was watch on silently as the love of his life was being led away from him and into the arms of that terrifying man. He felt useless. Was there really nothing that he could do to help her? As he walked home, the dark cloud which lingered over him intensified with every step he took away from her.

***

When he reached home, William wished that he could just bury himself in his work and forget about everything, but no matter how hard he worked, he wouldn't be able to get the image of Annemarie walking away with the squire out of his mind. He began his full muck out of the stables, cleaning out all the wood shavings and replacing them with a fresh layer. He felt sick to his stomach the whole time as he pondered how to help Annemarie. The work didn't help to distract him in the slightest. After finishing the job, he let out a frustrated groan and threw his pitchfork down.

"I don't understand it father. Why do people be treating them so fancy-like?" he asked, kicking a clump of the freshly strewn wood shavings against the wall in frustration. His father was hammering in a board on their stable wall which had become loose. Will's whining was the last thing from his mind as he focused on the task at hand. He uttered a gruff neutral grunt in response and continued on with his work.

"Why do they even be calling him 'Father'? He ain't anyone's pa. What even is a cleric anyway?" asked Will as he slumped over one of the stable windows. He looked down the road searchingly as though he'd be able to see the back of Annemarie and the squire who were by now long gone. His anxiety began to build up in his stomach until it formed a knot of rage. Watching Annemarie's parents leading her down the road towards that dark cleric filled William with anger. How could they do that to their own daughter?

"Why do they be going along with it like it's nothing? They know bloody well what he's going to do to her! I wonder how much copper that foul bastard offered her family…" grumbled Will as he sank deeper into his slumped posture over the window ledge. Upon hearing the sound of his father's hammer falling to the floor, Will knew that something was wrong. He quickly turned around, but before he had a chance to react, his father's hand was already in full swing towards his face. With no time to defend himself he took the slap across his right cheek, causing him to lose his footing and fall down into the wood shavings which lined the stable floor. He subdued a yelp of surprise as he was struck down. Now on the floor, he shakily placed his palm over his cheek and feebly tried to stop tears from welling in his eyes in front of his father. He looked up in fear, confused as to how he had spurred such an attack.

"That man is a cleric of Bethmael! How dare you disrespect him like that?! You will never be half the man that he is, and nor will I! He needn't offer gold; it's an honor for her family that he considered her at all! If your sister was of age I'd ask that he take her instead!" spat his father furiously. William knew that his antics had frustrated his father, but he had no idea how he'd somehow made the man quite this angry.

"Father I..." began Will, not sure how to atone for what he'd said. His father shook his head and took a deep breath.

"Look William, just drop it, okay? Forget about her, forget about Marcus and just do yer bloody job!" groaned his father. William simply stared up at him and nodded obediently. Disappointment flashed over his father's face for a moment as he stared down over Will sitting pathetically on the stable floor nursing his cheek. After a moment it was replaced by what seemed like remorse. He let out a sigh. He seemed like he was about to say something, but caught himself and left the stables in silence. William felt utterly miserable. He had never made his father this upset, and he still didn't even quite understand what he'd done wrong. He hugged his knees on the stable floor, fighting his urge to cry with every inch of his being. He'd disappointed his father enough for one day, crying pathetically in a pile of wood shavings would be the final nail in the coffin.

William's mother suddenly appeared at the stable door, investigating what the commotion had been about.

"Willy!" she exclaimed, hurrying over to him and squatting down beside him. She put a concerned hand on his back.

"Are ye okay?!" she asked. William nodded silently and got to his feet, still massaging his red cheek.

"Where has father gone?" he asked, the knot of guilt in his stomach tightening by the second.

"I just saw him take Bonnie out," said his mother, still looking over Will with concern. Bonnie was his father's personal horse which he kept tied up out the back most days.

"Are ye sure you're okay sweetie? Tell me what's wrong! What happened?" she asked. William started blushing as he realized how badly he needed somebody to comfort him.

"I upset pa," said William, still barely managing to hold back his tears. His mother looked surprised.

"Why, what'd you do?" she asked, looking around the stables for some obvious sign of error. William let out a sigh. He didn't want to have to explain the whole situation to his mother.

"I spoke badly of Father Marcus," said William quietly. Realization flashed across his mother's face.

"Oh..." she said, her eyes glazing over as she seemed to be thinking deeply.

"Come with me Willy," she said, walking towards the stable door and beckoning to him. He followed after her, fascinated by her unusually somber tone. She led him around the back of the house, past the privy and down the hill a short way. She took him towards a bush which she parted, revealing a wooden crate. William had no idea what was happening. He inhaled nervously as he anticipated what could possibly be inside. His mother opened up the lid of the crate, revealing its contents. Inside sat the fancy bridle and saddle which his father had made for Father Marcus. William stared speechlessly at it for a moment. He had absolutely no idea what this signified. He looked searchingly at his mother.

"Why is that here?!" asked William, looking at the wilderness around them as though it might shed some clues on the situation.

"I saw it still on the gift table this morning," said his mother solemnly.

"What?! Father Marcus didn't care for it?!" asked William in shock. Any Lakhdorian should be ecstatic to be gifted something with so much of their village's spirit etched into every inch of it.

"There's something wrong with him," said his mother darkly.

"That's not the Marcus I remember..." she continued, her eyes glazing over again as she seemed to be remembering something.

"I suppose you fancied him like everybody else," blurted out William, immediately realizing that he only knew about Annemarie's mother's story because he had eavesdropped. William's mother looked at him in surprise.

"Aye I did! But how did you know about that?!" she asked in shock.

"Did yer father say something?!" she asked, beginning to shine bright red. William let out a sigh.

"No ma, I've just heard some stories about him is all," he said. His mother nodded understandingly.

"I see. Well yes Willy, I'd be lying if I didn't say he was rather charming, but... there's something you should know. It's about your father and him," she began.

"Your father, he used to... well, he used to bully him horribly when we were kids," finished his mother, looking guilty for mentioning this. William was dumbstruck by this information. His quiet and reserved father? A bully? It seemed so unlikely that he could barely fathom it.

"What?!" he asked in shock.

"Aye… your father he… well he matured faster than the other boys. He didn't grow that big overnight you know," explained his mother. William wasn't sure why his mother was opening up to him about all of this.

"Marcus was very popular with the girls because he was quite… feminine. We felt like he understood us better than the other boys did. But of course, he was unpopular with many of the other village boys for the same reason," she explained. William listened on quietly, starting to realize how much of her story was corroborated by Annemarie's mother.

"If father was a bully, then why did you marry him?" asked William. Would it be the same answer as always, arranged marriage?

"Oh, he grew out of all that! Plus, I weren't that spotless myself back then, ye know!" admitted his mother, realizing that she hadn't explained herself properly.

"No, by the time we were of marrying age your father had become the sweet man that he is today!" explained his mother, shaking her head. William was shocked to hear that neither of his parents had always been as virtuous as they seemed to be today.

"You know Willy, he feels such guilt over the way he treated Marcus. Especially since he left the village and became a cleric of Bethmael. Your father never had a chance to apologize for the way he treated him. That's why he made this you see," explained his mother, gesturing to the saddle and bridle. William stared at it perplexed.

"So… why is it here?" he asked again. His mother let out a sigh.

"I wanted your father to think that it had been accepted," she said, again drifting off deep into thought.

"Father Marcus is too sick to receive gifts properly..." thought William aloud as he comprehended the situation.

"Aye. And on top of that, the meaning of this bridle is lost on those knights. They're not Lakhdorian, they couldn't understand..." said his mother, shaking her head.

"William. I just thought you ought to know, it's not your fault that you've upset your pa. He's got his own hang-ups concerning Marcus, and hearing you disrespect the man probably brought some of that back up for him," she explained. William suddenly realized how unfair it was for his father to have struck him, but immediately let go of his resentment. The situation was complicated. There was a moment of silence as the two pondered the situation.

"He's marrying Annemarie," said William quietly, fighting back tears which welled in his eyes as he uttered those cursed words. His mother looked shocked at first before realization dawned on her face.

"Oh sweetheart come here," she said, hugging him tightly.

"No wonder you're so upset!" she continued.

"What can I do about it?" asked William, desperate for somebody to give him an answer. His mother seemed to think about his question deeply. William was touched that she was giving him this much respect, considering that she could easily disregard this whole drama as teenage nonsense.

"William, I think you should wait it out," she said seriously. William let out a sigh.

"Because he's sick, right?" asked William, remembering this being the first solution which Eric had offered too.

"Well yes, there's something wrong with that man to be sure, but I think you should just wait. Wait and see what happens. These things have a way of working themselves out," said his mother, kissing him on the forehead.

"Aye. Thank you mother," said William, thanking her more for consoling him than for providing him with any realistic solution to the problem.

As the two of them walked back towards their house together, with their shared secret of the hidden bridle bonding them closer, William finally accepted the only solution to the problem that he could. He'd wait it out. He didn't care how long he was going to have to wait. He'd wait for Annemarie. He'd wait until their time was right. The two of them were soul mates, he could feel it, and he knew that she could too. It was only a matter of time before the timing would be right, and they could be together, but just how long was that going to take?

CHAPTER SEVEN

Crimson Springs

William waited for the three longest days of his young life. It felt like she'd been gone for an eternity, and when a wagon finally came rolling into town with but two lone figures on its back, he wasn't sure what to make of it. He simply continued grooming Bonnie, but when the wagon stopped right outside his doors, he stopped grooming the horse and peeked outside of his stables. His eyes opened wide in surprise at who he saw. There was Annemarie, and with her, a stranger. No knights, no Father Marcus, and no Eric. Just as he was about to call out, he caught sight of her face. She looked utterly disheveled. Her parents burst out from their front door to greet her, and as soon as she set eyes on them, she alighted from the cart, running into their arms and releasing a cascade of tears. William ducked down below the window of the stables. He had so many questions, but now wasn't the time to ask them. Why was she so miserable? What had happened? Where were the knights? Where was Father Marcus? Was Eric okay? From where he was in the stables, he couldn't quite hear the conversation happening around the corner. He stood back up and peeked cautiously around the edge of the stable window. The man who had been controlling the wagon also hopped down, having a brief conversation

with Annemarie's parents. After a few minutes the entire group began walking into town, rather than entering Annemarie's house.

William stopped looking out the window and turned back to his
half-groomed horse who was staring back at him expectantly. He
could feel his anxiety rising as he pondered all of the scenarios
which could take place in three days that could've led to this moment. As he continued to halfheartedly brush Bonnie, his mind was
whirring. There were so many questions that needed to be answered.
Luckily for Will, he would only need to wait fifteen minutes before
his prayers were answered. The town bell was rung, signaling an
urgent town meeting. He dropped his brush and rushed towards the
village center. As he expected, everybody else was doing the same.
This rare occasion appeared to have spurred everybody to drop
whatever they were doing to convene at the town gathering point.

As William approached the busy village center, he began to feel
a strange sense of nervousness. There, standing on the tiny wooden
stage which was used for these rare public announcements, was the
mayor. Behind him was Annemarie, being consoled by her parents.
Alongside her was the strange man who had come into town with
her. As the crowd gathered, the mayor waited patiently for a few
minutes until finally he deemed the crowd adequate to begin his
announcement.

"My fellow Lakhdorians, I have called you here today with some
very unfortunate news. As some of you may be aware, Father Marcus had traveled to the hot springs of Mistfall village to ease the
aches and pains of travel. It is there that he unfortunately, like so
many clerics of Bethmael before him, succumbed to the darkness of
that horrible gateway. It is with regret that I must inform you, that
as of yesterday, Father Marcus, the hero of our village, has passed
away," explained the mayor solemnly. Immediately everybody in

the village began chattering amongst themselves. After seeing the state of him at the feast the other night, nobody was utterly astonished by the news, but it still came as a surprise. William could feel a strange mixture of emotions swelling inside of him. He was mostly still worried about Annemarie, and of course he was surprised to hear about Marcus' death, however beneath it all lingered a guilty tinge of relief. Had fate somehow smiled upon him and Annemarie? It was only when William began to think about the circumstances in more detail that a little bit of panic crept into his heart. Could it have been Eric? Could he or Annemarie have done that dastardly deed that William had not seen fit to even bring up, yet had lingered in the silence between the ideas they had cast? Again, William didn't have to wait long to have this question answered as somebody in the village called out to the mayor.

"How did he die?" asked the man brazenly. The mayor raised his hands to call for silence once more. He took a moment to steady his nerves as the discomfort of his next announcement threatened to make his voice crack.

"Marcus has... well, he has done as I said, um... as many of the clerics of Bethmael do, he..." the mayor clearly didn't know how to phrase his answer.

"He killed 'imself," said the outsider man bluntly. The crowd erupted with gasps and hushed chatter at this revelation. William still had his gaze locked on Annemarie who was crying into her mother's shoulder. He wondered whether perhaps she had been the one to find the body, or worse yet, had seen him commit the deed. How had he done it? William both yearned to know the gory details, and also yearned not to.

"We will be holding a traditional cremation on the ridge of ashes this evening, hosted by Mister Cotswold here, a mortician from

Mistfall who has accompanied Marcus back to our village. All are welcome and encouraged to attend, to celebrate the life of Father Marcus, the hero of Lakhdorian. His sacrifice will be remembered by the history books, and on behalf of Lakhdorian I thank him for his service in keeping us all safe," announced the mayor. There was a moment of silence as everybody collectively reflected on Father Marcus' life before the crowd began to disperse. William felt a hand on his shoulder. He turned to see his father looking over him with concern. He must've arrived shortly after William had.

"Come on boy, let's head home," he said quietly. William nodded and followed after his father. The two silently walked back towards the stables as they both ruminated on their own relationships with the dead cleric, neither having the social skills to communicate their feelings with one another.

***

The next several hours went by in a flash. William's family had made the trek over to the ridge of ashes, which had been the location for funeral pyres and cremations since the village's inception. There they stood, with the majority of the other townsfolk and quietly watched as Father Marcus' funeral pyre was lit before the sunset. As William watched the flames burning, he once again felt that strange concoction of emotions in his gut. Had this all somehow been tied up nicely? He could see Annemarie quietly watching the flames herself too. She wore a dark expression which he hadn't seen on her face before. What in the world had happened at that hot spring? It was too soon for him to approach Annemarie and ask her any questions, but he needed to know if Eric was okay.

After the service had concluded, William made his way over towards the mortician that the mayor had called mister Cotswold. If he couldn't approach Annemarie with his questions, perhaps this blunt speaking outsider could give him the answers he needed.

"Good evening…" said William, feeling awkward about being a random village kid approaching him out of the blue. The man raised an eyebrow and looked down over him before giving a polite nod.

"I just had a couple of questions… about… you know…" began William. The man seemed surprised, but then a sly knowing expression came over his face.

"Interested in this kinda stuff are ya? Yeah. I was about your age when I started getting curious too," misconstrued the man, making William feel a little uncomfortable.

"Uh… yeah," said William, deciding to simply go along with it since it seemed to be a good way to get the guy talking.

"It weren't like I've ever seen before, I'll tell you that much," said Cotswold, looking over the remaining embers of the funeral pyre, deep in thought. William stayed silent, not wanting to interrupt the man.

"He'd made a right mess of himself. Cut off all sorts of things that ought to stay where they are. Things that as a man myself, I have to say, made even me a little squeamish," said Cotswold with a gravelly chuckle. William released a fake laugh of his own in response, deftly defying the feeling of sickness he could feel forming in his gut. If he'd understood what the man was getting at correctly, Marcus had done something which William shuddered at the thought of.

"It weren't just that though. He'd gotten into one of em' hot pools and opened veins in both his arms. Looked like a bowl of soup, it did!" said Mister Cotswold, again making himself laugh and again making William feel sick. He hadn't really wanted to know any of these gory details, the main thing he wanted to know was whether Eric was okay.

"Who found the body?" asked William.

"Blimey, I don't know," said Cotswold, looking at Will as though confused why he'd care about that.

"You didn't see my friend Eric there did you?" asked William.

"Nah, just a bunch of knights. I gotta say though, squeamish bunch if you ask me. With the taxes we have to pay to that bloody college of theirs you'd think they'd teach them how to look at a body without getting their knickers in a twist!" said Mister Cotswold with another chuckle. William smiled meekly in response.

"Oh, hold on a minute... your mate, would he be that big fat kid?" he asked tactlessly. William was excited enough to hear Eric mentioned that he let the remark slide.

"Aye that's him!" said William enthusiastically.

"Oh yeah, I saw that kid," he said simply. William waited for him to continue before he realized he was finished speaking.

"Was he okay?" asked William.

"Yeah, he looked alright, all things considered. They sent the girl home with me, but he had to stay and answer questions. You know, now that I think about it, maybe it was him what found the body," said Mister Cotswold, apparently only now thinking about the situation in more detail. William was filled by both relief that Eric was okay but also horror that he had to witness something so gruesome.

"Say kid, if you ever find yourself in Mistfall, I might be looking for an apprentice somewhere down the line. Head down to the morgue and I can show you the ropes," said Cotswold, looking down at William's calloused hands and muscular arms, clearly having identified him as a hard worker. William's heart skipped a beat as he imagined himself working with corpses. He knew himself well enough that the idea of working with cadavers, or anything gruesome, would completely overwhelm his delicate sensibilities.

"Aye!" said William politely. He would never outright turn down a job offer, as in times such as these it was a flattering proposal, no matter who it came from. He shook Mister Cotswold's hand before turning back and beginning his journey home. Eric was safe, Annemarie was safe, and on top of it all she wouldn't have to marry Father Marcus now. Everything seemed to have been tied up very neatly, so why did William still feel a knot of worry churning in his stomach?

***

It was over a week before William saw Annemarie again. He hadn't heard a peep from her side of the wall in all that time either. Her house had been dead silent. The disquieting stillness of the atmosphere lingered over him like a cloak. When he finally cast his eyes upon her again, his heart didn't skip a beat like it used to, and he wasn't quite sure why. Something had changed between the two of them. There she was, carrying a bucket of milk back from her cows. It was a rare opportunity to speak to her, so William decided to test the waters.

"Good morning Annemarie," said William with a smile through his stable window.

"Good morning William," she replied politely without stopping, and that was it. There was no awkward conversation, no magic in the air. Just a cold greeting, like they were any two random villagers who hadn't shared that amazing romantic dinner on the festival night. William knew that she'd been through a lot, but the complexities of breaking down the walls of this stifling situation were beyond his capabilities. All he could do was return to work and ruminate on the situation.

***

It wasn't until William was lying in bed that evening that an idea suddenly came to mind. Rather than randomly accosting her out in the street, perhaps if he knocked on the back of the wardrobe she'd feel more comfortable talking with him. That would be a more wholesome and safe place to rekindle their relationship than in the middle of a random workday. He cast a worried glance over at Sasha who was reading quietly on her side of the room. Talking about anything in front of her would be way too embarrassing. He'd gotten lucky the last time that she hadn't been there. He took a deep breath. Was he more concerned about Annemarie, or embarrassing himself in front of his sister?

"Sasha..." said William, already blushing at what he was about to do.

"Hmm?" she hummed without looking up from her book.

"Uh... look I'm a little worried about Annemarie, so I'm going to see if she wants to talk..." said William awkwardly. Sasha looked up from her book with a puzzled expression on her face.

"Okay?" she asked, confused about why he was bringing this up to her.

"I mean, I'm going to do it how we used to..." he said, his blushing intensifying. Sasha stared at him blankly for a moment before a look of realization came across her face, followed by a cheeky grin.

"You mean, like..." she began, gesturing towards the wardrobe. William nodded; mortified as he remembered how he used to tell his sister he would marry Annemarie when they were kids talking through the wardrobe.

"Wouldn't it be easier to just talk through the wall though?" asked Sasha, raising an eyebrow. She had a point, but the childishness and nostalgia of the wardrobe game provided a cute and comfortable padding on which to instigate the potentially difficult conversation. William didn't know how to put this into words so simply shrugged.

"Go on then," said his sister, with an amused smirk, nodding towards the wardrobe. William felt so embarrassed that he lingered for a moment, before reticently clambering into the tiny wardrobe. He sat in the darkness for a moment, listening to his sister's stifled chuckles while watching him. He let out a sigh. Here goes nothing.

Tap, tap tap.

William knocked on the back of the wardrobe. He waited for a short while, but there was no response. He let out a sigh and prepared to leave the wardrobe.

"Come on Will, try again," said Sasha.

"At least try to pretend you're not listening to me! Read yer bloody book!" replied William angrily. He took a deep breath and tried again.

Tap, tap tap.

He knocked again, but once again there was no answer. He was just about to get back out of his wardrobe when finally, he heard it.

Tap, tap tap.

"Annemarie?!" he asked excitedly. There was a moment of silence.

"Aye, good evening William..." she replied quietly. William's heart raced as he realized that this was actually happening.

"How are you?!" asked William. There was another moment of silence.

"I'm fine," she replied. William could tell from her tone that something was wrong. He wasn't sure how to approach asking her about what was on her mind.

"Are… are you?" began William, racking his mind for the correct way to get her to open up to him. There was another moment of silence.

"Look uh, I just wanted to check up on you is all. I've been a bit worried about you since you got back…" said William honestly, blushing in the darkness. There was silence, but with his ear pressed to the back of the wardrobe William thought he could hear her sobbing.

"Annemarie?! Are you okay?!" asked William, full of concern.

"Aye, I'm fine!" she replied shakily, clearly crying. William shook his head. How could he get her to open up?

"Look uh, Mister Cotswold told me about what happened. Did you get a chance to see if Eric was okay?" asked William, thinking that perhaps changing the subject a little might help.

"What?! He told you?!" she asked in surprise.

"Aye, he's a creepy old coot, isn't he?" asked William. It was at that moment that he heard the beautiful sound of Annemarie's laughter.

"Aye he is…" she said with a giggle. William laughed too, out of pure joy and relief.

"I've missed you William…" said Annemarie earnestly. William felt his heart racing. Not only because of what she said, but out of embarrassment that Sasha probably heard it too. He was in too deep at this point. He needed to stop caring whether Sasha could hear. He needed to focus on being there for Annemarie.

"Aye. I've missed you too," said William honestly.

"I just thought…" began Annemarie.

"I just thought that you'd hate me... for well... going..." said Annemarie solemnly. William gasped in surprise.

"Annemarie no! Of course I don't!" he began, stumbling to find the words to explain himself.

"I know you had no choice!" replied William, his heart aching for her to know that he understood. There was another moment of silence.

"William can we... meet outside?" asked Annemarie suddenly, causing his heart to skip a beat.

"Aye! We can!" said William enthusiastically. He clambered out of his wardrobe as fast as he could, but when he locked eyes with his sister the embarrassment of the situation suddenly overwhelmed him. She stared back at him expectantly for a moment.

"Well? What are ye waiting for? Are ye gonna make her stand out there alone?" she asked, raising an eyebrow. William felt relief swell in his chest that his sister wasn't teasing him. He nodded with a grateful smile, hurrying out the front door and around the back of their house. As soon as he rounded the corner and saw her in her white nightgown underneath the moonlight, with her long blonde hair falling over her shoulders, he finally felt that spark return.

"William..." she said, running over towards him and catching him in a hug. He hugged her back tightly, like he'd been yearning to since she'd left. Once again, her tears began to fall into his chest and she began to sob, freeing all of her pent-up emotion that she'd clearly been dying to release. He quietly hugged her back, feeling her pain and consoling her to the best of his abilities. He didn't know the details of what she'd been through, but he could tell by the veracity of her crying that she'd been through a lot. And so it was, there beneath the moonlight, that the two young lovers stood for what felt like an eternity, locked in each other's embrace. As they reconnected, they both finally felt the relief that only the other could provide.

CHAPTER EIGHT

Barley and Wheat

The next three weeks went by in a flash. Every single day was a joy. William would wake up and shovel his breakfast down as quickly as he could before running around the back of the house and being greeted good morning by Annemarie. The two were yet to kiss, but William didn't care. He just loved being around her. They were all but official at this point, and William couldn't imagine that life could get much better than this. If he were to simply work in his father's stable until he was old enough to take over the place, then go on to marry Annemarie and move into a house together one day, then his life would be perfect. He could wish for no more than for life to continue on exactly how it was, but alas; the twists and turns of young William's life would take him to many a blissful peak, but also, to many a deep abyss.

The first sign that something was wrong began with Annemarie not being there in the morning to greet him. They'd met like this every day until now, and without a warning, she was missing. Was she sick? It made sense that if she were ill, then she wouldn't have come around the back of the house, but he'd heard nary a cough from through their dividing wall. Would it be appropriate for him to ask her family? Should he wait? They weren't even officially dating.

As far as anybody else knew the two were simply happy neighbors. As was rapidly becoming William's default solution to all problems he encountered in life, he decided to wait. Perhaps she had simply forgotten. Perhaps she had simply overslept. They'd made no agreement to meet here each morning. This morning ritual had evolved naturally. William returned to his work, with naught on his mind except the perplexing disappearance of Annemarie.

***

It was only after three days of silence that William decided that he'd had enough. He needed answers, and it felt ridiculous of him at this point to not have simply knocked on her door to get them. As he marched his way determinedly towards her front door after work that night however, he was in for a shock. Right as he was nearing their doorstep, the traveling doctor and her mother suddenly emerged. He quickly pretended he was simply returning home, turning around and slowly walking towards his stables while listening intently to try to overhear some of the conversation.

"Well, is there anything that you can tell us for certain now that ye've seen her?" asked Annemarie's mother. She seemed quite concerned. The doctor let out a sigh.

"Listen, the blood flow in the area is irregular, but of course all bodies are different. Be sure that she uses the wheat and barley before my next visit," said the doctor, putting his hat back on.

"But why is she feverish?! It weren't like that for me!" questioned her mother, grabbing the doctor by the tail of his coat. He let out a sigh and turned back to her.

"As I have already explained to you, I can't begin to deduce whether the two are related yet. If it's just a fever, then she'll get over it soon anyway. I'll be back in Lakhdorian next week. I'll visit again and see how she's developed," said the doctor, pulling his coat tail out of her hand and hopping up onto his horse.

"Aye…" she responded despondently as she watched the doctor riding off into the sunset. William quickly made sure he was out of eyeshot lest she notice him listening in. So, Annemarie was sick. Should he be feeling so relieved? At least it meant that it wasn't something he'd done, but feverish? Irregular blood flow? What in the world could be wrong with her?

***

As William ate his dinner that night, he pondered the many ailments he'd heard of in his short life, trying to deduce what kind of state Annemarie was currently in.

"William, are ye listening to me?" asked his mother sternly. He snapped out of his thoughts and looked up at her.

"Aye?" asked William, his knee jerk reaction being to agree, yet somehow accidentally pronouncing it as a question. His mother shared an annoyed look with his father.

"What's gotten into ye boy? Where's yer mind at?" she asked, raising an eyebrow.

"It's nothing…" said William, stirring his bowl of soup absentmindedly.

"Out with it boy," growled his father sternly. William looked up at him and swallowed nervously.

"It's nothing, I swear… I was just thinking… why would somebody take barley and wheat?" he asked, hoping that perhaps his parents would have the answers he was seeking. The two shared another confused look.

"In bread?" answered his mother, confused by the question. William shook his head.

"I mean, if they were sick. Why would they take barley and wheat?" he clarified. Again, his parents shared a confused look.

"Maybe as gruel? If they can't eat solids?" guessed his mother, looking at him suspiciously.

"Who's sick?" she added, giving him a piercing gaze as though trying to work him out.

"Nobody!" defended William, hurriedly returning to his soup.

"Barley and wheat hey..." said his father, turning to give his wife a knowing look. Suddenly realization appeared on her face.

"What? What is it?" asked William, looking between the two in confusion.

"It's Annemarie, isn't it?" asked Sasha suddenly, causing the whole table to turn and look at her. William glared at her, as though daring her to keep bringing Annemarie up in front of their parents. She knew too much about his little love affair to be talking about her at the dinner table this brazenly.

"Well, if you won't tell him, I will!" said Sasha, pointing at William with her spoon. William stared blankly between Sasha and his parents. It seemed that everybody was on the same page except for him.

"What?! Tell me what?!" asked William, annoyed to be the only one in the dark here. Sasha let out a sigh after her parents stayed silent.

"She's probably pregnant..." said Sasha, looking at William apologetically. He screwed up his face in disgust and let out a laugh.

"Pregnant?!" he cried out in disbelief, looking between their three uneasy faces. All three remained silent.

"None of you know 'er! She ain't pregnant!" said William, still snickering to himself at the mere suggestion of something so preposterous. Again, his family stayed awkwardly silent.

"From who?!" asked William, bemused by his irritatingly quiet family. They looked between one another awkwardly again.

"Well I mean… she did go on a romantic getaway to Mistfall… right?" asked Sasha. William again screwed up his face and shook his head at the preposterous notion.

"Nay! She couldn't stand the guy, trust me!" explained William, still shaking his head.

"Come to think of it, when was the last time you took me to the hot springs?" asked William's mother, suddenly turning her attention to his father who choked on his mouthful of soup at suddenly being in the limelight. After coughing and spluttering for a minute he seemed to be stuck for words.

"I'll tell you when; before we were married!" admonished his mother angrily. William's father looked around at his kids, clearly hoping that one of them would save him. Sasha raised an accusatory eyebrow at him, clearly taking her mother's side.

"She ain't pregnant…" said William quietly, returning to his soup. For a moment his father was excited by the chance for a change of subject before realizing that there was nothing more for him to say on that matter anyway. The rest of the meal went on without Annemarie being mentioned again, but he still couldn't get her out of his mind.

***

William snapped his eyes open and shot up in his bed, looking around his room. He saw Sasha sitting in her bed looking just as scared as he felt. They'd both been woken by desperate screaming from Annemarie's room, which had now fallen into loud crying, with her mother consoling her.

"Are ye okay?" whispered William, concerned about his little sister. She nodded, but her expression was one of grave concern.

They'd been woken by Annemarie's night terrors for the last three nights in a row. Her screaming was always so desperate and full of fear that on that first night William was moments away from running to her front door to make sure she wasn't being murdered. It was only when they'd hear her mother consoling her that they'd realize it was nightmares that she was having. William's mother suddenly appeared at their door. Even she had been woken up by the screaming tonight. She looked at William and Sasha in concern and shook her head.

"Ma, is there anything we can do to help her?" asked William. His mother let out a sigh and sat down on Sasha's bed.

"Ma, is that going to happen to me too?" Sasha asked, looking up at her mother searchingly. Her mother started caressing her hair caringly.

"No sweetheart. It weren't like that for me. It weren't easy... but it weren't like that," she said, continuing to caress Sasha's hair lovingly.

"But... if she's nay pregnant, then what do you think's wrong with her?" asked William, thankful that her symptoms were not typical signs of pregnancy. His mother looked at him and shook her head.

"You stay away from her boy. We don't know if it's contagious," she warned, raising an eyebrow seriously. William rolled his eyes and slumped back down in his bed. His mother tucked Sasha back in and gave her a kiss on her forehead before making her way over to William.

"Willy, I know how you feel about her..." she said, starting to caress his hair, just as she had Sasha's. William rolled onto his side facing away from her.

"You don't," he said glumly. His mother let out a sigh.

"Listen Willy, I'm sure she'll be fine. You said they've got that fancy traveling doctor seeing to her, right? Don't you remember when your pa had that nail through his foot? Remember how the doctor pulled it out and saved his foot too?" she asked. William stayed silent as he recalled the incident vividly.

"We thought he were gonna lose it, but look at him now! He's good as new!" said his mother, continuing to caress him soothingly. She kissed the back of his head and stood back up.

"Both of you try to get some sleep and stop yer worrying. This is what happens when ye have a fever, there's a reason they call them fever dreams ye know," she explained as she left, putting William's heart at ease a little more. His mother was right. He should really be happy that she's showing signs of a normal fever. At the very least it indicated that the pregnancy nonsense was mere conjecture, but still he couldn't help worrying. Pestilence had been the primary threat facing humanity since the great war. Just because she wasn't pregnant, that didn't mean that there was no reason to worry. Sickness like what she was going through could end a life in the snap of a finger. As he closed his eyes and tried to go back to sleep, he couldn't help questioning, was Annemarie really going to be okay?

***

As days turned into weeks, things only seemed to get worse. Her night terrors continued just as ferociously as they had, however the roster of healers which William would see appearing at her door each day seemed to increase with time. The traveling doctor, who at first had seemed somewhat uninterested in her situation, had now become fascinated, and barely a day went by without Will seeing him pass the stable to enter her house in the morning. He was tired of being the only one not trying to help her. It was time for him to do something.

It was the middle of the day, so Sasha was busy at school and his parents were both busy with their duties, so it was the perfect opportunity for William to make contact with Annemarie. He'd been careful to take note of when the doctor had arrived this morning. Right now was his opportune moment to make contact, as the doctor had just left. Annemarie's mother had even gone with him. There would never be a better opportunity to do this. William rushed into his bedroom and over to his wardrobe. He quickly pulled open the door, almost causing the entire wardrobe to topple over from his vigor. He hurriedly knocked on the back wall, not wanting to waste any time.

Tap, tap tap.

He waited impatiently, looking over his shoulder to see if his father would come to see why he wasn't working. He decided to try again.

Tap, tap tap.

This time he waited for close to a minute before he let out a sigh. Was she ignoring him, or was she just too sick to answer? William's question was suddenly answered before he had a chance to follow the thought any further.

Tap, tap tap.

"Annemarie?!" William called out desperately, but the voice which croaked back at him was certainly not Annemarie's.

"William…" growled the strange, gravelly voice. It was unlike any voice he'd ever heard before. It was as though there were multiple people talking at once.

"Who is this?" asked William, a chill running down his spine as his pristine communication channel with Annemarie was suddenly sullied by this strange interloper.

"It's… it's me…" croaked the voice. William's eyes opened wide, and he swallowed in fear. Could it really be her?

"Annemarie?!" asked William, refusing to believe his ears.

"Yes," replied the voice. William jumped in fright. It was almost like the word was whispered directly into his ear, like there was somebody sitting in this wardrobe right beside him in the darkness. As goosebumps ran up his arms, William took a shaky breath.

"I… I know that you're very sick… but I just wanted to tell you that I'm thinking about you… and…" began William, wishing that he'd rehearsed what he was actually going to say to her. For a moment William sat, fumbling for the right words to say, overwhelmed by the moment.

"William… I forbid you to see me…" she suddenly interrupted. William sat in a stunned silence for a moment, not sure if he'd heard correctly.

"You…what?" he asked, confused.

"I couldn't bear to have you see me like this. Please William… forget about me," she finished somberly. William once again felt a chill run down his spine. If Annemarie didn't want him to see her, then there was only one explanation he could think of, and it was the last thing he wanted to hear. He took a breath, wondering whether he should even ask the question that was on his lips, but if not now, when would he get another chance?

"Is it… because you're pregnant?" asked William, closing his eyes in shame at the audacity of him asking this question at all. There was a long silence before the voice answered.

"I didn't want it," she said shakily. William felt his heart drop. So, this was the great cleric Father Marcus' final mark on the world? Impregnating a teenager and then gruesomely killing himself? Thoughts of loathing and resentment flooded William's mind.

"That filthy bastard..." said William, balling his hands into fists as his anger at Father Marcus grew to new depths.

"No William..." began Annemarie.

"He didn't want it either..." she finished. William wrestled to understand what that meant before his rage once again took over.

"If you're pregnant then he bloody well must have!" he shouted. There was a long silence as William thought he could make out quiet sobbing.

"He... he was crying... he kept saying... no... no, no, no..." began Annemarie, her usual voice suddenly becoming somewhat perceivable underneath the gravelly tones which were drowning it out. Her sobbing grew more intense.

"No, no, no, no, no!" she continued sobbing desperately.

"Annemarie!" cried William, putting his palm up against the back of the wardrobe. He was making her relive the worst experience of her life, all because he couldn't keep his stupid immature mouth shut.

"William..." she said, seeming to gather herself suddenly.

"I need you to promise me. Promise me that you won't try to see me," she said seriously, as she broke into a coughing fit.

"But... but Annemarie... I... I love you," said William, blushing as he finally uttered these painful words. There was a long moment of silence while his passionate words lingered awkwardly in the air.

"If you love me, then you'll make the promise," she replied, managing to quell her coughing. William let out a sigh. She didn't understand how much he cared about her. She didn't understand that he didn't care whether she had a pregnant belly or not.

"Annemarie, I saw my ma' when she were pregnant with Sasha. Trust me, I won't look at you any differently, I promise!" implored William desperately.

"**William**!" she yelled in frustration suddenly. The cold and dark voice which erupted from her sent another set of chills down William's spine. As it echoed in his head, he furrowed his brow nervously.

"It's not about the baby. I am sick William… and… it's changing me. This isn't how I want you to remember me…" she continued ominously before breaking into another fit of hacking coughs.

"Remember you?" asked William, suddenly feeling anxious butterflies in his stomach. He could hear by her coughing fit that she should be resting. The best thing he could do right now would be to put her mind at ease. He slumped his shoulders as he began to accept the situation.

"Okay. Fine," said William quietly.

"Say it properly," replied Annemarie. William let out another annoyed sigh.

"I, William Lakhdorian, hereby swear that I will not try to see you," he said with his eyes closed, disappointed by the outcome of their interaction. There was a tense moment of thick silence as the weight of his words hung in the darkness.

"Thank you, William. For everything," she finally replied quietly before he began to hear the telltale sounds of her exiting her wardrobe. William sat in silence as he heard her coughing grow more distant. He sat in that darkness for close to ten minutes, ruminating on their interaction and whether he could've done it differently. Little did William know, their conversation would come back to haunt him in ways he could never, ever have imagined.

CHAPTER NINE

The Progeny of Possession

As days turned into weeks, and weeks turned into months, William kept his promise, yet still a dangerous curiosity roared like a fire in his heart. As her condition worsened, both he and his sister had begun to be plagued by horrendous nightmares of their own. Although Sasha had taken to sleeping in their parent's room, William couldn't bring himself to move away from Annemarie's side.

With the variety of healers which had begun congregating at her house, they might as well have installed a revolving door. They had collectively deemed her illness strange, and without parallel, yet not contagious. There was little more any of them were able to do, and so they'd leave as spontaneously as they arrived. None of this stopped Annemarie's mother from keeping her doors open to all who might be able to help her daughter, such was her desperation. At this point it had unavoidably become the talk of the town, and many were calling it unbelievable that she was still alive at all.

William had taken Bonnie out for her morning exercise, trying to beat the dark storm which was brewing overhead. Upon arriving back in town, he immediately realized that something had changed. There was a large gathering of individuals outside of Annemarie's house, all engaged in deep and lively conversation. The majority were healers, however there were a few curious townsfolk who had joined the flock. William could feel his heart racing as he gently led his horse back into the stables. His father had not yet returned from his duties, so William was left alone in the stables with naught to do except to peer anxiously at the large gathering of people outside Annemarie's window. Ordinarily her curtains were closed shut, so he could only imagine that they'd been opened specifically to allow the other healers to spectate whatever was happening in that room. Beneath all of the hubbub, William could hear Annemarie moaning in that strange, gravelly voice of hers. He breathed a sigh of relief that she was alive, but his heart stung as he realized the desperation and pain in her voice. He couldn't just sit here and pretend he hadn't heard anything. He covertly slipped his way around the stable door and walked over to the crowd, hoping to hear what was going on.

"Poor girl."

"They should've let me perform the procedure…"

"So it's true. It really is the child of Father Marcus…"

"We don't know that!"

"She's just a girl, of course it is!"

"Well, I don't care. It might've saved her life."

"No, it wouldn't. Trust me, her sickness is not related to the baby."

"Trust you? Hah! You're not even a real doctor! Why would I trust a word you said?"

"How dare you?! Just because I don't use your big city, fancy medical journals, doesn't mean I don't know more than you about the human body!"

"Pah!"

William closed his eyes and tried not to let himself snap at these ignorant conversationalists. To them Annemarie was just a medical curiosity. To him, she was the love of his life.

"What's happening?" asked William to one of the arguing healers, who looked down at him and shook his head.

"None of your business, kid," he said, crossing his arms and raising an eyebrow.

"Oh, could you be more repugnant? The poor boy works in the stables right there, he ought to know!" yelled an out-of-town gypsy lady who had been arguing with a traveling doctor. She put an arm around William's shoulder and raised her tone as though speaking to a small child.

"Sweetie, your neighbor is having a baby," she explained, smiling at him understandingly. William's heart skipped a beat. He stared at the woman in shock.

"Already?! It's only been six months!" exclaimed William, counting on his fingers to make sure he hadn't somehow lost track of time. The other doctor rolled his eyes.

"Yes hon, sometimes the babies like to come early!" said the woman, sickeningly sweetly. William took a step back. This could be for the best right? Why was he feeling so much panic running through his body?

Annemarie's screaming suddenly intensified. The crowd fell into silence as her bone chilling shrieks filled the air. It wasn't just her strange gravelly voice that William could hear screaming though. It had an animalistic quality to it.

"Can't any of you do something for her?!" asked William desperately, looking at all of the healers standing around uselessly. They exchanged uneasy glances.

"Kid, we've gotten her drunk. That's the best we can do for her at this point. Shut your mouth and-" the doctor was suddenly interrupted by an explosive rumble of thunder erupting from above them. It was enough to make everybody look upwards at the horrendously dark storm which was brewing overhead. The clouds were as black as night, and they twisted and churned over the village as though guided by something more purposeful than mere wind. There was a moment of concerned disquiet before William snapped back to reality.

"Drunk?! Don't you people have medicine that you could give her?!" asked William, staring in anger at all of the healers around him.

"Where exactly do you think we are, kid? Oxgate hospital?" asked the doctor, snickering at William's ignorance. At this moment rain finally began to fall, causing some of the gathering to disperse and clear a path towards Annemarie's window. William stared at the opening. It was as though he was being called to that window, but no matter what, he couldn't go back on his promise. He'd sworn that he wouldn't try to see her, but as he stood in the rain, hearing her mournful shrieking, the urge to be by her side and make sure that she was okay was overwhelming.

"Get out of here!" said the doctor, shooing William away as he looked up at the terrifying storm which was now sending bolts of lightning throughout the countryside. Even now the atmosphere was getting darker as more and more clouds worked their way over the village.

"No," replied William, shaking his head resolutely. He didn't care about the rain, or the thunder, or even if lightning struck him right here and now. He needed to make sure that Annemarie was okay. As her cacophonic screaming intensified, so too did the storm overhead, sending bucket loads of water hammering down over all those outside. At this point most of the crowd began to scatter, leaving just two healers and William out in the rain. William looked around. What would be the worst that could happen if he did look through that window? It's not like she would see him. The clouds overhead were so dark that he'd have thought it was the middle of the night. He needed to make sure she had a capable doctor with her. He needed to make sure her parents were by her side. He needed to make sure that she was as comfortable as she could be. This is what he told himself as he took his first step towards that window. The winds which carried rain pelting through the sky were intensifying and changing directions seemingly on a whim.

"What kind of storm is this?!" yelled out one of the two remaining healers who were looking through the window. At this point the storm was becoming so intense that even these two healers who were fascinated enough by the case to stick around this long could no longer stand out in the elements. They both retreated, running towards the town hall. William was now alone, standing in the rain. Above all of the wind, rain and thunder, he could still hear Annemarie's otherworldly screams. He released a frustrated cry of his own. He couldn't do this. He couldn't stand here in the rain, listening to her suffer. He needed to see her. He needed to know what was going on in that room. He got to his feet and stared at the window that was calling to him like a flame to a moth. *Screw it.*

William marched determinedly through the mud, with rain pelting into his cheeks and lightning bolts striking around the town, his attention solely planted on that window. He took one last deep breath as he neared it, closing his eyes and centering himself for a moment. He'd be breaking his promise, but it didn't matter. He'd love her no matter how she looked. He determinedly took the final step over to the window. What he beheld on the other side of the glass was a cursed vision which would stay imprinted in his psyche for the rest of his life.

Annemarie's parents were by the side of her bed, with the doctor delivering the baby at its end, but the figure which lay atop its covers couldn't possibly be Annemarie. She was emaciated to the point of looking like a mere skeleton with skin draped over its bones. Her sickly green tinged flesh was covered in bruises and bleeding nail marks which ran down her arms and cheeks. Her eyes had giant bloody black bags under them and most of her teeth were missing. Her hair had clearly fallen out in clumps, leaving but mere strands dangling loosely from her oozing sore ridden scalp. She was bent over backwards, screaming her lungs out as the baby was beginning to crown. Annemarie had her palms and feet placed down on the bed, her frail body writhing in agony with the little strength that it had left. As she thrust her body upwards, her head hung upside down with its top resting on the bed. It was at this moment that she noticed him. William's horrified visage loomed outside her window, lit up by the flashes of lightning outside. Her expression changed from agony to horror as the two locked eyes for a moment which seemed to never end. William dropped down below the window, feebly hoping that perhaps somehow, she hadn't noticed him.

"No!" she screamed mournfully as the reality of the situation set in.

"You promised me! You promised!" she wailed. As she screamed, it was almost like she was a conductor, and the storm a symphony, with the raging lightning and swirling clouds intensifying with every breath. As she continued releasing a hail of mournful cries, William realized that he needed to get indoors. He scrambled to his feet and dashed towards the stables where his horses were releasing their own choir of panic. He had no time to attempt to calm down the horses. He was of no mind to tend to the animals. He ran straight past the stables and into his house, slamming the door behind him.

"William!" exclaimed his mother as he entered. She hurriedly ran over and grabbed him by the shoulders.

"Where have ye been?!" she questioned, looking fearfully at the windows which were being shaken by the storm outside. William didn't even know what to say to her. He looked at his sister who was curled up on the padded seat looking scared from the storm. His father was nowhere to be seen. His mother noticed his panicked saccade as he looked around searchingly.

"Your father was helping Wilton up at the farm, I'm sure he's fine!" she said reassuringly. William stared back at her, still in a state of shock.

"Take those muddy clothes off or you'll catch a-" but before she could finish, William caught his mother in a tight embrace. He fell to his knees, holding her as tightly as he could. She squatted down with him, hugging her back while William clutched on to her with his eyes open wide in panic. He was finally out of options. There was nowhere left for him to run. There was nowhere left for him to hide. There were no more half-cocked, childish, nonsensical plans for him to attempt to save her. All that was left was pure horror as he tried feebly to fathom the situation for what it was.

"William! Come now sweetheart, what's happened to ye?!" asked his mother, trying to pull him away from her so that she could assess him. He continued to cling on to her silently as his brain felt like it had stopped working. It was like the floor had been pulled out from under him and he was free falling.

William's mother led him over to the sitting area where Sasha was curled up and sat down next to her, pulling William down too so that the three of them were huddled together. It was here that William sat silently shaking as shock overwhelmed his body. The three of them sat huddled together, listening to Annemarie's screams beneath the cracks of thunder and lightning outside. They sat like this until Annemarie's cries slowly died out, and the wails of her mother took over.

"Is she..." began Sasha shakily as the cries of Annemarie's mother dug into their psyches like a pick into ice.

"No," said William, shaking his head assuredly. William's mother hugged him more tightly.

"William… I think it's time to…" began his mother.

"She ain't," insisted William, shaking his head vigorously. His mother and Sasha shared a worried look with one another as the two of them began releasing tears of their own. It took several minutes for the defensive walls in William's psyche to begin to crumble. He buried his face in his mother's shoulder, finally unable to stop himself from sobbing tears of mourning. When he'd looked into Annemarie's eyes, he had known it was the last time that he'd ever see her. Her body was not long for this world. Anybody who cast a mere glance at her could tell that. She'd looked as though she was already dead. The healers had been right. Even if the baby hadn't been making her sick, it might've somehow been the only thing keeping her alive.

CHAPTER TEN

Presence in Absentia

Silence had never been so loud. The echoes of her screams rang like tinnitus in the dead air. William lay emotionless on his bed. Upon her passing, he'd wept. Upon her cremation, he'd wept. Upon the spreading of her ashes, he'd wept. As he'd wallowed in the wake of her passing, he'd wept for each of those seven long days. But now, the well was empty. His soul was cold. Her absence thickened the air, strangling him with every breath he tried to take and filling his lungs with grief. His memories of her licked at wounds of their own making, threading scars of guilt and shame through his soul. Sasha entered the room, holding the book that she'd been reading today. It was about the knight's college. William hadn't seen her read a single fiction book since she'd taken her interest in the clerics of Bethmael.

"William…" said Sasha, coming over to his bed and sitting down on the end of it. William didn't look at her, continuing to simply stare absentmindedly at dust particles.

"I'm going to sleep in here tonight with you, okay?" she asked, placing a concerned hand on his leg. William didn't respond. He rolled his eyes around to look at his sister without moving his head. She looked very worried about him. Ordinarily his big brother instincts would kick in and he'd try to ease her mind, but he was far too immersed in his misery right now. He simply stared at her blankly. Her expression darkened slightly as she raised her eyebrows in concern at her older brother.

"Pa says ye don't have to go back to work until yer feeling ready for it," she said, clearly hoping that this would make him feel better. Work was the last thing he cared about right now. There was another short silence as William returned to staring at the dust particles.

"Hey!" said Sasha, slapping him on his leg. He looked up at her in surprise.

"I get that yer hurtin' Will but come on! At least say something!" groaned Sasha in frustration. William stared back at her silently for a moment before letting out a deep sigh.

"I thought you said it was too weird to sleep in here," said William, again looking away from her. Sasha took a breath and nodded.

"It is," she said earnestly, looking at the wall, her brow furrowing uncomfortably. William shifted his gaze to look up at the wall too. Was she also feeling it? Was the sickening ambience emanating from that room real?

"You can feel it too?" asked William, sitting up slightly in the bed as his brain suddenly began to question where his personal grief ended and where Sasha could perceive the vile ambience too.

"Aye," she said, her expression darkening again as she stared at the wall.

"Do you... do you smell it too?" asked Sasha, swallowing nervously. When the horrible odor had begun, he had thought that perhaps it was Annemarie. He didn't know how long it took for a body to begin to smell, but it had been three days before they'd cremated her. The only problem with this theory was that even now, the smell grew stronger.

"Something's probably dead in the wall," said William, lying back down. Sasha raised her eyebrow at him questioningly.

"In the wall? William, you do realize that partition is solid, right?" asked Sasha, clearly questioning her brother's intelligence.

"Of course I do!" replied William, frustrated by the question.

"You know you don't have to sleep in here either, right?" asked Sasha, again looking at her brother in concern. He scowled in annoyance.

"Go away would ye?" he asked, turning over onto his side and looking away from her. She let out a frustrated huff.

"Fine! Sleep in here alone then! I only wanted to sleep in here cos I was worried about ye, but yer obviously fine!" she said angrily, standing up and storming out of the room. William let out another deep breath and let his eyes close. His sister would never understand. William knew that from the outside looking in, it was weird for him to stay here, especially with that horrible smell becoming worse by the day. What they didn't know was that as long as he slept here, he somehow felt closer to her. He felt like moving rooms would somehow be admitting to something that he wasn't ready to accept, not that he even knew what that was. As thoughts and feelings vibrated through his mind and body, there was one question which stood out above all others: if Annemarie was really gone, then why did William still feel like he could feel her presence lingering on the other side of that wall?

***

Tap, tap tap.

William shot up in his bed, looking around the pitch-black room. Had he imagined it? Had he dreamed it? He could've sworn he'd just heard that impossible sound. It suddenly dawned on him how intense that horrible smell had become. After darting around the dark room searchingly, his eyes finally found a focal point where he could just make out a dull glow that was emanating from under his wardrobe doors. At first, he sat perfectly still in his bed. Was it the moonlight playing tricks on his eyes? He swallowed anxiously as he rolled out of his bed and tentatively placed his feet on the floor. Why did he feel so scared all of a sudden? The fear which flowed through his body was almost crippling. All he wanted to do was get back into his bed and hide under the covers, but his curiosity was too strong. He stood up and took his first step towards the wardrobe, keeping his arms crossed anxiously across his chest lest he some-how walk into something in the dark. He continued taking three more tentative steps towards the wardrobe before he was within arm's reach of it. His heart was beating fast in his chest, and he could feel his body shaking with anxiety. He could clearly see that dull light through the cracks of his wardrobe now. He took a deep breath which did nothing to steady his shaky nerves as he extended his right arm towards the door handle. As his hand grasped it, he took one last nervous breath before pulling it open.

Tap, tap tap.

"William?!" cried out Sasha suddenly.

William yelped in fright as he heard his name, falling backwards from the wardrobe and onto the floor.

"William, are ye alright?!" asked Sasha's voice from the dark-ness. William sat on the floor, huffing and puffing wildly as he tried to get his bearings as adrenaline coursed through his veins. He sud-denly felt a hand on his shoulder which made him whimper in sur-prise and grab the hand.

"It's just me, William!" said Sasha, placing her other hand on him too.

"What are ye doing?!" yelled William, angry that his sister had given him such a fright. Despite saying she wouldn't, apparently she'd slept in here with him after all.

"No, what are you doing?! Why are ye walking around the room in the middle of the night?!" asked Sasha in response, her voice quivering. William took a deep breath. He hadn't meant to scare his little sister, but clearly his midnight antics had done just that. The room suddenly filled with light as their mother appeared in the doorway holding a candle.

"What in the world are the two of ye doing?!" asked their mother angrily, squinting at the two of them after clearly having just been woken from her slumber. William stared back at his mother, not sure of what to say.

"Ma! William's acting weird!" said Sasha, looking over at him in fear.

"What?!" exclaimed William defensively, shocked by her betrayal.

"William…" began his mother, closing her eyes and shaking her head. William swallowed nervously.

"We've tried to give you time. We've tried to give you space. But this has to stop!" yelled his mother angrily.

"We understand that you cared about her, but enough is enough! Yer pa is struggling to pick up yer slack in the stables!" shouted his mother, with tears appearing in her eyes. William stared back at his mother in horror. He never wanted to make her cry, and he didn't even really understand how he'd done it.

"Enough is enough William! Can't ye see yer scaring ye little sister?!" asked his mother, nodding towards Sasha who also had tears in her eyes at this point.

"I…" began William, not even knowing where to begin to defend himself from what felt like a very unfair confrontation. No matter how unfair it felt, he could see that his behavior had clearly upset both his mother and his sister. He was going to have to quell his emotions from now on, at least so far as they could see.

"I'm sorry," said William, closing his eyes and letting out a sigh. His mother let out a sigh of her own, before suddenly sniffing and raising an eyebrow.

"Is it just me or is that smell getting worse?" asked their mother looking between the two of them. William and Sasha both silently nodded.

"Okay, well if William wants to sit in here with that stink then he can, but come on Sasha, you're sleeping in our room," said his mother, gesturing for Sasha to follow her.

"But Ma, I wanna stay with Will!" cried Sasha.

"Come! Now!" commanded their mother angrily. Sasha nodded obediently, grabbing her blanket and pillow.

"Come on William. Let's get you back into bed," said his mother, coming over to his side and helping him up from the floor. She walked him over to his bed and tucked him back in, kissing him on the forehead.

"I'm sorry ma," said William honestly.

"Hush now sweetheart, it's okay. Yer becoming a man now. Ye've got to start acting like one. Ye can't be scaring yer sister like that. Why don't ye try talking more with yer pa? I know he's quiet, but if you start the conversation, he'll answer ye. He just isn't good at speaking first," said his mother, kissing him on the forehead again.

"Aye mother. Goodnight," said William, just wanting the two of them to leave the room at this point. As the candlelight eventually worked its way down the hallway and back out of sight, William's room was plunged back into darkness. He rolled over onto his side and closed his eyes. He'd never intended to make his family worry so much about him. As he lay in bed questioning what was real and what was a mirage of his grief, he once again drifted off to sleep.

***

Tap, tap tap.

The moment William opened his eyes, he was immediately filled with a type of terror he'd never felt before in his life. There, standing before the open doors of his wardrobe, was Annemarie. She was ethereal and emitting a dull glow. Despite the strange form she'd taken, it was unmistakably her. William's first instinct would've been to scream in terror, but the fear which coursed through his body rendered him unable to move a muscle. As he beheld her standing in the middle of his room, he dared not even make a sound. She was staring directly at his bed with an expression of pure hatred on her face. It was an expression he'd never seen her adorn before. It looked positively unnatural on her. She suddenly flickered, momentarily changing to take her disheveled form like he'd seen in her sick bed before blinking back to normal. She flickered between the two forms randomly as she stared hatefully at William. As he could feel his heart-beating in his throat, William's body simply lay perfectly still. His adolescent mind was frozen in fear, unable to make a decision other than to not make a sound and hope that the threat would somehow pass him by.

As he stared back at her in terror, she slowly took a beleaguered step towards his bed. He didn't know what to do. Should he follow his instincts and lay perfectly still, hoping that she hadn't seen him? No. She was staring directly at him. Should he scream and cry out for his parents to come? No, he'd made his mother and his sister cry earlier tonight with these antics. He had promised his mother he'd be a man. He had no idea whether this was a dream, a hallucination, or somehow real. No matter which it was, there was naught his parents could do for him anyway. There was only one option for him; he was going to have to run. But how? She was approaching his bed from the side. If he somehow managed to dive off of the end of his bed he'd be able to sprint right out the door, but then where to? As Annemarie took one more beleaguered step towards his bed, he realized he had to make a choice now.

As his willpower finally managed to overwhelm his frozen body, he immediately dived over the end of his bed, throwing his covers to the floor as he scrambled over the foot, slamming his shin against the wood in the process. He had no time to lament over the pain however, as he yanked open his bedroom door and took off into the living room. He dared not even look over his shoulder as the fear coursing through his body overwhelmed his mind and sent him into a near psychotic state. He could still see the dull glow emitting from Annemarie casting its light into the living room, so he just kept running all the way to the front door and out onto the road. Once outside, he turned around to look back at his house. Through his bedroom window he could see Annemarie still standing there, staring at him hatefully. What was he to do now? He couldn't stay here, she was still clearly following him. He looked around the town road. It was completely silent. It must've been around three or four in the morning. There was nobody about in the town except for him, and apparently, Annemarie. He had no choice but to keep running.

As he sprinted down the road away from his house, tears began to fall from his eyes. He stopped by a low wall and grabbed onto it while he caught his breath. Was that really Annemarie, or was it some kind of hallucination? Suddenly a realization hit him, sending goosebumps running down his arms. On her deathbed, he'd promised Annemarie that he wouldn't look at her, and then he'd betrayed her in her final moments. Could it be that this really was Annemarie? Could it be that she was this furious at him? What was she going to do to him if she managed to get her hands on him? He sat on the low wall, sobbing silently in the night as he looked down the road half expecting her to still be following him. Was this a mere hallucination, or was this apparition real? If it was, then what in the world was he supposed to do about it?

CHAPTER ELEVEN

Decimation

As he was shaken awake, William let out a cry of panic, flailing about feebly as he tried to assess his attacker. It didn't take more than a few moments to realize that it was his father, looking over him with a mix of concern and confusion on his face.

"What has gotten into you boy?" asked his father, staring down over him with an eyebrow raised. William looked around to try to get a grasp of where he was, before it all suddenly came rushing back to him. He'd ended up taking cover from the rain in the privy behind his house and slept there last night. He'd resolved to wake up early considering that the morning light would shine on him, but apparently he'd underestimated both how drained he was and how early of a riser his father was. William stared back at his father, gaping his mouth dumbly while he tried to fathom what kind of excuse he could even come up with for his current situation. His father let out a sigh.

"Come on boy. Get out of there," he said, pulling William up and helping him off the floor. William looked guiltily at his father who seemed to be saddened by his son's pathetic behavior.

"William... your mother is very worried about you," began his father, clearly not knowing how to have an earnest heart to heart with his son.

"I... I know..." responded William quietly.

"If she knew ye'd slept out here, she'd have a breakdown," said his father sternly, shaking his head.

"Aye," responded William guiltily. There was an awkward moment of silence between the two of them. His father was waiting for William to explain himself, but he had no explanation to share. What could he possibly say? He saw Annemarie in his room last night? His father would think he was having a childish nightmare at best, or that he'd lost his mind at worst. There was no good in that. There was no real excuse for this strange behavior that his father would even buy. After a moment his father let out another sigh.

"Come on boy. Help me exercise the horses before your ma wakes up and gets breakfast ready," he said, gesturing back towards the stables and turning to lead the way. William nodded obediently, thankful that his father wasn't pushing the matter with him. As the two set off on their morning work, William's heart was filled with angst. He couldn't keep this up any longer, so what was he going to do? If he tried to sleep in the house again tonight, would Annemarie be back, or had he seen the last of her?

***

William sat leaning against the stable wall as he took a bite from the dark bread that he and his father were eating for lunch. He looked up uneasily at his father who was quietly eating while staring down at a logbook of the stable's horses. Was now an opportunity to discuss things? He could tell that his father was concerned about him based on how easy going he'd been today. His usual discipline had been conspicuously missing, and even in his own work his father had seemed absent minded. William remembered that his mother had told him he should make the first move if he wants his father to open up, so maybe this was the perfect chance.

"Pa... have you ever lost anyone?" asked William, blushing, as the idea of discussing something so sappy with his father made him feel like running out of the stables in embarrassment. His father looked slightly surprised by the question but sank deep into thought.

"Only ma and pa," replied his father, taking another bite of his own bread. William nodded understandingly and let a long silence form.

"You know... with Annemarie... we were closer than... well closer than I made it seem..." stammered William awkwardly. His father raised a surprised eyebrow and nodded understandingly.

"Aye. I figured as much," replied his father simply. William quietly chewed on his bread as he worked up the courage to approach an even touchier subject.

"Pa... about last night..." said William, swallowing nervously. At first his father seemed to have his interest piqued before he returned to dully looking down at his bread as he ate. William wasn't sure if he was uninterested, or if perhaps he just didn't want to scare Will away from opening up. Either way, he felt like it was okay for him to continue.

"I saw her last night," said William bluntly. His father raised his eyebrow and looked at Will quizzically.

"Well I mean... I don't know that it was her... but... well... I don't even know that it was real, but..." stammered William, regretting putting himself in the spotlight like this. He knew it was real. He had stared at her through that bedroom window from the road outside. In that moment he'd known he wasn't dreaming. Even if he knew this though, explaining it to his father as though it were a fact was not a tactful way to approach such an unusual subject.

"She were... she were in the room... I think maybe... maybe she hates me," said William shaking his head in dismay.

"What makes you think that?" asked his father, assessing him with concern. William felt anxiety rising in his chest. He was really going to have to open up here.

"Before she died... she told me that she didn't want me to see her. I promised her that I wouldn't... but... on that last day... I looked through the window..." began William, fighting back the tears which were aching to be released.

"She saw me pa. Right before she died. She saw me... I... I betrayed her..." said William, clenching his fist tightly. His father raised his eyebrows in surprise as he listened on intently.

"Well..." said his father, thinking deeply.

"That sure explains a lot," he said, turning back to his bread and taking another bite.

"What do ye mean?" asked William, confused.

"No wonder ye've been acting up. That's a heavy load ye've been carrying there," said his father. William stayed silent and nodded his head.

"William, let me say this. She don't hate ye," said his father assuredly. His words sent a chill down William's spine as relief flooded over his body.

"I saw the way she looked at ye. It'd take more than seeing her through a window to change her feelings for ye boy," explained his father with a confident nod. William once again fought back tears. Having his father's understanding made William's previous feelings of being all alone slightly dissipate.

"It weren't smart what ye did, but I'd have done the same if I were in your situation," said his father deep in thought. William nodded thankfully as his father's words sent relief flowing through every inch of his body. If his father would've done the same, perhaps William's actions hadn't been quite as evil as he'd thought.

"As for seeing her at night..." began his father. Immediately William felt that angst form again. Was his father going to think he was crazy? Was he going to think he was being childish? Was he going to yell at him for trying to discuss one of the forbidden topics?

"My pa used to tell me stories about the great war..." began his father, his expression darkening as he was clearly recalling some disturbing tales. He'd never shared a word of this with William. Perhaps he was waiting for him to be older before he shared any of this.

"But what yer going through, it's normal son. He told me that when me granda lost me grandma he'd see her at night too. He'd have all sorts of night terrors, seeing her face and all," explained his father. Again, relief flowed through William. So, this was a normal part of losing somebody? This was part of the grieving process. This information changed everything. William's self-doubt was crumbling by the second. His father finished the last mouthful of his bread.

"Come on boy. Let's get back to work," said his father, clapping his hands together to wipe off the crumbs as he stood from his chair. William shoveled the last of his bread into his mouth and stood obediently. As the two returned to their duties, William found himself smiling for the first time since Annemarie had passed. So, this was all normal. She wasn't really there; it was just night terrors.

This meant that he could sleep in his bed again tonight safely. Even if she did appear again, it would be totally normal, right?

***

William watched as his sister's candle flickered excitedly on the other side of the room. He had asked her if it was okay for him to use it tonight and she'd happily obliged him, overjoyed for him to be reading a book for once. Little did she know he was just using it to make himself feel safer. The flickering light brought him comfort, and despite his sister not being in the room with him, it made him feel like she was. He closed his eyes and tried to calm his racing mind down. Tonight was a night just like any other. He tried his hardest not to think about Annemarie, but every time he tried to force himself to think of something else, she immediately came bursting back into his mind. He couldn't unsee that terrifying gaze of fury which had plastered her ethereal face last night. Was his father right? Was she really not angry with him? Was seeing her really a normal part of losing a loved one? Either way, he was going to have to toughen up and just try to sleep here. He thought about his father. There is no way he could imagine his father worrying like this over something so silly. There is nothing scary enough that'd make him run around the streets crying at night before going to sleep in a privy. As William lay in bed chastising himself for his immaturity, his mind finally let go and allowed him to drift into a deep slumber.

***

Tap, tap tap.

The moment that William opened his eyes, he was immediately thrown into a panic. Annemarie was standing directly over him this time. She was standing right by the side of his bed, reaching out towards him with a dark and deep loathing in her eyes. He had no time to even scream, jerking away from her and smacking the back of his head on the wall beside his bed as he escaped her grasp. He threw his covers aside and jumped over the end of the bed backwards, not wanting to take his eyes off of her. Her expression darkened as she watched him escape her grasp, suddenly letting out a hurricane of furious unintelligible words which William heard as but a whisper. He didn't recognize the voice which reverberated through his soul and sent chills down every appendage. Despite not understanding them, the fear and dread that the incomprehensible words sent through his very spirit caused his legs to shake and give way. He collapsed to the floor in terror as the voice echoed in his mind. He felt warmth spread through his loins as he lost control of his bladder, the fear that this strange voice invoked overwhelming his mind and body. As he sat in a puddle of his own making, Annemarie glided her way around the bed towards him, the approaching threat finally kicking him back into gear.

He regained control of his shaking legs and managed to scramble to his feet, once again bolting through the sitting room and out the front door of his house. Once he was outside on the rainy street, he looked back through the window of his room and saw Annemarie standing on the other side, looking utterly furious. Her hair flowed strangely in the air behind her as she stared at him with the deepest hate he'd ever felt from anybody in his life. The killing intent which oozed from her clung to his heart and sucked every ounce of happiness and joy that he had left. William once again fell to his knees as his legs gave out. Tears streamed down his face as he cried in fear and confusion.

Annemarie suddenly looked away from William, turning her head to look directly at the wall between his bedroom and the living room. William sat up slightly, confused about what had drawn her attention away. Up until now she had always been entirely focused on him. A few moments later a dull glow radiated from the front door of his house as his father appeared in the doorway holding a candle.

"William?!" he called out, staring at his son who was sitting on the road outside of their house in the rain in the middle of the night. Before William could respond, Annemarie suddenly started to glide straight towards his father and out of view from the window.

"Pa! Pa! Watch out!" cried out William, struggling to regain control of his shaking legs as he scrambled to his feet on the wet earthy road. His father lowered his candle slightly, trying to get a better look at William. At this moment he saw Annemarie appear directly behind his father.

"Behind you!" yelled William, pointing towards Annemarie who was now floating directly towards him with her arms extended menacingly. His father turned around and adorned an expression of shock, but he was too slow. Her hands connected with his neck and immediately began to strangle him.

"Father!" cried out William, not sure of what he could possibly do to help him. He stood out on the street, frozen on the spot, fear gluing him to the patch of earth he was standing on as he watched his father gasping for breath. Before William's very eyes, his father fell to his knees, clutching his throat and gagging desperately. He stared at William with an expression of fear that he'd never seen on his father's face before in his life. The dramatic moment kicked William back into gear. He finally began to take back control of his body as he took a few steps towards the door, but at that very moment it suddenly slammed shut as if on its own accord.

William ran to the door, pulling at it frantically as he tried to get inside, but it was locked shut. He banged on it desperately, screaming for somebody to let him in. At that very moment, he heard a sound that shook him to his very core. His mother and his sister were screaming from deeper in the house. There was no time to lose. William had to do something to help them. He looked around desperately for something to ram the door with, but there was nothing he could use. There was only one option left for him. He ran around to the stables and grabbed his shovel before bolting his way around to his bedroom window. He had no time to waste, as he smashed straight through the locked window with his shovel, sending glass hailing into his bedroom. He hurriedly climbed through the smashed window and fell roughly onto his bedroom floor, cutting his hands and legs up as he climbed over the fractured glass. With no time to tend to his wounds, he ran around to his parents' room, immediately beholding a sight which would haunt him until the end of his days. William's father sat over his mother who was lying on the floor. He had his hands gripped around her neck and was squeezing as hard as he could. Her face was beginning to turn bright red as she helplessly gasped for breath beneath the gigantic man. His sister was in the corner with a red cheek from clearly having been struck hard. She was cowering in fear and screaming in horror as she helplessly watched on while her father strangled her mother to death before her very eyes. When William entered the room, his father snapped his head around to stare directly at him. His head jerked around for a moment as he seemed to be fighting with himself, before suddenly he made direct eye contact with William.

"Kill me boy!" demanded his father desperately. William watched on in shock, not sure of what to do. His mother's desperate punches at his father were beginning to falter as she lost consciousness.

"Wh-what?!" whimpered William, stunned.

"It's inside of me! Do it now boy! Kill me!" demanded his father again, tears streaking down his face as he could clearly feel his wife's life leaving her body through his hands.

"Stop him!" cried out Sasha suddenly, pulling William out of his stunned paralysis. He had to stop his father at all costs. He ran towards him and smacked him across the head with his shovel, but to the giant man this was nothing but a dull blow.

"Harder!" pleaded his father desperately. William took a deep breath before instinct finally overwhelmed him. He picked the shovel up in two hands and struck downwards at the side of his father's head like he was chipping at a boulder. As the blow sank into the side of his father's head, a chunk of flesh came loose from his skull, splattering the floor crimson. Despite the brutal blow, he kept his tight grip around his wife's throat. William screamed in horror as he finally fathomed the reality of what it was going to take to end this.

"More!" exclaimed his father desperately. William continued screaming in despair as he released a hail of strikes to his father's head, cracking his skull with the end of his shovel over and over again. His sister wailed in misery in the corner as she watched her father's skull be caved in and dismantled by William's brutal blows. William continued to scream in horror as he splattered the floor of his parents' bedroom with his father's blood. Finally, his father's grip around his mother's throat released as he fell to the floor. William stopped, the shovel raised in the air above his head, ready to release another strike if he needed to. He looked at his mother's lifeless corpse, her face frozen in a countenance of terror.

"K... kill me..." gurgled his father before releasing a terrible death rattle. A sickening silence filled the room broken only by

William's panting, as he and Sasha stared hopelessly at the ever-growing pool of blood and gore beneath their parent's corpses.

"Pa?... Ma?" stammered William, his young mind broken by the impossible scenario which had just taken place. Sasha suddenly released a cry of horror as she too processed the impossible situation. As she screamed, William let go of his shovel which clattered to the floor. His arms were shaking with shock and adrenaline as he caught himself in a futile embrace while he stared perplexed at his parents' corpses. William turned towards his little sister and took a few steps towards her, wanting to comfort her but causing her to retreat from him in fear.

"Sasha... I... I had to..." said William, unsure even himself of whether this was true. She stared back at him, with fear and confusion plastering her face as she stared at her own brother like he was a wild animal. Suddenly, her gaze shifted over his shoulder, and as it did, her expression changed to one of pure terror. William turned his head and felt his heart drop as he realized what she'd seen. There, rising from the corpses of their parents, was Annemarie, but this time she looked different. She no longer looked disheveled and weak. She no longer was flickering between her broken, sickly body and her white night gowned ethereal version. As she slowly rose from his father's corpse, it was as though she was formed entirely of shadow. She still wore her white nightgown, but her hair was now a deep jet black and her fingers ended with dark claws at least a foot long each. Her eyes were glowing a deep red and a tangled web of shadowy tendrils extended all around her like wings. This time William wasn't going to let himself be stunned by fear. He immediately snapped into action.

He lunged towards Sasha, grabbing her and pulling her towards him. She screamed in panic, but he didn't care how hard she fought against him. He had to get her to safety. He threw her over his shoulder and ran out the door without taking a second look at the monster which was still emerging from his father's body. As they ran, she stopped fighting him and simply clung to him for support. William carried her straight to the front door of the house, unlocking it and bursting through it in one quick motion before running around to the stables. He quickly readied Bonnie, leading her out of the stables and leaping up onto her bare back, pulling his sister up with him. Sasha continued to cling to his chest, hugging him tightly as she faced backwards on the horse. Just as they managed to climb their way up, the front door of his house burst open, blasted from its very hinges. It exploded out onto the street, revealing the dark, shadowy monster standing directly behind it. William didn't waste a second. He kicked his horse into action, getting her into a gallop as quickly as he could while he held his sister tightly. As the two of them rode off into the stormy night, Sasha screamed over his shoulder. William looked back and saw the monster leaving their house and heading onto the road. It began floating through the air, clearly following them. William kicked his horse again, spurring it to run as fast as it could. He didn't even know where he was going; all he knew was that they had to keep running.

The thunderstorm above intensified as the two bolted their way through the night and out of the village. William had no time to question what had happened in that house. He had to get his sister to safety, but where even was safety? The only place he could think of was his uncle's house. It was a fair way out of town, and if Annemarie was following William, perhaps he could drop his sister off there before leading the monster out of town and into the night. It wasn't much of a plan, but it was the best he could come up with on the spur of the moment. Bonnie raced through the night, clearly also sensing the dark entity which was pursuing them and achieving speeds neither William nor his father had ever managed to rouse in the beast. Within a matter of minutes they'd made it to their uncle and aunt's house. As soon as they neared the front doors, William reared Bonnie and lowered Sasha down, but she refused to let go of him.

"Sasha! Please! You have to get down! Go to Uncle Wilton. He and Aunt Genevieve can keep you safe!" pleaded William, looking over his shoulder as he knew that the monster was approaching.

"No!" exclaimed Sasha, tears streaming down her face as she realized what her brother's plan was.

"Sasha, please. She's after me. Not you. If I can lead her away from town, you'll be safe. Please, you have to go now! I can't lose you too!" cried William desperately. Sasha pressed her face into his chest, bawling her eyes out as the reality of the situation hit her. William hugged her tightly and kissed the top of her head.

"Sasha, please. If you don't go now it's going to hurt them too," said William softly. His sister continued hugging him for a few moments longer before her grip loosened. She pulled back and looked into his eyes to assess his expression.

"Promise me you'll come back," said Sasha, her face plastered with fear and desperation. William brushed her wet hair out of her eyes and smiled back at her.

"Aye. I promise. We have to hurry now!" said William, finally letting go of her. He dashed into his uncle's horse shed and stole his saddle. With what lay ahead of him, William knew that he wasn't going to be able to pull it off bareback. He hurriedly attached it to Bonnie, before hopping back up and watching Sasha retreating towards his uncle and aunt's house. He turned his horse around to face back towards the storm and took a deep breath. This chase was only just beginning. Over the horizon he could see the eye of the storm approaching. It was only at this moment that he realized that it was coming straight towards him, as though it were somehow following Annemarie. William had no time to question it. He kicked his horse back into action. He needed to make sure he had Annemarie's attention. For him to do that, he was going to have to gallop back towards it and lead it out of town. He took a deep breath before setting off. This might be the stupidest thing he would ever do, but for Sasha's sake, he had to make sure that it was following him and not her.

CHAPTER TWELVE
Storm Chasing

The closer that William's horse carried him towards Annemarie, the more intense the storm became. Just as he didn't think it could get much worse, he finally saw the silhouette of Annemarie on the horizon. There she was, with her cape of black tendrils flowing outwards in all directions. Never before had William felt such a deep and threatening aura of fear and destruction as the monster before him was producing. Bonnie clearly felt it too, as she reared up, whinnying and drawing to a halt.

"Whoa girl..." said William shakily as he tried to steady his own nerves. Nothing mattered right now except making sure this thing didn't go anywhere near Sasha.

As Annemarie drew closer, her form became clearer and clearer. The intense lightning which was swelling in the clouds above lit up the countryside enough for William to clearly see her. He'd heard horror stories throughout his life about the monsters that came out of that gateway, but even they paled in comparison to seeing this apparition with his very own two eyes. She was flying through the wilderness, several feet above the ground. A dark cloud of chaotic energy spiraled around her as she flew towards him. Even from this distance, William could make out those horrific glowing red eyes. It was time for him to run.

Once again William reared his terrified horse up, turning her away from Annemarie and towards the road out of town, leading down into the moorlands. As long as it followed him now, he could make sure that Sasha was safe. The monster had clearly seen him, as it released a shriek of rage and malice which echoed over the landscape, joined by several lightning bolts which demolished trees all around him. William had no time to spare, he kicked his horse back into a gallop, clinging low to her and bolting through the night. Would she take the road up the hill towards Sasha, or take his bait and follow him down into the moorlands? As William galloped on in anxious anticipation, he took one final look over his shoulder. It worked! Annemarie was still following him at top speed.

"Yes!" exclaimed William happily, so filled with relief that he somehow released a triumphant huff even in this horrific scenario.

"Hyah!"

William kicked Bonnie into the fastest gallop that she could manage on the difficult mountain path. She didn't need any convincing. She too could clearly feel the presence of that monster encroaching behind them and wanted nothing more than to run away as fast as she could. Now that he knew that it was following him, William didn't have to hold back at all. His horse flew down the mountain fast enough that the rain flying into his face stung like hornets. He didn't care about the discomfort; all he wanted to do was create as much distance between him and Annemarie as he could. As images of his dead parents penetrated his broken mind again, he had to shake his head and quell them for now. He had no time to lament, not yet. He still didn't even have a plan, but he did at least have a destination in mind. There was only one place that he'd ever been to in the moorlands: Eric's farm. He'd been so wrapped up in his own grief that he hadn't even found out whether Eric had made it back from Mistfall, but at this point he was out of options. He was going to have to take the gamble that Eric would be home. He had no other choice. He hated to bring this other-worldly horror to Eric's doorstep, but he couldn't do this alone.

***

After close to twenty minutes of artfully navigating their way down the muddy and rocky mountain path, William and Bonnie finally burst their way into the open moorlands. As soon as Bonnie noticed the even ground beneath her hooves she finally let herself go, breaking into a ferocious gallop down the straight moorland road. With the flat ground beneath them, they were finally able to put some real distance between themselves and Annemarie. William looked over his shoulder, the black storm swirling down the mountain with bright flashes of lightning erupting within it. Annemarie was still coming, and it seemed that she would stop at nothing to catch him. He turned back to the road ahead and narrowed his eyes nervously. The moorland fog made it hard to see more than a few feet ahead of them. If there were any obstructions on the road, both he and his horse would be sent flying without any recourse to stop themselves. He placed his hand gently on the side of her neck. The poor thing was utterly exhausted. William knew her limits; he'd been taking Bonnie out for exercise for months now.

"Come on girl. Not much longer," said William gently as he felt Bonnie's pace slowing. Thankfully, when Eric's great grandfather had moved down into the moorlands, he hadn't gone too far from Lakhdorian. Within fifteen minutes William began to see some familiar farmlands that indicated that they were nearing the Roth-

mane estate. As they continued through the mist, he suddenly spotted the entrance way into their land.

"There it is! This way girl!" exclaimed William, again gently
patting his horse on the side of her neck as he turned her off from
the main road and into Eric's farm. It would only be a couple of
hours until sunrise, but as William strained to see through the mist
at the encroaching storm, he knew that it wouldn't take that long for
Annemarie to catch up.

As soon as they approached the dooryard of the farmstead, William jumped from his horse, leading her over to a full drinking
trough where she began replenishing herself. He didn't have a second more to waste, bolting directly to Eric's front door and banging
on it desperately.

"Eric! Eric! Let me in!" cried out William frantically, pounding
at the door with his fist as he looked over his shoulder in the direction of the oncoming storm. It didn't take long before William
heard Eric's familiar voice on the other side of the door.

"Who goes there? I have a weapon!" he yelled threateningly.

"Eric! It's me William! Open up! Please!" William yelled desperately back through the door. The door was hurriedly unlatched
and swung open, revealing Eric standing there holding a butcher's
knife. As soon as William set eyes on him, a tsunami of emotions
ran over him. His body finally gave itself permission to buckle under the tremendous trauma it had endured. His legs gave way and
he collapsed into Eric, catching him in a tight embrace. He released
a cascade of tears into Eric's shoulder, finally not alone in facing
this terrifying experience.

"William! What's the matter with ye?!" asked Eric, pulling away
to inspect him in more detail. William didn't know how to respond.
Where could he even start? A deep booming thunder suddenly

growled over the countryside, snapping William back to reality. He jolted his head around and stared at the oncoming storm. Judging by the way the storm was churning up the mists, it looked like Annemarie had almost reached the moorlands. William shook his head and took a deep breath, trying to steady his nerves.

"Eric, I don't have a lot of time to explain..." stammered William, the hopelessness of the situation suddenly re-entering his psyche as he tried to piece together how he could even begin to form a coherent recount of the night's events.

"It's okay William, take a deep breath. I still have some of that fancy tea that the traveling merchant brought through from the desert the other day. Let me put on a pot and-" began Eric.

"No!" exclaimed William, again shaking his head to try to steady himself. He began slapping his cheeks to bring himself back into a more useful state of mind.

"There's no time for that!" cried William. Eric nodded understandingly.

"Okay. Come on then, tell me what's happening or I won't be able to help you," coaxed Eric calmly. William nodded, taking one final deep breath to steady himself.

"Okay so... Annemarie... she's... she's dead," said William.

"Oh no... I'd heard that she was pregnant, but..." began Eric, sorrow plastering his face.

"But... but..." William shook his head trying to figure out how to phrase it all.

"Something is wrong Eric. When she died, something was left behind. Something really bad," said William, a chill running down his spine as he tried to explain himself. Eric's expression darkened as he listened to his friend's story.

"It's like… her, but… it's not. It's something else. It took control of my pa and it… and it…" William couldn't hold it back any longer. Images of his father's skull splattering the floor at the end of his own shovel, while his mother was choked to death flashed back into his psyche. He pulled back from Eric, turning into the garden bed and dry retching.

"William!" exclaimed Eric, squatting down beside him and putting a concerned hand on his back. William convulsed and shook as he tried feebly to regain his composure.

"What do you mean it took control of him?!" asked Eric in confusion, his eyes only now settling on the blood which smattered William's wet clothes.

"I don't know!" screamed William, tears again erupting from his eyes.

"It went… inside of him! And it… it made him… it made him…" William couldn't even say the words. He shook his head.

"Look, it doesn't matter. All that matters is, that storm," began William, pointing through the mist towards the storm which was ever encroaching.

"It ain't natural," continued William, shaking his head.

"Aye," agreed Eric, looking up at it broodingly.

"She's in the center of it, and she's coming here… right… now," said William chillingly. He watched as Eric fathomed the urgency of the situation.

"What can we do then?" asked Eric. William thanked his lucky stars that his best friend was ready to believe his story without question. If Eric hadn't believed him, William wasn't sure what he was going to do. Even still, all William could do was stare back at him blankly. Understanding crossed Eric's face as he clearly realized that William was in over his head. His plan had ended at getting to Eric's farm.

"It's okay William. We'll think of something," said Eric patting William on the shoulder before standing up and adorning his expression of deep thought. With Eric on his side, maybe, just maybe, they'd be able to figure out a way to get out of this alive. Eric extended a hand to help William up, which he accepted gratefully.

"You think that this thing wants to get inside of you, right? Like it did your pa?" asked Eric. William nodded back.

"It tried to do it while I was asleep, but... I managed to get away..." said William, shuddering as he remembered waking up to Annemarie standing over him. Eric nodded again.

"In all of granda's journals, I've never heard of anything quite like that I'm sorry to say..." admitted Eric shaking his head. William nodded understandingly. He'd never heard of anything like it either.

"But..." began Eric, immediately rousing William's spirits with hope.

"My granda, he talked about his shield..." said Eric, deep in thought.

"In his journal, he talked about a sigil he painted on his shield. He said that as long as his shield had that sigil painted on it, monsters from the gateway couldn't break through it..." he continued.

"Monsters from the gateway?" asked William in surprise.

"It's got to be, right? Have you ever heard of something like that coming from anywhere else?" asked Eric. William stared back at him blankly. How would a monster from the gateway have made it into Lakhdorian?

"Wait a minute..." breathed William, taking a step back from Eric as realization hit him.

"You don't think it was Father Marcus who did this, do you?!" asked William, his eyes widening in realization. Eric nodded solemnly.

"We could tell that there was something wrong with him, right? Maybe he brought it with him from the gate. Maybe it transferred from him into Annemarie somehow..." guessed Eric. William placed a hand over his forehead as realization struck him. So, they might be dealing with one of the denizens of the otherworld here after all. How had a bunch of peasants had the misfortune to be on the receiving end of something so horrific?

"William. Stay with me now!" implored Eric, looking up at the encroaching storm.

"If that sigil works on shields, what if it works on other things?" asked Eric cryptically. William raised an eyebrow unsure of what Eric was getting at before it finally sank in.

"What if we could... paint it on me?" asked William, causing Eric to snap his head around to stare at him.

"No brother, the paint could just wash away, and I don't have any pigments in our farm right now anyway!" said Eric, shaking his head assuredly.

"What about a tattoo?" asked William, feeling like this idea of applying the mark directly to his body was their best bet. Eric thought about it for a moment and then shook his head.

"Do you know how to tattoo? I certainly don't. I don't even have the tools required for that, or the know-how. Plus, we've not the time!" said Eric decisively. William let out a groan of frustration. Was there nothing that they could do here? Suddenly Eric's eyes lit up with realization.

"William... I've got it..." said Eric, clapping his hands together excitedly.

"A brand! We brand our cattle! I can make a brand of that symbol and... and we can..." began Eric, suddenly recoiling slightly as he imagined trying to brand it into William's flesh. William grabbed Eric by his shoulders and stared into his eyes seriously.

"Eric. I can handle it. This is it. This is the plan. So, what is this symbol?" asked William. Eric looked at William with uncertainty on his face for a moment, but when he saw the determination in William's eyes he nodded in agreement. Eric suddenly moved past Will and began to run down the garden path, beckoning for William to follow him. William hurried after him eagerly to a nearby garden shed. Eric immediately pulled out a shovel and threw it to William who was hit with a wave of disgust as he remembered the last thing he'd done with a shovel. Eric then appeared back at the door of the shed with a shovel of his own.

"What's this supposed to be for?!" groaned William, not having wanted to hold a shovel ever again in his life.

"I told you that the sigil was on my great granda's shield, right?" asked Eric. William nodded in confusion.

"Well... he was buried with it," said Eric seriously. William was lost for a moment, before realization hit him and he let out a groan. How was this night still getting worse? As the two boys got ready to set off into the farmland, the rain from the storm finally began to reach them. Would they really be able to do all of this on time? Even if they did, would it really work?

CHAPTER THIRTEEN
The Brand of Malice

"What's taking so long?!" asked William impatiently, the rain beginning to pick up slightly. The wind from the storm had by now begun to churn up the mists around the farmstead so it was harder for William to tell how far away Annemarie was. Every second they waited she drew nearer, and so every moment spent dilly-dallying in the shed filled William with intense anxiety. Eric suddenly popped back out of the shed holding a lantern.

"It took you that long to light a lantern?" asked William.

"Course not! I had to make sure the coals will be hot when we get back..." said Eric ominously. William swallowed nervously as he fully grasped the situation. They were going to go and rob a war hero's grave, create a makeshift brand to mimic the sigil on his shield, and then brand it into William's flesh. All of this while a horrific monster encroached on them, drawing nearer by the minute. The reward at the end of this? They would still be face to face with the monster, but hey, at least it wouldn't be able to take control of their bodies and make them murder each other. As he exited the shed, Eric slapped him on the back and gave him a confident nod. William let out an anxious groan and shook his head as the two boys hurried off into the moorlands. Just as they were entering the fields, Eric suddenly handed his shovel to William.

"What are ye handing it to me for, I've already got one!" said William, holding up the shovel in his other hand.

"I need my other hand for this," said Eric ominously, grabbing an enormous hammer that was leaning against the side of the field's fence and resting it over his giant shoulder.

"What could you possibly need that thing for?!" asked William, surprised.

"The moorcrawlers have been acting up lately..." said Eric ominously as he led the way out into the field.

"Ain't that hammer for culling pigs?!" asked William, staring at the pig hammer that was as large as he was. William struggled to keep up with the pace Eric was setting despite carrying the giant weapon.

"Aye. But me pa and I use it on the moorcrawlers too. They get stuck in our traps when they're going after our pigs..." said Eric, staring anxiously around the swirling mists as he jogged onwards.

"But I thought moorcrawlers were just like... foxes or something..." replied William, assuming that the pig hammer was a little overkill.

"No brother, they're as big as us," clarified Eric with a serious nod.

"Ay?!" exclaimed William in shock.

"And ye just... use that thing to..." William trailed off as he tried to figure out how to phrase his question as he stared at the giant hammer in Eric's hands. Eric nodded stoically as the two boys continued their jog, before he suddenly pointed with the lantern out ahead of them.

"There it is!" he said, quickening his pace slightly. A tree suddenly came into vision through the fog, and as the two boys dashed towards it, William noticed a small wooden grave marker. Eric leaned his hammer up against the tree beside them and took one of the shovels from William.

"Sorry granda," said Eric with a sigh. He dug his shovel into the dirt, his farm boy strength showing as he effortlessly penetrated deep into the moorland earth. He tossed the soil aside and went back for a second shovel full.

"Come on Will, don't just stand there!" said Eric expectantly.

"Aye!" exclaimed William, swallowing back his disgust at the memories of his last shovel swing, before also showing his own strength by managing to easily penetrate through the soil too.

"Yer great grandma isn't in here too is she?" asked William anxiously as he shoveled. Eric shook his head solemnly.

"The monsters got her..." said Eric quietly. William returned his focus to the task at hand and quickened his pace.

After a few minutes of the boys hurriedly digging to disentomb Sir Heinrich Rothmane, William's shovel finally hit something solid.

"I think we've found him!" shouted William, almost allowing some semblance of excitement to enter his psyche. The two boys dug a little more and unearthed enough of the old knight's coffin to be able to lift the lid.

"Here goes nothing..." said Eric, pulling the lid from the coffin before immediately regretting not covering his nose.

"Oh, that's dank..." said William, spluttering as the stale air from inside the coffin filled his lungs.

"But hey look! There it is!" said Eric. Inside the coffin was his great grandfather's skeleton. His arms were crossed beneath his full tower shield which was lying over him.

"That thing's enormous!" exclaimed William in shock, both referring to the skeleton and the shield itself. He'd never seen a full tower shield before. The giant shield must've weighed at least fifty pounds. It stood as tall as William, and wider than his shoulder width. William realized at this moment where Eric had inherited his stature from. Just as Eric had described, the shield bore an iron sigil on the front of it. It looked like nothing William had ever seen before. The sigil looked like a combination of basic, but beautifully crafted geometric shapes arranged in a very specific pattern.

"Help me lift it out..." said Eric, looking anxiously towards the horizon at the ever-encroaching storm. He was clearly uncomfortable with pilfering his great grandfather's grave, yet painfully aware of their time limit. William nodded understandingly and crouched down, lifting the lower half of the shield off of Eric's great grandfather's corpse. Between the two strong boys they managed to heave the enormous old shield out of the grave. Eric pulled it upright and leant on it, looking down over his great grandfather while he and William momentarily gathered their breath.

"Sorry granda, we've no time to put ye back under..." said Eric guiltily as he stared at old Rothmane's open jawed skull in the coffin slowly being filled with rain.

"Come on. Let's get back, we haven't much time..." said William, extremely conscious that the storm was almost upon them. Eric nodded in agreement, but then suddenly stopped in his tracks.

"Wait a minute..." he said, his eyes narrowing. William followed his gaze down into the coffin, only now noticing what Eric had seen. Clutched to the old knight's chest, beneath both of his enormous skeletal hands was some kind of trinket. Between the boney fingers, William could make out a red gem wrapped in an intricate metal design.

"What is that thing?!" asked William, looking up at Eric searchingly. Eric shook his head as he lowered the shield down to the ground. He crouched down next to the grave and slowly reached a hand down towards his great grandfather's closed fingers, looting the trinket from within.

"What is it?!" asked William, walking over to his side and looking down at the object. Eric pulled it up and inspected it closely. William could just make out that it looked more like a badge than anything, and on its outermost layer there was a design with a large capital 'R', a hammer and a flower. Hidden beneath that was a strange sigil similar to that which was on the shield. The entire design was wrapped intricately around a ruby-like gem at its center.

"It has our family crest on it..." said Eric, rubbing a finger gently over the large letter R. Suddenly a bolt of lightning from the storm brought the boys' attention back to the matter at hand. Eric snatched his hand closed and stood back upright.

"Come on. We'll worry about this later. Let's get back to the farm!" said Eric, pocketing the trinket as he looked up to the horizon. William nodded in agreement, casting one last worried look at the open grave before turning away and running back towards Eric's farmyard.

***

When they finally made it back to the shed, Eric wasted no time, immediately beginning to get busy preparing to make the brand. William knew that he needed to help or there was no way they'd be able to get this done on time. He looked around and saw a grimy old sack of green sand leaning against a wall, which he hurriedly grabbed and carried over towards Eric.

"What are ye doing with that?!" asked Eric in confusion.

"Don't we need it to make a mold?" asked William. Eric shook his head.

"We don't have time to make things the proper way. How long do you think it'd take for the iron to cool?" asked Eric, turning back to the workbench that he was clearing. William shook his head and tried to regain his composure. He wasn't thinking straight. As the walls of the shack began to shake from the ferocious winds and rain which were growing stronger outside, William let out an anxious groan.

"Come here," said Eric, as he lifted the enormous shield up onto the work bench and leant it against the wall. William nodded, slapping his cheeks to regain his composure again before standing by his friend. Eric picked up a bucket from under the bench and poured its contents over the worktop.

"Iron scraps?" asked William.

"Aye. Look, we don't have the time to do this any other way. We'll have to bend these scraps into the shapes that we need," said Eric distractedly, as he rifled through the scraps looking for appropriate pieces.

"But… but how do we connect them up into one shape?" asked William, not yet understanding how this was going to work.

"Brother… we can't. With the time we have, making a single brand as complicated as this is impossible," said Eric sincerely. William stared back at him blankly.

"Look at the design of the sigil," said Eric, nodding towards the shield leant up against the wall. William stared at the shield, still not quite following.

"It's made up of a few basic shapes, right?" asked Eric, raising an eyebrow. William finally realized what he meant, and suddenly dread filled his heart once again.

"You mean..." began William.

"Aye brother. We can't make a brand of that shape, so we'll just have to brand that shape into you piece by piece. We'll need to be branding you six times..." said Eric in an apologetic tone. William had no time to lament. He took a deep breath and nodded understandingly.

"Okay, what do we need to do?" asked William.

"Looking at that sigil we need... three different sized circles... two different sized triangles... and one straight piece," said Eric assuredly, nodding his head as he assessed the design.

"Okay, you do the circles, I'll work on the triangles," said William, picking up a pair of metalworking pincers from beside the forge. Eric nodded, and without wasting another moment, the two boys got to work. They rifled through the metal scraps, picking out the most appropriate pieces and hastily trying their best to bend them into the shapes that they needed. Each time that the boys finished bending one of the pieces of metal into the shapes that they needed, they'd move it over to the forge and place it over the coals, heating it up in preparation for burning it into William's flesh. As William bent the final angle into one of his triangles, he looked over at his best friend hammering a long metal scrap into a circular shape. There was no person he trusted more than Eric to get this crazy plan of theirs to work. He was glad that it wasn't him that had to figure out how to brand that shape together, as under the current circumstances he knew that the pressure would make his mind freeze up.

Crashes of lightning were exploding all around the moorlands surrounding the farm. Both boys knew that they had barely minutes left before she would arrive at their doorstep. As Eric finally finished hammering out his final circle and placing it in the fire, both boys stared at each other anxiously. Neither of them even knew whether this plan would work, but the next step was by far the most harrowing. William nodded to Eric assuredly.

"I can handle it. Just hurry," said William, pulling off his shirt and taking a seat on the stool by the forge. Eric put on his thick heat resistant leather gloves and took a deep breath.

"Are you sure about this? Last chance to back out now," said Eric, placing a concerned gloved hand on William's shoulder.

"I'm sure," said William gallantly, staring at the door of the shed in front of him that was rattling enough to almost come off its hinges. There was no backing out now, she was almost here.

"And just to make sure… ye've not lost yer mind, right? This is all real, yeah?" asked Eric warily. William snapped his head around to look at him.

"What?! Of course it's real!" yelled William indignantly. Eric held up his hands.

"Okay. Okay. Well, you have to stay still, no matter how much it hurts," said Eric.

"Aye," responded William stoically. Eric leant over to grab the first shape from the hot coals. Suddenly something occurred to William.

"Wait!" he said, turning to face Eric.

"I need you to promise me something. When she gets here… you'll grab that shield and sit behind it in the corner of the room," said William. Eric nodded nonchalantly and reached towards the metal again.

"Eric!" yelled William, grabbing his arm.

"Promise me now! If she comes, you'll get behind the shield, whether we've finished the design or not!" implored William desperately. As Eric looked into his eyes, he could see the conviction that William held. Eric nodded reticently.

"Aye. I promise," said Eric. William let go of his arm and nodded thankfully.

"Okay. Let's do this," said William, closing his eyes and taking a breath to steady his nerves.

"The first shape is the largest. It's the large circle which surrounds the sigil. You need to stay perfectly still William. Are you ready?" asked Eric anxiously.

"Aye," replied William nervously. The two boys both took one last anxious breath.

"I'm branding it in three... two... one..." Eric counted down, holding the giant circular ring of red-hot metal just behind William's bare back. The moment that the metal touched William's skin, every instinct in his body told him to jolt away from it. He was expecting a cold feeling before the pain hit, but the agony was instant. William couldn't hold it back. He screamed in anguish as he heard the sizzling of flesh and smelled his own skin being cooked. Despite the pain, he knew how important it was that he sat still. He clutched onto his stool, tensing every muscle in his body as the hot iron melted the circular shape into his back. After a moment or two Eric removed the iron circle, throwing it back into the coals and looking at William.

"William are ye-" began Eric.

"Hurry up! Do the next one!" implored William as tears of pain streamed down his face. All he wanted more than anything was to run outside and lay down in the horse's cold trough of water, but as the storm hit its peak, he knew that he had no time. It was now or never. The agony that he had to endure had only just begun. Eric nodded and got to work. The next shape was a giant triangle.

"Okay William, here we go. Three, two, one…" Eric counted down again. William breathed rapidly, almost hyperventilating as he prepared for the pain, but regardless of how much he prepared himself, the pain was overwhelming. He screamed in agony again as the triangle was burned inside the circle. This time Eric didn't waste any time asking William if he was okay. The storm had hit its peak, and they both knew what that meant: Annemarie was here. Any minute now she'd be upon them. There was no time to waste. Again, Eric threw the shape back into the coals and withdrew the next one.

"William, this one is going to hurt a bit more…" warned Eric.

"What?!" exclaimed William in confusion. How could anything hurt more than the last ones?

"This triangle intersects with the previous shapes…" said Eric solemnly. There was no time to lament.

"Just do it!" yelled William, grabbing a rag from the shelf beside him and putting it inside his mouth. No amount of preparation would be enough. When the iron once again connected with his skin, the pain was just too much. William's vision began to blur as he was overwhelmed with agony. The cloth that he'd been biting down on fell from his mouth as he shrieked his lungs out. Even after Eric had removed the brand from his back, there was no relief. How much longer could he go on like this? This was a torture that no boy should have to endure.

"We're halfway there William," said Eric. William didn't have the energy to respond. All he could do was hold onto his stool for dear life. As the storm suddenly calmed slightly outside, a familiar feeling washed over him. The hair on his arms stood on end and goose bumps appeared on his skin. William's eyes opened wide. He knew this feeling. Suddenly that putrid smell that had filled his bedroom stung his nose, and William now knew it for sure.

"She's here…" said William, swallowing nervously, as his fear of Annemarie overwhelmed his pain temporarily.

"She's-" began Eric in response.

"Hurry up! Just finish it!" interrupted William desperately. Eric didn't waste another second. He didn't even bother counting down this time.

"Get ready," he said, pressing another circle into William's back, causing him to wail in agony.

"Okay two more to go," said Eric, again casting aside the previous circle and leaning in with the smaller circle as the penultimate shape.

"Here we-" began Eric, when suddenly the doors of the shed blasted open. It was as if time stood still. There at the door of the shed, in all her horror, was Annemarie. William froze in fear as he stared at the horrific being standing before him. He hadn't seen her up this close since she'd transformed after murdering his parents. She was even more horrifying than William had realized. Never in all his years could he have imagined something as terrifying as the monstrosity that was currently looming mere feet away from him. Suddenly he felt that familiar feeling of hot iron being pressed into his back. His senses were overwhelmed, and for the first time since the branding had started, he could barely feel it. There was just too much fear and adrenaline coursing through his veins.

Within moments of opening the door, Annemarie began to descend upon him. There was nothing he could do. They were too late. The sigil wasn't finished. They still had the final brand to place, and Eric had promised him that when Annemarie entered, he'd hide behind the shield. Even if he didn't, there was no time to place the final brand before Annemarie got to William. This was it. It was over. They'd lost.

CHAPTER FOURTEEN

Tautomerism

As Annemarie reached out towards William, her hands wrapped around his neck and he immediately felt himself unable to breathe. A terror unlike anything that he'd felt in his life filled his body as he began to try to grab at her ethereal hands which were choking him to death. The closer that she drew to him, the less control he felt like he had over his body, until finally she was down, face to face with him. He could feel her ice-cold breath against his face as he gasped for breath and began losing control over his body. As a strange paralysis began to set in, he felt pins and needles running up his legs and spine. The supernatural aura of fear which the monster emitted began to completely overwhelm his young mind. Before his eyes, the ethereal abomination suddenly began to slide itself down his gasping throat. As its otherworldly visage began to disintegrate into a fine red mist, he uncontrollably breathed it in and felt it filling every inch of his body. He gasped for breath, but it was no use. The only thing that filled his lungs was Annemarie. As the pins and needles grew stronger and stronger, he felt himself losing consciousness until finally, his world fell into darkness.

***

When William opened his eyes, he didn't recognize his surroundings. As he tried to move his arms, he realized that he was in some way bound up. His arms were extended upwards in either direction, seemingly tied up or restricted. With his head nodded downwards, he could see that his body wasn't composed of his normal flesh. Instead, he was somewhat ethereal, as though composed by a shimmering mist of sorts. As he regained consciousness, a million questions spun in his mind. He was less filled with fear than confusion. This didn't last long however, as when he raised his head to look up, he beheld an almost unfathomable monstrosity. There, looking down over him, was a behemoth of positively titanic proportions. The leviathan loomed higher than the mountain on which Lakhdorian resided. It was so preposterously large, that William's heart was filled overwhelmingly with fear, while at the same time, awe. The creature had countless twisting appendages which sprawled about the abyss in which they were currently residing. William knew not where most of these appendages even ended. They were so large that they twisted off into the darkness and out of sight in all directions. The body of the beast was equally unfathomable. The titanic figure was long and grotesque like a centipede, seemingly unending as it extended out into the inky depths of the abyss. It was made of a kind of chaotic flesh which flexed and moved about, ripping and tearing itself, bubbling and flowing like there were a billion ants crawling under its skin. The creature bore an untold number of tusks and horns chaotically erupting at random throughout its body. On top of its enormous head, sat two horns, each the size of a small village, which extended sharply into the sky above it. Its face was a muddled explosion of fleshy bubbles and growths that assumed an almost brain-like quality. The enormous pink tumorous growths pulsed and wobbled as the beast moved itself. Amongst the tumultuous mess of flesh was a muddled field of glowing eyes which all seemed to be focused down on William. Beneath its eyes sat a grotesque maw of a mouth which extended hundreds of meters downwards, drooling blood from its teeth which grew with such chaotic disregard that they pierced its own flesh on the opposite side of its hideous mouth. Many of its appendages seemed to have claw or hand-like qualities, but the nature of its form made little sense to William. It was like a creature made of pure chaos; an explosion of flesh that never quite settled in any particularly ordered form. Beneath its corpulent exterior, and also erupting around it like lightning, was some form of anarchic energy, assuming many different colors depending from where it vented. The monster was of such mythic proportions that William could hardly even feel the same kind of fear that he'd felt before when he'd been face to face with Annemarie. It was just too absurd. The monster itself and the entire situation were just so preposterous that William could barely even take it seriously. As he stared up at the behemoth, the reality of the situation finally set in for him. What he was looking at was the true form of the monster that had been taking the shape of Annemarie, and the abyss they were inside was William's body.

The monster had clearly noticed him staring up at it. It craned itself downwards, assessing him with its innumerable eyes with laser focus. It had no discernable expressions, so William had absolutely no concept of what it was feeling or thinking, but he felt nothing but malice from the thing. The amount of malevolence which oozed from every pore of its being created an overwhelming aura of animosity which William could barely handle. How could something this preposterously evil even exist? Suddenly William noticed something out of the corner of his eye. Down below the creature, in front of William, floated a large spectral orb. Through the orb William could see the open door of Eric's shed. A chill suddenly ran down William's spine. The orb was showing what his body was seeing in the real world. He watched on in horror, as his real-life body began to look down over itself, raising its hands and flexing them, seemingly testing its own control over itself. William's heart was filled with despair as he realized that it wasn't him that was controlling his body; it was this monster. A horrible thought suddenly crossed William's mind: is this what his father had been seeing? Had he been bound up like this, in front of that horrendous monstrosity, having to watch his beloved wife be strangled by his own hands?

As William's body suddenly began to straighten itself up, his heart was filled with dread. Eric was alone in that room right now, probably hiding behind the shield like they'd agreed. Was William going to have to watch the monster murder his best friend? There was nothing he could do. He was completely bound up. He couldn't move a muscle. But that's when he suddenly remembered something. When William had burst into that bedroom and seen his father with his hands wrapped around his mother's neck, his father had spoken to him. He'd begged William to kill him. How had his father managed to regain that much control over himself? He knew that his father was a strong man, but even when facing a monster of these mythic proportions, he'd somehow managed to free himself enough to relay his message.

William stared up at the evil abomination towering over him. His father had really gotten the last laugh over this thing. If his father could do it, so could William. He had to. He had to make his father proud. He took a deep breath and filled himself with determination. He'd do exactly what his dad had done.

William suddenly began fighting with all his might to free himself from his binds. As soon as he started squirming, the titan before him became agitated, moving its head down to inspect him closer. William didn't care. He had to get free. He had to regain control of his body before this monster made him hurt Eric. How had his father managed to do it?

"Eric!" screamed William desperately, his voice erupting as barely a whisper. The monster shrieked loudly, its impossibly deep roar exploding over the abyss in which they sat like an earthquake. William ignored it. His father must've gotten this far at least. The fact that he was pissing the thing off told him that he was on the right track.

"Eric! Kill me!" cried out William desperately, his voice somehow becoming a little louder this time. Suddenly, another voice echoed over the abyss in response, cold and distant like a memory.

"Sorry William, but we're not done yet," said Eric's voice. Before William could even process what Eric had said, a blinding white light erupted over the abyss. The sound of sizzling flesh echoed all around him, and as the light and sound intensified, the monster released a horrendous shriek which shook the very earth beneath their feet. Just what in the world had happened? William couldn't open his eyes, as the light which was erupting over the abyss blinded him. After a moment William tentatively forced his eyes open anyway, and what he beheld filled his heart with horror. The monster was still screaming. It almost sounded panicked. The beast was twisting and turning its head around in all directions, seemingly looking for something. As the white light started to die out, the monster suddenly exploded into action. Its millions of appendages carried it scuttling around the abyss like a cockroach trapped in a glass jar. It was shrieking and screaming in a way that made William feel like it was somehow in fear. What had happened? Just what had Eric done to somehow incite fear in a beast of such unfathomable proportions? Regardless of how it had happened, the monster was now flailing and scuttling about; its attention finally having left William. This was his chance to regain control. He pulled with all his might at whatever was binding him, and as he focused his willpower like he never had before, he felt something beginning to tear away. After a moment his arms were freed, and he fell to the floor of the abyss. Immediately the behemoth turned back around to face him. For a moment the two of them were frozen in place, as William stared between the monster and the floating orb to the real world. The monster suddenly released a roar, clearly not of fear this time though, but of fury. William had to act fast. He raced as quickly as his ethereal legs would carry him towards the orb as the mountainous behemoth scuttled upon its countless appendages after him, quaking the earth as it galloped. As William stretched out his arms and dived towards the orb, some of the beast's enormous appendages extended towards him. At this moment a smirk crossed William's face. He knew he'd beaten it. His world suddenly faded into blinding white light, and he felt an intense vacuum like sensation. As he regained consciousness, he reeled in nausea as the overwhelming light of the dimly lit garden shed hit his eyes. It took him a moment to comprehend where he was. He had fallen from the stool that he'd been sitting in and was face down on the floor. As he shakily managed to right himself up onto his hands and knees, he was once again filled with overwhelming agony. His central nervous system blasted waves of pain up his spine from his fresh branding wounds. William cried out in pain as he returned to reality.

"William?!" exclaimed Eric's voice in concern. William's world flashed white and red as he was overwhelmed with pain. He fell forwards onto his face, groaning in agony. He managed to turn his head around on the floor and looked up at his friend. There was Eric, holding the final piece of red-hot metal in his calipers. It was the single long vertical piece which extended up through the middle of the sigil. For a moment William stared at him with a mixture of confusion and relief. Relief that Eric was okay, but confusion about what exactly had happened.

"Where did it go?!" asked William, clenching his teeth as he tried to get the question out through groans of agony. He looked around for Annemarie but was hit by a wave of nausea which sent him toppling back down onto his forearms.

"William!" exclaimed Eric, throwing aside the calipers and running to William's aid. William tried to center himself, fighting against the nausea and overwhelming pain on his back. It was only now that he suddenly noticed that the storm was finally letting up. He looked up at Eric.

"The… the storm?" he asked. Eric nodded.

"Will, I don't know how but… I think somehow… we did it…" said Eric, tentatively as he helped William up. As a cautious sense of relief started to spread over them, they continued to look around, expecting to see Annemarie hiding in a corner somewhere. At least for now, it seemed like they'd really done it. Somehow, the monster was gone.

CHAPTER FIFTEEN
The Break of Dawn

Eric stared down at his friend as his mind whirred with a million thoughts. After cleaning William's wound and applying some honey to it, he'd bandaged him up and set him down on his father's bedroll in the kitchen. Despite how painful his wound must be William was in an extremely deep sleep. Eric's eye twitched when he thought about being face to face with that abomination. Never in a million years could he have prepared himself for what he was confronted with last night. His thoughts were suddenly interrupted when he heard the distinct sound of a galloping horse entering his farmstead. It was too early to be his father returning, so could it be somebody from Lakhdorian? He stepped out onto his porch and looked out curiously to see who it could be. As they came into view, he felt a sense of relief enter his heart.

"Ahoy!" waved Eric, extremely happy to see William's uncle Wilton. As Wilton neared the front porch, he reared his horse up to a stop before trotting around to where Eric was standing. He nodded to Eric in greeting with a stern expression on his face.

"Eric…" began Wilton, in an uncharacteristically serious tone. Eric suddenly felt a pang of worry run down his spine. This whole horrific event had started in Lakhdorian. William had said that the monster had taken control of his father, but he'd never elaborated on the details.

"I'm afraid I come bearing some horrible news," said Wilton, catching his breath for a moment as he seemed to be thinking about how to approach the conversation.

"Is your father home?" he asked, peering over Eric's shoulder.

"I'm afraid not. What's the news?" asked Eric anxiously. Wilton seemed to center himself for a moment.

"Last night, William was involved in something..." began Wilton cryptically. Eric suddenly felt his anxiety rising again.

"I know that he must be scared, and I know that he can't return home. There's only one other place that the boy knows..." continued Wilton looking around the property searchingly.

"Why can't he return home?" asked Eric curiously.

"Have you seen him?" asked Wilton, ignoring Eric's question.

"Is he in some kind of trouble?" asked Eric, dodging Wilton's question in return. Wilton let out a sigh.

"Aye, he is. So have you seen him?" asked Wilton again. To Eric, it almost sounded like William had done something wrong. He assessed Wilton's demeanor. Not only did the man look exhausted and disheveled, but he bore a curiously stern expression on his face. He'd never seen Wilton so serious in his life. If Eric did say yes, how could he even begin to explain why he'd branded his nephew's flesh six times? Could he just explain that a horrific monster wanted to take control over him? There was no way he'd buy that. Eric needed more time to think, but with Wilton standing right in front of him he had to act on impulse. It was at this moment that Eric made a very important snap decision which he could only hope was the right call.

"No, I haven't seen him," replied Eric flatly. Wilton inspected him suspiciously.

"He didn't come by last night?" asked Wilton again.

"No, I haven't seen him since the feast," replied Eric with a shrug. Wilton exhaled with frustration and grumbled to himself before turning his horse back around towards the entrance of the farm.

"Would you like to stay for some morning tea?" asked Eric daringly.

"No, I haven't the time. I have to find William. If he comes by here, please, bring him back to Lakhdorian," said Wilton seriously.

"May I ask what kind of trouble he's gotten himself into?" asked Eric with concern. Wilton adorned a dark expression and paused momentarily.

"He's… I think he might know something about the murder of his father," said Wilton, his voice cracking slightly with emotion. Eric felt his head spin with shock. William? Playing a role in the murder of his father? There was no way. Even if he'd wanted to, the man was far too enormous. Surely it was that monster that had done it. Eric needed to know more.

"What?! Steinar's dead?! What about Sasha and Mary, are they okay?!" asked Eric fearfully. Wilton sucked his teeth and looked down at the ground as his expression darkened even more.

"Mary's dead too," said Wilton grimly, swallowing to hold back tears as the words left his mouth. Eric was too shocked to know what to say. He'd had no idea that William had lost both of his parents last night. Just how much had the poor boy suffered through?

"As for Sasha, William dropped her off at our cottage last night before making off into the night…" explained Wilton.

"What? She was with William? Then does that mean she saw it happen?!" asked Eric, genuinely concerned about Sasha having been face to face with that monster. Again, Wilton's expression darkened.

"Aye. She's not coping well. A mind as young as hers ain't equipped for what she saw last night. Says that the dead girl next-door did it," said Wilton, shaking his head incredulously. Eric felt his heart drop. So there it was. Sasha had seen the monster, but people weren't believing her story. Would Eric corroborating it help the situation at all? If Eric told them that he'd seen it too, also adding the details of what transpired here, would they believe him? He didn't have enough information about what had happened to know for sure. Perhaps if he'd divulged the truth before Wilton had told him about Sasha's monster story it would've held more weight, but now it'd seem like he's just clutching at straws to exonerate William. He took a deep breath. He needed to get the full story be-fore he knew how to properly help him. Whether Wilton took Wil-liam home now or later, it wouldn't change the fact that William's parents were dead. On top of everything, Eric didn't even know if the monster was truly gone yet. If he sent William home with Wil-ton and the monster was still inside him, it could pose a huge threat to the entire village. The last thing that he wanted was any more death. Eric closed his eyes and nodded understandingly.

"I'm so sorry for your loss. Send my love to Sasha and Gene-vieve. My father and I will be thinking of you all," said Eric genu-inely, shaking his head sadly as he fondly remembered William's parents. Wilton nodded appreciatively before turning his horse away and setting off back into the moors. Eric narrowed his eyes as he watched him riding away. Had he made the right decision? Should he have just told the truth? No. He knew what he had to do, as difficult as it would be. He let out a sigh and got to work making preparations for what lay ahead of them. As he walked towards his garden shed, he still couldn't help questioning his decision. Was it really okay to have lied like that to Wilton, or had he made things even worse for William?

***

William woke up with a jolt, adrenaline coursing through his veins. It took him a few moments to figure out where he was and calm down, realizing that he had been having a nightmare. His relief was short lived however, as reality then came crashing down on him as the pain in his back reminded him that in actuality; it wasn't just a dream. His mother, his father, and Annemarie were all dead.

"Good morning!" said Eric suddenly, pulling William from his dark thoughts and the precipice of a complete emotional breakdown. William tried to roll over onto his back but immediately discovered that it was far too painful for him to be able to do that right now, so simply stayed plastered to the floor on his stomach like a slug. He groaned in pain as he rolled around on his belly, feebly trying to figure out a position that might be more comfortable than his current one. He got onto his hands and knees which freed up the pressure on his chest and allowed him to breathe a little more easily.

"Here, let me help you," said Eric, coming over and putting an arm down to support William up onto a chair. William thankfully accepted his help and felt relief run through his body as he was finally able to breathe more easily. For a few moments William sat in simple disbelief at the pain he was in. He looked up at Eric, who was watching over him with concern.

"How did the wound look when you saw it?" asked William, shaking his head miserably. Eric let out a sigh and shook his head.

"I'll be honest, it's a bloody mess back there..." admitted Eric. William slumped his shoulders and nodded understandingly.

"How long until it heals?" asked William, terrified of the answer. Eric's expression darkened slightly.

"For the cows... it takes weeks..." replied Eric, looking at William apologetically. William let out a sigh of frustration. He'd already known what the answer would be but hearing it out loud somehow made it feel worse.

"Just wait until we do yours..." William said with a cheeky wry smile, as he tried to find a comfortable position to sit in. At first Eric looked surprised, but then smiled and shook his head.

"Aye, we'll do mine, but it'll just be a small one right here," said Eric, raising his eyebrow and patting himself on his left shoulder.

"What? Why does yours get to be so small?" asked William in surprise, gritting his teeth and wincing in pain as he accidentally pressed his wound against the back of the chair.

"I've had time to make a smaller brand. It's already cooling off in the shed as we speak. Unfortunately, we couldn't have made yours any smaller. Not with the iron scraps that we had, and not in the time we had," said Eric, his expression darkening as he recalled the experience. It was already midday and Eric hadn't rested yet.

"We barely managed to get it done in time, you know. It looked like it almost managed to take control of you," said Eric. Did Eric really not realize that the monster had in fact taken control of him for a moment there? He had to tell him the full story, he owed him as much.

"It did," said William simply.

"What do ye mean?" asked Eric, his unease apparent. William let out a sigh.

"It got me. I don't know what happened but... for a moment there it had control over me. I saw what it really looks like... it's terrible Eric," revealed William, shaking his head as he recalled seeing the monster in its most complete form.

"Whatever you did when you finished that sigil, it sent it into a panic. While it was distracted, I had a chance to regain control over myself," explained William. Eric's expression darkened again as he fell back into deep thought.

"We need to learn more about all of this," said Eric seriously. He wore a troubled expression as he clutched the bridge of his nose, deep in thought.

"Aye, but how are we meant to do that?" asked William wearily. Eric took a deep breath and looked around the room for a moment deep in thought.

"There's only one place that could possibly have the information we need…" said Eric, placing his hands on his hips and raising an eyebrow decisively.

"Where's that?" asked William in confusion.

"Oxgate library," he replied, staring down at William seriously.

"Ey?!" spluttered William in surprise.

"And how exactly are we supposed to get in there? You have to be a fully-fledged knight to even have a chance, right?" asked William, trying to recall what little he knew about the place from his sister's ramblings. Again, Eric simply nodded in response.

"Aye William. We'd have to be knights," replied Eric. Before William could even respond, they both suddenly heard the sound of a horse and cart entering the property. Eric stood up straight and let out a frustrated sigh.

"Sounds like dad's home…" he thought aloud as he began walking towards the front door. William shifted in his chair nervously. How far would word have spread about what had happened in Lakhdorian last night? What would the townsfolk think of it all?

Sasha was the one that William was most worried about. He was thankful that he'd managed to deliver her safely to Wilton's cottage, but he couldn't get her out of his mind. He desperately wanted to check up on her to make sure that she was okay. He'd left her safely in the hands of his uncle and aunt, but the amount of confronting questions the town was going to have for her was something he hadn't honestly thought about until right now.

"Good morning Mr. Harlowe!" called out Eric from the porch, bringing William's mind back to the present situation. How would Eric's father react to William being here? Was he going to have to go back to Lakhdorian? He wasn't sure whether he felt up to the trip yet. He painfully stood up and walked his way over to the front window and looked out of it nervously. Barty Rothmane was arriving onto the property barely able to keep himself upright in the back of a cart. A frustrated looking middle-aged man was leading the horse and stopped the cart in front of Eric. He didn't respond to Eric's greeting and instead simply glared at him.

"This top-heavy bastard stole from me!" shouted the man angrily, gesturing to Eric's father who was attempting unsuccessfully to sit up straight in the back of the cart.

"Who are ye calling top-heavy ya toffee-nosed twat?!" shouted Barty in response, again feebly trying to stand up and falling over onto his face.

"Ahh, I do apologize sir!" said Eric, bowing his head slightly.

"Bullocks with your apology! I'll be expecting the usual payment for hauling this useless pig back to his sty, plus an extra silver piece for the booze he guzzled," growled Harlowe angrily. Eric gasped in surprise.

"A silver?! Are ye mad? Surely he didn't drink that much!" reasoned Eric, walking over to the side of the cart to assist his father.

"Take a look at him! It were the good stuff too ye know!" spat Harlowe furiously.

"Tasted like piss to me!" slurred Barty, hiccupping mid-sentence and falling over Eric's shoulder as he was lifted down from the back of the cart like a toddler.

"Aye sir. Give me a moment," said Eric, leading his father inside. As soon as Barty caught sight of William, his face adorned an expression of shock.

"What's this runt doing 'ere?!" he growled grumpily.

"He's helping me with some work pa. Let's get you down into bed," said Eric, trying to lead his father towards the bedroll on the floor that William had been using. Suddenly William realized why it was in here. Getting his drunken father any deeper into the house would've been significantly harder. This must've happened quite often. As he was led past the table, his father swiped at the bottle of spirits that was still out from Eric cleaning William's wound. Eric pulled him out of arm's reach before he could grab it.

"Not now pa, it's time for bed," said Eric calmly. Barty again swiped desperately at the bottle as Eric lowered him down towards the bedroll. The second that Barty's body collapsed into the bedroll he seemed to forget about the bottle of alcohol, as his eyes began to droop closed.

"Ya... fat..." Barty didn't manage to finish his sentence before he'd fallen asleep. There was an awkward moment of silence before Harlowe smacked on the side of his cart impatiently.

"Chop chop! I haven't got all day!" he yelled.

"Aye sir!" called Eric back, hurrying off into another room of the house before returning with a handful of coins. He went out onto the porch and handed them to Harlowe. As soon as Harlowe had the coins in his hands his disposition changed immediately. He looked down at Eric with a sympathetic expression on his face.

"Ye can't be running this farm alone and taking care of him too," said Harlowe, shaking his head. Eric looked down at the ground in embarrassment.

"Aye sir…" he replied flatly.

"Yer a good kid. Ye know the only reason we put up with his shite is 'cos of you," continued Harlowe, letting out a sigh.

"Thank you, sir…" responded Eric, again averting his eyes in shame. Harlowe put a hand on Eric's shoulder and patted him roughly.

"Yer a strong lad, and so were yer pa before… well…" Harlowe pulled his hand back and shook his head uncomfortably.

"Anyway. I'll be off. Take care o' yerself young Rothmane. Don't let him screw up yer life, ye hear?" asked Harlowe sternly, raising an eyebrow.

"Aye sir," responded Eric with an understanding nod. With that, Harlowe spurred his horse into action and set off back up the road towards Mistfall. Eric let out a deep sigh and stared after him before turning around and heading back inside. The two boys shared an awkward silence for a moment as the reality of how Eric had been living hit William.

"Eric, you should've told me things were this hard…" said William, looking at Eric compassionately. He shot William an incredulous glance.

"I appreciate it brother, but who would I be to take pity on myself at a time like this?" he asked, looking down at his father who was now deep asleep and snoring loudly.

"He might be daft, but at least I've still got him..." said Eric deep in thought. He suddenly seemed to snap back to reality and looked up fearfully at William.

"Oh William, I... I'm so sorry, that was stupid of me to say..." stammered Eric. William stared back at him in confusion for a moment before he suddenly realized why Eric was being so awkward. Tears began to well in William's eyes as last night's events again overwhelmed him.

"I just meant, because I've lost my mother you see, I didn't mean..." began Eric, again seeming frustrated by his own lack of tact. William took a shaky breath and tried to wipe the tears out of his eyes, but it was no use. The dam had been opened once again, and William was assaulted by an overwhelming torrent of sorrow. Eric put a consoling hand on his shoulder, trying his best to avoid the brand. William sobbed, unable to stop himself from crying miserably as the last night's traumas were reignited in his psyche and he was finally able to face the loss of his parents. It was there, standing in Eric's kitchen with the midday sun shining through the windows, that the two boys finally confronted the traumas that they'd been faced with last night.

CHAPTER SIXTEEN
Revelation in Flames

William took a moment to steady his nerves. For now he'd some-how been able to quell his tears. As he started to ground himself, his mind went back to what Eric had just said as he'd been comforting him.

"Uncle Wilton was here this morning? Did he say anything about Sasha?" asked William.

"Aye, he said that Sasha is okay. They don't believe her story about Annemarie though," explained Eric. William let out a sigh and leaned back in his chair, immediately jumping forward again when his brand touched the wood.

"I've got to go up there and explain what happened," he said, standing from his chair.

"William no! Think about it!" reasoned Eric, also standing. William stared back at him expectantly as panic coursed through his veins.

"What are they going to think? Are they going to believe that a monster that looked like Annemarie came and started murdering your family?" asked Eric expectantly.

"Well, it's the truth!" replied William defensively.

"Aye it is! But what's more likely? Yer pa was the largest man in the village, and there ain't a soul who don't know that he were a bully. People have always gossiped about him working you and yer sister too hard. Is it really that much of a stretch, that maybe big old Steinar Lakhdorian were beating his wife?" asked Eric. William stared back at him in horror.

"Eric, what are ye on about?!" yelled William furiously. Eric shook his head.

"William, think about it from their perspective! You said yer ma was strangled. Yer sister has already told them that it was yer pa that did it. It won't take a genius to see that it were his hands around her neck. What if little Sasha Lakhdorian were trying to protect her brother from being hung for patricide? What if that's why she made up her ghost stories?" asked Eric. William couldn't hold back his anger. He groaned loudly in rage and slammed his fist down on the table, almost waking Barty from his drunken slumber.

"William! Calm down for a second!" cried Eric.

"How can you speak about my family like that?!" yelled William.

"Come on William! You know I love your family! But please be realistic with me for a second here!" begged Eric desperately.

"What good is you going back to that village going to do? All ye'd be doing is putting yer life in jeopardy, and for no good reason!" explained Eric, trying to appeal to William logically. William let out a frustrated groan.

"What about my father's honor? He loved me ma. He'd never have laid a hand on her. Never!" cried William, tears streaming down his face.

"Aye! I know that! And if you don't go back to that village, what happened in that house last night will remain a mystery. Nobody will know. They won't know where William Lakhdorian went. They won't know what happened to yer parents. All they'll know is that it were a tragedy that broke yer sister's young mind," said Eric shaking his head sadly. William stared back at Eric, earnestly taking in his words. He was right. The only thing that going back to Lakhdorian would achieve was putting William's life in danger. He had no evidence, as the monster was gone. All he had was a disgusting wound on his back and a ghost story. He groaned in frustration.

"I can't stay here forever. What am I supposed to do?" asked William, goose bumps appearing on his arms as the futility of his situation dawned on him.

"William, I have a plan. I ain't leaving you. Ye hear me?" asked Eric, looking into William's eyes searchingly. William nodded appreciatively.

"What's yer plan?" asked William quietly. Eric stood up and put his hands on his hips. He closed his eyes and took a deep breath.

"There's only one place where the forbidden knowledge we need can be found. We're going to Oxgate," he said definitively. William rolled his eyes.

"Eric, we've been over this. We can't get into that library we'd have to be-" began William.

"Aye. We'd have to be knights," interrupted Eric. William stared back at him blankly for a moment.

"Have ye forgotten something? We're a couple of farm boys, Eric. We're not nobles. They don't let people like us become knights," said William, shaking his head dismissively. Eric raised an eyebrow and looked down at William haughtily.

"No William, you're the one who's forgotten something. I may be a farm boy, but I'm also a Rothmane," said Eric.

"Wait…" began William, the reality of the situation finally hitting him.

"Aye William. My great grandfather may have chosen to live out his last days on this farmland, but it didn't make him any less of a noble," said Eric shaking his head. William's eyes widened as he stared at Eric.

"You're… you're a noble…" said William in awe.

"Aye William. So get yer things ready. We're going to Oxgate," said Eric.

***

"You don't have to do this you know…" said William, feeling guilty as he watched his friend turning his life upside down to help him. Eric finished tightening the last strap around one of the packs before he stood up and dusted his hands off triumphantly.

"I know, but ye can't talk me out of it now brother," he replied with a wink before turning around and heading back inside to collect his final items. William looked over the tightly packed cart and let out a guilty sigh. A loud crash suddenly erupted from inside Eric's house, pulling him from his thoughts. He hurried to the front door but stopped in his tracks when he realized what had caused the ruckus.

"What do ye think yer doin'?!" exclaimed Barty who had woken from his nap just as drunk as when he'd entered it. The crash had been the sound of him stumbling into a kitchen shelf, knocking down some pots and pans. Eric stood on the other side of the living room rifling through a small chest that had been hidden behind some books.

"Father, I'm leaving," said Eric flatly, taking the contents of the small chest and pouring it into a coin purse.

"Get yer filthy hands out of my money!" shouted Barty drunkenly, trying feebly to right himself and falling over in the opposite direction into the kitchen table this time.

"I'd wager you didn't know I was keeping this chest of savings…" said Eric, his eyes glazing over as he stared at his drunken father unable to right himself.

"If you'd known, it'd all be gone by now," finished Eric, closing the chest and putting it back where he'd found it.

"Give me my money ye fat pig!" shouted his father, still unable to let go of the kitchen table that he was clinging to desperately for support. Eric shook his head in disdain.

"I'm going to Oxgate to become a knight," said Eric, turning and looking up at a portrait of his great grandfather which hung on the wall. Barty released a howling cackle of laughter in response.

"You?! A knight?! What are ye going to do?! Eat them to death?!" exclaimed Barty, his laughter turning into a coughing fit followed by some dry gagging.

"It's what granda would've wanted for me," said Eric honestly. Eric's father managed to catch his breath, standing up shakily and pointing a finger towards Eric threateningly.

"You don't have the balls to be a knight, you ungrateful tike!" spat his father furiously, taking his first drunken stumbling step towards Eric without the table's support.

"Now give me my money, or I'll turn ya face upside down ya great fat…" Barty slurred, taking another shaky step towards Eric before stumbling into one of the kitchen chairs and falling down to the floor. Eric took a few steps towards his father and looked down over him flailing about on the kitchen floor.

"I'm only taking the savings I've set aside since I took over control of the farm. I'm leaving the rest for you. It'll be more than enough to keep the farm running, as long as you don't drink it all away," said Eric, looking down over his drunken father.

"You wouldn't dare... I'll smash ya face in, come 'ere!" murmured Barty from the kitchen floor. Eric shook his head.

"If mother could see you now..." said Eric, furrowing his brow with disdain.

"Don't you dare speak about her..." said Barty, pointing a finger up at his son.

"Don't you dare!" he yelled at the top of his lungs, inciting another hacking coughing fit.

Eric hesitated for a moment, clearly wanting to help his father up. He eventually seemed to change his mind and took a step away. He took a few more tentative steps towards the front door before he turned around and looked back at his father.

"I really am leaving, father. I trust you remember how to run this place," said Eric as Barty flailed about, trying to sit upright. He paused for another moment.

"I love ye pa. I really hope you find your way out of this nonsense. I'll come back and visit you someday... and... I hope when I do, I can make you proud," said Eric, his expression darkening. He closed his eyes for a moment and turned away.

"Proud?!" yelled Barty.

"Proud?! You've never made me proud a day in your good for nothing life, ye hear me?! Yer dead to me boy. Dead!" bellowed Barty, sitting upright and pointing at Eric. William wasn't sure what to do. He'd never felt so awkward in his life.

"Come on Will..." said Eric, nodding to William as he walked towards the door.

"Oh..." said Eric, suddenly stopping and turning back towards his father.

"If you've any decency left in you at all… you won't tell any-body that William was here," said Eric, nodding to his father one last time before walking out the door.

"You're dead to me boy. If you come back here, I'll kill ya! Do you hear me boy?! I'll kill ya!" screamed Barty from the kitchen floor. William followed Eric silently out the door and out towards the cart.

"You okay?" asked William once they reached the cart.

"Aye…" said Eric, closing his eyes and nodding his head.

"It's like I said. At least I've still got him," he said before hopping up onto the cart. William nodded understandingly and hopped up into the cart onto the seat beside Eric.

"Nope," said Eric suddenly, shaking his head. William looked around in confusion.

"You need to rest. Hop in the back," said Eric nodding over his shoulder.

"Oh come on, after all you've done today, surely you should be the one resting!" argued William.

"You don't even know where we're going!" retorted Eric, crack-ing a wry smile. William crossed his arms and released a groan in defeat.

"Fine, I'll just rest for a short while. Wake me up before dusk," demanded William as he crawled painfully over into the back of the cart.

"Aye, aye…" said Eric with a smile. William tried lying down on his side, but on the bumpy road his back simply hurt far too much. With a grunt he adjusted to lying uncomfortably on his stomach. He couldn't imagine that he'd be able to fall asleep while lying on his stomach in the back of a bumpy cart anyway, so he re-ally would only rest his eyes for a short while.

It took less than a minute for William to fall into a deep sleep.

***

William was woken with a jolt. The wagon seemed to be bumping even more heavily than he imagined it would. As he sat up on his hands and knees, he noticed that dusk had already fallen over the moors.

"Hey!" exclaimed William.

"Oh, you're awake!" said Eric cheerfully.

"I told you to wake me up before dusk fell!" said William, leaning his head on the back of Eric's seat and groaning with pain as his brand wound was stretched by his motion.

"Whoops!" said Eric chuckling to himself. William looked around them and immediately realized why the wagon had been bumping more than before. They had turned off of the main dirt road through the moors and were traversing a rough, rocky path up a heather laden hill.

"Hey, where are we going?!" asked William, looking around at the endless fields of heather stretching all around them.

"I know some people that live out here. They'll let us stay in their commune overnight, trust me," said Eric with a confident nod. William inspected their barren surroundings curiously. Sure, there were a lot of hills, but William supposed that there couldn't possibly be any towns around here. As it were, he could see no signs of settlement.

"They… they live out here?" asked William, confused. Eric gave him a sly look out of the corner of his eye as they neared the top of the small hill that they were traveling up. Atop a slightly smaller hill just beyond this one sat a congregation of colorful tents.

"Gypsies…" thought William aloud in awe as they continued towards the encampment. Eric gave him a knowing nod in response.

It only took the boys a few more minutes to arrive at the camp right as night was falling. Upon their arrival, several people congregated over to inspect the boys mysteriously arriving at their camp.

"Good evening!" called out Eric as they approached. The gypsies were reticent at first, but upon realizing that it was Eric, immediately lightened up and waved back.

"Young Eric! It's good to see you, my boy!" called out one of the men enthusiastically. As soon as he reached the camp, Eric pulled Bonnie to a halt and hopped down from the cart, exchanging greetings with the gypsies. He suddenly turned around and gestured towards William.

"This is my friend William, from Lakhdorian!" announced Eric. Everybody waved merrily to him and welcomed him into their camp. William felt himself blushing as the attention was turned on him, waving back and smiling awkwardly.

"What brings you to our camp?" asked one of the older gentlemen curiously.

"Aye, you aren't due for another week are ye son?" asked one of the gypsy ladies looking at him with concern. Eric let out a sigh and nodded.

"Yer right, I'm not, but next time it'll be my pa bringing your delivery," replied Eric. A few of them exchanged surprised looks.

"Are you sure he's up to it?" asked the lady.

"Aye. I believe he is," Eric nodded confidently.

"Well then, what brings you boys to our camp then?" asked the older gentleman again.

"Now that is a long story... but we're here requesting that we stay with you just for the night. We're traveling to Oxgate and we need a place to rest," explained Eric, bowing his head politely. The gypsies exchanged some unsure glances with each other.

"Oh! Right!" said Eric, turning towards William.

"Pass down that green sack in the corner, would ya Will?" asked Eric. William scrambled to find what he was talking about. Once he found it, he passed it down to Eric who received it eagerly.

"I've brought a gift! Some fresh pork!" said Eric happily. Immediately the gypsies' faces brightened up.

"Well then, what are you waiting for boys? Come in, come in! I'll get a campfire started!" said one of the gypsies excitedly as the whole group spurred into action. William smiled and shook his head in surprise. Eric had really planned ahead. Would William ever be able to think as clearly as Eric always did? He didn't have much time to ponder this, as the gypsies suddenly came over and led Bonnie and the cart into their camp site.

***

The atmosphere around the campfire was extremely jovial. It was a much-needed distraction from the grim adventure that William and Eric had been sharing. After they'd all had their fill of pork, a few of the gypsies had taken to playing music by some lanterns a short way away from the fire. Coming from Lakhdorian, William had never had a lot of exposure to music. Only on winter solstice night, or when traveling gypsies had come through town on occasion. There were four gypsies playing instruments, one a fiddle, another a lute, one a flute and finally one with a small animal skin drum. As they played their enchanting music, William was positively captivated. A gypsy lady in a beautiful red dress was dancing to their music in the firelight, her skirt spiraling all around, rendering William spellbound. This was exactly the kind of distraction he and Eric needed. He turned to his friend to see how he was enjoying the music but found him fast asleep on the floor by the campfire. He smiled, happy to see him finally lying down. It was a well-earned rest.

"So, William is it?" asked the elderly gypsy who was sitting by the campfire beside William.

"Aye!" stammered William with a nod. The gypsy smiled at him politely before casting a curious gaze down to his clothing and raising an eyebrow.

"My boy that tunic is far too large for you!" said the old man, shaking his head as he regarded the tunic which was indeed, several sizes too large for William.

"Aye, it's one of his," William laughed, nodding towards Eric who was fast asleep. The gypsy nodded understandingly.

"Melina!" called out the old man suddenly, taking William by surprise. After a few moments a middle-aged gypsy lady came out from one of the nearby tents.

"Aye father?" she asked.

"Please find a tunic for young William here," asked the old man, catching William off guard.

"Oh, no! No, that's okay! I'm perfectly comfortable!" lied William in his giant tunic which went down over his knees. The gypsy lady raised an eyebrow at him before turning around and disappearing into one of the tents.

"Please, you really don't have to trouble yourself!" insisted William after her, feeling overwhelming shame at taking advantage of these gypsies' hospitality. After a few moments the lady came back out holding a vibrant green tunic.

"Really, I'm fine!" insisted William.

"Try this one on," she said, ignoring him. He finally obliged, but when he removed his oversized tunic both of the gypsies gasped in shock.

"My boy, what has happened to you?!" exclaimed the elderly man, looking at William's extensive bandaging. William blushed abashedly.

"I uh… I had an accident…" lied William, not sure of what kind of excuse to use. The two gypsies exchanged concerned looks with one another.

"When did this happen, dear?" asked the gypsy lady, walking closer into the campfire light beside Will to look at his bandages. When the two were face to face in the light, for a moment they both paused and curiously inspected one another.

"Wait a minute… don't I know you from somewhere?" asked the lady, tilting her head curiously. William felt like he recognized her too, but he wasn't quite sure where from, before suddenly it hit him. She was one of the healers that had been unable to help Annemarie. He'd talked with her briefly outside Annemarie's window. It felt like that had all happened an eternity ago at this point. In reality it had only been a little over a week ago. William leaned back nervously.

"I… I don't think so…" he lied. He looked down at Eric who was still fast asleep. Just how much trouble was William going to get himself into while Eric couldn't do the talking for him? Suddenly the gypsy lady's eyes opened wide and she gasped.

"You're the boy! The stable boy! Oh sweetheart, I'm so sorry!" she said, extending her arms to embrace him but then realizing there was no real way to hug him, so simply laid a concerned hand on his cheek.

"I heard what happened to her, my love. I'm so, so sorry," she said again, rubbing his cheek gently. William felt tears well in his eyes. He couldn't cry. Not in front of these strangers. Not now. No matter how hard he tried, he couldn't quite quell the tears though. Why was he crying? Was it just because of her motherly warmth? Was it because she had mentioned Annemarie? He wasn't sure. Something about how she'd tried to console him opened the fresh wounds in his heart and suddenly he felt tears falling from his eyes that he couldn't stop.

"Thank... thank you..." said William desperately wiping at his tears.

"You've been through a lot, haven't you son?" asked the elderly man. William nodded, continuing to wipe away the tears that were rolling down his cheeks. The two gypsies exchanged concerned glances with one another.

"Son, why don't you let her take a look at that wound of yours?" asked the elderly man suddenly. William shook his head as a feeling of panic ran down his spine.

"No, it's okay, I'm fine, really!" said William, again looking down at Eric who was still fast asleep. He reached down towards the large tunic that he'd already pulled off, wanting to put it back on, but the gypsy lady grabbed his arm.

"I'm a healer. Please, let me help you," she implored, staring into his eyes with concern. William wavered for a second. Would it really be that big of a deal if she looked at the wound? As William hesitated, the gypsy lady led him over to a tree stump that was by the elderly man.

"Come, come," she said, leading him by the hand to sit down. Before William could even think, she'd started unwrapping his bandages.

"What kind of accident did you have?" asked the old man, watching on curiously. William tried to slow his rapidly beating heart while he thought of an excuse.

"Uh it was... um..." stammered William, not sure of what kind of excuse he could even use. As soon as the gypsy lady set eyes on the wounds, she immediately gasped.

"What in the world is this?!" she exclaimed in horror, her confusion and worry intensifying with every layer of bandage she unwrapped. There was no excuse William could even come up with at this point. As the bandages were unwrapped, revealing the extent of his wounds, all William could do was wince in pain and try his best to angle his burn wounds away from the campfire. As he turned his head, he suddenly caught sight of the elderly gypsy. The old man's eyes and mouth were open wide with an expression of horror on his face. He looked over at Eric again, desperate for someone to help him out of this awkward situation, but he was still in a deep sleep. The gypsy lady looked at her father with concern. He knew that his wounds were shocking, but he'd not been able to see them himself as they were on his back. Just how bad was it?

"My boy, who has done this to you?!" asked the old man, crawling towards him and inspecting the sigil more closely. Upon taking a closer look, the old man fell backwards in shock.

"Father, what is it?" asked the gypsy lady suddenly, placing a concerned hand on her father's arm. He was visibly shaking with fear. William knew that the wounds were confronting, but this reaction was very extreme. It was a level of fear that a mere wound shouldn't instill in somebody.

"This is... dark... magick..." said the man, scrambling a little bit further away from William. His daughter ran over to her father and put an arm around him to comfort him.

"What do you mean?!" she asked, looking over at the sigil on William's back. The man was positively shaking with fear at this point.

"The boy... he wears the language of the gateway on his skin..." said the old man, tears of fear falling from his eyes. William felt his heartbeat racing as a chill ran down his spine. The language of the gateway? Just what had he and Eric done? What really was this mysterious sigil, and what kind of mistake had they made in using it?

CHAPTER SEVENTEEN
The Keeper of the Key

The old man stared at William, taking a shaky deep breath and pulling the blanket his daughter had given him tighter over his shoulders. The mere sight of William's wound hadn't been what scared him, it was the sigil itself.

"For something so evil to be branded into the flesh of a child..." muttered the old man, shaking his head in disbelief. His tanned skin had paled, since setting sight on the mark. William hadn't said a word. He didn't know what was even appropriate to say at a time like this. He had many questions, but he didn't know which to ask first.

"Please, help the boy and then cover it. Such a thing should not be out in the open like this. It's not safe," said the old man. The lady rifled around in a satchel that was leaning against the side of a tent before withdrawing a mortar and pestle. She then withdrew a bag of herbs and walked over towards William.

"What's that?" asked William apprehensively.

"This one..." began the woman, holding up one handful of herbs.

"It relieves pain. It'll help to numb the wound so that it won't give you so much trouble while it's healing," she explained, placing it into the mortar.

"This one…" she said again, holding up a different kind of herb.

"Will help the wound to heal," she continued, also placing that into the mortar.

"And this one…" she said finally, holding up a third kind of herb.

"This one will help to keep the wound free of infection," she finished, adding that into the mortar too. William nodded, swallowing nervously as he anticipated how much it may hurt to apply these to his wound. The gypsy lady immediately got to work, bashing and muddling the herbs together with the pestle until they'd formed a thick paste.

"Why didn't you give any of these to Annemarie?" asked William, his expression darkening as he remembered back to that fateful day. The woman's bashing slowed and she let out a mournful sigh.

"My boy, what was wrong with her went far too deep for such ointments to help. Even the medicines of Oxgate's finest apothecaries couldn't have helped her," said the lady, shaking her head.

"The Lakhdorian girl…" said the old man suddenly as he finally realized who they were talking about.

"Aye," confirmed William. The old man nodded in realization.

"That's where this all started, isn't it boy?" he asked. William nodded solemnly in confirmation. The old man closed his eyes and mulled over the situation for a moment.

"So, was it the cleric's baby after all?" asked the lady, returning to bashing and muddling the herbs. William nodded again. The lady shared a concerned look with her father.

"As I suspected, this sigil does harken back to that cursed gateway…" said the old man, shaking his head with disdain. William regarded him quizzically.

"No sir, the brand on my back is not from the gate. It was upon a relic, a shield from the great war. We used it to protect us from… well…" William realized he'd said too much. He didn't want to come off as crazy. He remembered Eric's warnings about how saying too much could lead to him being hanged for patricide. He had to be more careful with his words. The man's eyes suddenly widened again.

"A shield from the great war? There's only one thing this evil mark could be used to protect against. Oh my child, what dangers have you brought to our camp?" asked the old man, suddenly looking over his shoulder anxiously. William stammered for the right words to defend himself.

"No sir! Please, don't get me wrong! What I was running from is gone! This mark saved my life," said William honestly. The old man shared another concerned look with his daughter.

"Do you see now Melina? This is why the kingdom forbids knowledge of these things. It is not safe," said the old man, shaking his head disdainfully.

"Get ready boy, this will hurt a little," said the lady suddenly, preparing to apply the ointment to William's wound. He couldn't help but groan as the searing pain erupted once again as she applied her ointment.

"If you're not running from something, then what's sending you to Oxgate?" asked the old man curiously. William let out a sigh.

"As you say, the knowledge we need is forbidden. Oxgate is the only place that we can find it. We're looking for answers. We still don't know what really happened in Lakhdorian. We don't know what was really chasing me. All I know is that my loved ones are dead, and I should be too. He's the only reason I'm still alive," said

William, pointing to Eric who was still fast asleep. The old man nodded understandingly.

"If it's answers that you're seeking, perhaps I can help a little," said the old man, causing William to snap his head around in surprise. Upon seeing William's enthusiasm, the old man held up his hands.

"I don't know much! But I can share what I know about that cursed mark," said the old man. William nodded patiently.

"When I was a child, our people still hadn't yet found their place in these western lands. After the war, we had wanted to return to our homeland. Upon arriving there, we discovered that the war was in reality, still far from over. Those creatures from the gateway, my parents used to say that they're drawn to arid, empty places. Nowhere is drier than our homeland in the eastern deserts. I was lucky enough not to see them, but the knights out there told us that it was still too unsafe for our people to return home. Even with the gateway closed, the monsters which still lingered here wandered the desert, lusting for a way for their vile brethren to join them. The desert which we called home was the very same desert in which that cursed gateway was opened. When my family returned there, they hadn't finished building that monastery around the gateway yet... so I was able to see it with my own two eyes..." the old man suddenly trailed off as he ruminated on his harrowing childhood experiences. William waited patiently for the man to recompose himself while the lady began re-bandaging his wounds.

"Upon the rocks which make up the gate, a message is engraved. A message in a language not of our world. It is through this language that the gateway was opened, and the monsters spilled forth. It is this very same language which you have branded into your flesh," said the old man chillingly. William felt the hairs on his arms raise as goose bumps ran down his whole body. How were he and Eric supposed to have known any of this? Something suddenly occurred to William. A symbol over which monsters of the gate can't traverse? How had he never realized it until this moment. Clearly this was magick.

"Wait, does that mean that I've practiced witchcraft?" asked William, suddenly gulping as realization dawned on him. Not only had he committed patricide, he'd also somehow managed to commit the single other most deadly sin that their society condemned. The old man let out a sigh.

"The boys didn't know! Surely it can't be considered real witchcraft!" insisted the man's daughter, sliding the fresh tunic over William's shoulders now that his wound had been attended to. The old man once again shook his head solemnly.

"I'm afraid that by the sounds of things, whatever it is that these boys have been involved in goes far deeper than mere witchcraft..." said the old man chillingly. There was a moment of silence as the three of them wallowed in the severity of the situation, while the wildly juxtaposed cheery music carried on in the background. The lady placed a concerned hand on William's shoulder again.

"My boy, you can stay here tonight, but..." began the lady. William held up his hand.

"Trust me. I understand. We'll be gone as soon as the sun rises," said William solemnly. The trail of destruction in their wake was so dark and harrowing that William couldn't blame them. He wouldn't feel comfortable being involved in it either. The old man stood up from his stump and looked at William compassionately.

"May your curse be broken, my son. May these deadly omens be mere coincidence. May the gateway remain forever closed," he said with a nod, before turning away and retiring into a tent. William stared despondently at his back as he left. He had learned a lot more about his situation, but it had only made him feel even more helpless.

"I too must sleep now," said the lady packing her satchel back up.

"Thank you for tending to my wound!" said William earnestly. She smiled and nodded politely in response.

"What can I do to repay you?!" he asked, unsure of what he even had to give. The lady let out a sigh.

"To repay me... please, just never return to our camp," she said earnestly with an expression of concern on her face. William swallowed, unsure of exactly how to respond to her. He nodded somberly, relieved that despite the harsh sentiment, it was a payment he could actually afford.

"Aye," he replied simply. With that, she too retired to her tent. William lowered himself down from the stump that he'd been sitting on and sat down on the floor by Eric. So once again Eric had been right. It all harkened back to the gateway after all. There were a million questions that William had spinning in his mind, but at this point he was too overwhelmed to even know where to begin. As he lay down on his side, watching the embers dancing in the night, his eyelids slowly closed and he drifted off into a deep, deep sleep.

***

Tap, tap tap.

William shot up straight in his bed. As he looked around his room, he found himself barely able to see anything. He rubbed his eyes, trying to clear his vision. When he opened them again, he still found himself struggling to see things clearly. It was as though his whole room was swirling around, like he was drunk.

Tap, tap tap.

William gasped with surprise. Annemarie was knocking at his wardrobe door. How long had he been asleep? He tried to remember what he'd been dreaming about but couldn't recall anything. He definitely got the vibe that it had been a nightmare though.

Tap, tap tap.

"Aye, I'm coming!" called out William enthusiastically, trying to stay steady on his feet in his swirling world. He took a few shaky steps towards the wardrobe before suddenly stopping on the spot. He felt like he'd forgotten something really important. For a moment he simply stood still, trying his hardest to remember what it was. No matter how hard he strained himself though, he couldn't remember. He shook his head and continued towards the wardrobe, reaching out and grabbing the handle. As soon as he tried to pull on it, he realized that something was wrong. No matter how hard he pulled, the door remained closed.

"William..." whispered Annemarie from inside the wardrobe.

"Aye! I'm here!" he called back breathlessly.

"I'm locked in here William..." she whispered again shakily. William felt his heart sink. How had Annemarie managed to get locked inside his wardrobe? What would happen if his parents found out that she was in his room? Wait, his parents? Suddenly, horrific images from his memories flashed before his eyes: his mother's mottled face as she struggled for air, his father's final death rattle as he bled out on the floor. William screamed and clutched his head as the horrific memories flooded over his mind.

"William!" yelled Annemarie angrily from in the wardrobe, banging on the door from within. He fell to his knees, the images haunting his mind beginning to overwhelm him.

"Let me out! Let me out!" screamed Annemarie desperately, shaking the wardrobe furiously all the while.

***

Eric was woken from his slumber, feeling a burning sensation on his thigh like he'd rolled over onto a hot coal. He rolled away from the campfire and onto his other side before he suddenly heard William murmuring in his sleep.

"Mother... father..." murmured William. Eric's heart sank as he realized the trauma his friend was dealing with. He opened his eyes to check up on him, but as soon as he did, he felt his heart leap up into his throat. There, looming over William in the darkness, were six enormous moorcrawlers. Eric caught himself before he instinctively cried out in fright, placing his hand over his mouth just in time. All of them were slowly creeping closer to William, inspecting him curiously as he slept. Their empty, expressionless, human-like faces and bald heads were craned down as they studied him. They tilted their heads around like puppies hearing a new sound for the first time.

Eric tentatively shuffled backwards slightly away from William but felt his back bump against something. He slowly turned his head and noticed that there was another moorcrawler right over his shoulder. His heart began racing and his body began hyperventilating and shaking as the reality of the situation set in. The moorcrawlers varied in size from five feet to well over seven. They all had the same distinctive features. Gray skin which extended down each of their six arms, each ending in humanlike hands upon which they walked through the moors. Hair like that on a man's arms sprouted from every inch of their gray bodies which slinked closer to William by the second. As Eric looked around the camp, he realized that the six moorcrawlers looming over William were just the tip of the iceberg. The entire camp was surrounded. Every-where that Eric looked, he saw another one of their empty, soulless, expressionless faces, looming in the darkness. Luckily for him, right now they were all entirely captivated by William.

What could he possibly even do right now? He turned around and looked over at Bonnie who was fast asleep on the ground by the cart. Eric needed an escape plan of some kind here. Would Bonnie freak out if he woke her? She wasn't attached to the cart anymore, so Eric would have to reattach her before they could even think of somehow escaping this situation. Eric slowly stood up, get-ting up to his feet and looking around at the moorcrawlers anxious-ly. They were so focused on William that they were ignoring Eric completely. Eric held his breath nervously as he tiptoed his way through the moorcrawlers towards Bonnie. As soon as he neared her, she began to stir in her sleep. Eric placed a calming hand on her head and patted her soothingly.

"Hey girl... everything's okay. Everything's fine..." he whis-pered, praying that she'd somehow keep her composure around all of these moorcrawlers. When she first opened her eyes, she seemed a little discombobulated, exhaling with a small amount of panic. Immediately a few of the moorcrawlers turned their heads to look directly at Eric and Bonnie.

"Shh, sh sh sh..." said Eric, rubbing her head soothingly as he looked around nervously at the curious moorcrawlers.

"It's okay girl. These are friends... friends..." said Eric, sweat beginning to pour down his anxious brow. Bonnie got up onto her knees and struggled to stand, still exhaling disconcertedly as she looked around the campsite at all of the strange creatures that had surrounded them. Eric continued to stroke her comfortingly as she stood up and shook her body.

"Yeah! See… they're just normal… friendly people…" said Eric, praying that she'd maintain her composure. As she hadn't yet begun to panic, he realized that this was his only chance to reattach her to the cart.

"Come on girl… that's a good girl…" said Eric quietly. She was still fully harnessed, but she wasn't hitched to the cart. As he began hitching the cart back up to Bonnie, he watched William out of the corner of his eye. This was still the easy part. He didn't know how he was going to get William out of this. He just needed him to stay asleep for as long as possible before he could formulate a plan to get him out of here.

***

"Let me out! Let me out!" shrieked Annemarie, shaking the wardrobe furiously and pounding on its doors from the inside. William was still kneeling down, clutching his head as the disturbing images continued.

"I… I can't!" cried William, as tears began to pour from his eyes.

"Let me out!" she continued to scream, pounding on every inch of the wardrobe.

"It's locked!" exclaimed William, crawling towards the wardrobe and placing his palm against it. Suddenly the banging and screaming stopped.

"You have the key…" Annemarie whispered. William looked around his room. He couldn't see the key anywhere.

"I don't! I don't have it!" said William tearfully. Suddenly, that's when he noticed it. There was a heavy object weighing down his right pocket. After rifling about in there for a moment he finally found it and pulled it out. It was a giant brass key.

"Annemarie, I've found it! I've got it!" said William excitedly. As dizzy as he was, William focused his mind as he lifted the giant brass key up towards the keyhole of the wardrobe. As it slid in, he suddenly felt another image burst into his mind. It was Annemarie on her funeral pyre. He couldn't see her, as she was covered by a white sheet, but he knew it was her under there. Her parents had confirmed it.

He suddenly snapped back to reality. Annemarie was dead.

"Let me out William…" she whispered. William let out a shaky breath and closed his eyes. Annemarie wasn't dead. That was impossible. She was locked in his wardrobe. She wasn't dead, she was right here. His parents couldn't be dead either. That made no sense.

And with that, he turned the key, feeling the quintessential dull clunk of the mechanism unlatching. He'd done it. The door was unlocked.

***

Eric hastily managed to clip the last of the buckles on Bonnie's harness, but suddenly she began to panic a little. She was staring straight towards William. Eric placed a comforting hand on her head, turning to see what was suddenly riling her up. As soon as he cast his eyes upon William, his jaw dropped in shock. William was slowly beginning to hover upwards above the ground. His hair was floating about as though he was under water, and a dull red glow was being emitted all around his body. The moorcrawlers were becoming agitated, slowly moving away anxiously from William. Eric had to do something fast. Whatever was happening to William was threatening to cause the entire camp to explode into chaos. He looked around at the moorcrawlers who were all starting to twitch uncomfortably. Eric let out a quiet moan of discomfort when he realized what he was going to have to do. He needed to work his way right into the middle of the pack if he wanted to wake William up. As he began turning Bonnie and the cart around, for but a moment, the thought of simply hopping up into the cart and disappearing into the night crossed his mind.

Eric shook his head and turned back, taking a determined step towards William. Just as he began to move, suddenly a black mist started erupting from William's mouth. His body twitched and twisted in the air, flipping around so that his chest was facing upwards. There was a white light burning beneath his skin, exposing every vein in his body as he lifted upwards into the sky. The moorcrawler's signature dull, vacant, soul dead expression that they all had always worn suddenly began to change. Their brows furrowed, and their dull eye sockets darkened, their faces beginning to twitch sporadically as their expressions twisted. Some of them began releasing a disgusting throaty growl as their bodies pulsated as though energized by something. Bonnie was becoming extremely restless, taking a few panicked steps away from the camp and taking the cart with her. Eric had to act now.

Just as he was about to snap into action, a gypsy suddenly emerged from her tent. As soon as she emerged, she froze for a moment, taking in the horrific scene before her. Immediately she let out a heart chilling shriek of horror as she beheld the terrifying monstrosities that had infested their camp. Every single moorcrawler's head snapped around to stare at her, their faces twisted into an expression of malicious fury and hatred. She stopped screaming, realizing that she'd drawn the attention of every single moorcrawler, but she was too late. The moorcrawlers released a disgusting guttural war cry, the likes of which Eric had never heard in his life. Immediately every single moorcrawler in the camp charged towards her. Eric had no time to waste. He couldn't save her, but this was the only opening he was going to get to grab William. He ran as fast as his legs would carry him into the middle of the camp while the woman shrieked in terror, continuing to attract the attention of the moorcrawlers. As the moorcrawlers reached her tent, her screams began to wake the other gypsies who all began to emerge from their tents too. Eric grabbed William who was still floating ominously in the air and tried to pull him down to the ground, but he couldn't overpower whatever force was keeping him there.

"William! William! Wake up!" screamed Eric, shaking him desperately. The gypsy woman's tent was torn open by the voracious moorcrawlers who descended upon her, ripping and tearing at every inch of her body with their enormous humanlike arms. She screamed and gargled her final cries as the monsters tore her to shreds. The other gypsies were beginning to emerge from their tents, some holding weaponry, and some simply screaming in horror as they beheld the horrific sight outside.

"Come on William! Snap out of it! I need you to come back to me!" pleaded Eric desperately.

CHAPTER EIGHTEEN

The Dance of the Gypsies

The moment that the key rotated in the lock, the doors of the wardrobe burst open, knocking William backwards onto the floor. He couldn't see what was inside, but he felt a horrifying chill running down his spine. Whatever was in there, it wasn't Annemarie. He could feel its presence. It was something dark. Something evil. As William watched on in horror, a thick red fog burst out of the Wardrobe and started filling the room. It seemed to have energy pulsing all through it like a thunder cloud. William gasped in horror, scrambling away from the wardrobe as the red fog pulsated unnaturally around his room. After a moment it suddenly focused itself inwards, shooting down towards William's open mouth. Before he could even figure out what was going on, the red smog was working its way down his throat and filling his lungs. William's eyes opened wide with fear as he tried his hardest to close his mouth, but couldn't. As the red fog was filling his body, his vision began to fade, and he felt his eyes lulling shut as he slowly lost consciousness. Suddenly, a sound reverberated in his mind. It was a sound that he clung to for dear life. It felt like he was drowning, and it was his only hope of surfacing.

"William! William! Wake up!" screamed Eric desperately. William focused all of his willpower on opening his eyes.

"Come on William! Snap out of it! I need you to come back to me!" screamed Eric's voice desperately. Eric needed him. None of this was real. He was in a nightmare, and it was time for him to wake up.

William snapped his mouth closed, stopping the red mist in its tracks as a horrific shriek erupted throughout the entire dream world he was in. It shook the very walls of his room with its fury. William didn't care. He wasn't going to let this continue. He needed to get back to Eric. He slowly struggled back to his feet as the furious shrieking continued, blasting the windows of the room out and causing the walls to begin to splinter and crack. As William struggled his way back towards the wardrobe where the red fog was still escaping from, he could feel the smoke pushing against him, trying to keep him back. He wasn't going to let it. Eric needed him. He needed to wake up. He could feel in his heart that there was only one way for him to do that. With a final war cry of his own, William charged at the wardrobe door like he was trying to break it down, finally managing to barge his way through the red mist and begin closing the door. Again, the gargled shrieking intensified, the entire world shaking like there was a hurricane and an earthquake all at once. The walls of his room were blasted to pieces sending splinters of wood flying all around him in a vortex as he pushed against the wardrobe door with all his might. Both William and the dark presence screamed as they worked against each other, with William trying to close the door and the presence trying to open it. With one final overpowering push, William managed to slam the door shut before reaching down to the floor where he'd dropped the key when he'd fallen. The shrieking intensified as the wardrobe was smashed against from the inside. It was being attacked so forcibly that the wardrobe was bouncing on the floor as the monster within banged against every inch of its walls trying to get out. William leant his back against the door which was springing open slightly with every desperate pound from the monster. He slowly slid down until he could reach the key on the floor. As soon as he felt it in his grasp, he slid his way back up, turned around and gave the wardrobe door one last firm push shut, before ramming the key into the keyhole and twisting it forcibly. The monster inside released another furious scream, followed by a torrent of indecipherable garbled words being hurled at him from within. It slammed desperately at the wardrobe doors hard enough that the entire wardrobe moved around on the floor.

"William!" exclaimed Eric's voice again, pulling at William's psyche. He felt this nightmare world beginning to fade away. It was finally time to wake up.

***

As soon as William opened his eyes, he saw Eric's panicked face looking down over him. Suddenly the reality of their situation hit him, as the symphony of screams and violence set in. He looked in horror at the scene around them, as tents and gypsies were being torn apart by the moorcrawlers. He looked back up at Eric who seemed to have caught him in midair.

"William! Come on!" shouted Eric, standing him on the ground, then grabbing him by the arm and pulling him towards their cart. Bonnie was already part way down the hill, fearfully whinnying as the horrors of the camp intensified. She was in a combat of her own, rearing up on her front two legs as a moorcrawler lunged at her.

"What's going on here?!" gasped William in terror as he narrowly dodged a moorcrawler that went skittering past him towards a gypsy who had shot it with a crossbow. It dived on the man, shoving a thumb into each of his eye sockets and wrenching at his face, cracking his skull and tearing his face in half while its other arms disemboweled him. William cried out in fear as Eric dragged him through the carnage towards Bonnie.

"Watch out!" exclaimed William, pulling Eric back from a moorcrawler that had launched itself at him. The two narrowly missed the creature, falling backwards down onto the ground. William immediately felt an explosion of searing pain emitting from his wound, but he had no time to lament. They immediately picked their pace back up and sprinted towards Bonnie. As soon as they neared the cart, the two boys jumped onto it for dear life. As they dangled from the back of the cart, Bonnie finally seemed to get the best of the moorcrawler that was lunging at her. As it jumped up at her, she kicked it in the face with both of her front hooves and sent it falling onto its back. As soon as it was down, she broke into a sprint, trampling the thing and carrying their cart with her. As their cart bumped roughly over the fallen moorcrawler, William was tossed up into the back. The moorcrawler which the boys had narrowly dodged was still after them though, diving onto Eric and grabbing ahold of his legs from behind the cart.

"Eric!" screamed William, clambering to the back of the moving cart to grab ahold of Eric's arms. As Eric continued to dangle, dragging the moorcrawler along the ground behind them, he looked up at William. For the first time in his life, William saw Eric's face holding an expression of pure, unadulterated terror as he looked into his eyes.

"Hold on Eric! No matter what, hold on!" exclaimed William. Eric cried out in pain as the moorcrawler's grip on his legs intensified as it tried to drag itself up his body and into the cart. William pulled at Eric's torso, working with him to heave him upwards closer onto the cart which was now moving much faster as Bonnie broke into a full gallop. The moorcrawler which was being dragged behind the cart worked its way further up Eric's body, grabbing onto the sides of his torso with its front hands and releasing a blood churning, guttural cry. William wasted no time, jumping over the back of the wagon and kicking at its face desperately. Every time he struck its face, the thing seemed to just get angrier, as it was unable to release its front pair of hands from Eric to fight back without falling. William released one final cry, kicking into the side of its face as hard as he could, finally causing it to lose its grip and go tumbling backwards into the moors. William grabbed hold of Eric, pulling him up into the back of the cart, before again falling onto his back, causing him to cry out in agony. He rolled around onto his side, catching his breath for a moment. Eric lay on his belly also recouping himself, before suddenly snapping back into action. He shot back up onto his hands and knees, trying to keep himself balanced in the back of the cart that was still blasting its way through the bumpy countryside. He grabbed hold of Bonnie's reins and began trying to steer her back towards the main road through the moors. She was still in a desperate panic, and so she was incredibly hard to direct, but after a few moments Eric managed to regain control. He guided her down the hill and back onto the main road, looking over his shoulder fearfully towards the campsite in their wake.

William, struggling to his feet, immediately felt his heart fill with panic again. He could see countless moorcrawlers still chasing after them in the darkness, with that twisted expression of fury plastered across all of their faces.

"Don't slow down!" yelled William, as he watched the six-armed creatures failing to keep up with their cart now that they were on a flat road. After several minutes of charging through the night, the many moorcrawlers had been left behind in the darkness. As Bonnie began to slow down a little, William finally let himself take a deep breath. He had no idea what had happened at that camp while he was asleep, but he'd never seen creatures as terrifying as those which they'd just encountered. He climbed over from the back of the cart onto the seat beside Eric and placed a concerned hand over his shoulder.

"Eric, are ye okay?" asked William, still shaking with shock and adrenaline but suddenly realizing that Eric was bleeding.

"Eric!" exclaimed William, lifting his tunic to assess his wounds.

"I'm fine," said Eric with a dark expression on his face. They'd just been through what was certainly Eric's most harrowing experience yet. William could tell that Eric was far from fine. He decided to give him a few more moments to calm down before he tried talking to him again. The two rumbled along in silence as William caught his breath for a short while.

"What were those things?" asked William, breaking the silence after a few minutes of quiet travel.

"Moorcrawlers," replied Eric quietly. William turned and looked at him quizzically.

"Those were moorcrawlers?!" asked William in shock. Aside from having six arms, they didn't match Eric's descriptions at all. Rather than the dull, solitary, lumbering animals he'd made them out to be, they were fast, vicious, and clearly operating as a pack. Their faces and limbs were also oddly humanlike. This was not what William had been envisioning based on Eric's descriptions.

"William. I need you to be honest with me," said Eric suddenly.

"That thing…" he began.

"It's still inside of you… isn't it?" asked Eric, continuing to simply stare straight ahead. William nodded.

"Aye," he responded quietly. There was a long silence before William decided to speak again.

"Eric…" began William, turning to face his friend before he suddenly noticed that Eric was crying.

"Hey!" he exclaimed, putting a concerned hand on Eric's shoulder. Eric shook his head and wiped at his tears.

"Can we just… not talk for a while?" asked Eric. William nodded understandingly. As the two of them rode on in silence, dawn was beginning to break over the horizon. They'd barely even managed to spend a single night in that gypsy camp before it had fallen into chaos and horror. The night had taken its toll on the boys, but their troubles were far from over.

***

The three knights sat in awkward silence, staring across the mahogany desk at the chancellor who was still reading over the paperwork with a puzzled expression on his face. August and Azalea shared an uncomfortable glance with one another as the deafening stillness loomed over the room. A guard cleared his throat, breaking the silence and drawing the attention of all three knights. Flustered, he immediately bowed apologetically.

"I'm confused by this part here. Would you please explain to me again why you traveled to Mistfall?" asked the chancellor, looking up from the paperwork for the first time in minutes. Ivar took a nervous sip from his goblet, drawing the ire of his compatriots as they were plunged into having to explain the situation that he'd gotten them into.

"Well, you see…" began Azalea, clearing her throat and sitting up straighter in her chair.

"The cleric requested it, sir…" piped up Ivar suddenly. Azalea stared at him in surprise. The chancellor raised his eyebrows.

"The cleric did?" he confirmed, looking between the three of them in confusion.

"Ah, yes-" began Ivar, his voice cracking as he choked on the wine he'd not yet finished swallowing. As Ivar broke into a subdued coughing fit, Azalea sat back in her chair, scowling at him resentfully.

"Yes sir, it was Father Marcus himself who fondly recalled the hot springs he had dearly loved when he was a child…" lied Ivar, continuing to clear his throat awkwardly. Azalea shook her head and rubbed her eyes in disdain at the needless fictitious details Ivar had added.

"Father Marcus… whom… as you all say… was rendered unable to communicate effectively due to a particularly acute case of gateway sickness…yes?" asked the chancellor, turning his head to look at the physician who was standing up among a cohort of relevant individuals.

"Y-yes, that is correct sir," replied the physician, clearly feeling out of place in this awkward meeting. The chancellor looked around at each of the knights again with an eyebrow raised.

"Can you understand why I am confused?" he asked expectantly. The three knights nodded their heads empathetically. The chancellor leaned back in his chair and let out a sigh.

"After all that the three of you have accomplished, I must say that I am shocked. A simple escort to and from a country town, barely a few days' journey from Oxgate, and this is the task three heads of knightly orders found too difficult to carry out?" asked the chancellor in frustration. All three knights hung their heads in shame.

"Each of you are in line to become knight commanders, are you not?" he asked in frustration. Again, the three knights simply nodded.

"And? Do you honestly feel that this is an appropriate title for you at this point?!" asked the chancellor animatedly. All three knights snapped their heads up to look at him in concern.

"Sir, if I may, he really was very difficult to work with and..." began Ivar before the chancellor interrupted him with a brash laugh.

"Difficult to work with?! Are you telling me that three first class knights can't keep a single sickly cleric alive for a single week, just because he-" mid-way through his sentence the chancellor stopped as though he'd bitten his tongue. He was looking over the knight's shoulders with an expression of surprise on his face. He hopped up to his feet and bowed his head politely. The three knights looked over their shoulders, only to see that the Duke himself had entered the room. The three knights instantly stood up and bowed their heads politely.

"Your Grace!" exclaimed the chancellor.

"Good morning," said the Duke politely. As the whole room struggled to regain their composure, he walked over towards the large mahogany desk and gestured towards one of the chairs on the side of the room. Immediately one of the guards carried it over for him and he sat down at the side of the desk, looking over the paperwork curiously.

"Please continue," said the Duke distractedly as he read the paperwork. The three knights shared worried glances with one another.

"Ahem... as I was uh... saying..." stammered the chancellor, trying to adjust to their new company. He stared blankly at the three knights as he tried to recall where he had left off.

"Oh yes! Knight commanders! I must say, I do not foresee a promotion to such a role in any of your near futures!" admitted the chancellor, shaking his head and glancing at the Duke for approval.

"B-but sir, if you'd just-" began Sir Ivar before suddenly he was interrupted.

"What is this?" asked the Duke, shifting his gaze up from the paper in confusion. All four members of the meeting exchanged fearful glances.

"The way this is worded is rather peculiar... what does this mean?" asked the Duke, pointing to a line of text.

"That means that he um... dismembered his own genitals your Grace..." stammered the chancellor, unsure of how to politely phrase it.

"The man castrated himself?!" asked the Duke in shock. All three knights hung their heads in shame once more.

"Yes, your Grace," confirmed the chancellor, averting his eyes awkwardly. The Duke screwed up his face and looked at the knights in disbelief. He stared at them for a moment before shaking his head angrily.

"Three first class knights," said the Duke, holding up three fingers and looking at the three of them expectantly. The three knights blushed.

"Actually your Grace, technically they're knight officers..." added the chancellor. The Duke raised his eyebrows in surprise.

"Three knight officers no less?!" he confirmed, again causing the three knights to hang their heads even lower. The Duke put down the paperwork and rubbed his face in frustration.

"Why were three knight officers sent to escort a single cleric on respite in the first place?" asked the Duke, raising an eyebrow and turning to face the chancellor. The chancellor sat up straight in his chair and cleared his throat, caught off guard by the Duke's focus suddenly shifting onto him.

"Well, you see your Grace... the first college semester didn't begin until the following month, and these knights are in line to become commanders. They requested being sent on a quest of some importance while they had free time, to boost their renown and such..." stammered the chancellor, realizing that he too could come under fire in this conversation.

"So, you're telling me the treasurer approved this too?" asked the Duke in surprise.

"Yes, your Grace! We saw it as the best use of their time, considering the amount of exposure and approval the cleric himself was getting from the towns that he traveled through. We considered it important to show that we shared the values of the people and..." the chancellor tried to explain before the Duke held up his hand for him to stop.

"You didn't show that we shared the values of the people! You showed that the dissidents are right in questioning where their taxes are going!" yelled the Duke angrily, slamming his hand down on the desk in frustration, causing a few of the chancellor's expensive desktop trinkets to topple over. The chancellor gulped anxiously as the three knights stayed silent.

"I must admit, how three knights could let a cleric do this to himself..." began the Duke, gesturing towards the paperwork with an expression of disgust.

"...is beyond me... but..." the Duke suddenly stopped and turned around to look at the out of place cohort of individuals standing around the sides of the room.

"Who are all of these people?" he asked abruptly.

"They're peripherally related to the situation, your Grace," stammered the chancellor. The Duke turned back around and looked at him quizzically.

"Peripherally?" he asked in confusion. The chancellor simply nodded and swallowed anxiously. The Duke closed his eyes in frustration.

"Out! All of you, get out! Now!" he demanded, pointing towards the door. Everybody bowed before hurriedly taking their leave and closing the door behind them. The Duke turned back to the table.

"Do you have any idea what kind of ire the common folk are holding towards the college right now?" asked the Duke, looking between the four of them expectantly.

"Your Grace, if I may..." began the chancellor, before being silenced by the Duke's hand once again.

"I've been in discussions with the royals themselves over how concerned we all are about the rumors that taxpayer money is being squandered on the college. Now you've gone and made a big show of sending three knight officers on a pointless escort mission of an invalid to a pile of mud in the moors! That would've been bad enough on its own, but then they somehow failed at the task too!" yelled the Duke, again slamming his fist on the desk angrily. The chancellor managed to catch a small golden pheasant statuette before it fell off onto the floor, while the three knights again hung their heads in shame.

"I mean, perhaps we are as ridiculous as those southerners say we are..." said the Duke with a sigh, leaning back in his chair and shaking his head as he watched the chancellor sheepishly trying to right his toppled trinkets. When he realized he was being watched, he stopped and retracted his hands back down into his lap and cleared his throat daintily.

"Well unlike them, at least we actually have a knight's college..." said the chancellor, raising an eyebrow as he was clearly thinking spitefully about the Castellian kingdom to the south. The Duke looked at the chancellor in disbelief.

"Should we really be so proud of that? The gateway has been closed for over a century now, chancellor. What are we even doing here? If this is the quality of the knights our kingdom is producing, then perhaps they're right in investing their money into their military instead!" shouted the Duke, gesturing towards the three silent knights once again. The three knights exchanged glances, each wanting to defend themselves but being too wise to do so.

"I'm lucky my aide keeps an eye on your schedule, or I'd have never even known about any of this. Why did this meeting take you months to arrange?" asked the Duke suddenly, turning his ire directly upon the chancellor. He squirmed in his chair for a moment, gaping like a cod as he looked around searchingly at the three knights for somebody to blame.

"Well, I wanted to afford the knights some time to write up an effective report, considering the, ahem, importance of the situation. Since the semester had begun, these three were obviously quite inundated with work in the college, so I decided to give them until the mid-year break!" stammered the chancellor. In reality, his provision of so much time to write their report had come out of his own inability to recognize its importance more than out of any kind of charity from the man.

After a moment of awkward silence as the Duke processed the chancellor's shallow excuses, he let out another disappointed sigh and stood up.

"You know what? You deal with it," he said suddenly, shrugging emphatically. The four of them exchanged dumbfounded looks.

"The four of you are to solve this problem," said the Duke, taking a few steps towards the door of the room.

"B-but your Grace..." began the chancellor, standing from his chair. Again, the Duke held up his hand.

"How can the college win back the hearts of those who doubt its value? How can we assure the taxpayers that the college is worthy of the taxes it receives from them? I must admit, at this point even I am among them," said the Duke, holding his hand up preemptively as the four of them all wanted to ask for clarification.

"After such a monumental failure from all of you, this is the least you could do to atone for it. I expect a solution within the week. If you are unable to do so, I'll strip you all back to the rank of mere squires, do you understand me?!" threatened the Duke commandingly. The three knights nodded understandingly while the chancellor stared back nervously. The Duke turned to leave again before August suddenly piped up with a question.

"Your Grace, the chancellor is not a knight, the role of squire would-" began August before being interrupted by the chancellor shushing him and kicking his leg under the desk.

"Ah yes..." said the Duke turning back around and assessing the nervous chancellor intensely.

"I'll have to decide on your punishment, but I promise that you won't like it. That'll be all," said the Duke before turning back and leaving the room. After he'd left, a heavy silence fell over them all, as each of the four quietly felt the weight of the burden the Duke had dropped on their shoulders.

"Well... there's somewhere else I need to be, so..." began Ivar, standing up before Azalea grabbed his arm and pulled him back down. The chancellor stared at Ivar furiously.

"Well, I suppose we'd better start brainstorming then..." said Sir August, leaning forward in his chair and scratching his chin, deep in thought. As the weight of the responsibility that had just been passed down to them found its grip around their hearts, the four silently pondered how they could possibly achieve what the Duke and the royals could not.

CHAPTER NINETEEN

Counseling

"And as soon as I got the key back in the lock, it seemed to seal it in there. It didn't like that at all. It got really angry, banging on the sides of the wardrobe and all... but anyway, that's when I woke up and you know the rest..." explained William, finally stopping to take an eager bite of his bread. Eric hadn't said a word while William was recounting his experiences from the previous night. The dark expression on his face was hard for William to even look at, so he continued to avert his eyes as Eric silently stared down the road ahead. The moorlands had ended rather abruptly, surrounded by a small stone edge which stretched out as far as the eye could see in either direction. Beneath the stone edge was significantly greener, beginning to look more like grassy knolls than moorlands. As they crossed the precipice from the moorlands and began traveling downhill, William could see small fences and stone walls separating clearly divided farmlands stretching as far as the eye could see. He looked over at Eric who was still wearing a cold, dark expression on his face.

"Where are we now?" asked William tentatively.

"We're entering the Bleaklands," he responded quietly. William looked around at the grassy fields which extended out all around them with the beautiful farmlands in the distance.

"Doesn't look that bleak to me..." said William.

"That's just because we're coming from Lakhdorian," Eric replied. William let them travel in silence for a few more minutes before the awkward air over their little cart overwhelmed him.

"I know you're angry Eric, but I swear that I'm not trying to keep secrets from you! I didn't even know myself that the thing was still inside of me... not until last night at least..." admitted William. Eric let out a deep sigh.

"So, anger is what you think I'm feeling right now, huh?" asked Eric without taking his eyes off the road.

"Well, I don't know... I thought it was that, and just, you know... last night was really scary and all..." stammered William, feeling his sublimely inadequate emotional intelligence once again showing itself. Eric furrowed his brow as his expression darkened once more. William swallowed nervously.

"So, what's really on your mind then?" asked William uncomfortably.

"Am I talking with William right now?" asked Eric intensely, finally turning to look him in the eyes.

"What are ye talking about? Who else would I be?!" asked William defensively. Eric shook his head.

"I don't know William... I don't know..." said Eric, releasing a deep sigh.

"Trust me, you'd know if that thing had taken control of me," admitted William, washing his bread down with a sip from Eric's flask of ale. Eric watched him as he screwed up his face at the taste of the beer.

"Aye. I suppose I would…" he said, sinking deep back into thought.

"Something strange happened last night. Something with you…" said Eric, shifting his gaze back up to assess William darkly. William suddenly felt his anxiety rising.

"I didn't do anything! I swear!" exclaimed William defensively. Eric continued to assess him curiously.

"William, while you were having that dream, you were floating in the air," said Eric. William raised his eyebrows in surprise. This was the first he was hearing about it, although he did remember Eric holding him when he'd first woken up.

"What?! Floating?!" asked William in shock. Eric nodded quietly in response.

"It were you what attracted those crawlers. They were all looking at you… like you were… I don't know. It weren't like you were food… it were more like… you were water…" said Eric, clearly unsure of how to phrase himself properly. William raised an eyebrow in confusion. Eric eased up slightly, as he looked back at his perplexed friend. He let out another sigh and sat back in his seat.

"William… last night we watched an entire camp of people be massacred," said Eric, catching William off guard. He leant forward in his chair and gave Eric a serious nod.

"Aye," he replied. Eric looked straight ahead, his eyes fogging over slightly as he was recalling last night's events.

"They weren't just people to me though William. They were friends. I'd known them for years…" said Eric, still sitting back in his chair with his eyes glazed over. William finally realized why Eric had been acting so suspicious of him. He didn't think that William was disturbed enough by last night's events. Did he not think

William cared about what had happened to those gypsies? He leaned forward and stared Eric in the eyes.

"Eric. Look at me," said William seriously, raising his eyebrows and staring at his friend. He immediately saw Eric's eyes snap back to reality as he looked back at William.

"The night before last, I watched my father strangle my mother to death. Then I caved his head in with a shovel and rode off into the night, being chased by a monster born from the womb of... well... the girl that I loved," said William, his expression darkening as he recalled his experience. Eric's expression began to soften as he listened to William's words.

"It's a wonder that I'm able to talk at all. I remember how it felt when Annemarie first died. I mean, it were only last week," said William, continuing to stare seriously into Eric's eyes.

"I'm numb Eric," admitted William, shaking his head solemnly. Eric looked back at him with concern.

"They were good people. They fixed my bandages. Treated me right..." said William, looking down at the nice tunic that they'd given to him.

"Maybe it's the monster living inside me. Aye. But maybe I just don't have any more tears to cry right now Eric. Maybe I'm all out of tears. It don't mean I'm a monster though. It don't mean that I think what happened last night was okay," said William, shaking his head and taking a deep swig of the ale. When he looked back up at his friend, he realized that Eric had finally let go. Tears were rolling down his face as he listened to William's words.

"They were good people, Will," croaked Eric, shaking his head as he looked back down the road ahead.

"Aye. They were," replied William softly.

"They didn't deserve to die like that..." continued Eric, shaking his head solemnly.

"Aye. They didn't," agreed William.

"It was my fault William. I'm the one who led us there. I'm the one who-" began Eric.

"No," said William, shaking his head.

"It weren't your fault. It weren't even my fault. It was the monster that did this," said William earnestly. Eric looked back at him and after a moment nodded his head in agreement.

"We need to get to that library Eric. You were right all along. Whatever this thing is, it needs to be stopped, and we're the only ones who can do it," said William, staring intensely at his friend. Eric began to wipe the tears out of his eyes. William held Eric's flask out to him expectantly.

"To the gypsies," said William. Eric grabbed the flask.

"Aye. To our fallen friends," said Eric, toasting with William before taking a long swig of the ale. With a newly fueled sense of purpose, the determination of the two boys intensified. They were going to get into that library no matter what it took. It was only two days more travel until they could reach Oxgate and they were going to stop at nothing to get the answers they needed.

***

"How about a festival? Commoners love festivals!" suggested August, raising his hands enthusiastically as he remembered how happy everyone had been at the feast in Lakhdorian. Ivar's eyes lit up suddenly.

"A festival you say..." he said, seemingly intrigued by the idea. August looked at him suspiciously.

"You wouldn't just be hoping for exotic wines now would you, Ivar?" asked August, raising an eyebrow suspiciously and looking around the mostly empty pub that they were day drinking in.

"I would never!" exclaimed Ivar, placing his hand over his heart dramatically as though deeply hurt by August's words. Azalea's eye twitched as her frustration began to climax.

"Where did that stupid chancellor go anyway?" she asked suddenly, taking an angry swig from her tankard and dropping down, resting her head on the table with a frustrated sigh.

"Probably finding some way to weasel his way out of having to help us..." guessed Ivar.

"I don't think we've entertained my festival idea enough yet," said August, leaning back and crossing his arms. Ivar let out a frustrated sigh and Azalea grunted glumly as she swirled her tankard around pointlessly.

"Where would the money for the festival come from, dear August?" asked Ivar, raising an eyebrow expectantly.

"Hello? We have the chancellor on our side, right? He ought to be able to pull some strings!" retorted August. Ivar shook his head.

"It's all tax money, August. They may be commoners, but they're not stupid. Throwing some kind of lavish festival will raise their cheer for a single night, but then they'll come at our throats even harder. We'd have wasted their tax money on a festival to try to distract them from worrying about us wasting their tax money!" yelled Ivar.

"Well then dear Ivar, how do you propose we do this then, hmm? How are we to show that the college deserves its funding if we can't spend any money to do so?" asked August, raising a combative eyebrow.

"If I knew the answer to that, I wouldn't be wasting my mid-year break sitting in this dank pub in the middle of the day listening to you prattle on about festivals now would I, dear August?!" asked Ivar angrily.

"Does it really deserve its funding?" asked Azalea glumly.

"Of course it does!" defended August, standing from his chair dramatically.

"Who is sent in when the forces of nature wreak havoc on a village?" asked August.

"The knights are…" responded Ivar with a shrug.

"And who is at the front of the battlefield, leading the charge when a war breaks out?" asked August, tilting his head expectantly.

"The knights are…" responded Azalea, sitting up straighter.

"And who is standing by the King, protecting him with combat skills unparalleled in all the kingdoms of the world?!" asked August passionately.

"The knights are!" responded Azalea enthusiastically.

"That's right! The knights are! The knight's great library holds knowledge that can't be found in any corner of the world but right here! We hold military might beyond comparison; strategies of war passed down through generations of the biggest, baddest fighters this world has ever seen. We alone turn the combat of farmers flailing pitchforks around in the mud into an art form wielded by the world's mightiest warriors. Our names alone strike fear into the hearts of our enemies. The mere sight of a knight on the battlefield could send an entire army of those southern Castellian whelps running in the opposite direction! The only reason the commoners have forgotten this is because we are so preposterously mighty that no one has dared cross us for half a century!" lectured August passionately, raising the spirits of his two compatriots. Azalea cheered and applauded excitedly at his rousing speech while Ivar nodded his head approvingly.

"Why don't we just get him up on a stage in town?!" asked Azalea, gesturing at August enthusiastically.

"Mere words aren't enough to sway the hearts of the masses. They need to see how strong we are. They don't realize the gap between an ordinary soldier and a knight, they have no clue," said Ivar, thinking about August's speech deeply.

"Well then can't we show them that? Can't we show them how mighty we are?" asked August, looking between his two fellow knights. Ivar mulled it over.

"How?" he asked after a moment, raising an eyebrow.

"What do you mean, how? We could hold some kind of battle. Some kind of show to demonstrate our power!" suggested August excitedly.

"Between whom exactly?" asked Ivar, still confused.

"Between the knights of course! We've been sparring with one another for years!" responded August.

"If it's knights fighting other knights, that won't exactly demonstrate the power gap now, will it?" chipped in Azalea.

"Well fine! We can have a show match between ordinary soldiers and knights!" compromised August, still excited by his idea.

"Surely that wouldn't be safe for the soldiers though..." reasoned Ivar in concern.

"The knights could hold back! Come on, we've been sparring for years, we know how to hold back!" insisted August.

"But if we're holding back, they won't see our true might, so what's the point? Also, wouldn't this just make the soldiers look bad? We'd just be shifting the taxation concerns on to the army. There's no way the Duke would be satisfied with that solution..."

said Azalea, her shoulders drooping a little as the cracks in the plan started to show. August stared back at her, stammering for a retort, but not really being able to think of one. The three knights sat in despondent silence for a moment as they realized why the Duke had dropped this responsibility on to them. What could they even do? If a Duke couldn't solve the problem, what hope did the three of them have? Ivar let out a loud sigh.

"What do commoners want!?" he groaned exasperatedly, as though it were one of life's great mysteries.

"It's not like they're foreign creatures, Ivar, they live in the same city as we do..." responded Azalea, rolling her eyes. August's face lit up again.

"You're right!" he exclaimed, slapping his hand against the table, startling both of the other knights.

"They're in the same city as us! Why don't we just ask them what they want?" suggested August with a shrug. Ivar and Azalea looked at each other and raised an eyebrow. Ivar suddenly slapped the table himself, again startling Azalea.

"Fantastic idea August! While you're doing that, I'll go to the taxation office and ask the archivists there what past kings have done to solve similar problems!" volunteered Ivar, standing up and finishing the last of his drink before beginning to make his exit. Azalea and August exchanged a knowing glance.

"Not so fast Ivar..." said August, stopping Ivar in his tracks.

"Let's put it to a vote. Whoever gets the most votes has to go and gather information from the commoners..." suggested August. Ivar suddenly became flustered.

"B-but hold on a minute-" began Ivar.

"Three... two... one..." interrupted Azalea enthusiastically. August and Azalea both immediately pointed at Ivar. He lowered his hand and let out a defeated sigh.

"Fantastic! Great work Ivar. If you need Azalea or I, you'll be able to find us at the taxation office!" said August happily as he and Azalea stood from the table. Ivar raised a finger to object, but then lowered it again and shook his head in defeat. It looked like he was going to the Oxgate markets, but how in the world was he supposed to fit in with the commoners?

CHAPTER TWENTY
Oxgate

Ivar looked around at the bustling marketplace uncomfortably. He let out a defeated sigh as he watched the commoners milling about busily. He had come here undercover, wearing common clothes and all, but it had taken him mere seconds to realize that short of bathing in horse shite, there was nothing he could do to truly camouflage himself among the commoners. Every mannerism he had screamed that he was a noble. He looked around reticently at his fellow Oxgateans. What did they want? What made them tick? He tried to put himself in their mind frame but was found wanting. Who could he even approach to talk to here? He looked around, but everybody was so busy going about their business that he felt like randomly accosting one of them would be an extremely out of place exchange. That being said, standing here awkwardly at the side of the marketplace made him seem just as out of place. The only other people who didn't seem to be doing much were a few vagrants and vagabonds. Perhaps he'd seem least out of place approaching one of them? Everybody else seemed to be avoiding them like the plague, so that'd certainly be a good place to start if he didn't want to draw attention to himself. He saw a one-legged pauper sitting on a canvas sack beside a baker's stall, tucking into a mostly rotten apple. He cleared his throat and approached the man.

"Pardon me for interrupting your meal good fellow, but might I proposition you for some information regarding your day-to-day life within our fair city?" asked Ivar politely. The pauper stared up blankly at Ivar, before looking over his shoulder to see if he'd been talking to someone else. After a moment of silence, the pauper screwed up his face in confusion.

"You what?" he asked. Ivar shifted uncomfortably on his feet and cleared his throat again. Clearly, he hadn't quite gotten the knack of the common tongue.

"Uh... tell me... matey... uh... friendo.... what is it that you want in life?" asked Ivar awkwardly, trying his best to mimic the common tongue. The pauper looked up at the hawker at the stall beside them who had by now stopped shouting about sweet rolls and was also staring at Ivar, just as perplexed as the pauper was.

"What are you on about?" asked the pauper confrontationally, clearly not sure of whether he was being insulted or not. Ivar raised his hands defensively.

"I'm just asking you, if you could have anything, what is it that you'd desire?" asked Ivar, frustrated that he'd been tasked with this troublesome job.

"Coins," replied the pauper, holding out his muddy hands expectantly. Ivar rolled his eyes.

"Besides that!"

"Food," replied the pauper, again holding out his hands expectantly.

"Food you say..." thought Ivar aloud, bringing his hand up to his chin as he began absent-mindedly stroking his goatee while he considered the pauper's request. Food. It seemed simple enough, but ultimately it would equate to the same thing as money as far as the Duke was concerned. Ivar let out a sigh.

"What about in a more general sense. What do you want from life, overall?" asked Ivar, looking between the pauper and the baker. The two of them looked at each other perplexed by his question.

"Right now?" asked the baker. Ivar turned to him excitedly.

"Yes! Right now! What is it that your heart desires?" asked Ivar.

"For you to sod off and stop causing trouble around my stall!" said the baker, waving a dismissive hand at him. Ivar gasped in surprise, flabbergasted that a commoner would speak to him in such a way. He suddenly remembered that he was dressed up as a commoner and appeared to be bullying a random vagrant. He let out a groan of frustration and reached into his pocket, withdrawing a silver piece.

"Here. Give him a sweet roll then!" offered Ivar, flicking the silver piece towards the baker who caught it eagerly.

"A sweet roll?! With that you could buy me five!" insisted the pauper, sitting up on his one good knee and his stump as he looked up expectantly at the baker.

"Nope, you heard the man, one sweet roll," said the baker, raising an eyebrow and tossing a sweet roll down to the pauper who caught it eagerly but continued to stare up at the baker angrily.

"He gave you a silver piece!" exclaimed the pauper.

"Uh, now now..." began Ivar, holding up his hands as he watched the situation unravel before his eyes.

"Yes, and he told me it was for a sweet roll! I gave you one! Now beat it!" shouted the baker shooing the pauper away in frustration.

"You bloody crook! Give me my sweet rolls!" demanded the pauper, clutching at the baker's legs. The baker kicked back at him angrily as the two began hurling insults at one another. Ivar slowly backed away from the scene that he'd created and disappeared into the crowd. After walking away around a corner, he leant against a wall and let out a defeated sigh. Put him at a table of aristocrats or in a war room and he'd shine, but here in Oxgate's bustling market district he was completely lost. He decided to continue walking around, silently watching the commoners, overwhelmed by the responsibility that had been given to him. How in the world was he supposed to reach these people?

***

"What happened here?" asked William, looking around in shock at the squalor which surrounded them. The quaint rural villages that they'd been passing through had been relatively familiar. They'd had similar layouts to Lakhdorian, and although lacking some of the quality of life that the Lakhdorians were blessed with, William hadn't thought much of it. The further that they'd delved into the Bleaklands however, the serene surroundings of farmlands and windmills had slowly begun to disappear. Now that they were entering the villages closer to Oxgate, things had really taken a turn for the worse. He'd never seen so many people in his life. Most of them looked miserable, milling about, arguing and bartering, tending to animals and selling their goods and services every which way. Every direction that William looked was more captivating than the last. The place was in utter shambles. There was certainly a sense of order beneath the chaos, but to William's untrained eye it was impossible to grasp.

"To be honest, I kind of expected worse," admitted Eric as Bonnie tried her best to navigate her way down the busy main street.

"Worse?!" wheezed William in surprise. He'd expected things to become more and more lavish the closer that they drew to Oxgate.

The thought that dreary old Lakhdorian had a higher quality of life than these less agrarian villages was something that he'd never have imagined.

"Aye. Me granda's journal talked about the time before the great war, it were horrible," said Eric shaking his head.

"Ey?!" huffed William in disbelief.

"How could things have been worse before the great war? I thought the war was what ruined everything!" said William, confused. Eric's expression darkened and he nodded understandingly.

"A lot of the problems society was facing were… well, let's just say they were ironed out by the great war. Issues of who owned what land, who owed money to whom, what part of society people were from; these kinds of things don't matter when the world is ending," explained Eric, grimacing as they passed a man covered from head to toe in boils. William felt like his neck was beginning to hurt from snapping it around to look every which way at the fascinating sights to take in.

"After the war, there was more land to go around since, you know, so many people were dead and all. People were on more equal footing and the knights had become better too. My granda talks about the knights before the great war like… well like they were villains," explained Eric, shaking his head as the two of them somehow managed to work their way out of the thick of the chaos.

"Eric, look!" exclaimed William as they finally managed to get a clear view of the road ahead. There, in the distance they could finally see it. Oxgate, in all its glory. The enormous city was surrounded by huge walls on all sides. It was constructed on a giant hill, with Oxgate castle at its very pinnacle. Beneath that was the knight's college and noble districts, then the market district, followed by the common district. Outside the city walls were the surrounding villages and farmlands which Eric and William were currently travelling through. The boys shared an excited look with one another. Neither of these two farmboys had ever imagined that they'd actually get a chance to travel all the way to Oxgate, but here they were.

"William! Look! There it is!" shouted Eric excitedly, pointing towards an enormous old, ruined stone gateway that was in the middle of a wheat field.

"What is that thing?" asked William, confused as to why such a thing existed at all. It was clearly exceptionally old, having been weathered away considerably. Whatever structure it had been attached to had completely crumbled away. All that remained were the enormous stone pillars with what seemed to have once been intricate designs, weathered away to the point of being indecipherable. Eric's eyes were lit up with awe.

"That's the Oxgate!" exclaimed Eric as the boys passed by the field that was housing it.

"Huh?" asked William dully as he looked at the giant, although to his eyes, unremarkable ruined archway in the middle of the wheat field.

"There used to be enormous ox heads sculpted into that archway. No one knows what kingdom was here before, but the Oxgate is all that remains of it. The crown has forbidden its destruction, so I suppose the farmers are having to work around it," guessed Eric as they passed by. William smiled happily as Eric excitedly regaled him with the history of their land. He was glad to see excitement back on Eric's face. There was no telling what awaited the boys when they entered Oxgate, so William relished the moment, as for the first time in their trip, they were but two innocent farm boys enjoying their exciting adventure to the capital city.

***

When the two boys finally arrived at the walls of Oxgate, they both immediately felt a chill of realization run down their spines. Never had they seen walls so enormously high. These very walls had kept the people safe during the great war. These were the very same walls that served as the last bastion for the knights who had managed to fight their way all the way from Oxgate to the gateway in the desert. The significance of this location loomed heavy in the air above their little cart as they slowly worked their way down the busy main road.

As the two boys passed beneath the enormous Oxgate main entranceway, they were filled with awe at how many people there were in the common district. They'd thought that the villages of a hundred or so people that they'd previously traveled through were enormous. As soon as they'd crossed the precipice into Oxgate, they realized that the surrounding villages paled in comparison to the thousands of people who called this place home.

"Eric, this is…" began William, looking all around them at the busy townsfolk going about their daily business.

"Incredible," finished Eric, also looking around in awe at the bustling city. After a few moments of being lost in thought, as he gazed around in all directions at the incredible place they'd found themselves in, William suddenly snapped back to reality.

"Wait a minute. How exactly is this going to work?" asked William suddenly, turning to Eric with a puzzled expression on his face.

"Hmm?" asked Eric, still distracted by their surroundings.

"You're a noble," said William. Eric turned to face him quizzically.

"Aye. Technically," confirmed Eric unconfidently.

"How can you prove that to the people at the great library?" asked William, still confused.

"I've brought my scroll of pedigree with me," answered Eric, nodding over his shoulder towards the gear he'd packed in the back of the cart.

"Aye... and so?" asked William. Eric raised an eyebrow.

"And so... it proves my pedigree. It shows that I am a noble. It's an official record. It'll match what they have in the city records," explained Eric with a nod. William stared at him blankly for a moment.

"And... what about me?" asked William. Eric swallowed nervously.

"Uh... what?" he asked, averting his eyes.

"Eric... what about me?" asked William, tapping him on the shoulder to regain his attention. Eric let out a sigh.

"Look there are a few options here. Don't worry, we'll get you into that college, no matter what," said Eric with a nod.

"What are ye talking about?!" asked William in panic.

"What do ye mean, options?!" he asked, feeling himself beginning to hyperventilate with worry. Eric patted him reassuringly on the shoulder.

"It'll be okay! Calm down! One thing at a time. We have to see how stringent the admissions process even is first. Don't forget everything I know is from really old books. Most of 'em are from me granda, but that means they're from his days, or even older. A lot has changed. They might allow commoners in these days," explained Eric positively.

"And if they don't?" asked William, unconvinced.

"We'll cross that bridge when we get to it," said Eric with a confident nod.

"Eric!" exclaimed William, dread creeping over him.

"Look William, I do kind of have an idea but, I'm going to level with you here. I didn't exactly have time to come up with a solid plan! I thought I'd have had time to think of something between leaving home and arriving here, but with the moorcrawlers and all, I haven't had a chance to come up with anything solid yet!" admitted Eric guiltily. William let out a sigh.

"I'm sorry Eric. I didn't mean to freak out. Obviously, I haven't thought of anything either," admitted William, feeling guilty for relying so heavily on Eric.

"It's okay. Like I said, I do have a plan, sort of…" said Eric, narrowing his eyes, deep in thought as the two continued their way uphill towards the market district.

***

Ivar stared at a pointy hatted woman mashing away at the brew in her giant cauldron. She'd likely been mashing and stirring away since long before he'd gotten here, and didn't appear to stop for a second. He mused over how even some knights he'd met wouldn't have the stamina to carry out her duties every day.

"Oi!" exclaimed an older lady at him, snapping him back to reality.

"Are you buying or not then, handsome?" she asked, raising her eyebrows and looking him up and down.

"Uh…" he wasn't sure how to politely decline, but upon catching a waft of that signature scent of barley and hops, he couldn't resist.

"Oh, go on then," he said, sighing and looking around for a price listing.

"It's two coppa for a pint," said the lady, reaching into a cupboard and withdrawing a tankard.

"Can I drink it here?" asked Ivar, looking around for somewhere to sit.

"Course ya can love," she said with a wink, filling the tankard with ale and holding out her hand expectantly.

"Oh uh, here," said Ivar, reaching into his pocket and withdrawing a silver piece which he tossed over to her.

"Oh my!" exclaimed the lady, her eyes lighting up when she caught the silver.

"For that price... could it be that yer expecting some other services from me too?" she asked, lifting her dress suggestively.

"What? No!" exclaimed a very flustered Sir Ivar. She immediately cackled.

"I'm only joking, let me get yer change love," she said, turning to access her coin pouch.

"No, no, that's fine you keep it," said Ivar with an awkward smile, not wanting a bunch of useless copper pieces jingling around in his pocket. She raised her eyebrows in surprise.

"Thank ye sir!" she said earnestly, handing Ivar his tankard.

"Ye can keep the tankard at that price!" she said with another cackle. Ivar smiled politely as he began searching for somewhere to sit down. Although she'd said he could drink it here, he didn't want to hang around awkwardly at the front of her business. He let out a sigh and walked over to a random wall and leant against it to drink his ale. He had to admit, despite being low quality stuff, it tasted pretty good being this fresh.

He closed his eyes and let out a deep sigh after taking a swig from his tankard. If Azalea and August were going to force him to be here, the least he could do is try to enjoy himself a little, but what had he even accomplished so far? He'd caused a fight to break out, got lost in the markets and then bought some cheap ale. It wasn't exactly going to solve the Duke's problem. He cringed as he imagined how August and Azalea would react if he went back completely empty handed. He struggled to communicate with the commoners at the best of times, but approaching them at random and questioning them about their political concerns? That went way beyond anything that he was comfortable doing. He was just going to keep his eyes peeled and see if he could find an opening to provide him insight into the hearts of the commoners.

He opened his eyes back up and began to look around again. As he looked downhill, that's when he saw it. There, slowly working its way up the main street of the market district, was a horse and cart carrying the Rothmane boy that he'd hoped he'd seen the last of back in Mistfall. He stared at Eric and William's cart with his mouth agape as it slowly wobbled its way up the hill towards him. What in the world were those two rural farm boys doing in Oxgate? He furrowed his brow nervously. There was only one reason he could imagine for them being here, and that was to sell information about the Mistfall incident. If those two were to tell the chancellor's office the full story of what happened in Lakhdorian, he and both of his knightly compatriots were totally screwed. The secrets that they'd left out of their report could easily be spilled by the mouth of the Rothmane boy, and if it was, then being stripped back to the rank of squire wouldn't just be a mere threat; it'd be a guarantee.

CHAPTER TWENTY-ONE
The Deadly Secrets of Mistfall

"Halt!" shouted a guard, holding his hand up in Bonnie's face, causing her to draw to a stop. William looked over at Eric fearfully but was relieved to see that he looked quite confident.

"What business have you in the upper district?" asked the guard, rounding the side of their cart and looking over it curiously.

"I am Eric, of the house Rothmane. I am visiting Oxgate from my farmstead in the Mistfall moors," stated Eric assertively. William was once again in awe of Eric's aptitude when it came to knowing the right thing to say. If it were William doing the talking, they'd have ended up being thrown out of Oxgate by their bootstraps. The guard looked up at him suspiciously.

"Rothmane?" asked the guard, narrowing his eyes.

"I have my papers here," replied Eric, reaching into his satchel and withdrawing a sealed and stamped scroll. The guard took it and looked it over in detail.

"This is my first-time hearing of a Rothmane in Oxgate…" said the guard absentmindedly, continuing to scrutinize Eric's paperwork.

"Yes, well as I said, I'm visiting from our farmstead in the Mist-fall moors," reiterated Eric, watching over the guard keenly as his pedigree was examined.

"Hmm..." the guard hummed, still reading the paperwork in detail. After a moment he looked back up at Eric and William suspiciously.

"You don't look like nobles..." he thought aloud. William blushed as he remembered that he was still wearing the vibrant green tunic that the gypsies had given to him.

"Again... I am coming from our farmstead in the moors..." reiterated Eric, seeming a little unsure of what else to say at this point. The guard continued to assess him suspiciously.

"This birth date would only make you fourteen!" exclaimed the guard incredulously. William and Eric stared back at him blankly. An awkward silence formed as the guard stared back up at them silently for a moment.

"Are you only fourteen?" asked the guard, raising an eyebrow as he looked Eric's enormous body up and down. Eric nodded his head slowly. The guard looked even more surprised by this than by his claim of being a noble. After a moment of pondering Eric's size, he cleared his throat and lowered the scroll slightly.

"Well, your papers certainly look authentic but..." thought the guard aloud, again looking over the contents of their carriage.

"Wait here," he said, turning around and approaching another guard who was sitting in the guard post. The two seemed to be having a detailed conversation, with the guard inside the post writing something down with a parchment and quill. William exhaled nervously and shared an anxious glance with Eric.

"It's okay," said Eric with a confident nod. William felt his racing heartbeat slowing down a little as Eric's aura of calmness resonated with him. After a few moments of deliberation, the guard came back over to their cart. He looked anxiously at the small lineup of horses and carts that had begun to form behind the boys.

"We're going to have to formally verify your documentation before you can enter. Please feel free to leave your horse and cart in the waiting area over there while we undergo this process," said the guard, handing Eric back his documents. Eric nodded obediently and began to steer Bonnie around towards where the guard had gestured, before the guard suddenly piped up again.

"Hey, wait a minute. Your friend there, if he's a noble I'll need his documents too," said the guard. William again felt his heart beginning to race.

"He's my aide," replied Eric simply. The guard looked William up and down once more before nodding and stepping back from their cart. William breathed a deep sigh of relief as Eric led Bonnie away from the gate and over to the waiting area.

"Eric, that was…" began William.

"Don't celebrate too soon," interrupted Eric, shaking his head.

"It ain't over yet," he said, looking over towards the guard post. The guard inside the post handed whatever he'd been writing to a young page boy who was standing by, next to the post. Immediately the boy set off, sprinting into the upper district.

"Where do you think he's going?" asked William, looking after the boy as he disappeared into the crowd.

"Probably to check my details against the official census…" said Eric, seeming to have centered himself a bit better now.

"Will it be on there?" asked William, suddenly feeling a little more worried. Eric was about to reply, but then caught himself.

"I've never filled out any census details. I don't think they take census of people living in the moors since… well it's pretty much

just me and pa. I know me pa's never been to Oxgate either, so…
maybe it'll still be in granda's name?" thought Eric aloud.

"Do you mean your grandad? Or your great grandad?" asked
William. Eric shrugged.

"I honestly have no idea whether me great granda even had to
fill out paperwork to set up his farm in the moors. Nobody owned
the land back then, and he was a war hero so… we'll just have to
wait and see," replied Eric with an anxious sigh. William looked
back towards the entranceway to the upper district anxiously. Just
where was that page going, and would they have the records that
the boys needed?

***

As the two knights approached the gate out of the noble district,
they were buried deep in an engrossing discussion.

"So, let's get this straight then. If he walks through those gates
without having gathered any information at all, you have to give my
eldest squires a private combat training session before their exams,"
said Azalea, raising an eyebrow expectantly at August.

"Yes, precisely. But if he returns to us having gathered some
completely unrelated, entirely useless information, you have to take
my eldest squires to one of those fancy tea parties and teach them
proper etiquette," parried August, raising his own eyebrow combatively.

"You're on!" said Azalea, shaking August's hand enthusiastically. As soon as the two turned back towards the gate and took in the
sight on the other side, their merry mood immediately dropped.
There on the other side of the gate were William and Eric sitting in
the waiting area by a guard. Just what were they doing here, and
what kind of trouble was it going to cause for the three knights?

***

"How long do you think they'll be?" asked William, his stomach rumbling with both hunger and anxiety. Eric shook his head.

"I've no idea..." said Eric with a sigh. Suddenly somebody grabbed Eric by his arm, causing him to jump in his seat and cry out in surprise.

"Shh!" hushed Ivar, looking over his shoulder as he held onto Eric's arm.

"Sir Ivar!" exclaimed William and Eric in tandem.

"Yes, it's me..." said Ivar, shaking his head. Eric and William exchanged a confused glance with one another.

"Why are you dressed like a commoner?" asked Eric, looking over Ivar's floral scented, pristine brown tunic and trousers which he'd clearly never worn before.

"That's... a private matter," replied Ivar, raising an eyebrow.

"Why are you here Rothmane? I thought we had an agreement!" he suddenly hissed, again looking over his shoulder anxiously.

"What? I'm terribly sorry, but I don't recall that!" said Eric, genuinely trying to remember ever agreeing with Ivar that he wouldn't come to Oxgate. Ivar let out a knowing chuckle before crossing his arms, seemingly impressed.

"Hah! So that's how you're going to play it, huh?" asked Ivar incredulously. William and Eric shared another confused look with one another.

"What do you want Rothmane?" asked Ivar with a sigh.

"We're trying to get into the upper district," replied Eric, holding up his scroll of pedigree and showing it to Ivar, who raised an eyebrow.

"That's it?" he asked. Again, Eric and William shared a confused glance.

"Fine. And let's say you manage to find your way into the upper district... I don't suppose you'd be heading to the chancellor's office by any chance now, would you?" asked Ivar, staring up at the two of them smugly, as though he'd caught them red handed.

"No?" answered Eric, confused.

"No?!" exclaimed Ivar in surprise.

"Surely not... the Duke?!" gasped Ivar, seemingly flabbergasted by Eric's audacity.

"What?! No!" replied Eric again, confused about how he'd even get an audience with either of these aristocrats.

"We just want to get into the knight's college," added William suddenly. Ivar looked up at him, apparently having considered him part of the architecture until he'd spoken.

"The college?!" exclaimed Ivar, looking back up at Eric who nodded affirmatively. Ivar looked at the two of them skeptically.

"And why do you want to go there?" he asked warily.

"We want to enroll," replied Eric honestly. Ivar seemed surprised at first, but then a knowing expression crossed his face.

"Fine! You win, but this is it, Rothmane. If I help you get into the college, we're even," replied Ivar sternly.

"Even? But you don't o-" began Eric, before William interrupted him by elbowing him in his side.

"Okay, we have a deal," replied Eric, shaking hands with Ivar who seemed quite proud of himself.

"Great, follow me then," said Ivar, grabbing Bonnie by her harness and beginning to lead her back over towards the guard post. As they approached, the guard who'd initially greeted them let out an annoyed sigh.

"I told you to wait! We're still processing your documents!" shouted the guard in exasperation.

"That won't be necessary!" announced Ivar, drawing the guard's attention. He looked Ivar up and down.

"And who might you be?" asked the guard. Ivar looked extremely offended that he hadn't been recognized.

"How dare a lowly guard-" began Ivar, before he remembered that he was in his commoner disguise.

"Oh, right," he said, reaching into his pocket and withdrawing an intricate, platinum and gold medallion before showing it to the guard. Immediately the guard's demeanor changed.

"I'm incredibly sorry sir! I had no idea! You're dressed so..." began the guard, looking Ivar up and down. Ivar raised an expectant eyebrow.

"...humbly, sir," finished the guard tactfully, swallowing nervously when he met Ivar's gaze. Ivar nodded approvingly.

"These boys are with me," said Ivar confidently, gesturing towards Eric and William who smiled awkwardly down at the guard.

"Of course, sir. We were simply waiting on the archivists for-" began the guard before suddenly the page boy re-emerged from the crowd and sprinted over to the guard's side, handing him his parchment.

"...well, for this," said the guard with a polite smile, beginning to unravel the parchment. As soon as he read it, his eyebrows raised in surprise.

"I'm afraid your documents didn't clear..." began the guard, looking between Eric and Ivar, not sure of who he should be addressing at this point.

"And? I demand that you let them through. They are my guests," demanded Ivar assertively.

"Of course, sir. Please, pass through," replied the guard with a polite bow, before stepping out of Bonnie's way so they could pass by the guard post. As the little cart began to trundle its way into the upper district, Ivar suddenly caught sight of his two knightly compatriots.

"Oh! There you are!" chirped Ivar merrily.

"Good afternoon Sir August, and Dame Azalea!" greeted Eric politely, as he and William bowed their heads to them both. The two knights were still in a stunned silence. August yanked Ivar aside and grabbed him by the collar.

"What do you think you're doing?!" he exclaimed furiously.

"Calm down August! I've made a deal with the boy!" defended Ivar, pulling August's hands away and straightening his common tunic.

"Another deal?! How many deals are you going to make with the kid?!" asked Azalea, looking over her shoulder at the two farm boys who were awestruck, looking all around the upper district.

"He shook my hand. He agreed that if I got him to the college, he'd keep his mouth shut. Trust me. They just want to enroll," said Ivar, looking over his compatriot's shoulders at the farm boys who were now enthusiastically breaking a piece of stale bread together.

"We heard it all, Ivar! Their documents weren't cleared anyway! They wouldn't have been able to even get into the upper district, let alone tell anybody about Mistfall, if you hadn't let them through!" said Azalea angrily. Ivar shook his head.

"You really think so little of me? I saw the documents myself. They would've gotten through eventually, trust me; they're legitimate," said Ivar with a sigh.

"Look, it doesn't matter. They're here now. Let's just get them to the college and figure out the rest later…" said August, crossing his arms and letting out a sigh. The three knights nodded in agreement as they watched the two farm boys babbling excitedly about the big city that they'd found themselves in. Would they really be able to get them enrolled? Even if they had the Rothmane name behind them, would that really be enough to turn two farm boys into knights?

CHAPTER TWENTY-TWO
The Trials of Rothmane I

William smiled politely at the three knights, blushing abashedly as he cleared more space in the messy cart. Ivar had hopped up into the seat that William had been occupying next to Eric and had begun giving him directions. The other two knights had climbed up into the back of the cart, along with William. He looked awkwardly between the two knights who were inspecting Eric's luggage curiously.

"Is that what I think it is?" asked August, nodding towards Eric's tower shield which was wrapped up in canvas.

"Aye sir! It's his great granda's shield!" replied William eagerly, immediately biting his tongue when he remembered that he was supposed to be using fancier words.

August kicked the shield lightly before chuckling.

"An old-world full metal scutum. How our ancestors got by with such unwieldy armaments is beyond me. You won't be using that at the college, trust me," he said, shaking his head. William stayed silent. He remembered the old gypsy man's reaction to seeing the shield's sigil. It was best that these knights simply thought they were fools for bringing a giant old shield along rather than knowing anything more about it.

"You really are just here to enroll in the college, aren't you?" asked Azalea, looking around at Eric's humble belongings. William tilted his head in confusion.

"Aye," he confirmed.

"I mean, yes!" he corrected, blushing at his lack of etiquette. Azalea and August exchanged an amused glance.

William looked around in awe at the beautiful jettied buildings which loomed over them, some three stories high. Azalea smiled warmly as she watched him looking around curiously.

"Have you ever seen buildings like these before?" she asked. William shook his head.

"Never. Back home a few people had two levels on their houses, but it weren't common. I never knew they got even bigger than that!" recalled William, craning his head to see the tops of the buildings. Azalea let out a sigh of relief as she watched Eric listening intently to Ivar's instructions while William was being mesmerized by the city around him.

"So, you two really want to enroll in the college?" asked August, drawing William's attention. He nodded affirmatively.

"Yes, that's right," he said, silently congratulating himself on using the correct words. August raised an eyebrow.

"You're a bit old to be pages, aren't you? I suppose, considering that the Rothmane name still holds some weight, and with the three of us on your side you may be able to convince them to let you enter in the next intake of squires instead. Might I see your papers?" asked August expectantly. William looked back at him blankly.

"Papers?" he asked, confused.

"Yes, your scroll of pedigree," confirmed August expectantly. William began blushing.

"I uh… I don't have one…" replied William meekly. Azalea and August shared a concerned glance. Even Ivar turned around and started listening in to the conversation at this point.

"Pardon?" asked August, thinking that perhaps he'd misheard him.

"I'm a commoner, sir… so…" confirmed William.

"But, you told me you wanted to enter the college!" exclaimed Ivar, suspecting that he'd been hoodwinked in some way.

"I do!" confirmed William.

"Commoners can't be knights!" yelled Ivar exasperatedly.

"I know that but… Eric didn't you say you had an idea?!" asked William, desperate for some help. Eric cleared his throat awkwardly.

"I mean…" he stammered.

"Would you perhaps be able to help us enroll William?" asked Eric to Ivar hopefully. Ivar recoiled dramatically.

"What?! We might be administrators, but that doesn't mean we can change the rules!" yelled Ivar. Eric looked like he wanted to respond but was suddenly distracted by something ahead of them.

"Is that it?" he asked suddenly, pointing to another enormous wall with yet another guard checkpoint and a small office. Ivar let out a sigh.

"I really wish you had told me that you weren't a noble sooner…" said Ivar in frustration.

"I did!" replied William defensively.

"When?!" exclaimed Ivar.

"Back in Lakhdorian!" explained William earnestly.

"Lakhdorian?! You expect me to remember that far back?!" asked Ivar, dumbfounded. William suddenly felt a pang of distaste shoot through his body. Had these three supposed knights really already put the happenings of Lakhdorian behind them? Did they not care about the destruction that had been left in their wake? Did they not care about what had happened to Annemarie when she was supposed to be under their watch? How dare they move on with their lives as though they hadn't ruined his? He was suddenly pulled from his thoughts when Eric drew Bonnie to a stop and hopped down from his seat as a guard approached them.

"Good afternoon," said the guard, bowing his head politely to each of the three knights.

"We're here to enroll two new students," said Ivar. The guard looked at Eric and William with his eyebrows raised.

"Three first-class knights? Here for an enrollment?" he asked, confused. The three knights simply stared back at him. He cleared his throat and shuffled awkwardly on the spot.

"Of course! Please, head straight through into the office!" said the guard, bowing awkwardly and stepping away from their cart. After the motley crew disembarked, leaving Bonnie in a bay to the side, Ivar led them into the small office building by the gate. Eric and William exchanged a nervous glance with one another. This was it. It all came down to this moment. Without enrollment in the college, their chances of accessing the library records were practically zero. They had to somehow make this work.

***

William opened his eyes in surprise as he entered the small, cramped office. The archivist on duty was clearly of Zarubian descent. Being from the endemic town of Lakhdorian, William had never had the privilege of meeting any outsiders aside from the gypsies. Even foreign traveling merchants skipped their unnoteworthy dot on the map. As the group filed into the tight office space, the archivist dropped what he was doing and stood up in surprise. Three first-class knights being in his little office was quite unusual, especially when accompanied by a couple of farm boys.

"Good afternoon, how may I help you?" asked the archivist nervously, looking over their shoulders through the window at the guard stationed outside who simply shrugged.

"We're here to get these two boys enrolled," said August, stepping forward confidently.

"Oh, certainly!" said the archivist, sitting back down in his chair at the front desk, relieved that it wasn't something more serious.

"May I see their papers please?" he asked. William and Eric exchanged a nervous glance with one another.

"Come now, is that really necessary?" piped up August suddenly, taking another step forward. The archivist looked quite confused.

"… yes?" he confirmed, looking around at the bunch as though he'd missed something.

"I'm afraid the boys have lost their papers! That's why we're here! We can confirm their identity for you!" said Azalea, also stepping forward and smiling warmly at the archivist. He furrowed his brow nervously, looking up at the three knights.

"I'm afraid… that's not quite how this works…" said the archivist, clearly uncomfortable. As the three knights continued to argue the point, William nudged Eric.

"What?" whispered Eric.

"I think you're going to have to try that idea you had…" said William, noticing that the three knights were getting nowhere. Eric's face went a little pale.

"It's a terrible idea William… really…" admitted Eric, shaking his head.

"What idea?" asked August suddenly, drawing all attention back to the boys. Eric swallowed nervously as the entire room focused their attention on him.

"Well... I mean..." began Eric, stammering under the pressure of the situation. He let out a sigh and tried to steady his nerves before stepping forward towards the archivist's desk.

"It wasn't always the case that commoners couldn't enroll in the college, right?" asked Eric. The archivist looked back at him confused.

"You're commoners?" he asked. Eric immediately realized he'd misspoken and stammered to correct himself, but William put his hand on Eric's shoulder and took a step forward to join him.

"He isn't, but I am," admitted William shamefully. The archivist raised a puzzled eyebrow.

"Look!" began Eric, pulling William's hand from his shoulder.

"Back when my great grandfather enrolled, he wrote about how there were ways to become a knight that weren't just from being of noble birth!" claimed Eric desperately. The archivist shook his head confidently.

"No. Perhaps he was simply alluding to the entry exams. All new enrollments must go through the entrance exams, but they have to be noble to qualify for those in the first place," said the archivist, continuing to shake his head.

"That's not what he was talking about!" shouted Eric, realizing that he was becoming a little too worked up.

"He... well he said..." trailed off Eric as his face again became a little pale as he tried to find his words. The archivist let out a sigh.

"I'm afraid I can only process enrollment requests from-" began the archivist.

"What about the trial by combat?" interrupted Eric suddenly. The archivist recoiled in surprise.

"Trial by what now?!" exclaimed August.

"No, no, no. Again, you're thinking of the combat exam, part of the graduation process from squires to-" began the archivist. Eric shook his head confidently.

"No, I'm not talking about that. When the great war was first beginning, they needed to train more knights. They ended up amending a clause to the college's constitution which stated that the most talented fighters of the common class may be accepted into the college if they passed a trial by combat," recited Eric conclusively. The three knights exchanged searching glances with one another, each shrugging as they'd never heard of this either. The archivist chuckled nervously.

"Boy, I'm impressed by your research. You'll be a good fit for the order of the owl, but I'm afraid you're confused. Firstly, that amendment was intended to allow the strongest fighters from the military ranks to be promoted into knighthood, not for random commoners to become squires. Secondly, amendments from that long ago can hardly be upheld. I assure you an amendment as obscure as that has long since been revised. I mean, come on. We could never uphold such an ancient, obsolete, and frankly, barbaric clause in the modern day!" reasoned the archivist emphatically. There was an awkward silence as the archivist's words lingered in the room.

"Come on boys, we tried our best," said Azalea, putting a hand on each of their shoulders.

"Challenge," replied Eric simply.

"What?" asked the archivist, surprised.

"I challenge your word. By the name of house Rothmane, I challenge your ruling," said Eric, placing his scroll of pedigree down on the desk before the archivist. The archivist looked expectantly at the three knights, but each of them simply stared back in confusion.

"You're challenging my ruling?! What is this, a court of law? What are all of these obscure, archaic rules you're enacting here?! Challenges haven't been a thing for eighty years!" exclaimed the archivist.

"Are you sure about that?" asked Eric, raising a combative eyebrow. The archivist looked back at him, tilting his head in disbelief at Eric's boldness.

"Rothmane huh? I guess it really does run in your blood..." muttered the archivist with a sigh. Eric nodded, with a proud smile.

"Fine! I honestly don't recall ever hearing that 'challenges' had officially been declared obsolete, so I suppose I'll have to uphold your challenge for now," replied the archivist, shaking his head in annoyance.

"Pardon me, but what does all of this mean?" asked August suddenly. The archivist let out a sigh.

"Challenges are a very antiquated way for a noble to put their family's name on the line to challenge a ruling. It was typically used in the court of law, but... I suppose there's nothing to technically forbid its use in a menial legal matter like this," explained the archivist. The three knights shared some intrigued glances.

"Basically, the boy's claim that trials by combat have never strictly been struck from the college constitution must be officially fact-checked in the great library," the archivist concluded, realizing that the majority of the room was still not quite following what was happening. There was a moment of silence as everybody caught up.

"What happens if his challenge is met, and it turns out he was incorrect?" asked Ivar, curiously. The archivist shrugged.

"I guess in some cases it could mean that his family would lose some of their titles, or in the absolute worst case, that they're stripped of their knighthood..." the archivist looked up and raised an eyebrow at Eric, who clearly didn't have much to lose.

"You really would be a good fit for the order of the owl you know," he reiterated, impressed. Eric bowed his head appreciatively.

"So, what now?" asked August.

"Now..." began the archivist, standing from his chair and closing the book he'd been writing in.

"...we have to go to the great library," he finished with a sigh, looking around at the three knights.

"But... surely you have a copy of the constitution somewhere nearer than that?" asked Ivar, hopefully. The archivist shook his head.

"Even if the specific clause relating to trials by combat aren't on the modern-day copies which I have access to, that doesn't mean they've necessarily been removed. The copyist may simply have deemed it unimportant to include in our handouts, it really is quite an obscure and archaic rule. Plus, if the boy is right, I've got a long evening of reading century old legal manuals about combat trials ahead of me there anyway..." admitted the archivist with a disappointed sigh. As everybody in the room began to walk towards the door, William grabbed Eric by the arm.

"Hey!" exclaimed William quietly. Eric looked at him quizzically.

"Trial by combat?" asked William, panic starting to rise in his chest. Eric gestured for him to calm down.

"Don't worry, this is all going to plan…" said Eric assuredly. William stared back at him perplexed. How could this situation possibly end in their favor? Either they were going to end up being rejected from the college, or in the best-case scenario, William was going to have to engage in some kind of trial by combat. He'd never so much as touched a sword in his life. How was he supposed to pass any kind of combat trial?

CHAPTER TWENTY-THREE
The Trials of Rothmane II

As their small group worked their way down the peaceful road, William and Eric looked around in astonishment. Beyond the guard post and some initial administration buildings was an expanse of open, well-tended grassy fields.

"How large is this city?!" asked William in awe.

"More than six miles," replied the archivist proudly.

"Six miles?!" exclaimed William, gobsmacked.

"Feels like more than that…" said Ivar, annoyed at having to make the trek to the college campus and the great library.

"Come on, aren't you at least a little curious about how this is going to work out?" asked Azalea, elbowing Ivar. He shrugged.

"I suppose so, but not as curious as I am about how the bottle of wine I'd bought for this evening tastes…" replied Ivar despondently. Having left Bonnie happily stationed at a water trough by the guard post, their group was traveling on foot. They'd already been walking for close to ten minutes and were only now nearing the walls at the far end of the greenery.

"Whoa…" said Eric, as they approached the walls and were finally able to see the full extent of what lay beyond them. The walls had been blocking the view of the enormous marble building ahead of them. The giant circular building was a hub of activity, sur-rounded by scholars going in and out, chattering quietly with one another in the golden afternoon sunlight, and going about their dai-ly business. The front of the building was supported by a giant line of marble pillars which extended magnificently high to support the heavy marble tiled roof. A large ornate fountain stood out the front featuring a sculpture of a bearded man with an owl on his arm.

"Is that…" began William, awestruck.

"Yep. That's the Oxgate library," replied the archivist proudly. As their group approached the front steps of the grand building, the weight of the situation once again began to settle on William's shoulders. He took a deep nervous breath as he looked up at the in-timidating building ahead of them. Did Eric really have a plan? How could this end in anything but disaster? William was pulled from his thoughts when the archivist suddenly turned around to face their group.

"Now, there are some important rules of etiquette when entering the great library," he began. The three knights all let out frustrated sighs, as they'd heard the spiel a million times before.

"Firstly, for non-librarians or researchers, you may not delve any deeper than the entrance hall," explained the archivist. Eric nodded knowingly in response, having read these rules a hundred times himself.

"You must remain respectfully quiet. All weapons must be left with the guards stationed at the entrance of the library. No food or drink is to be brought into the library. If your hygiene standards are deemed inadequate, you will be asked to leave. Everybody under-stand?" asked the archivist. William and Eric nodded their heads enthusiastically. The archivist looked down at the two of them in thought for a moment.

"You may be asked to leave, but we'll see..." he thought aloud, looking over their muddy, low classed, heavily worn commoner clothes. Eric and William both blushed shamefully, but were reassured by a pat on the shoulder by August. William winced as the pressure sent a wave of pain through his brand, but he managed to keep himself from showing how much it had hurt by simply smiling and continuing on walking. As they approached the front door, they were halted by guards who requested that they give up any weapons they may be holding. William, Eric and the archivist showed that they had no weapons, but all three knights were forced to hand over daggers which they had hidden away on their person. It was the first time that William had seen any of them holding a weapon before, and the fact that they were actually knights began to set in again. He and Eric were actually being guided into the great library by three knights right now. Goosebumps ran down his arms as the enormity of the situation dawned on him. He looked over at Eric and saw that his face was several shades paler than usual. He must've been feeling the same thing.

As soon as they entered the building, both William and Eric gasped audibly in shock. The interior of the library was the most lavish, intricate and beautiful architecture that either of the boys had ever seen. Even here in the mere entrance hall, the enormously high, curved marble ceiling was painted with elaborate works of art. Gold trimming ran down every inch of the beautifully carved interior walls. The design of the building meant that the natural light from the golden afternoon sun was lighting up the room in an enchanting way, the vibrant colors of the room reflecting from its shiny marble tiled floor. Librarians sat at desks all around the room, quietly discussing books and research papers with visitors to the library. They all sat at beautiful mahogany desks with ornate golden lanterns lighting up their work-stations. Eric and William shared a gob smacked glance with one another. Coming from their common homes out in Lakhdorian, to be standing in a place as lavish as this was almost unfathomable.

"Okay, follow me," said the archivist, approaching a desk that was administered by an older looking, bearded librarian. He was wearing a badge bearing the crest of the order of the owl. The librarian looked up in surprise at the unusual group that had approached his desk.

"Good afternoon," said the archivist. The librarian didn't respond, simply continuing to look over their group quizzically.

"We're here because this boy has issued a challenge to a ruling I have made," explained the archivist. The librarian's head snapped back to look at the archivist.

"A what now?" he asked in surprise. The archivist chuckled knowingly before letting out a sigh.

"Yes, I was surprised too..." admitted the archivist. The man looked at Eric and tilted his head in confusion.

"A challenge?" asked the old librarian. Eric simply nodded in response. The librarian looked him up and down, raising an eyebrow as he sized up the scruffy boy who stood before him.

"How have you even come to learn of such a thing?" asked the librarian. Eric shuffled nervously on his feet.

"Well... I've read through all of my great grandfather's old books and journals from during the great war..." explained Eric.

"Your great grandfather was a knight?" asked the librarian, intrigued.

"Sir Heinrich Rothmane," confirmed Eric with a nod. The librarian's eyebrows shot up in recognition as he looked Eric up and down once more. William couldn't help but smile in adoration at

Eric. The fact that he'd even managed to get them this far was astonishing. He was every bit as brilliant as William had always known he was, and finally other people were recognizing it. The old man hummed, deep in thought before looking back up at the archivist.

"Well, I suppose it's possible that challenges must still be upheld, but it's the first I've heard of them since I was a mere page..." admitted the man. It was at this moment that it suddenly dawned on William that every single one of the librarians here were knights too. He looked around at all of the intelligent looking nobles stationed around the room and felt a chill run down his spine again. How had Eric managed to get them so close to their goal already? The old librarian leaned forward in his chair.

"So, what was the ruling which is being challenged?" asked the librarian, dipping his quill into his pot of ink in preparation for documenting their exchange.

"Well..." began the archivist, clearing his throat awkwardly.

"The ruling is that commoners may not be enrolled into the college via trial by combat..." said the archivist shaking his head in disbelief at the words which were coming out of his own mouth. Immediately the librarian snapped his head back up and stared at the archivist in shock. There was a short pause while the man simply sat open mouthed, looking over the bunch in confusion while his readied quill dripped ink on his parchment.

"Trial by combat?!" gasped the man, looking Eric up and down again, before tilting his head as he seemed to be deeming him suitably sized for such a task.

"The college hasn't seen a trial by combat since... well since before even my parents' time..." said the old man, shaking his head.

"Yes, but the boy's challenge is that they may still be written in the college constitution," explained the archivist. The old man laughed.

"Preposterous!" he exclaimed, shaking his head.

"Yes, indeed... but still..." replied the archivist, uncomfortably shifting on the spot again. The man shook his head at first, but then tilted his head deep in thought, looking back at Eric again.

"Sir?" asked the archivist after waiting for a moment. The old librarian was pulled back to reality, letting out a sigh.

"I suppose we'd better check the constitution then," said the librarian. The archivist bowed his head thankfully as the old librarian reached over to the side of his desk and pulled a small piece of silk rope. The rope was attached to a mechanism at the top of his desk which, when engaged, raised a little flag with the order of the owl crest upon it. William jumped back in surprise when the little flag popped out, bumping into Azalea who giggled at his antics. Suddenly a young man who couldn't have been much older than William hurried over to their desk. He was wearing similar blue robes to all the other librarians, but he was considerably younger. As he reached the side of their desk, he bowed politely to their group before closing the flag mechanism back up with his hand and looking at the librarian expectantly.

"Squire, fetch us a copy of the current college constitution," commanded the librarian. The squire nodded obediently and went to set off, but suddenly the archivist grabbed him by his sleeve to stop him.

"What about the trial by combat?" asked the archivist. The librarian let out a sigh.

"We're not going to need to go that far," said the librarian, shaking his head. The archivist looked at Eric, seemingly sizing him up before turning back to the librarian.

"I wouldn't be so sure. On the off chance that the boy is right, I certainly don't know those rules by heart, do you?" asked the archivist. The librarian seemed to consider his words, before once again releasing an annoyed sigh.

"Fine. Squire, also fetch..." the librarian seemed to stop in his tracks. There was a long moment of silence as the squire patiently awaited the librarian's order. The librarian looked searchingly at the archivist who simply shrugged in response.

"The pathway of pedigree IV: a modern manual to the art of chivalry, written by Magister Ulfric ... first edition, Sir..." said Eric suddenly, bowing his head apologetically. The librarian swallowed nervously.

"Magister Ulfric's pathway of pedigree you say?" confirmed the librarian uneasily. Eric nodded confidently. The librarian stared back at him for a moment before once again letting out a sigh.

"Yes, that... but whatever edition is newest," he said, clearing his throat awkwardly. The squire nodded obediently before hurrying off and disappearing down a hallway at the back of the room.

"Don't get your hopes up boy," said the librarian suddenly, raising an eyebrow at Eric. The archivist nodded his head in agreement.

"Even if it turns out that you've found a tricky little loophole here, that's all it'll be," said the librarian conceitedly.

"What do you mean?" asked Eric, confused.

"Look, even if these things haven't technically been officially removed from the college's guidelines, that doesn't mean they're obligated to follow through on any of this," explained the archivist.

"If it's in the college constitution, how could they not follow through?" asked Eric, bewildered.

"Something as groundbreaking as a commoner entering the college would need to go through the magister's office at the very least. It would likely require that the rector himself sign off on it. Even still, if somehow you managed to get the rector's approval, which you likely wouldn't, the idea of a commoner in the college would be quite offensive to many high-ranking officials," explained the archivist soberly. William felt his hope at the situation leaving his body more and more with every word that came out of the archivist's mouth.

"None of that will matter anyway," said the librarian dismissively.

"Want to bet on it?" asked Eric, combatively. The librarian scowled at him disdainfully.

"Listen boy, if you're so smart, I suppose you realize that a trial by combat was actually held between man and monster, yes?" he asked, smirking at Eric smugly.

"Yes sir, I'm relying on it," replied Eric confidently, surprising everybody, but most of all William.

"What?!" exclaimed the librarian.

"Yeah, Eric. Um, what?" asked William, suddenly feeling his doubt in Eric's plan intensifying. At that moment the squire emerged back into their room and hurried over to their desk holding a scroll and a book. He handed both to the librarian before running back over to his station at the side of the room. The librarian and archivist hurriedly got to work reading through the constitution. As soon as the group descended into silence, Ivar turned around and began walking towards the door.

"Don't go anywhere," said the archivist, looking up at the knights.

"You're going to make us wait here?" asked Ivar, despondently.

"Yes, for my report I need to interview you on how the three of you have become wrapped up in this situation," replied the archivist absent mindedly. August and Azalea exchanged worried glances.

"Report?" asked Ivar nervously.

"No…" said the librarian suddenly, stopping rifling through the scroll he was reading. He and the archivist both stared at the scroll speechlessly for a moment.

"There it is…" said the archivist, swallowing nervously. There was another moment of silence before he slapped a hand on his forehead in exasperation.

"Do you have any idea what this means for me?! If word gets out that challenges are still a thing, I'll be buried in paperwork until the day I die! I'm the first line of defense for those snob-nosed noble parents to come to with their complaints about the college! They'll challenge me about all sorts of trivial affairs! I'll never get another day of rest!" groaned the archivist in despair.

"Shh!" hushed the librarian, annoyed by the archivist's theatrics.

"That's nothing! Look!" he said, his eyes open wide in shock. He was pointing to another section, buried deep in the bowels of the constitution.

"The college shall uphold all enrollment processes set forth by the magister's office…" read the archivist. William and Eric exchanged excited grins.

"It's actually there…" said the archivist, dumbstruck.

"Hold on now, we still don't know if this applies to the trial by combat!" insisted the librarian, putting the constitution scroll aside and picking up the book.

"Okay, let's see, let's see…" said the librarian, opening the book and searching for any kind of contents page or appendix.

"Page 347, Sir," said Eric helpfully. The librarian took the time to scowl at him before reluctantly scrolling to page 347 and raising his eyebrows in surprise. Both the librarian and the archivist silently stared at the words in the book, their jaws dropping more with every line.

"What does it say?!" asked August curiously. The entire affair really had become so bizarre that even the three knights were invested at this point. The fact that they'd been following the boys with suspicions of being extorted at first had apparently completely left their minds.

"The trial by combat is a newly approved process by which the kingdom's mightiest fighters may join the ranks of knighthood, should they prove their value in battle with the denizens of the gateway. An event shall be held by the college, in which applicants will face off in one-on-one mortal combat with a denizen of the gateway. The monster is to be provided by the college. The event shall be held within an arena such that neither man nor monster may flee. The battle is deemed to have been a victory when only the fighter remains on the battlefield. If the gateway creature provided by the college is of a breed which separates into smaller beings upon being slain, or features any similar characteristics, the fighter may only be declared a victor when a monster has been completely defeated," read the archivist aloud, also beginning to draw the attention of some other nearby librarians who had begun listening in. The librarian looked back up at Eric.

"Surely you see how this can't happen," explained the librarian with a shrug.

"I see no such thing," replied Eric confidently. The librarian stared at him dumbfounded.

"Boy, have you lost your mind? It clearly states that a gateway monster must be provided by the college. Magister Ulfric wrote these rules in a time when the gateway was still open. I don't know if you'd forgotten, but it's been closed for a century!" shouted the librarian. Eric smiled assuredly.

"That's not our problem," he replied flatly. The librarian and archivist exchanged a flabbergasted look.

"What?!" exclaimed the librarian.

"Our task is simply to pass the trial. The text clearly states that the trial will be passed once William here is the only one left standing in the arena. If you can't provide a monster for him to face... well then... I suppose he'd just win by default then, right?" asked Eric. William felt that familiar feeling of awe and pride at Eric welling in his chest. Even the three knights exchanged shocked laughs at his audacity.

"The rector would never allow this. Never!" yelled the librarian, clearly offended by the way that Eric was twisting the college's constitution to his favor.

"Are you sure? Judging by the statue of the man stationed directly out the front of this very library, I would've thought that the rector would've held Magister Ulfric's rules in quite some high regard," poked Eric.

"Preposterous! This is an affront to the college! An attack on chivalry itself! I have personally met the rector many times, and I can assure you that you'll never get his signature on this. Never!" bellowed the librarian, banging his fist on the desk angrily, startling some of the other library workers.

"Get out! All of you, get out!" commanded the librarian, angrily waving his hand for their group to leave. The ruckus was drawing the attention of the guards who began walking towards their desk.

"You can't kick us out! You must follow through on this! It's your job!" exclaimed Eric angrily. The archivist grabbed him by the arm and began leading him away from the desk.

"Don't worry boy, you're right. He might be angry, but he still has to pass this on. Come on," said the archivist, looking anxiously at the approaching guards. Eric reluctantly backed away from the table as their group began retreating towards the front of the library.

"Come on," said the guards, appreciating that the group seemed to be cooperating. Everybody silently walked back out the front doors of the building and out into the dusk light on the marble stairs outside. As the knights retrieved their confiscated weapons, Eric released an angry grunt, looking back over his shoulder at the door of the library as though he wanted to run back inside.

"Eric, it's alright. You heard him, he has to send it on to the… guy," said William, already forgetting the title of the man that had been talked about in the previous conversation. Eric looked at William and let out a frustrated sigh.

"It's not about that. It's not fair… because he's right," said Eric despondently. The archivist put a consoling hand on Eric's shoulder.

"I must say, as much as I wanted to see your plan come to fruition, the rector would never sign off on this," agreed the archivist.

"How can that be?!" asked William.

"What's the point of having all of these rules if some high up noble can just say no anyway?!" he questioned, starting to inherit some of the anger and frustration that Eric was feeling.

"Welcome to Oxgate," said the archivist with a wry smile. As the three of them continued to discuss their predicament, suddenly

Ivar grabbed August and Azalea by their arms and pulled them aside. The three knights began chattering away together excitedly, a plan of their own beginning to form. Just what were William and Eric going to be able to do from here, and how would the rector respond to their challenge?

CHAPTER TWENTY-FOUR
The Trials of Rothmane III

Evening was beginning to fall, and the last rays of the golden hour were dancing on the water of the ornate fountain in front of them. William, Eric and the archivist stood on the marble steps, quietly discussing their options. The archivist suddenly noticed that the three knights were huddled together having an excited, whispered conversation.

"Hey!" exclaimed the archivist, suddenly drawing them out of their conversation with a jolt.

"What are you going to do with these two?" asked the archivist, gesturing to William and Eric.

"Right!" said Ivar, suddenly hurrying over towards Eric and William.

"Listen boys, we're going to need you to stick around for a while…" said Ivar, looking between the pair of them. William stared back blankly.

"You want us to stay here?" asked Eric confused. Ivar nodded affirmatively.

"Where are we to stay?" asked Eric, looking around at the lavish library surrounded by naught but empty fields.

"There's a decent Inn called 'the blue lantern' within the noble district not too far from this fellow's office," said August, nodding towards the archivist.

"It's Roland," said the archivist despondently.

"No, it's definitely called the blue lantern," replied August assuredly.

"My name! My name is Roland! We've been over this so many times, August! We studied together for crying out loud!" yelled the archivist.

"Forgive him Roland. The only thing this man cares about is how hard you can swing your sword. He's never remembered the name of a single knight who chose the research route," said Azalea, rolling her eyes.

"Is that so wrong of me?! What can I say? I love to battle!" defended August with a shrug.

"What about Bonnie?" asked William, bringing their attention back to the topic at hand. A long silence formed as August stared at him blankly.

"Our horse," added Eric helpfully.

"Oh! The blue lantern has an attached stable of course," replied August with a nod.

"Wow, an Inn with an attached stable?" exclaimed William, awe struck by the facilities provided in the city.

"Yeah, about that. An Inn in the upper district? We don't have that kind of money," admitted Eric honestly. William hung his head shamefully. He was leeching off of the little hard-earned money that Eric had brought with them. He'd left his own home with nothing but the clothes on his back. Thus far he'd contributed nothing to their journey but woe.

"Ivar, you already have a running bond of debt with them, yes?" asked Azalea expectantly. Ivar looked around desperately at everybody else, but eventually let out a defeated sigh.

"Fine! I'll pay for it, but only until… well until I tell you to get out, do you understand?" asked Ivar. Eric and William both nodded obediently.

"Well now, we have somewhere we need to be, so…" began Ivar, beginning to turn away before Roland grabbed him by the arm.

"Not so fast. You have to come back to my office. I need to write my report, remember?" asked Roland. Ivar groaned in frustration.

"Now is not the time!" exclaimed Ivar, looking at the other two knights expectantly.

"Roland dear, can't we please do this another time?" asked Azalea, smiling at him pleadingly. Roland let out a sigh.

"This is a big deal, you know. All of this. I still don't have the foggiest idea of how the three of you are even wrapped up in this," explained Roland, looking at them suspiciously.

"We'll come by your office tomorrow to sort it all out," offered Azalea. Roland reluctantly nodded his head.

"If I get reprimanded for this, you must take the fall then. If they ask why you haven't been interviewed, I'll simply tell them that you refused," said Roland. The three knights nodded in agreement.

"Well, come on then you two. I'll point you towards the Inn," said Roland, beginning to walk back down the road. William and Eric bowed politely at the three knights, who at this point were already chattering excitedly and leaving in another direction.

"What do you suppose they're up to?" asked Eric suspiciously.

"I don't care. We're staying at an Inn for nobles tonight Eric!" said William excitedly. The two boys shared a sweet moment of unbridled excitement. Even if Eric's plan to get William enrolled wasn't going quite as smoothly as he'd hoped, the two of them had already made it further than they could've ever dreamed on their first day in Oxgate.

***

The chancellor leaned back in his chair and took a sip of port from his fancy golden goblet, washing down the last of his celebratory turkey dinner. He'd done well. He'd done very well. Not only were all of the next semester's academic programs budgeted, finalized, and signed off, but he'd secured an enormous stipend from a Castellian noble family for a new enrollment in the college. The lion's share of their preposterous international student fees generally ended up in amenities funds, however with a payout this large his office would certainly be seeing some new furnishings too. He looked around at the beautiful room bathed in rich mahogany furniture and intricate golden ornaments. For every new foreign noble child that was shipped over here to begin training as a page, the chancellor would be able to add a new article to its contents. What more did it even need though? Perhaps a new rug? He was suddenly pulled from his musing as a ruckus began to erupt from downstairs. He sat up anxiously in his chair, listening intently to try to hear what the arguing voices were yelling about. It didn't take long however for the argument and accompanying stomping footsteps to work their way directly up to his closed office door. It was thrown open roughly, revealing the last three people in the world he wanted to see right now.

"Gertrude! I told you not to let them in!" growled the chancellor furiously at his aide who was standing behind the three knights, looking rather flustered.

"I tried, Sir! I'm sorry!" she cried, fluttering about anxiously behind them as she tried to make eye contact with her boss over August's hulking shoulders.

"Aha! I told you she was lying! He is here!" exclaimed August, pointing at the chancellor.

"Why are you in my office!?" asked the chancellor furiously, standing up from his desk.

"Why are you trying to keep me out?!" retorted August, looking around the room suspiciously.

"Why do you think?!" asked the chancellor angrily. Azalea squeezed her way past August.

"I'm sorry sir, but we have very important news that can't wait!" she explained, bowing her head respectfully to the chancellor. As Ivar sheepishly joined his comrades, the chancellor looked over the three of them and let out a frustrated sigh.

"Fine! Gertrude, close the door…" said the chancellor reluctantly, sitting back down in his chair and rubbing his temples. His aide nodded obediently and closed the door gently behind the knights.

"What's so important that it couldn't wait until tomorrow?" asked the chancellor, looking out of his window at the twilight shadows beginning to fall over his fancy back garden.

"We know what to do about the tax problem!" declared August confidently. The chancellor returned to his desk and assessed the three of them derisively.

"That's not my problem anymore," he said, leaning back in his chair and crossing his arms.

"What?!" exclaimed August.

"I had the matter looked into. Such responsibilities do not fall under the purview of my position as chancellor," he explained smugly.

"But… it falls under our purview as knights?" asked Ivar, raising an eyebrow.

"Of course. A knight's purview is to carry out whatever task the kingdom asks of them. A chancellor's responsibilities revolve specifically around the workings of the college. They are somewhat more specific I'm afraid," explained the chancellor, taking an arrogant sip from his goblet.

"The Duke asked for you to be involved directly! We were all there! We all saw it!" yelled August. The chancellor laughed.

"I'm afraid that's inconsequential! He simply got caught up in the moment!" replied the chancellor with a shrug. The three knights exchanged incredulous looks with one another.

"Will you at least hear out our plan?" asked Azalea. The chancellor shook his head.

"I'm afraid it's not my problem. Now if you'll excuse me, I have a hot meal waiting for me at home," lied the chancellor, subtly nudging his empty plate aside while looking at the knights expectantly. The knights wanted to object, but at this point there was little they could do. He'd really managed to worm his way out of accepting any responsibility for the matter at all. After exchanging a defeated glance, they reticently stood up to leave.

"Well, thank you for seeing us anyway…" said Azalea politely. The chancellor nodded his head as he watched the knights turning to leave.

"I guess we have no choice then," said Ivar hesitantly to Azalea.

"Do you think he'll still be in his office?" asked Azalea.

"He's the rector. I'm sure with the college having received such an unprecedented request he probably has quite a lot on his plate right now…" reasoned Ivar on his way out the door.

"Wait!" exclaimed the chancellor suddenly. The three knights stopped in their tracks and turned back to face him expectantly.

"The rector, did you say?" asked the chancellor, his voice cracking. The three knights nodded as he cleared his throat awkwardly.

"And you said something about an odd request?" asked the chancellor curiously. Again, the three knights exchanged unsure glances with one another.

"We probably shouldn't be discussing the rector's business with other people," said August, bowing his head apologetically. Immediately the chancellor felt his blood beginning to boil.

"It involves the taxation issue too, so as you said; it's not really your problem. This should probably be kept between the rector and the Duke. Please, just go ahead and enjoy your meal sir," said Ivar, bowing his head politely before turning to leave. The chancellor pounded his fist on the desk angrily, causing some of the golden statuettes which littered it to topple over. He instantly realized how uncomely his outburst was and reached out to straighten up the figurines. He looked back up at the three knights and took a deep breath.

"Alright, get back in here!" he said angrily, beckoning for the knights to close the door and come back. The knights obliged him, coming back and sitting down.

"Listen, we need to get one thing straight. I am sick of people thinking that the rector is somehow above me. The only thing he controls is the library. All other college matters are my responsibility. Do you understand?" asked the chancellor, looking each of them in their eyes intently.

"Hmm..." hummed Ivar distrustfully. The chancellor again raised his fist to bang on his table angrily but caught himself and simply rubbed his bald head in frustration instead.

"You said something about an odd request that the college received. If it's a request for the college it should come straight to my desk, not his!" yelled the chancellor furiously. The three knights feigned surprised glances with one another.

"Oh, we didn't know that!" lied Azalea. The chancellor shook his head angrily.

"Does he do this a lot? Taking college matters into his own hands?" he asked. The three knights shrugged. The chancellor let out another sigh.

"Go on then. Explain the situation to me," said the chancellor, leaning back in his chair and taking an angry sip from his goblet. And with that, Ivar's plan started to come to fruition, as the three knights began to explain William's bizarre trial by combat enrollment request.

***

The chancellor leaned his head on his fists, listening intently to their story.

"...and so the request has been passed on to the rector, who will surely decline to sign it," finished Ivar, leaning back in his chair, exhausted from his monologue. The chancellor nodded his head and leaned back in his chair too. He thought about the situation deeply before responding.

"I certainly hope you didn't come here expecting me to approve the idea of this 'trial by combat' nonsense," said the chancellor. The idea of a commoner enrolling in his college sent a wave of distaste flowing through his chest. He'd lose the respect of swathes of nobles if he allowed such a thing.

"No sir, of course not. We'd never do that to the rector. We just wanted your council on the matter," lied Ivar. The chancellor immediately bit the bait, staring straight at him, invigorated by his words.

"What do you mean? Do what to the rector?" asked the chancellor curiously.

"Well sir, of course, this whole affair being the result of him not striking outdated clauses from his records, in addition to his staff members not knowing what's written in their own constitution. It's... well it's not a good look. It would look even worse if we went above his head and had you sign off on the matter after he's already refused it. Imagine if a commoner was allowed to enroll in the college and it was all because of his oversight! All of the blame could surely only fall on the rector's shoulders considering the circumstances. All would begin to doubt his prowess..." said Ivar, expertly manipulating the chancellor's mind like a puppeteer. The chancellor once again took the bait, his eyes lighting up in delight at the mere thought of the idea.

"Now, hold on a moment," began the chancellor, standing up and beginning to pace behind his desk, unable to stay still in his excitement.

"You said that this trial by combat was held between man and monster, yes?" asked the chancellor, confused.

"Yes sir," confirmed Ivar.

"So how could it be held at all? The gateway has been closed for over a century," said the chancellor, pausing his pacing for a moment to stare at Ivar quizzically. Here it was. This was where Ivar really needed to get things right.

"Yes sir, well..." began Ivar.

"There technically are still gateway monsters crawling about. It's just that they're only in one place. Any knight that has been stationed in the desert has seen them, including us! They're nothing compared to what our ancestors faced, so we typically wouldn't call them 'gateway monsters', but to those who have never seen one before, they are like horrors straight out of their wildest nightmares. No one from Oxgate has ever seen anything like them, I assure you," explained Ivar.

"All who set eyes upon the beasts would surely be terrified! I still remember my first time. I felt like running back to Oxgate!" added August, the word of one of the kingdom's mightiest warriors carrying quite some weight on the matter. The chancellor seemed to be nodding along. He looked almost excited by the idea.

"Indeed, I had forgotten about those strange desert creatures. The mere descriptions I've heard of those foul beasts is enough to send a chill down my spine just thinking about them. But if we hold a demonstration out in the desert, there's no point in any of this. The only people out there are clerics and knights anyway," thought the chancellor aloud.

"That's why we want to bring one of the monsters here," explained Azalea with a confident nod.

"Bringing a gateway monster to Oxgate? That's madness!" exclaimed the chancellor, flabbergasted.

"Indeed, we've all sworn an oath in our knighthood that we shall never allow there to be a monster within the walls of Oxgate," agreed Ivar.

"But, this is why we want to hold the event in the barracks. It's outside of Oxgate's walls. The infantry stationed there are all commoners and low nobles, and it already has an arena. This is where the taxation issues might be solvable. Perhaps this is all a serendipity..." said Ivar, again capturing the chancellor's attention.

"What do you mean?" asked the chancellor, ceasing his pacing to stare at Ivar, captivated by his words.

"The barracks is close enough to Oxgate that those nobles who are interested can come and watch. Word about the event would spread quite well. Whether the boy succeeded in his trial or not, the masses should be satisfied that there is still a need for a college," said Ivar. There was a short silence while the chancellor considered their plan. They had a point. If the people of Oxgate got a firsthand look at one of those monsters, their doubts in the need for the college would surely be largely abated.

"How exactly would you get one of those beasts to Oxgate? That's not a minor concern. Who would go to the desert to do it? Would it be you?" asked the chancellor. The three knights exchanged a knowing glance.

"Slaying one of those monsters is one thing, but capturing it and safely transporting it all the way here? That's a totally different story…" said Ivar, shaking his head. The chancellor nodded in agreement.

"But…" Ivar then began, raising a finger.

"What if the one man who could do this without a doubt was already out there? What if it was a knight outclassed by none, who the commoners literally sing songs about?" asked Ivar, raising an eyebrow as he saw realization dawning on the chancellor's face.

"Surely there's no way he'd come back for something like this!" exclaimed the chancellor, unconvinced.

"The challenge of wrangling one of those things and bringing it back to Oxgate might be the exact kind of excitement he's looking for, don't you think?" asked August eagerly. The chancellor thought about their plan.

"If word spread that he was coming home for this event, that might be enough to get everybody in Oxgate excited about it…" thought the chancellor aloud.

"This is one of the places where we hit a bit of a wall. How are we supposed to contact him? We don't exactly have Kane's contact details written down. Even when we were students together, the man barely said a word to any one of us except August," explained Ivar. The chancellor let out a frustrated sigh.

"I must admit, even I have trouble contacting Kane. Just take a look at his order! It's chaos! His students have barely ever even set eyes on him! His own son included! No matter how many times I write to him, he doesn't seem to care. If he won't even come back to manage his order, what makes you think he cares about the college enough to help us with this?" asked the chancellor despondently.

"Well, if he received a letter from the Duke, perhaps he wouldn't have a choice..." thought Ivar aloud. The chancellor's eyes opened wide in realization. He looked between the three knights suspiciously before leaning back and releasing an impressed sigh.

"Well, well, well. You really got me!" admitted the chancellor shaking his head in disbelief. The three knights feigned ignorance, tilting their heads and looking back at him like three, confused, innocent puppy dogs.

"You didn't come here for my council at all! You just want me to contact the Duke for you!" said the chancellor in disbelief.

"Sir, if I may. I know that you said solving this taxation issue was not your problem, but would this not be ideal? It would be cleaning up the mess that the rector has made, and at the same time solving a problem for not just the college, but the whole kingdom. How could the Duke look at this in any other light than as an absolute win?" asked Ivar earnestly. The chancellor seemed intrigued by his words, but still a little unsure.

"Listen, if I do this, I need you to give me some assurances," said the chancellor, filling all three knights with excitement.

"Firstly, if it seems like this commoner boy might pass the combat trial, I need you to step in and finish the beast off. I want this event to undoubtedly demonstrate that a knight is needed to combat such a creature. If the boy manages to do it himself, the impact of the event will be diluted. I also need to be able to assure the Duke that no commoners will truly be making their way into the college as a result of this," explained the chancellor.

"He's never even held a blade before sir, I don't think we need to worry about that," explained Ivar.

"He's a very timid boy," agreed Azalea.

"One sight of that monster and he'll be banging at the gate with wet pants," agreed August with a haughty chuckle. The chancellor seemed relieved to hear this.

"Secondly, if anything goes wrong. Anything at all, you three will take all of the blame," said the chancellor, looking at the three of them seriously. For a moment, the three knights exchanged an uneasy glance with one another, but after considering their circumstances, reticently nodded in agreement. They didn't have much of a choice. If they didn't want the Duke to reprimand them for the happenings in Mistfall, this was the best solution they had to the taxation problem. The chancellor suddenly clapped his hands together.

"Good! Well then, I have some preparations to make. Firstly, I'll be issuing a formal request to the library that the rector update the college constitution to remove this trial by combat nonsense," said the chancellor, his eyes gleaming excitedly by the prospect of reprimanding the rector. He suddenly looked up at the knights.

"Why are you still here? Go on. Get out! I've got work to do!" he exclaimed, shooing the three of them out the door. The three knights obliged him happily, taking their leave with polite bows. As they walked out of the chancellor's office and into the night, they continued their excited babbling about their wildly successful meeting with the chancellor. The air around them was filled with zest, as even they found themselves excited by the show they were planning to put on in the college's name.

CHAPTER TWENTY-FIVE
The Blue Lantern

The inn was abuzz with activity. Everywhere the boys looked was another table packed with animated noble folk, laughing and conversing loudly.

"Alright, this is where I leave you," said Roland suddenly, patting both boys on their shoulders. William spun around to look at him desperately. He felt like they were being dropped in the deep end here. When Roland saw the look on his face, he smiled reassuringly.

"Don't worry kid, you'll be alright. Ivar said he's paying for everything so…" said Roland, suddenly seeming to get an idea. He abruptly made his way over to the bar.

"Gerald!" he shouted, attracting the attention of the man working behind the bar.

"What can I do for you Roland?" asked the barkeep, pouring a beer for another customer.

"These two boys need a room for the night, courtesy of Sir Ivar. They'll also need a bath, and a fresh change of clothes. Add it to what he owes!" said Roland. William suddenly felt even more self-conscious as he looked around at the well-dressed nobles who were regarding him and Eric disdainfully. William had never even so much as dipped a toe in a hot spring. He'd certainly never had a proper bath.

"Maud! Room and a bath!" called out the barkeep, handing a man his beer and beginning to fill another. Roland looked over his shoulder nervously.

"Ivar would also like a bottle of your finest Castellian red..." said Roland, clearing his throat awkwardly. The barkeep shot him a quizzical glance but then shrugged. He handed the second man his beer before reaching under his counter and pulling out a nice-looking bottle of wine. Roland accepted it eagerly and then seemed to remember that the two boys were still watching him. He laughed nervously as he looked between the two of them.

"Don't worry he uh... he owes me..." said Roland, beginning to back away towards the door.

"Wait-" began William before somebody whistled suddenly from behind him. When he turned around, he saw a stout middle-aged lady with short auburn hair looking him and Eric over with her hands on her hips.

"Are you boys in town for the squire exams?" asked the lady curiously. William looked to Eric and saw him nodding sheepishly. She shook her head as she assessed their dirty, torn clothes in disbelief.

"What have they had the two of you doing? I swear, they're expecting too much from young pages these days!" she exclaimed, turning around and beckoning for the two of them to follow her. She led them around a corner and up some stairs. William was still in awe at how large this Inn was. Back at home they had an inn, but it was not much more than a small cottage with two rooms for the occasional traveling merchants to stay in overnight. This place was enormous by contrast. Upstairs was just as fancy too, with serene artworks along the walls and nice lanterns and candles lighting the halls.

"My youngest boy's a page too. Bit young for the exams still, but when he's old enough I'm hoping for him to be an owl like my oldest. Safer that way. Course, his father's hoping for the lion," said the lady, rolling her eyes and shaking her head. She continued to lead them up yet another staircase before stopping at one of the rooms. She opened the door with her key and led the way in.

"Here we are boys," she said, beckoning for them to come in with her. When the two entered the room, both of their mouths opened at the spacious, beautiful, cozy abode that had been provided for them. Unlike their cots at home, the beds featured proper mattresses and even fancy linens with down pillows.

"We get a lot of students here, so we've got the beds separated. If you have any more joining you then you'll need to pay more. Don't go trying to sneak any extras in here, trust me, I'll know," she said sternly, looking between the two boys. Both nodded obediently. William suddenly felt tears unexpectedly welling in his eyes. He wasn't sure what caused it, so quickly turned and wiped them away while the lady was walking towards the wardrobe.

"Now, you've only got the one chest, but the wardrobe is a nice big one," she said, approaching the wardrobe and reaching out to open it. William felt butterflies suddenly form in his stomach as soon as she opened the wardrobe doors.

"No…" he murmured, reaching out to stop her. Luckily, all she revealed inside was an empty wardrobe, but he had half expected to see Annemarie.

"We have all of our gear in our cart in the stables…" said Eric, not having noticed William's subdued antics. Immediately the lady held up her hand.

"Don't you worry dear, Gerald will be sending one of the boys up with it in no time. If I were you I'd worry more about having a bath," said the lady, raising her eyebrows and looking them over. Both boys blushed in embarrassment.

"Oh worry not my dears; I'm not one to judge. They've got you pages doing all sorts of dirty work. Now, will you be needing fresh gowns? That'll cost extra," said the lady looking at the two of them expectantly. Eric reticently nodded his head, clearly guilty about adding even more deficit to Ivar's bond with the Blue Lantern Inn.

"Alright! I'll let them know downstairs. Here's your key," she said, handing Eric their room key.

"There's only the one. If you lose it, it'll cost you," she said, looking at the two of them sternly. Again, the two boys nodded understandingly.

"Really, you'd be surprised how often students lose their keys," she said, shaking her head.

"Anyway, that's about it! For the bath, just bring your key over to the bathhouse next door and leave it with them at the desk until you're finished. If you're staying here, you're free to use their facilities as you please," said the lady, giving the boys a smile as she walked towards the door.

"Any questions?" she asked. The two boys felt like they had a million questions, but none specifically came to mind at that moment, so they both just simply shook their heads.

"Alrighty! I'll be downstairs if you need anything. If you can't find me, ask my husband Gerald behind the bar. Well, enjoy your stay!" said the lady, closing the door behind her. For a moment William and Eric simply stared blankly at the door before they turned to each other. As soon as William made eye contact with Eric, for whatever reason, the two of them suddenly couldn't hold back laughter. William leant on Eric as the two of them laughed uncontrollably while they both succumbed to the absurdity of their situation.

"Trial by combat?!" wheezed William, looking at Eric in disbelief. Eric shrugged, continuing to laugh.

"I don't know Will, but it's gotten us this far at least, right?" asked Eric, shaking his head and sitting down on his bed. William sat down on his bed too, immediately being caught off guard by how deeply he sank into it. Eric's expression suddenly sobered a little.

"Look William, I don't know what's going on with those knights but…" began Eric. William tilted his head curiously.

"All of this?" said Eric, gesturing around at the nice lodgings they'd found themselves in.

"They must have a reason for it. Why would they be so interested in keeping us in the city?" asked Eric, deep in thought. William raised his eyebrows at his friend.

"Wow Eric. I think I need to cherish this moment!" said William, taking a deep breath while Eric looked on in confusion.

"Have I actually figured something out before you?" asked William smugly. Eric raised his eyebrows in surprise.

"Why? What is it?" asked Eric curiously.

"It's because, ye know what happened in Mistfall, right?" asked William. Realization finally dawned on Eric's face. He shook his head in dismay when he realized that William had likely hit the nail on the head.

"That must be what Sir Ivar was talking about when he mentioned us having an agreement," thought Eric aloud before letting out a sigh.

"He paid me. He paid me a lot. Our agreement was that I wouldn't tell anybody about what happened there with Father Marcus dying and all..." said Eric guiltily, averting his eyes. William felt a chill run down his spine as his mind once more traveled to that harrowing night in Mistfall and the events of Lakhdorian.

"I thought he were just talking about, ye know, me pa and that... 'fraid of rumors among the common folk. I suppose he must've really been scared of word getting out here in the city..." thought Eric aloud. There was a long pause before William broke the silence.

"Eric, I know what really happened in Mistfall," said William. Immediately Eric's eyes shot up to stare back at William in surprise.

"Ye do?!" asked Eric, a guilty expression suddenly appearing on his face.

"Aye," confirmed William solemnly, his mind wandering back to his final conversations with Annemarie.

"William, I... I was so in over my head, I..." began Eric. William held up his hand.

"Do ye really think I'd blame you, Eric?" asked William earnestly. Eric stared back at him with guilty tears beginning to well in his eyes.

"It were those knights who were supposed to protect her. Not you," said William, shaking his head disdainfully.

"That's not true Will. I should've been there for her. When she needed me the most; I wasn't. I knew that she were alone with Marcus. I knew that she didn't want to be. But I still didn't do anything. The knights told me to leave them be, and I obeyed them," admitted Eric, finally breaking down as his guilt began to overwhelm him.

"Eric, they're knights! Of course you obeyed them!" exclaimed William.

"Do ye really think that helps me sleep at night?" asked Eric, staring back at William expectantly.

"The fact of the matter is, I could've helped her, but I didn't. When she needed me the most, I wasn't there for her. What kind of person does that make me William?" asked Eric, staring back at his friend with tears streaming down his face. William's expression darkened too. He shook his head.

"At least ye weren't her neighbor Eric. At least ye didn't sit in your room for months, listening to her screams. Hearing her pain. Knowing how desperately she needed you and ignoring it. All because ye were scared. All because ye weren't man enough to just walk in there and be by her side…" said William, tears beginning to form in his eyes too. The two boys sat in a sad silence as they collectively pondered their guilt and anguish. Neither of them had a word of comfort for the other, as they were both feeling the same pain.

"Those knights have forgotten she even existed. The only thing they care about is covering their asses about that cursed cleric," said William scathingly. Suddenly there was a knock at their door. The boys hurriedly wiped the tears from their eyes as William made his way over and opened the door up to reveal the inn lady standing there with two college gowns in her hands.

"I wasn't sure if this one was large enough, but after your bath, try it on and let me know if you need a larger one sweetheart!" said the lady, barging into their room and hanging the two gowns from the handles of the wardrobe. The two boys nodded their heads thankfully as the lady wandered back out of the room. There was an awkward silence after she'd left as they gathered themselves.

"Come on William. Let's finally get a good night of sleep," said Eric, standing from his bed and investigating the gowns.

"Aye," agreed William. With that, the two boys prepared themselves for their first night in the city. They waited until late at night when there were less people at the bath house before enjoying their first ever warm bath. As they babbled excitedly over how much hard work it must take to keep the waters clean and warm, they finally felt that foreign feeling of calmness wash over them. As he poured the ewers of warm water over himself, William had to keep his wound dry, but still managed to scrub every other inch of himself clean. Once back in their cozy room, the two boys tried on their fancy new college gowns before carefully hanging them up again, crawling into their comfortable beds and drifting off into a deep, well-earned slumber.

***

As William opened his eyes, it was as though time was standing still in his same old Lakhdorian bedroom. That familiar, dull gray light from the overcast sky outside was peering through his window. It felt like it had been there forever. His curtains blew in the breeze, sending dust particles swirling drearily around his room. He let out a sigh. How long had he been lying here? How long had she been gone? How long had she not?

"I'm right here," said Annemarie, pulling him from his thoughts. William sat up in his bed and rubbed his eyes sleepily. She was standing in the opposite corner of the room with her back to him. She was wearing her beautiful white solstice dress which always made William's heart flutter. She turned around to face him, revealing that she was holding a bouquet of tansies.

"I thought you were locked away…" said William, looking at his locked wardrobe. Annemarie slowly walked towards him and put a hand on his cheek, staring down into his eyes.

"I am," she said softly, taking his hand and placing the bouquet of tansies into it. William looked down and inspected the flowers curiously. There was something hidden in its center. Annemarie sat down on his bed and reached into the bouquet, removing a single black rose which had been buried beneath the tansies. She closed her eyes and lifted the rose to her face, inhaling deeply.

"I miss you so much..." said William, watching her gracefully smell the flower as the wind from the open window gently blew against her long golden locks. She slowly lowered the rose and turned to face him.

"We can be together again," she said softly, sidling slightly closer to him on the bed and taking his hand in hers.

"How?" asked William, lost in her eyes.

"I can't let you out," he said, feeling for his key which was still in his right pocket.

"You don't have to let me out. All you have to do is let me in," said Annemarie. William slowly shook his head.

"It don't feel right. I can't unlock that door," said William looking at his wardrobe, sure in his heart that he shouldn't unlock it, but unsure of why.

"Forget about that. Look," said Annemarie, grabbing him by the chin and turning his head back to face her.

"I'm already here. All you have to do is let me in," said Annemarie, staring deeply into his eyes. He swallowed nervously. All he wanted to do was to let her in, but every instinct he had was telling him that something was wrong. Suddenly William heard a loud knocking sound erupting from nowhere in particular. Annemarie looked around, her face adorning an expression of deep annoyance.

"What's that-" began William, looking around for the source of the sound. The world was starting to fade away into pale white around him.

"Hey," said Annemarie, again turning his head back to face her.

"Just remember. If you let me in, we can be together," her voice echoed as she faded away with the world around him.

***

Eric sleepily walked his way over to the door of their room as the banging continued. The second that he unlocked the door, Ivar immediately burst in, looking around their room searchingly.

"Castellian wine?!" he exclaimed, looking at Eric in disbelief.

"What?" asked Eric groggily as he tried to wake up fully enough to process Ivar's wrath. Ivar turned to look at William who was only just stirring from his slumber.

"Where is it?!" asked Ivar, squatting down and looking under their beds.

"Are you talking about the wine that Sir Roland ordered?" asked Eric, still confused. Ivar snapped his neck around and looked over at Eric. He got up to his feet and dusted off his robes, gathering himself.

"Roland you say…" murmured Ivar, deep in thought.

"How'd you sleep boys?" asked Azalea warmly as she entered the room past Eric who was still standing by the door. Before either of them could respond, August barged his way forward.

"Great news!" he exclaimed.

"We've spoken with the chancellor! And guess what; the Duke himself is personally going to see to it that your request is honored! You'll get your fight!" finished August enthusiastically. William and Eric both stood in a stunned silence as his words settled on them. Azalea drooped her shoulders and huffed in frustration at August's lack of tact.

"What?" asked William flatly, looking to Eric who seemed as shocked and confused as he was.

"The... trial by combat?" asked Eric, an expression of dread suddenly adorning his face.

"Yes!" confirmed August. Again, the room was plunged into an awkward silence as the weight of the situation settled on the boys.

"Sorry, just to clarify... I am going to actually be put into a trial by combat?" asked William, still not quite coming to grips with the situation.

"Yes!" confirmed August again.

"With a monster?" clarified William.

"Yes!" confirmed August once again, a beaming excited smile on his face. He looked around searchingly at everybody else.

"Why are you not cheering?" he asked in confusion.

"No, wait, hold on just a minute. We agreed that it was impossible for that to happen, since the gateway is closed there's nothing for him to fight!" reasoned Eric, walking over to William's side and looking over at the knights in confusion. Ivar let out a sigh.

"The circumstances have changed. It is in the college's best interests to see that the trial by combat does happen, so they'll be bringing in one of the monsters from the desert for you to fight," explained Ivar flatly, his expression quite telling as to his awareness of how unideal this situation likely was for the boys. Again, there was a moment of awkward silence as William and Eric stared speechlessly at one another.

"At least your challenge was heard though, right? Isn't this what you wanted?" asked Azalea brightly, trying to lift their spirits a little.

"I don't know how to fight!" said William as panic began to settle in. It felt like the floor had dropped out from under him. He sat down on his bed and grabbed handfuls of his hair as he felt himself beginning to hyperventilate.

"No!" exclaimed Eric, shaking his head.

"This doesn't make any sense! Why would the college go to all that trouble?! Why would the Duke care about..." began Eric, before his eyes began to wander as his brain whirred into action. Suddenly his gaze rose up to meet Ivar's, who gulped in anticipation, averting his eyes awkwardly.

"This is about taxes, isn't it?" asked Eric, looking between the three knights searchingly. August and Azalea exchanged a surprised glance at Eric's deductive reasoning. Eric shook his head in disdain.

"Taxes?" asked William, looking up at Eric and tilting his head.

"It's all people have been talking about lately. You hear it all the time, right? People complaining about the taxes that go to the college?" asked Eric, turning to William. The last that William had heard about taxes was back in Lakhdorian when mortician Cotswold had told him that he was unsatisfied with the amount of tax that was paid to the knight's college.

"They want this to be a spectacle, don't they?" asked Eric with a sigh, sitting down on his bed. Azalea stammered for a tactful response before simply nodding her head.

"Why do you boys look so glum?!" asked August, raising an eyebrow in confusion.

"I'd have killed for a chance to battle one of those things when I was your age!" he exclaimed, a fire lit behind his eyes.

"I've never even touched a sword in my life..." said William, shaking his head and rubbing his face in despair.

"So what?" asked August, still confused. William looked up at him incredulously.

"Those things really aren't that bad you know! Naught mightier than a wild dog! Half the time you approach one it gets all scared and tries to bury itself in the sand! Really! They're nothing to be afraid of!" he said assuredly. William and Eric exchanged an unsure glance with one another. William remembered what the gypsies had told him about the monsters in the desert being dangerous enough that they were still unable to return home. He'd never imagined that they were talking about actual gateway monsters.

"Listen boys, we have a plan. Those things might look scary, but they're sheepish creatures. They'll only fight if cornered, and even then, they're far more inclined to run away than to engage," explained Azalea, squatting down and putting a reassuring hand on William's shoulder.

"We won't let anything happen to you. If it seems like the monster is getting the upper hand, August here will come into the arena and finish it off," explained Azalea, again looking between the two boys as she tried to reassure them both. William and Eric remained quiet as they processed her words.

"I don't know the first thing about fighting..." admitted William shamefully. August let out a pained sigh, looking at the other two knights deep in thought for a moment.

"I can teach you the basics," he said with an assured nod. Ivar immediately kicked him in the shin and shook his head desperately.

"Come on, it's just the basics!" exclaimed August. Eric watched the two of them intently before realization suddenly appeared on his face.

"Okay! We accept!" he shouted suddenly, hopping up from the bed and clapping his hands together, much to the chagrin of Ivar who let out a frustrated sigh.

"William will fight in the trial by combat, guided by the training of Sir August!" declared Eric enthusiastically. William stared blankly at Eric. He clearly knew something that William didn't. Whatever it was seemed to have given him an incredible boost of confidence. Even though William still didn't feel any confidence in himself, he was smart enough to know that going along with Eric's plans usually ended far better for him than trusting his own instincts. He stood up and faked an enthusiastic smile for the knights too.

"I'd be honored to be your student!" announced William, holding his fake smile as he tried to hide his fear.

"Great! Well, come and meet me in the fields near the library in an hour. I'll be there training some of Azalea's eldest squires, so you're either there or you miss out," said August, looking down at William seriously. William gulped and nodded his head understandingly. August patted him roughly on the shoulder and then turned away to follow Ivar who had already begun leaving. Azalea nodded to the two boys before following after her compatriots. As she was leaving, she looked over her shoulder at the boys one last time. William noticed a look of concern come across her face momentarily before she disappeared. Once they'd left, he turned to Eric uneasily.

"Eric, I sure hope ye've got a plan, cos I've got to be honest with ye; I'm kind of soiling my pants over here," admitted William, panic coursing through his body. The idea of being locked in a cage with a gateway monster filled him with nothing but horror.

"So you didn't notice it after all..." replied Eric cryptically, grinning and beginning to make his bed.

"Notice what?!" asked William, his interest piqued. Eric raised a mischievous eyebrow as he fluffed his pillows.

"When Sir August said he'd train you, did you see how worried the other two knights were?" asked Eric. William thought back to that moment. He remembered that Ivar had kicked August in the shin.

"It was a bit strange..." said William, scratching his chin as he thought back to it. Eric nodded his head.

"And what about all that taxation business? How would having you compete in a trial by combat help them with that?" asked Eric, tucking in his blanket. This time William was completely stumped. He felt shame rise in his chest once more that he was again showing how intellectually out of his depth he was.

"I don't know Eric. I'm a moron, in case you hadn't noticed!" exclaimed William, sitting back down on his bed in a huff.

"Hey! No William, yer not a moron!" said Eric, turning around and staring down at William seriously.

"This is exactly my point! There ain't no reason that having you complete the combat trial would help them. Not unless you were to fail and need a big tough knight to save ye," explained Eric, punching William lightly on the shoulder. William raised his eyebrow curiously.

"Ye mean like... to prove how strong they are?" asked William.

"Aye. Now yer gettin' it," replied Eric with a cheeky grin, turning away and starting to don his new college robes. William thought back to what Azalea had said again.

"She said that the monster was going to be real weak, right?" asked William. Eric nodded his head. Suddenly William's expression darkened.

"That means they think I'm gonna be a pushover, don't it?" asked William. Eric stammered for a moment, turning to William and looking over him with concern.

"William, it don't matter what any of these nobles think of us. Do you see how they've been treatin' me just because of my name? I'm no different than you. I'm just a farm boy too," said Eric earnestly. William shook his head, his mind a million miles away. If they had any idea of what he'd been through they'd never underestimate him. He didn't care if they were knights, if they'd come face to face with Annemarie that night they'd have pissed themselves and ran in the opposite direction. A feeling of conviction suddenly washed over him. They may think that he's a weakling, but they had no idea how hard he'd fought for his life. They had no idea what he'd endured. He was going to show them that commoners aren't pushovers whose lives can just be thrown aside for political gains. He was going to show them all what commoners were really capable of.

CHAPTER TWENTY-SIX
Proving Grounds

"Hey, just wait a minute William!" implored Eric, grabbing at William's shoulder to get him to stop. William pulled his shoulder away and let out a groan of annoyance as he turned back to face his friend.

"Look, just take a deep breath before we get over there, okay?" implored Eric, looking over William's shoulder at the group of squires who were sparring together. William rolled his eyes and began to turn back around.

"William, come on! You need to do this the right way! This is training with a real knight! Look at this as the opportunity of a lifetime!" reasoned Eric. William suddenly stopped in his tracks and turned back to face him.

"The opportunity of a lifetime? After all that I've been through, now I'm being forced to try to learn how to fight because I'll be locked in a cage, fighting to the death with a monster. Am I really supposed to be thankful for this? It's all well and good for you to say that with yer noble heritage Eric, but things aren't so easy for me now, are they?" asked William angrily, turning back away. Eric let out a sigh and continued walking after William silently. As the two boys continued towards the small group training in the field,

Eric looked at his friend with concern. He hoped that William would be receptive to Sir August's training, but right now he seemed far too emotional to be a good student.

***

As William approached Sir August, he looked around at the people who were gathered with him. There were three other people, all of whom looked a little older than Will, and seemed to know their way around a sword. August was locked in combat with one, explaining sword techniques as he fought, while the remaining two watched. Sir August parried his opponent's attack, then suddenly stepped forward and cut down into their shoulder with his wooden training sword, ending the fight.

"So, do you see how I stood with my right foot forward for that cut?" asked August, taking a step back from his sparring partner.

"Yes, but it made no sense. With your right foot forward, you shouldn't have broken line to the right. For a right shoulder from the roof like that, you should have been standing with your left foot forward," replied the defeated squire, catching her breath.

"Aha, but why? Why should I not have had my right foot forward?" asked Sir August, assuming the right foot forward position once more. The defeated squire raised an eyebrow and looked to her compatriots for solidarity.

"Well of course it's fundamentally incorrect," she replied assuredly.

"And why is that?" asked Sir August, raising an eyebrow.

"Because of the distance of the footwork of course. We're to be knights soon Sir August, surely you're not underestimating us just because you landed that blow? I got confused because you were using the wrong footwork is all," she defended incredulously.

"And now we've arrived at my point. You're reading my cuts based on my stance. If we behave exactly by the book, then we can also be read like a book. It's important to master the fundamentals of course, but you can't expect your enemies to always fight so mechanically. Maybe they're amateurs. Maybe they're not. Either way, you need to be able to adapt. You've only sparred against other squires from the college who've had the exact same exams as you. It's important to remember that you won't be squires for much longer. You're going to start facing opponents who don't fight exactly like you do. Moving into your knighthood is going to require you using your head more when you're in combat," explained Sir August. The squire let out a defeated sigh and nodded appreciatively.

"Now, why don't the three of you keep practicing what we've covered, I've got a new student to attend to!" said Sir August, resting his sword over his shoulder and smiling brightly at William and Eric.

"You made it!" exclaimed August merrily. William nervously cast his gaze towards the squires who were beginning to spar with one another.

"Oh don't mind them, they're here to learn, just like you," said August, nodding hello to Eric who waved back politely.

"So, tell me, what experience have you with combat?" asked August, raising an eyebrow and looking over the two boys curiously. As soon as William thought about the question, suddenly he saw the image of his father's cracked skull in his mind. He tried shaking his head to dispel the image but felt himself starting to become short of breath as his muscles began tensing up in panic.

"Let me in. I can make it stop..." whispered Annemarie's voice in William's ear suddenly. Although startled, he somehow managed

to subdue his instinct to shout. Surely he'd imagined it. Surely it was just part of his childish antics. He shook his head again, trying to dispel his panic attack.

"Ah," August's expression sobered when he saw William's reaction to his question about combat experience.

"I know that look. You've got a warrior's heart boy. Don't feel ashamed of it. There's naught a knight worth his salt who doesn't suffer the same. How about you then Rothmane? Any experience in combat?" asked August, shifting his gaze to Eric who was immediately caught off guard by the question. He stammered for a moment before clearing his throat to answer.

"No sir," replied Eric earnestly.

"What about the moorcrawlers?" asked William, still trying to steady his nerves. August raised an eyebrow curiously.

"That don't count," replied Eric assuredly.

"I'll be the judge of that," said August.

"Well, sometimes the moorcrawlers come after the pigs on my farm. I set traps for them but I have to use my pig hammer to finish them off," replied Eric reluctantly. August tilted his head in confusion.

"Moorcrawlers?" he asked, looking between the two boys searchingly. Eric nodded affirmatively.

"Do you mean wolves? Foxes?" asked August, still confused. Eric and William exchanged an unsure look before shaking their heads. August looked between the two boys searchingly once more before shrugging.

"Well, it sounds like both of you have come face to face with death anyway. That's important. That's the part that we can't teach you. That's the part most of the squires in this place graduate without ever having experienced. Regardless of how mighty you are with a sword, it's what's in your head and your heart that really counts. In your combat trial, that's what is going to matter the most," replied August, turning away and picking up a wooden training sword from the ground.

"Trust me, whatever hardships you boys think you've faced out in your farms pales in comparison to how it feels to be locked in combat," said August nonchalantly.

"He has no idea what you've been through. How dare he?" whispered Annemarie's voice in William's ear. Sir August turned back and tossed the training sword to William who was too preoccupied to catch it. The sword toppled to the ground at his feet. William shook his head again, realizing that perhaps he wasn't just imagining the voice after all. He slowly squatted down and picked up the sword as he began to feel a deep anger swirling in his chest. He took a deep breath and stood back up to face August. Whether he was imagining the voice or not, it was right. It didn't matter how friendly and wise August was pretending to be. He was one of the knights responsible for all of this, and he was still standing there smugly having no idea what he'd put them through. It was his fault that Father Marcus had been brought into his life. It was his fault that Annemarie had suffered how she did. It was his fault that William's family were dead. It was his fault that William had that horrific brand on his back, and it was his fault that William was having to fight this monster at all. Even after all of this, he had the gall to act like what they'd faced was trivial. As William stared back at Sir August with hatred suddenly swirling in his gut, he saw Sir August's expression change.

"Now, now boy. That's no way to approach combat. You need to empty your bowl before we start," said August, raising his training sword in one hand and pointing it at William.

"What's that supposed to mean?" asked William spitefully, holding his sword out in front of him.

"When you've seen as much battle as I have, you begin to be able to feel what your opponent is feeling. What I feel from you is that your mind is full of chaos right now. You need to relax and empty that bowl of emotion you have going on there," said August seriously. William's fury was only ignited further by his words. How dare he tell him not to feel angry after all that he'd been through? After all that he had put him through?

"Let's just get on with it," said William, taking a step forward. August looked like he was about to say something, but caught himself.

"Fine then. It looks as though you'll need to learn this lesson the hard way. Show me what you've got. Try to land a hit on me," said August, letting out a disappointed sigh and readying himself. William felt rage flowing through his entire body. August had just given him permission to attack him. He wasn't going to pass up on the opportunity. He ran towards August with his sword above his head, swinging down at him with all his might. August took a springing step backwards and swiped his own longsword to the left, easily parrying William's bold attack and sending him toppling forward and down onto his knees as his overly aggressive strike carried him off center. He fell onto the ground, collapsing roughly into the grass.

"When your opponent comes at you strong and hard, you must become soft and light in response," said August, gently lowering his sword. William felt his anger amplifying in his chest again. He reached out and grabbed the grip of his sword once more.

"I sense that you're not done yet. Again!" said August, raising his sword up once more. William didn't need to be told twice. He got up to his feet, this time holding his sword over his right shoulder rather than directly over his head. As his anger got the better of him, he couldn't hold back from yelling with exertion as he ran towards August. He slashed down at him with all his might once again. This time August sprung to the left, holding his own sword horizontally and parrying William's blow down to the ground. William wasn't done yet. He pulled his sword back up over his left shoulder and kept charging at August, taking another wild slash down with a loud yell of exertion. August expertly hopped aside from the slash, towards William's right side, swiping down with his own sword and sending the tip of William's sword directly into the ground. He continued his motion into William, colliding roughly with him and sending him off balance and down into the grass.

"Swordsmanship is an art form. Relying on sheer strength alone will not help you. You're coming at me like a buffalo," said August, taking a step back from William. Every word he said sent a wave of loathing through William's core, amplifying his hatred and deepening his resentment for the man.

***

As Eric watched on, he suddenly realized how far out of hand things had become. As William sat on the ground, catching his breath and reaching back for his sword again, Eric suddenly caught sight of that look in his eyes. He hadn't seen it since that night on the back of the cart, but looking at him now, Eric realized that things were just about to spiral completely out of control.

"William, stop! You need to keep control of yourself!" cried out Eric desperately from the sidelines. He couldn't say too much in front of Sir August, but Eric needed William to realize that if he continued like this, he was going to lose himself to the monster within.

***

Eric's words echoed in the back of William's mind.

"Forget about him, he doesn't matter right now. Focus..." whispered the voice in William's ear. Again, the voice was right. It didn't matter what Eric was saying. Right now, all that mattered was destroying the man standing before him. He reached for his sword again, the anger and loathing swelling in his stomach like a ball of energy.

***

Once William had gotten back up to his feet, he looked up and stared August in the eyes. What August saw within those eyes shook him to his core. He hadn't seen this look in somebody's eyes for many years. He'd certainly never seen it in the eyes of one of his students. It was a look of animalistic fury. The boy wanted him dead. He didn't just want to land a hit on him, he wanted to destroy him, and August could feel it.

"Hey now, you need to calm down boy," said August seriously, tightening his grip on his sword. William snarled angrily, holding his sword out to his side and beginning to charge at August again. This time the speed with which the boy came bolting towards him took August a little off guard. He was charging at him in a sloppy kind of tail guard stance, ready to swipe his sword upwards into August's side. August waited for the moment that William's blade began to rise. As soon as it did, he took a step backwards and swung his sword down to defend the swipe. The amount of resistance he felt when his sword collided with William's sent a shock through his body. Just how strong was this kid? He might be coming at him with the wild disregard of a buffalo, but he was somehow mustering the strength of one too. Without a moment's hesitation, William kept running directly towards August, yelling furiously with exertion as he turned his deflected sword back around and above his head. He was ready to cut down at August with a ferocity that he had never seen from any of his students before. August's innate reaction was to get ready to block the blow, but just as he was about to raise his guard, he caught sight of William's eyes. What he saw behind them were not the eyes of a man, but of a monster. For but a second, he could've sworn he saw someone else. Something else. In this moment it was like time froze. He felt a chill run down his spine as a strange feeling of fear began to grip his heart. The smell of tansies burst over his senses, overwhelming him with confusion and nostalgia. As the momentary trance threatened to pull his mind from the battle, his years of experience suddenly kicked back in, drawing him back to the present and dispelling the trance that almost overcame him. With but a moment to spare, he managed to focus back on William's incoming blow. His instincts had spoken; and they'd told him that he shouldn't try to block this blow. August let the point of his sword fall to the ground as William's attack from overhead came cutting down at lightning speed. He barely had time to hop nimbly to the side, the blade whistling straight down in front of his face and into his own sword with alarming power. The force of the blow was enough that William's wooden practice sword cracked in the middle, the blade splitting into two, sending an explosion of splinters into the grass. William was also sent toppling forward into the grass yet again. August's eyes opened wide in shock. Even with a training sword, if that had connected with him, he'd surely have been gravely injured.

"You need to calm down!" reiterated August, taking a step backwards from William whose animalistic rage only seemed to be growing. William reached out for the handle of the sword lying in the grass beside him. With the split blade in his hand, William turned and looked up hatefully at August. Once again, August felt that chilling feeling of dread grip his heart, the smell of the tansies once more exploding over his senses. The boy wasn't done. William snarled again, springing forwards at August with the broken sword hilt in his left hand. The point of the sword was now a sharpened stick due to being snapped off and splintered. It was like William was coming at him with a dagger. As William dove at him with the wooden dagger in hand, he took a step to the left to dodge. William flew towards him, attempting to drive his wooden dagger into August's neck. August quickly dropped his sword and grabbed William's wrist, using his momentum to guide him down to the ground. He expertly twisted around the boy and knelt on his back, pinning him down into the grass in a wrestling hold. William snarled and yelled as he struggled to break free from the hold, as August's knee dug into his brand wound.

"What has gotten into you boy?!" asked August in disbelief as he felt the raw animalistic strength of William pushing back against him as he writhed in agony on the floor. He couldn't believe that the amount of power he was feeling beneath him was coming from a teenage boy, and a small one at that.

"Hey! Get off him!" cried Eric. He ran over and pulled at Sir August, managing to wrench him off from William's branding wound.

"William! Can you hear me?! William, please! I need you to get a grip!" shouted Eric, running around and kneeling in front of William.

***

The second that August's knee had dug into William's brand the agony sent a shock coursing through his entire body. His vision faded to white as the excruciating pain overwhelmed his nerves.

William suddenly felt himself regaining control over his body. As Eric's words burst into his psyche, he felt his mind returning to the present. He looked around at the three squires who had stopped their training to spectate the dramatic scene which had unfolded beside them. He looked around at Eric who still had a hand placed on William's shoulder, and finally up at Sir August who wore an expression of unease on his face. Now back in control of his body, William suddenly felt a wave of emotion wash over him. Wrath, shame and anguish. Wrath for how the knights had behaved, shame at how he'd just made a fool of himself, and anguish over those he'd lost. As the floodgates opened, William couldn't hold it back. Tears began streaming down his face. Sir August let out a sigh, untensing his muscles and seeming to relax slightly when he saw that William didn't appear to be a threat anymore. A silence overcame the entire scene as William tried to regain his composure while the three spectating students looked on awkwardly. Sir August finally let out a breath of his own, shaking his head in disbelief.

"Would you care to explain what that was all about then?" asked August in disbelief. William sat up slightly, still catching his breath. After what he'd just pulled, there was no holding back anymore. He was going to have to confront Sir August head on.

"Why are you helping me?" he asked shakily, tilting his head up and looking at August distrustfully. Eric helped him to stand.

"Why do you think?" asked August, placing his hands on his hips and shaking his head.

"I know that you want me to lose the fight. I know that you've organized this whole thing because you don't think I can do it," said William earnestly. Realization crossed August's face and he let out another sigh.

"So that's the root of all this anger? Listen kid, what kind of knight would I be if I sent you in there completely untrained?" asked August seriously. William stared back at him, not sure of how to answer.

"Where would be the honor in that? I wouldn't be respecting my own code, and I certainly wouldn't be respecting your honor as a fighter either. As a knight, I could never do that," said Sir August earnestly. William was taken aback by how sincere August's answer was, but it reignited some of the anger which lingered in William's heart. He closed his eyes and shook his head incredulously.

"Honor? You care about honor? Where was your honor when Father Marcus was hurting Annemarie? Where was your honor when she died because you didn't protect her?!" asked William spitefully, opening his eyes back up and staring at August condemningly. August's eyes opened wide in surprise.

"What are you talking about?!" asked August, looking between William and Eric in confusion.

"You probably don't even remember her, do you? She was probably just some commoner girl to you," said William spitefully. Sir August held up a finger and pointed it at William.

"Hey now, don't jump to any conclusions. I do remember who you're talking about. She was that sweet girl that came with us to the hot springs. Of course I remember her," he said defensively.

"Well, while the three of you were off frolicking in the springs, Father Marcus was having his way with her!" cried William furiously, his voice cracking with emotion. August's face dropped into an expression of shock.

"You were supposed to protect her from him! You knew there was something wrong with him, and you still left them alone together!" shouted William, once more having to hold back tears. For a moment August was unable to respond.

"I... I had no clue. He didn't even seem in any fit state to do such a thing. She never said anything... I thought she was just upset because of what the cleric did to himself..." stammered August, the true extent of his failures in Mistfall only now revealing themselves to him.

"She was only fourteen years old. She died giving birth to his child. Her blood is on your hands. All three of you," said William spitefully. Eric's consoling hand on William's shoulder tightened as he too was overwhelmed by this emotional exchange. Sir August's expression darkened, and he looked down at the ground in shame.

"I had no idea that any of this had happened. I don't even know where to begin. I am truly sorry to you both for your loss, and... yes. I do accept full responsibility for what happened to her. You're right. It was my duty to keep her safe, and I failed. Her death is on my shoulders," admitted August, closing his eyes and taking a deep breath. Sir August's words sent a chill down William's spine. As he watched the crestfallen knight accepting responsibility for the pain he'd caused, he didn't feel anything like relief. Watching August learning of Annemarie's death brought William nothing but more misery. There was no rewarding feeling of justice, or victory like he'd expected. Just more pain. Always more pain.

There was a long moment of silence as August's words lingered in the air, the Mistfall tragedy once again spreading its tendrils of sorrow. Eric suddenly let go of William's shoulder and took a step forward.

"Sir August, you asked William what kind of knight you'd be if you sent him into that arena untrained," began Eric.

"How do you explain your two friends then? They seemed to be perfectly okay with him going in there and losing the fight. You might be able to tell why Will and I have our reservations about knights, given what we've seen from the three of you," finished Eric intensely. August nodded understandingly.

"I can't defend our negligence in Mistfall, but when it comes to the combat trial, let me try to explain. What you need to understand about Ivar is that he's too cunning for his own good. He gets his head wrapped up so deeply in his schemes that he loses sight of the little things. Azalea's the opposite. She's too short sighted. Truthfully, it would be her who would suffer the most if anything happened to you in that arena. I can guarantee that. She just hasn't thought that far ahead yet," said August earnestly, letting out a deep breath. William stood silently as he gathered his emotions and listened intently to August's words.

"When you did inevitably lose the fight, we planned to push the case that you showed enough bravery and honor by stepping into that arena at all that you should be granted admission to the college," admitted August, cringing at his own words as he spoke. William and Eric both shook their heads, realizing how ill thought out this plan was.

"We were lying to ourselves. I knew that the chancellor would never accept that. If I'd realized it, I'm sure the others have too. The truth is simply that we just didn't care whether some commoner boy was enrolled into the college or not," admitted Sir August bluntly. William and Eric exchanged a look of sad realization as they listened to his words. There was yet another long silence as August's admission lingered in the air. August's other three students were still simply standing by, uncomfortably listening in to their theatrical exchange.

"So, what now?" asked Eric suddenly, breaking the awkward silence. August brought his gaze back up to face him.

"Now…" began August. He looked between William and Eric intensely.

"Now our training really begins," he said, looking William in the eyes.

"If you'll allow me, I think that offering you training for the trial is the least that I can do," offered Sir August earnestly. Eric looked at William expectantly. Who would William be to throw a spanner in the works now? If Eric had been willing to throw his life into shambles to make it this far, he deserved that William make a similar effort. He took a deep breath. For Eric's sake, he was going to follow his lead and try to make the right decision.

"We all played our part in letting Annemarie down. It wasn't just your fault. Thank you though… for taking responsibility for your part…" said William abashedly. Sir August nodded his head appreciatively. William cast another glance at Eric, making up his mind. This was something he could do. Finally, he had something that he wouldn't need to rely on Eric for. Eric had done his part by getting him this far. If William wanted to get into the college and find the answers that he needed, it was now going to be up to him.

"If you'll put aside how I've acted today, I would greatly appreciate your training," said William earnestly. Sir August's expression brightened upon hearing William's brave words. He nodded excitedly.

"You're going to win that fight boy. I'll make sure of it. I don't care what the chancellor has to say about it; you're going to win that fight!" said Sir August with an assured nod. After a moment, a look of concern suddenly appeared on his face.

"Just… don't tell the others… okay?" he asked sheepishly.

Despite the failures of the three knights, it was going to be up to William and Eric to put it all behind them if they wanted to move forward with their plans in the college. After a searching glance was shared between the two, William and Eric nodded in agreement. They had to keep their heads on task from now on. All that mattered now was passing this combat trial. William had a strong work ethic, and his tutor was a world class fighter, but would he really have enough time? There was no telling how long it would be until the combat trial was held, and as proficient at the basics of swordplay as William may become, would it really be enough when faced by not merely a man, but a monster?

CHAPTER TWENTY-SEVEN
The Exam

William and Eric walked beside Azalea with a dark cloud hovering over their heads. It had been two weeks since William had begun training with Sir August.

"Come on boys, pluck up. I'm sure you'll be fine!" said Azalea, looking down over the two crestfallen boys. They had been so focused on preparing William for his combat trial that they'd forgotten about something which had been staring them in the face since the first day they'd entered Oxgate. Be it the excitement of the training, or the horrors that they were running away from, neither boy had thought about the fact that they too would have to sit the academic exam. All who were entering the college as squires were required to go through the process, even William.

"Aren't we supposed to spend months preparing for these exams?" asked Eric, his face falling a shade paler as he imagined how complicated these exams were likely to be.

"Oh come now, after seeing you school the librarians on their own constitution I have no doubts that you'll do fine!" said Azalea assuredly.

"What about me though?! I can barely even read!" exclaimed William in desperation. Azalea shot an uneasy glance at Ivar, who sighed and rolled his eyes.

"Look boy, I'm not going to fluff it up for you. You're going to fail," said Ivar flatly. Immediately William felt a swell of dread lurch through his stomach.

"Ivar!" exclaimed Azalea angrily at his bluntness.

"But..." he began, raising his eyebrows at Azalea.

"The academic exam means nothing for you anyway. It means nothing how you perform on that thing. You're entering the school on a loophole with this combat trial business," said Ivar aloofly as they walked onwards towards the exam hall. William actually felt surprisingly reassured by Ivar's words. His relief was unfortunately short-lived however, as when they drew closer to the exam hall, William felt his anxiety rise again. There were a sea of pages his age all gathering outside of the hall.

"And here we are!" said Azalea, drawing to a halt and putting a hand on each of the boys' shoulders. William looked over at Eric expectantly for reassurance, but immediately noticed that he seemed to be even more anxious than William.

"Hey, are you okay?" asked William, nudging Eric. He turned to face William and slowly shook his head.

"This is where we leave you boys!" said Azalea, patting them on their heads and ruffling their hair. William and Eric stared back at her in stunned silence. As Azalea looked over them one last time a look of concern came across her face momentarily.

"Look, Ivar is right. Don't worry too much about the exam. Focus your energy on that combat trial. And as for Rothmane, I'm sure you'll do fine! Listen, you're well ahead of these other pages in knowledge, trust me. What you boys have been doing for work is very similar to what they've been doing in their page duties too. Dare I say, it goes beyond in most cases. You're not beneath these nobles, no matter how it seems, okay?" asked Azalea, her expression of concern seeming to fade to one of soft admiration for the two strong boys before her. They both nodded appreciatively at her kind words.

"Goodluck!" she said, balling her fist up supportively before hurrying off to catch up with Ivar who had already begun walking away. The two boys stood in a shook silence for a moment, watching the crowd from afar before William realized that for once, he was going to have to take the reins where morale was concerned.

"Hey!" said William, patting Eric on the shoulder roughly. Eric slowly turned to face him, his face still wearing a forlorn expression of dread.

"Come on brother! You heard them! There's nothing to worry about, let's do this!" said William, mustering his best attempt at fake enthusiasm. Eric was unmoved by his bogus fervor, simply staring back at him silently. William let out a sigh.

"Don't you realize it Eric? We're about to sit the exams to become squires! Look how far we've come!" exclaimed William, gesturing around them. Eric nodded in agreement, following William's lead and looking around them in awe.

"Let's get in there and show these noble bastards what us Lakhdorians are capable of!" said William enthusiastically, raising his fist expectantly. Eric's expression seemed to soften, and a small smirk appeared on his mouth as he exhaled shakily. He raised his fist up, reciprocating William's fist bump. With that, the two of them set forth to join the crowd of pages.

Everybody was gathering in a small courtyard outside a beautiful old stone hall. William was getting used to the fact that all of the architecture here was superb. He hadn't seen a single building, or even a stretch of road that was not perfect and clean. Obviously, everything paled in comparison to the great library, but even something as quaint as this little hall was beautifully upkept, despite clearly being quite old. Upon joining the mass of students gathering in the courtyard, William was immediately struck by how little attention he and Eric were garnering. He'd expected it to be a tight knit community with existing friendship circles of judgmental toffee-nosed spoiled brats who would be resistant to outsiders, but as he and Eric made their way into the mass and found a section of the courtyard's low stone wall to sit on; nobody paid them a second glance. Be it the gowns that they were wearing, or simply the fact that they were in the noble district at all, they somehow seemed to be blending in. William knew that the difference between nobles and commoners was far more complicated than what they were wearing, or where they were standing, but at this moment it really did all feel quite imaginary.

"Hey…" said Eric, tapping William anxiously.

"I'm going to deliberately fail the exam," he said, releasing a shaky anxious breath.

"What?! Eric no! Why in the world would you do that?!" asked William in surprise.

"This exam is all about figuring out which order to put us in. We have to get the same scores in the same areas if we want to be eligible for the same orders," explained Eric. A chill suddenly ran down William's spine. He hadn't even thought about the orders yet. If he and Eric were in different orders, what would that even mean? William didn't know the first thing about the knight's college. He hadn't even thought about what all these orders meant.

"Is that important?" asked William, swallowing nervously. Eric took a breath and nodded his head.

"If we're in different orders we'll have different classes, live in different order halls, and tread entirely different pathways into knighthood..." said Eric, thinking aloud as he looked around at all of the pages chattering excitedly amongst themselves. William once again felt his stomach sink. If he and Eric were in different orders that would leave William on his own amongst all these nobles. The idea of being cut off from Eric and his wisdom filled William's heart with panic. Eric placed a consoling hand on William's shoulder.

"Hey. Relax. As I said... I'll... I'll fail my exam," said Eric. William took a moment to gather his nerves and tried to think about the situation more clearly. They were here to learn as much as they could about the gateway, Annemarie, and the brand on William's back. That was the most important thing. In the worst case scenario, one where they were separated, they could still work together towards that common goal, surely... How different could the orders be? They were all in the same city. It's not like they'd be countries apart. He took a deep breath and looked at Eric quizzically.

"Eric, do you remember what those signs in the library said about only allowing students from the order of the owl in?" asked William. Eric seemed to be caught off guard, averting his gaze and not answering the question. William's heart began to sink.

"Eric! What about what Sir Roland said?! He said you'd be perfect for the order of the owl!" insisted William, pushing Eric's shoulder roughly to get him to make eye contact.

"If you fail your exam, will you be able to get into the order of the owl or not?" asked William, suddenly realizing the conundrum that Eric was facing. Eric slowly shook his head, letting out another anxious breath. William let out a frustrated sigh of his own. He couldn't hold Eric back. The most important thing was getting the information they needed. It didn't matter how scared William was, he couldn't put his own fear ahead of their mission.

"Eric, you don't have to baby sit me. I'll get by fine on my own, even if we're in separate orders. Don't you trust me?" asked William, looking at Eric quizzically. Eric stared back at him, his reticence obvious in his expression.

"Eric, promise me that you won't fail your exam," said William seriously. Eric seemed to be considering his words deeply.

"William, I-" began Eric, before suddenly a man shook a small handbell, drawing the crowd into a silence as they all turned to look at him. He was a short, bald man who was adorned with some extremely fancy turquoise ceremonial regalia and a pompous cap. The lavish robes included a plethora of badges worn proudly across his chest.

"Welcome everybody to your squire exams!" began the man excitedly from atop the hall's tiny front steps, looking over all of the students.

"I am Chancellor Graham Hedley, and I am in charge of this college. For many of you this is my first time meeting you, but hopefully not my last. Allow me please, to first congratulate you all on making it through your duties as pages!" said the chancellor, stopping his speech to allow for applause. William and Eric joined in awkwardly, feeling dishonest at sharing this undue praise.

"I know that it has been a very difficult few years, but if you're still here then that means you've made it through! I'm proud of each and every one of you!" announced the chancellor, looking over all of them with a beaming smile on his face. William and Eric exchanged an uncomfortable glance.

"This exam is simply used to gather some information about you all to help us better decide which order you'll be placed into. Please, relax! If you're here, you've already made it into the college! So wipe those forlorn expressions off your faces!" the chancellor continued warmly, earning a relieved chuckle from some of the students. William shuffled anxiously on the spot. He was the only student among them to whom this truly didn't apply. He would only actually be enrolled in this college if he completed his trial by combat.

"After completing today's exam, you will be presented with offers from orders to which you are eligible in the coming weeks. I wish you goodluck! I look forward to meeting you all individually, and to seeing your bright futures begin within the walls of our college!" finished the chancellor warmly, earning an appreciative applause from the crowd. With that, the crowd began to slowly mill towards the entrance of the hall. The chancellor seemed to be looking searchingly through the crowd, but William's mind was a million miles away by this point. The panic of entering into an exam of any kind was suddenly filling every inch of his body. He'd never sat any kind of exam in his life. Anxiety was running rampant all over his body. As the boys entered the hall, they were immediately separated in the sea of students.

William searched for Eric in the crowd but was distracted as he was herded into the exam room. He was filled with a sense of awe as he entered the hall and saw the banners of all the knight's orders hanging on the walls. He hadn't imagined that there would be so many different orders to choose from. Each banner was different, and they were hanging on every wall of the hall. A crest was displayed on each banner including a lion, a horse, a wasp, a serpent, a fox, and all sorts of other intricate iconography. He didn't have much time to think about it however, as he spotted an empty table which he staked his claim to quickly, before anybody else could. As soon as he sat down, he began looking around for Eric, who he eventually managed to locate sitting at a table on the far end of the hall. He was looking up at a blue banner with an owl on it, deep in thought. William let out a sigh as he watched his friend considering his conundrum. William hoped that Eric would make the right decision, but he had a sinking feeling in his gut that he was going to tank the exam. William had given him no indication that he was able to take care of himself. He had been leaning on Eric far too much. Because of his own lack of autonomy, Eric was going to have to pick up his slack as usual. William rested his head in his hands as he ruminated on his shortcomings.

After all the pages had taken a seat, a small handbell was rung from the front of the room, garnering everyone's attention. The staff member at the front of the room put the handbell down on the desk and cleared her throat before beginning to explain the rules of the exam. Each word that came out of her mouth made William feel more and more hopeless. He hadn't even learned how to read and write properly yet, and now he was sitting in an exam hall in the knight's college listening to a confusing set of instructions which he was already struggling to remember.

Somebody suddenly approached him from behind and dropped an exam booklet onto his table before continuing down the row of students. William stared at the closed exam booklet in front of him. Before he even had a chance to read what was written on the cover, the bell was once again rung. As soon as it hit its first chime, the hall erupted with the sound of a hundred booklets being opened. William tentatively reached out towards his booklet and opened the first page. It was a contents page which listed each of the sections of the exam. His jaw dropped at what he saw as butterflies immediately began fluttering furiously in his stomach. Algorism? Rhetoric? William was already lost and so far he'd only seen the section titles listed on the contents page!

***

The panic that had been building in Eric's mind was showing no signs of desisting. The more that he looked around at the banners plastering the walls, the more that he felt the weight of his ancestors on his shoulders. Could he really fail the exam? Where was the honor in that? Where was the chivalry? He had no doubt that William could take care of himself. That wasn't what was concerning Eric. He had seen firsthand the insidious force which lurked within his friend. He'd seen it not only when it had first come to his farmstead, or when William had been at the gypsy camp, but during the moments in between. He'd seen it in William's eyes when he'd pulled him up onto the cart as they were escaping the moorcrawlers. He'd felt its presence during William's fight with Sir August. He'd felt it in his nightmares as he'd slept mere meters from him. William was radiating a deep and powerful darkness which was only becoming stronger by the day. Eric needed to be there when things went wrong. He needed to be there not just to keep William safe, but to keep those around him safe. Whoever was unlucky enough to find themselves sharing a dormitory with William would be facing nightmares unlike any that they'd ever faced in their life. Eric had still not told this to William. He already had enough on his shoulders, bearing such a burden in the first place. The night terrors that Eric had been suffering had only gone unnoticed due to William's own nightmares keeping him preoccupied.

He closed his eyes and tried to steady his frustrated mind. Until they knew more about the darkness inside William, what was there that Eric could do for him? Even if they were sharing a dorm, if things really escalated any further, there was little more Eric could do to help. He'd exhausted his shallow knowledge of the gateway when he'd used his great grandfather's sigil. Without learning more, when that worst case event did happen, Eric was going to be useless. It didn't matter whether he was sharing a dorm with William or not. He needed to learn more. He needed to find answers, and he wouldn't be able to do that if he was stuck in some lowly order with William and the other low scorers. He turned and looked over at his friend. He had an open mouthed expression of pure fear on his face as he was reading his exam booklet. Eric let out another sigh. He turned back down to his own exam booklet and opened to the contents page. He was immediately shocked by what he saw. Algorism? Rhetoric? A lot of these sections were going to be far easier for him than he'd expected. These older fields of study remained unchanged for centuries. His great grandfather's textbooks that he'd grown up reading would be enough to carry him through most of these more general sections. He immediately got to work. He might as well read through the exam questions at least. He couldn't resist. The idea of challenging himself academically like this was exciting. Even if he aced the first sections, he could always fail the last sections and still arrive at a low overall score. He hurriedly buried himself in the exam paper, feeling his anxiety beginning to ease. The comfort and joy he was getting out of testing his knowledge was just the distraction he'd needed from his woes.

***

William turned yet another page without understanding a single question. He kept reminding himself of what Sir Ivar had said about this not mattering for him, but he still couldn't quite put his anxious mind at ease. As he looked around at all the other students his age voraciously writing out their answers, he was filled with shame. How, in the same years of life as he'd lived, had all of these people learned so much? He knew he was far behind, but he hadn't quite realized the extent of it. As he rifled through page after page, there was naught a single question that he could answer in the entire exam. History, geography, heraldry, aristocracy, instruments of war, chivalry, William knew nothing about any of it. Just as his shame and despair was reaching its peak, he finally turned to a section of the exam which caught him by surprise. It had a diagram of a horse's anatomy, with each muscle and bone labeled with numbers. William felt excitement swell in his chest. Finally some questions that he could answer! He looked at the title and noticed that the section was labeled 'animal husbandry'. As far as William could see, most of the questions were related to horses. Some questions were about breeds, some were about horse care, and some were just about anatomy. William got stuck into answering every question that he could.

By the time that he was done with answering all the horse related questions, he realized that he'd taken up the majority of the exam's time limit. Even just reading the questions had taken him a while. He'd taken up a large amount of the space on his parchment with his excessively large handwriting in his answers too. He hadn't so much as touched a quill since he was taken out of school as a young boy. He looked around the room at all the stressed-out students hurriedly trying to answer as many questions as they could before the time ran out. How were they answering all these sections on the same amount of parchment he'd used? William's heart was filled with relief when he saw Eric excitedly scrawling away at his exam sheet too. It looked like he'd decided not to fail the exam after all. William let himself relax and breathed a sigh of relief, sinking slightly deeper into his chair. As his eyes wandered, he looked to the front of the room. The staff member there was looking back at him quizzically. William immediately straightened up in his chair and cleared his throat awkwardly. Everybody else was still scrawling away at their exams. He suddenly felt a tap on his shoulder.

"If you're finished, please leave the hall," whispered a staff member from over his shoulder. William nodded obediently, standing from his chair, and scraping it loudly in the process, drawing the ire of many nearby students. He hurried out of the hall as quickly as he could, blushing at his lack of etiquette.

***

Eric stared blankly at the question in front of him with panic beginning to rise in his chest. He'd worked his way through the entire exam booklet and simply skipped over a few questions that he hadn't immediately been able to recall answers to. He'd quite early on discovered a real hurdle for himself. The questions pertaining to current aristocracy were really stumping him. The fact that all the books that he'd read were extremely old was really showing. How could he not know the name of the current Viscount of the Bleaklands? He'd literally traveled through their county on his way to Oxgate. It was barely a stone's throw from the moorlands as it was. He could forgive himself for missing a few questions about Castellian nobility, or the northern kingdom's social structure, but the thought of missing something so close to home hurt. Suddenly he was pulled from his thoughts as a chair scraped loudly from behind him. Eric turned his head and saw William hurriedly leaving the room with a blushing red face. Eric smiled upon seeing how out of place William clearly was in such scholarly surroundings. Suddenly the answer to his question came bursting into the forefront of his mind. William! Count William Terrowin! Eric hurriedly wrote down his answer when suddenly the sound of the handbell erupted over the room.

"Quills down, now!" instructed the staff member at the front of the room, standing from their chair and looking over the students seriously.

"That includes you, Mr. Strathmore..." she continued, raising her eyebrows seriously at a boy who was sitting beside Eric that hadn't stopped writing yet. Eric looked at him in surprise. Strathmore? If the boy sitting next to him really was of the Strathmore family, then he was practically seated beside royalty. There were literally questions in the exam about the boy's family. The Strathmore family were about as high up the chain of nobility as one could get. The mere fact that Eric had heard of them in his great grandfather's books showed how old and powerful their family was. The Strathmore boy sighed in frustration and dropped his pen before raising his own eyebrows back at the staff member challengingly. She cleared her throat uncomfortably before looking back over the hall.

"You may now leave the exam hall. Please leave in an orderly fashion!" she announced as all of the students stood up and began to stampede towards the front door.

***

As soon as William caught sight of Eric, he called out and beckoned to him. As Eric approached him, William could tell that he'd brightened up considerably since before the exam.

"How'd you go?" asked Eric, looking expectantly at William.

"How do you think?!" asked William glumly. Eric chuckled in response.

"Those questions were impossible!" grumbled William. As Eric seemed to be considering how to respond, he was interrupted by somebody tapping him on the shoulder. It was the boy that William had seen sitting next to Eric. He had pale skin, jet black hair and intense brown eyes.

"Hey, thanks for the answers, big guy. How'd you know all that stuff about ancient heraldry? Did they have you stationed in the archives?" asked the boy. William raised his eyebrows in surprise. Eric had given this guy answers? If he could've given anybody answers it should've been William.

"What?" asked Eric, seemingly confused. The boy laughed at him.

"Look I don't know if you were trying to or not, but you made it real easy to copy you," said the boy, shaking his head.

"Either way, just wanted to say, I'm impressed. What family are you from? I've never seen you before," asked the boy curiously.

"Oh, I'm Eric Rothmane!" replied Eric, scratching the back of his head awkwardly and extending his other hand to shake the boy's hand.

"Rothmane? I thought the Rothmanes were dead…" said the boy in surprise, reciprocating Eric's handshake. William chuckled to himself. Everybody seemed to say the same thing when they met him.

"What are you laughing at?" asked the boy suddenly, glaring at William.

"Oh! Nothing! It's just uh, everybody says that is all!" answered William defensively. The boy looked William up and down suspiciously.

"And you are?" he asked. William stammered for a moment, his awkward childhood memories of being a social outcast suddenly flashing back before his eyes.

"This is William, my best friend," said Eric flatly, taking a step closer to William. The boy looked between the two of them curiously.

"William who?" asked the boy. William was not getting good vibes from this guy. He really didn't want to reveal his commoner ancestry to him. He stammered again when it came to answering the question.

"Lakhdorian. And you're a Strathmore, yeah?" answered Eric, his tone slightly more serious than before. The boy tilted his head and furrowed his brow, seemingly deep in thought.

"I swear I've heard of the Lakhdorians before, but I can't remember where from. I never was good at memorizing the lower houses. Oh well," said the boy with a shrug. William and Eric both decided to stay quiet. It seemed like the thought of a page being a commoner was so unheard of that it might not even occur as a possibility to most people.

"Yeah, I'm a Strathmore. Aamon Strathmore," replied the boy with a bored tone, looking around distractedly. There was a sharp whistle from behind them which caught William's attention. When he turned, he beheld the fanciest black and gold carriage he'd ever seen in his life.

"My family's here. Thanks again for the answers, Rothmane. Hope you choose the drake," said the boy, walking over towards the carriage. A butler in fancy dress who had blown the whistle opened the door of the carriage and let down a mechanical staircase for Aamon to walk up. Inside the carriage William could see a lord and lady wearing extremely fancy black clothes looking at him and Eric suspiciously.

"Come on William, let's get some lunch," said Eric, turning away from the carriage and beginning to walk back towards town.

"Who are those people?" asked William, looking over his shoulder curiously as the carriage began to leave.

"They're the Strathmores. Best not to get on their bad side, yeah?" suggested Eric, drifting off into thought. William nodded affirmatively.

"What did he mean about the drake?" asked William, looking over his shoulder again as he watched the carriage rolling away.

"Did ye see the red and gold banner with the dragony thing on it in the exam hall?" asked Eric. William tried his best but couldn't recall any one banner in particular. There were so many that he'd become overwhelmed. He shook his head.

"Well, that's the order of the drake. Ain't no high up noble in power what came from any other order," said Eric, seeming to drift off into deep thought. William looked at his friend and narrowed his eyes. If Aamon had told him to choose the drake, then that confirmed that the Rothmane name wasn't just any noble house. It was one of the high houses. Had Eric just never told William about how important his noble heritage was, or had he not yet even realized it himself? He was always so intelligent and keen minded until it came to his own accolades. If Eric ever did realize how powerful his name was, how long would he stay by William's side? How long would he be willing to hang around with a commoner from a pile of mud in the moors with a monster living inside of him?

CHAPTER TWENTY-EIGHT
The Black Knight

The chancellor looked around unhappily at the busy scene taking place in the grassy knolls which expanded out all around them. It had been a month since they'd heard word from Kane, but from what the Duke had told him, he would be arriving today.

"Where is Terrowin?!" asked the chancellor grumpily, looking around amongst the crowd of busy workers searchingly.

"The Viscount is otherwise indisposed sir," replied Gertrude, rifling through her notes.

"What could he possibly have going on that's more important than my event being hosted in his county?!" asked the chancellor angrily.

"His aides sent a missive to the Duke regarding sporadic cattle mutilations around the county sir," said Gertrude, narrowing her eyes as she read the missive.

"Cattle mutilations?! For crying out loud, why are we even in this ghastly gongpit of a county?" asked the chancellor, looking down at the ground and lifting his fancy academic regalia lest they rest in anything undesirable.

"Because I requested it," answered a voice from behind the chancellor. He turned around, immediately feeling hatred well up in his throat when he saw who it was.

"Rector!" exclaimed the chancellor in surprise, looking at the fancy brigade of aides he was traveling with. The chancellor was suddenly extremely self-conscious that he'd traveled here with Gertrude as his only aide. The rector nodded his head smugly down at the chancellor from his horse.

"Graham," greeted the rector distractedly. The chancellor sucked his teeth. Addressing him by his first name? He'd already taken the back foot. He really needed to win back some ground here.

"Well, *Wulfgar*, I must say I am surprised to see you so far away from your ivory tower! How ever will the library manage without you? You wouldn't want them to accidentally sort the books in reverse alphabetical order now, would you?" asked the chancellor, placing a concerned hand over his mouth mockingly. He quietly reveled in his punchy delivery. He'd been rehearsing that one for weeks.

"We use a numerical system, and it's Rector Cynesige," replied the rector, looking past him at the scene being organized around them. The chancellor again felt hatred seething through his veins. This time he was really going to hit him where it hurt.

"Quite the entourage you've brought along with you today. I can imagine you must've been feeling quite scared about traveling through the common district. I myself only brought along my assistant Gertrude, for you see, I'm not afraid of being robbed by the common folk," said the chancellor smugly.

"Yes. I can't imagine you'd have reason to be," replied the rector nonchalantly. Again, the chancellor felt a wave of loathing flow over him as his attack was so easily parried.

"Why are you here?!" asked the chancellor, his polite façade falling slightly as his annoyance showed through in his tone.

"That's privileged information I'm afraid," replied the rector with a bored sigh.

"Why you!" exclaimed the chancellor for a moment, before catching himself. He stopped and steadied his nerves.

"I had suggested the military barracks as the location to host this event. They already have a full arena set up there as a permanent fixture, it's closer to Oxgate and features all of the amenities required to host a function such as this. Will you at least explain why you've chosen to change the location to this... paddock?" asked the chancellor, gesturing around in frustration at their agrarian surroundings.

"No," replied the rector flatly. The chancellor opened and closed his mouth like a cod out of water. He stood in silence for a moment while he tried to process how angry this response had left him.

"Perhaps I can shed some light on that," said a lone hooded man on a horse who had quietly approached them while they were talking. The man lifted up his baggy hood, revealing his handsome face and thick blonde locks of hair.

"Prince Alexander!" exclaimed the chancellor in surprise, immediately prostrating. The Prince held his hand out and made a motion for the chancellor to stand back up.

"Please, try to keep it down. I'm here incognito as I didn't want to cause a scene," explained the Prince, donning his hood again as he looked around anxiously.

"Your highness, preparations are coming along well," said the rector, nodding his head politely.

"Yes, I can see that, well done to you both," said the Prince tactfully. The chancellor bowed appreciatively despite feeling like he'd done far more than the rector in organizing the event thus far.

"Chancellor Hedley, let me say that we did appreciate your idea of having the event be held in the military barracks. It was only upon discussions between the Duke, the rector and myself that we discovered an issue. It was against the code of chivalry, and even my father's coronation oath, that one of those monsters be brought into Oxgate county. For this reason, Rector Cynesige suggested we host the event here, in the Bleaklands festival grounds instead," explained the Prince. The chancellor nodded understandingly, indignation sweeping over him that he'd not been invited to this secret meeting of theirs.

"I had interpreted that part of the code as meaning the walls of the city, not the entire county itself! My apologies!" said the chancellor, bowing his head.

"Come now, we can't expect every potter and smithy in Oxgate to understand these matters so deeply now, can we? And please, your highness, call me Wulfgar," said the rector, placing a hand over his chest and bowing politely. Before the Prince could respond, a horn suddenly sounded from nearby.

"He's here!" exclaimed the chancellor excitedly, looking towards the road behind the Prince. Sure enough, rolling down the road was an imposing brigade of knights. The brigade was led by none other than the black knight himself, Kane. His enormous jet-black Percheron stallion carried him at the front of the pack. He emitted an intimidating aura, his giant stature and long jet-black hair noticeable even from here. Behind him was a large brigade of intimidating looking battle-hardened knights. They were from the order of the serpent; those who were responsible for keeping control of the treacherous desert surrounding the gate. Behind them, in the middle of the brigade was a giant cube shaped carriage covered by a canvas tarpaulin. The chancellor swallowed nervously as he took in the impressive brigade which had also clearly garnered the interest of the common folk of the Bleaklands. A crowd of intrigued commoners had formed as the brigade had travelled through their county. They followed behind the rear guarding knights, chattering excitedly amongst themselves.

"He's really done it..." said the Prince quietly. He adorned a concerned expression as he eyed off the covered carriage in the middle of the brigade. The rector rode towards Kane, halting his horse on the side of the road as Kane approached.

"Welcome home Sir Kane. Congratulations on-" began the rector. He may as well have been a part of the scenery. Kane didn't even bother glancing at the man as he led his brigade straight past him and towards the field that the chancellor was still standing in beside the Prince.

"Now, hold on just a moment!" exclaimed the rector hurriedly as he became lost in the brigade of knights. The Prince reared his horse and slowly trotted towards Kane, pulling back his hood and shaking loose his signature blonde locks, revealing himself for all to see. As Kane approached the Prince, he finally drew his brigade to a halt, holding up a fist to signal a stop as he looked the Prince in the eyes.

"Welcome home," said the Prince, nodding his head in greeting.

"Where do you want it?" asked Kane flatly, doing away with any pleasantries. The chancellor was shocked by his insolence. The Prince on the other hand seemed perfectly fine with Kane skipping the formalities, chuckling slightly even. The Prince turned his horse towards the chancellor and raised an expectant eyebrow. The chancellor suddenly realized that this was his cue.

"Oh! Yes! Right this way please!" said the chancellor, picking up his robes slightly and hurrying through the grassy field towards where the makeshift arena was being erected. The brigade followed him as he hurried his way through the mud with Gertrude by his side.

"Why did we leave our horses in the town?!" groaned the chancellor in frustration.

"You thought the festival grounds were in the town, sir!" exclaimed Gertrude, beginning to become puffed out from their hurried rush through the field.

"I knew exactly where the festival grounds were!" lied the chancellor, looking over his shoulder anxiously at the intimidating brigade in their wake to make sure nobody had overheard them.

***

After a few minutes of walking, they finally arrived at the center of the still under construction arena. The wooden stands had mostly been erected by now. In design it wasn't dissimilar to the kinds of arenas that would be erected for jousting tournaments. The standout feature was the large metal bar confines for the arena center which were currently being erected, separating the stands from the actual battle ground.

"In here please!" exclaimed the chancellor, shooing any builders out of the way as he led the brigade into the arena's center. He turned around to wait expectantly while the brigade filed in, and as he did, he was reminded of just how scary a man Kane actually was. Covered in scars and tattoos from head to toe, even his face was battle worn. He had an enormous scar running from his forehead, all the way down between his eyebrows, and onto his left cheek.

The chancellor watched on nervously as the brigade of frightening knights gathered along the sides of the arena as the central carriage was brought to the far end of its center. As soon as it drew to a halt, Kane and his knights dismounted and got to work detaching the enormous crate from its carriage before heaving it down onto the arena floor.

"So, there's… there's really a… one of those things… in there?" asked the chancellor nervously, craning his head to see if he'd be able to catch a glimpse of the monster. After lowering the crate to the ground, Kane stood upright, turning to face the Prince.

"Anything else?" asked Kane, ignoring the chancellor's question. The Prince seemed to catch himself before responding, thinking deeply about something.

"I'd like to see the beast," said the Prince. Kane stared back at him blankly.

"Sun's out. They don't like that," replied Kane. The Prince looked back at him with confusion on his face for a moment, clearly unsure of how this was relevant.

"I need to see the beast so that I can confirm that you really have delivered upon what you were asked," said the Prince, looking at Kane expectantly. After a moment of silence while the two men simply stared at each other, the rector dismounted his own steed and stepped forward.

"Gentlemen, if I may-" began the rector.

"Fine," said Kane to the Prince, ignoring the rector. He turned and walked back to his horse, withdrawing a lantern which he lit before turning back around to face the Prince.

"Come," he said simply. At first the rector and the chancellor stood back, watching as the Prince and Kane began walking towards the crate. The two of them suddenly caught eye of one another, and regaining their respective composures tentatively scurried forwards, trying to beat each other to catch up with the other two nobles.

As the group approached the giant crate, Kane suddenly turned around.

"Keep your hands away from the bars," said Kane, looking at all three men expectantly. Having finally had their presence acknowledged, the chancellor and the rector nodded sagely. The Prince also nodded, swallowing nervously. Some of Kane's knights brought over yet another canvas tarpaulin, extending it from the top of the crate down to the ground behind their small group. They'd have been immersed in darkness if not for Kane's lantern. Kane handed the lantern to the Prince before turning around and beginning to untie some of the binds which were holding the canvas down around the crate. The moment that Kane lifted the corner of the canvas covering up, the chancellor felt a chill of dread run down his spine. The monster looked exactly how it had been described. What really took the men by surprise was the fact that the beast immediately sprung into action. The moment that Kane appeared at the side of its enclosure, it scurried away to the far corner, curling up and covering its eyes from the light. The deep fear that the chancellor had initially felt was suddenly replaced by a feeling of being underwhelmed.

"Is... is that it?" asked the rector, breaking the silence. Kane didn't bother answering, continuing to simply look at the Prince expectantly.

"Will this really be enough to send fear into the hearts of the common folk?" asked the Prince, looking at the pathetic creature which had balled itself up in the corner of the enclosure.

"I did what you asked of me," replied Kane enigmatically, simply continuing to stare at the Prince, seemingly awaiting his cue so that they could leave. As an awkward silence started to overcome them, the chancellor cleared his throat.

"Well, I for one wouldn't want to be in the arena with such a beast! You've done well Kane!" declared the chancellor.

"Yes, I can't imagine you would fare well," agreed the rector, gesturing towards the pathetic, quivering creature. The chancellor glared at him hatefully for a moment before the Prince suddenly piped up again.

"Speak candidly please. As my old sword master, I want your opinion on the matter," said the Prince to Kane, who simply continued to stare back at him for a moment before responding.

"Who is the fighter?" asked Kane. The Prince turned to the chancellor expectantly.

"Oh, he's-" began the chancellor.

"He's a commoner!" interjected the rector spitefully.

"Unless you know the details, please let the chancellor reply," said the Prince with a sigh. The rector blushed as he realized that he'd overstepped the mark by interrupting.

"Who is he?" reiterated Kane, staring directly at the chancellor this time.

"Well yes, he is a commoner, a stableboy from Lakhdorian," said the chancellor, raising a judgmental eyebrow at the rector.

"How old?" asked Kane.

"I believe he is fourteen years old," replied the chancellor with a nod. Kane turned to look at the monster for a moment.

"Well?" asked the Prince, after an awkward silence had developed.

"I think it's stupid," replied Kane flatly. The chancellor gasped at Kane's blunt response, looking at the Prince and wanting to do some damage control, but not being able to find the words.

"Quite!" agreed the rector, crossing his arms and nodding at Kane. The Prince looked a little dejected at hearing this.

"Stupid why?" asked the Prince.

"A commoner in the college..." muttered the rector under his breath.

"I don't care about that," replied Kane, turning back to face them.

"Any man entering the college should be able to defeat this thing. Look at it," said Kane, gesturing towards the monster.

"They try to run and hide from us until their last breath. It's the only reason they've survived for so long," continued Kane.

"Blessed with experience as you are though. If you were setting your eyes on this thing for the first time, perhaps it wouldn't seem so 'stupid'?" suggested the chancellor, unable to hold himself back from defending his well-planned event. Kane considered his words for a moment.

"Perhaps, but hear me well; if this fight goes on long enough for that crowd to realize how pathetic this thing is, they will see straight through your farce," said Kane coldly.

"I've kept this thing hungry for weeks, but you'd still best hope that this stable boy is as weak as you think he is. If the beast doesn't see him as prey, you won't even have a fight to watch," finished Kane. The chancellor paled in realization of Kane's chilling words. Had he monumentally screwed up here? If William was able to intimidate this creature into submission, the entire event would be a failure. Not just a failure, but it would make the monsters appear weak and the knights even less necessary. Just what kind of mistake had he made here, and was William really as weak as the knights had told him that he was?

CHAPTER TWENTY-NINE

A Wolf in the Hen House

"Any day now boys!" exclaimed Maud brightly, clearing the table where William and Eric were sharing an after-lunch pint. Eric smiled abashedly up at her, his anxiety showing a little on his face.

"Not for me..." said William with a sigh, swirling the dregs of his beer in his tankard.

"Oh, come now Willy, pluck up! I'm sure you'll get plenty of order invitations! Perhaps not the owl but... plenty of others!" insisted Maud, raising an eyebrow. Despite having stayed here for over a month now, William and Eric still hadn't revealed to her that William was in fact, the mystery combat trial fighter that the whole city was abuzz about. It would only worry her if she knew. Before William had a chance to respond, she suddenly gasped, looking down at Eric's plate which was in her hand.

"Eric! Finish your carrots!" commanded Maud, putting the plate back down in front of him and looking at him expectantly.

"Aye miss! I just... I'm not so hungry," admitted Eric, reluctantly reaching for the remaining carrots on his plate and stuffing them into his mouth to appease her.

"Next time I'll tell Sir Ivar that you're wasting his money..." threatened Maud.

"It's just because of these stupid exam results. Eric's getting pretty anxious about it all..." added William, earning a sigh from Eric. They understood what was happening in William's case, but mysteriously, Eric was also still to receive any offers. Dame Azalea had said she'd look into it for him, but he hadn't heard back from her in days.

"I don't care! The boy's going to waste away if he doesn't eat properly! Look at him! He's half the size he was when he arrived here!" exaggerated Maud, reclaiming the now empty plate. Eric had been joining in on William's training every day, so naturally his fitness had been improving. Compared to his previous diet which had consisted almost solely of pork and bread he'd prepared for himself, the more well-rounded meals provided by the Blue Lantern had lost him some weight since staying there. It was still certainly a wild exaggeration to say that he was wasting away however.

"I did have a few pounds to spare, you know!" responded Eric through his mouthful of carrots.

"Seeing you getting smaller every day doesn't send the right message about my food to the other patrons!" exclaimed Maud, pointing a fork at him threateningly before turning away back towards the kitchen. The two boys chuckled. They had grown quite close to the staff at the Blue Lantern since they'd been staying here. Maud and Gerald felt more like an uncle and aunt of theirs than strangers at this point. Albeit temporary, the warm atmosphere had led the two of them to actually manage to fall into somewhat of a comfortable lifestyle.

The more comfortable William became however, the more he yearned to send a missive to Sasha back in Lakhdorian. He was desperate to see if she was okay, and to let her know that he was alive. Eric had explained to him countless times by now that any missive he sent would surely be intercepted by Wilton and would potentially make Sasha's situation worse. It could even bring authorities searching for William if Wilton knew where he was. All William could do was be thankful that his aunt and uncle were there to provide support for his sister, and try to forget how traumatized and alone she must feel. The last she saw of William he was galloping off into the storm with a monster chasing him. As far as she knew, her whole family was dead and nobody believed her story.

William's rumination was suddenly interrupted by a commotion brewing out on the street. As they walked over to the window and peered out curiously, their eyes widened at what they saw. There was a unit of the biggest, scariest knights that either boy had ever seen in their lives. Each member of the crew was larger and more intimidating than the last, everyone wearing black gear bearing a green sigil of a menacing open-mouthed snake. Each of them were battle scarred, tattooed, and riding enormous war horses. The scariest member of the group by far was a man of immense stature with long black hair leading at the front of the pack on a giant black Percheron war horse.

"Who are they?!" asked William in awe.

"I don't know for sure but... that guy at the front? I think that might be Kane..." said Eric, swallowing nervously. William's eyes opened wide in fear. If Kane was here, that could only mean one thing; so was the monster. The knights had told him that 'Kane', the fabled knight of legend, would be the one bringing the creature. Until that moment William had thought that Kane might just be a fairytale parents told their children to get them to stop worrying about the gateway.

"I thought Kane was the head of the goats order hall, why does he have a snake on his crest?" asked William as he assessed the menacing knight approaching them.

"Aye, he is the head of the goats but he's also in charge of the vipers. The vipers aren't actually an order, they're just a group of knights that work out in the desert..." answered Eric distractedly.

The mid-day patrons of the Inn had immediately started moving away from the door, some tipping their hat and evacuating the building all together. Before William and Eric had decided what to do, the brigade had begun to dismount in front of the Blue Lantern.

"Why are they coming here?!" asked William.

"Shh! You boys stay quiet. This lot are dangerous. Stay out of their way," warned Maud, straightening her outfit and taking a deep breath as she prepared to greet the guests. William and Eric nodded obediently, retreating back to their corner table where they'd been eating their lunch, and waited anxiously. A moment later the front door of the Inn burst open and Kane strode his way in.

"Welcome to the Blue Lantern!" greeted Maud politely, curtseying at the brigade of enormous knights. They ignored her, walking straight past her and following Kane deeper into the Inn. He took his seat at the head of a table facing the door. He pulled a dagger from his belt and began absent-mindedly playing with it while the rest of his troop filed in and filled up empty chairs around the Inn. The existing patrons who had elected to remain in the tavern drew their conversations to a stop, watching on anxiously as the brigade of vipers entered their nest.

"What can I-" began Maud after sharing a concerned glance with her husband behind the bar.

"Drink."

"Food."

"Whores," answered voices from the brigade, all watching her expectantly.

"Drinks coming up," answered Gerald, beginning to fill tankard after tankard with ale.

"And I'll get the kitchen to start preparing you some food!" answered Maud, beginning to hurry off towards the kitchen.

"Whores?" asked Kane, stopping the twisting of his dagger for a moment and looking up at the retreating Maud expectantly. She stopped in her tracks and cleared her throat awkwardly, sharing a concerned glance with her husband.

"You've been gone for quite a while sir. It's not that kind of establishment since we've taken over I'm afraid," she answered nervously. The knights immediately started murmuring amongst themselves, displeased with the news.

"I suppose he'll have to do..." said one of the female knights sitting at the bar, running a hand down Gerald's arm. William and Eric sat up straight in their chairs, extremely discomforted by the scene unfolding around them. Maud looked like she wanted to come to her husband's aid, but he shook his head and nodded towards the kitchen. She nodded in return and quickly hurried back there.

"You heard her. Ain't that kind of place since we took over," said Gerald, removing the viper's hand and continuing to line up the tankards on the bar.

"Oh, but you're so my type..." said the knight, slumping her shoulders and staring him in the eyes. A few of the vipers exchanged chuckles.

"If there aren't any whores then I'm-" began one of the knights standing by the entrance, before suddenly he was interrupted as the door was kicked open, slamming straight into his face. In the doorway appeared Sir August, standing there with his hands on his hips and a giant keen grin plastering his face. He took a step forward and looked straight at Kane.

"Kane!" bellowed Sir August, grinning from ear to ear and raising an eyebrow as he stared down at the black knight.

"What the-?!" cried out the knight who had been clobbered in the face by the door, shining red with fury and approaching August angrily.

"You've finally returned!" continued August, still not having noticed what he'd done. The angry viper took a furious step towards August, balling up his fist and pulling back his arm to strike. Before William could shout out to warn August, the viper had launched his attack. As the viper's fist flew towards the side of August's head, he caught it with an open hand, stopping him in his tracks. William was in awe that he seemed to have been able to do this using peripheral vision alone.

"Now, now!" said August, turning his head to face the viper and raising an eyebrow. The viper angrily pulled his arm back, tensing up furiously but seeming to be too intimidated by August's fast reflexes to attempt striking at him again.

"You hit me with the door!" growled the knight, immediately seeming to realize how childish he sounded in this room full of mighty warriors.

"Oh, I did? Sorry about that mate!" apologized August jovially, slapping the man playfully on the arm.

"So, the lion lives," said Kane, stopping his knife twisting and looking up at August.

"Indeed!" answered August cheerfully.

"It had been so long since I'd heard any stories of your deeds, I had assumed that you were dead," said Kane, looking back down at his dagger distractedly. August erupted into hearty laughter.

"Well, I could really say the same about you! Surely those creatures in the desert aren't enough to keep you lot busy?" asked August, looking around the room searchingly. The knights all murmured, straightening up in their chairs.

"There's more going on in that desert than those things, you know..." said Kane cryptically, snatching his dagger back off the table and putting it into his belt.

"Of course. Still, I can imagine that bringing one of them here was no easy feat. Well done," replied August earnestly, looking around the room at all of the knights. He suddenly noticed William and Eric at their corner table.

"Oh! And there he is! The very boy who will be facing the beast!" said August, gesturing to William and Eric. The two boys waved back coyly as they suddenly found the entire room staring at them. Kane abruptly stood from his chair.

"Which one?" asked Kane.

"William!" said Sir August, pointing at William. A smirk suddenly appeared on Kane's face as he looked William up and down.

"Maybe the fight will be worth watching after all," said Kane, earning a chuckle from his compatriots. William didn't quite understand what he meant, so decided to stay quiet.

"Don't underestimate the boy," said Sir August, raising an eyebrow. Kane suddenly stopped in his tracks, genuinely reassessing William. It seemed like August's opinion had actually swayed Kane's judgment a little.

"We'll see," said Kane, gesturing with his head towards the door that he and his fellow knights should leave.

"Your drinks, sir?" asked Gerald, gesturing to the line of tankards waiting on the bar. Kane ignored him, as the black knights began filing out of the Inn.

"Ain't no point if you've got no whores," replied one of the vipers as the group exited the building. August shook his head as he watched them leaving.

"Richard," said August sternly when Kane was the last knight left in the room, suddenly causing him to stop in his tracks.

"See your boy while you're here," said August seriously. Kane stayed still for a moment without turning around, before continuing out the door and closing it behind him. There was a long moment of silence in the bar before Maud suddenly burst out from the kitchen.

"William!" exclaimed Maud, angrily pointing a wooden spoon at him as she rushed to Gerald's side. William stared back at her nervously, not sure what he'd done to garner her ire.

"You're not really involved with that nonsense down in the Bleaklands, are you?!" she asked, as her husband silently reassured her that he was fine. Eric and William exchanged a nervous glance before William let out a sigh.

"Aye," confirmed William ashamedly. August looked between the two of them in confusion.

"He'll be facing off against Kane's monster! Do you need tickets? I can get you seats!" offered August, missing her tone entirely.

"This is what you've been training him for?!" yelled Maud at August angrily, whipping him with her towel.

"Yes!" exclaimed August merrily in response.

"How could you?! Look at him! He's... he's..." stammered Maud, catching herself before she finished her sentence. William let out a frustrated sigh.

"I'm not even that small you know," said William defensively.

"Oh, I know sweetheart, it's just... I wouldn't let either of my boys near that thing! Not even my eldest!" she explained. William felt his heart warmed that her motherly instincts were kicking in on his behalf.

"Oh, don't worry! I've trained him well. He's more than capable enough of defeating the thing; I can assure you of that. I've sparred against him, and slain some of those things myself, so I should know!" said August, beginning to walk towards the door. Maud seemed a little reassured by his words.

"Well, you be careful not to upset those black knights too! They're dangerous," warned Maud as August was reaching for the door. He nodded appreciatively to her, waving goodbye to the boys as he left. Maud let out a deep sigh as she looked at the tankards lined up on the countertop and began quietly discussing matters with her husband.

William felt anxiety churning in his stomach. If Kane was here, that meant the fight could happen any day now. Had Kane been right? Was William really going to lose? Every time he'd told August he was worried, August had reassured him that he'd win if he just mastered the basics of swordsmanship. After seeing the most famous knight in the kingdom doubt him however, Will couldn't help but feel worried that Kane was right. Had William bitten off more than he could chew here, or would August's training be enough?

***

The second that the Prince entered the room he knew this was not going to be an easy conversation. His father was clearly not in a particularly receptive mood, but Alexander needed to report back to him anyway. The King was playing with what appeared to be some kind of exotic kitten, dangling a toy above it and watching it prancing about after the feather on a string. Alexander glanced over at his younger brother who was sitting in the corner on a fancy sofa looking incredibly bored. He was shelling some rare foreign nuts. After shelling each nut he'd toss the shell towards one of the stationary guards on duty, seeing if he could make it ricochet off his helmet and into a nearby vase. Alexander closed his eyes and let out a sigh.

"Stop that, Edward," said Alexander as he entered the room. His brother simply rolled his eyes and continued throwing the nuts at the guard who looked quite uncomfortable with the whole affair.

"Oh, let the boy have his fun," said the King, not taking his eyes off of the kitten he was playing with.

"That man is a knight, not an ornament. He deserves your respect!" stated Alexander, again imploring his brother to stop. Once more Edward ignored him, staring him in the eyes as he threw a nut directly into the knight's face to prove a point.

"Look what the Zarubians have gifted to me! They're only found in Zarubia. Isn't it positively wonderful?!" asked his father, continuing to ignore Edward's antics. Alexander let out a sigh, turning back to the King and nodding his head.

"Yes, quite charming indeed," answered Alexander, glancing back over his shoulder at his brother's activity before his father let out a grumble.

"Do at least try to fool me by feigning a little interest," said the King without looking up from the cat. Alexander looked down at the small black and white striped kitten rolling about on the smooth royal tiles of the throne room. He rubbed his face tiredly.

"Yes, please forgive me father, it's lovely. I've had a very long day. I have only just arrived here from the Bleaklands. I bring news of the combat trial which I wish to discuss with you," said Alexander, looking at his father expectantly. His father's eyes suddenly lit up. He looked up at Alexander and opened his mouth to say something before catching himself and looking around towards a corri-

dor to the left of the room. He clapped his hands twice and a Zarubian aide ran to his side.

"Yes, your highness?" asked the lady politely.

"Bring me the... the... oh I forget what it's called. That queer
mask of yours!" he requested excitedly. Alexander felt his spirits
drop the moment he realized that his father hadn't listened to a
word he'd said. The aide hurried off around a corner.

"Okay, so father-" began Alexander, before the King held up a
finger for him to wait. Alexander rubbed his forehead tiredly as he
waited for his father to be done with this train of thought. After a
moment his aide returned holding a large wooden tribal mask. She
handed it to the King, bowing respectfully before taking her leave
once more.

"Look at it!" said his father, chuckling at its design. He held it
over his face, dancing about in his throne.

"Ooga booga!" he exclaimed, laughing hysterically at himself.
The Prince feigned a smile at his father's antics.

"It's a very nice artifact, father. Very nice indeed," said Alexander.

"Isn't it?!" asked his father in response, putting the mask back
down in his lap and inspecting it adoringly.

"I take it that your relations with the Zarubians are as strong as
ever?" asked Alexander, realizing that if he wanted to get his father
to engage in a conversation, he'd have to use mention of his beloved distant kingdom as bait.

"Oh yes! Swimmingly!" chirped the King brightly, straightening
up in his chair. He suddenly let out a mournful sigh.

"Why is it that we can't be bordered with them? We've pompous
Castellians to our south, useless cave dwelling brutes to our north
and that cursed desert and its sand folk to the east. If only our an-

cestors had taken the opportunity the gateway had provided them with. They could've taken Castellia when such things were less scorned. We'd be but a canal away from Zerubia..." said the King, drifting off deep into thought. Alexander realized he was on the verge of losing him again.

"Yes! A fabulous observation, father! Talking of the gateway-" began Alexander.

"Father, can I leave yet?!" asked Edward suddenly, throwing his final handful of nuts straight at the guard with no particular target in mind.

"My sweet boy, you're here to witness how I keep our kingdom running! This is important! You're getting older. You're of a squire's age now! You need to start learning about these things!" replied their father, smiling adoringly at his youngest son.

"What things?! Neither of you are saying anything useful!" shouted Edward. Alexander let out a groan of annoyance.

"Father! Can I please just tell you about the progress of the combat trial so that we can all go?!" asked Alexander, frustrated. His father raised a judgmental eyebrow.

"You may be my son, but you're still talking to your King. Watch your tone," warned his father. Alexander immediately bowed his head.

"You are right. Please forgive me father. As I said, it's been a long day," replied Alexander. An awkward silence formed before his father let out a bored groan.

"Fine! Out with it then! What news do you have?" asked the King, leaning back lazily in his throne and giving a loose wristed gesture for Alexander to hurry up.

"Kane has arrived with the monster, and progress on the Bleak-lands festival grounds is coming along nicely. It should be ready for the event to be held on schedule next week," informed Alexander, thankful to finally be given the opportunity to share his message.

"Next week?!" piped up Edward suddenly, jumping up from his chair. He walked over angrily towards his brother and father.

"That's my birthday!" exclaimed Edward furiously. Prince Alexander and the King exchanged a confused glance.

"I forbid this! I forbid it!" shouted Edward, stomping his feet furiously.

"My dear boy, this won't interrupt your birthday! If anything, it will make your birthday even more extravagant! We can declare this part of the festivities!" suggested the King. Edward shook his head furiously.

"Have you forgotten father? I'll be on a hunting trip! My friends won't want to come if that combat trial is happening!" yelled Edward.

"Oh of course they would! Nobody would miss your party for the world!" reasoned the King.

"You can always come to the trial for your birthday instead," suggested Alexander. His brother stared at him hatefully.

"I don't care about that stupid trial! I have the whole trip planned! I've already told Aamon and everyone! How would it look if I changed it all now?" asked Edward, looking between his father and his brother searchingly.

"Edward please do try to be reasonable-" began Alexander.

"No! You'll have to delay the trial," decreed Edward, crossing his arms with a huff.

"But my sweet boy, we can't delay the trial! The college semester will be starting the week after next. Next week is the final time that the trial can be held!" reasoned the King.

"Well, we're scheduled to head up to the lodge the day after to-morrow, so you'll have to hold it tomorrow," decreed Edward cate-gorically.

"It can't be held tomorrow, it's not ready. I've just come from the arena; they've only just begun assembling the barricades. The safety of the audience must be our number one priority," explained Alexander. The King stared between his two sons deep in thought for a moment.

"The way that Duke Archamond explained things to me, this creature merely looks frightening. It is in fact quite docile, yes?" asked the King. Alexander nodded reluctantly, remembering seeing the monster curled up in the corner of its crate. His father suddenly clapped his hands together.

"Very well then! The event will be held tomorrow!" he ex-claimed, hopping up from his throne. Alexander looked between his brother and father exasperatedly.

"The arena won't be finished by then!" reasoned Alexander.

"As long as it looks sturdy that's good enough. If the creature is as docile as I've been told, then proper precautions need not be tak-en anyway. There will be plenty of knights in attendance. Those vi-pers are about, yes? Send them along. That should be safety enough. If it weren't, then I'd simply declare that the dissidents were clearly correct, reduce the college's funding and cancel the event all to-gether," explained his father, clapping his hands twice for his aide to come back in.

"But father-" began Alexander.

"Enough! The event will be held tomorrow, and your brother will have his birthday uninterrupted!" decreed the King, handing the mask back to his aide.

"Honestly Alexander, the gateway has been closed for a century anyway. Whatever happens to the college, I can always find other ways to import foreign talent to our kingdom. Now if you'll excuse me, I must prepare for dinner," said the King, wandering away down a hallway and out of the throne room. There was a moment of awkward silence as Alexander processed how little his father truly seemed to grasp the importance of the college.

"You're not invited by the way," piped up Edward, breaking the silence before turning away and leaving the room. Alexander shook his head and let out a deep sigh as he watched the house keepers hurry into the room and begin sweeping up all of the nuts his brother had left on the floor. Would it really be okay for the event to be held tomorrow? Would it really be okay to not have proper safety precautions? His father had a point. The monster was supposed to be quite weak; Kane had told them as much. But if that were the case, why did Alexander have a feeling of unease churning in his gut over the whole affair?

CHAPTER THIRTY

The Day of the Trial

There she was. A dark presence in the corner. Again. He felt his breathing intensifying. He tried to close his eyes but found himself, of course, unable to.

"N…" he tried his best, but no matter how hard he tried the word wouldn't come out.

Annemarie took a step closer to his bed. Suddenly the visions flashed before his eyes.

There she was, being dragged by her legs out the door, with her hands clawing at the door frame and her nails breaking as she tried feebly to resist their pull.

"Heinrich!" she screamed desperately, staring him in his eyes. Just like that, she was abducted away into the night. Taken to that unspeakable place.

He snapped back to reality, trying his best to scream, but all that came out was a dull whimper. Annemarie stepped closer, right up to the end of his bed. He struggled to lift himself up, but he couldn't move a muscle. She placed her hands on his legs. Again he tried to scream for help, but all that came out was a dull groan. Her insidious intent was clear, as she crawled her way on top of him, dragging herself up his body slowly.

"N... No..." he stammered, putting every inch of his willpower into trying to move a muscle, but it was no use. He was completely paralyzed. He knew what came next. He wriggled and squirmed, trying to scream at the top of his lungs but expelling nothing but hot air. He couldn't see it again. He couldn't. As Annemarie dragged herself over him, sitting on his chest, she bent down, staring him in his eyes. Her face was full of pure hatred and malice. Here it was. Right on cue, the vision suddenly flashed before his eyes and once again, he was taken to that awful place. The place where his great grandmother had been taken.

A swirling red mist. A choir of anguish. The squeals of joy and the cries of horror. A putrid carpet of gore, old, and fresh. Layers of despair. A mountain of flesh. Neapolitan. Stapled glottises silent and overflowing. Pithed and flayed, they suffered. Glabrous scalps and splintered stubs, avulsed and burst, they flumped and floundered. A terrified saccade 'neath cherry clogged lids. Furred. Congested. Peeled. Nerve-knots emitted an ebullition of thick crimson waste. Though scorched, they shivered, scarred and seared. Forced to live and doomed to die. Coerced emulsions intermingled. New life and death, cursed in sordid variegation. Among the fertile horror, his screams adorned the ambience. Unseeable, unspeakable, unthinkable. He screamed.

***

Eric was suddenly shaken awake. The first thing he heard was his own voice, still wailing in horror.

"Eric!" exclaimed William, continuing to shake him. Eric grabbed onto William's arm, catching his breath as he shot up in bed, looking all around himself as he regained his bearings.

"Eric, it's okay! I'm here!" said William, looking him in the eyes searchingly. Eric continued to cling onto him for dear life as the visions faded and reality cascaded back over him.

"I'm... I'm okay..." murmured Eric, swallowing between panicked breaths. William shook his head as he looked over his friend with concern.

"Eric, this is getting a little scary," said William, drooping his shoulders slightly. Eric nodded his head understandingly, taking a deep breath and steadying himself.

"Aye William. It's just anxiety... over the exams," lied Eric, dodging William's searching gaze.

"Is that really all it is?" asked William distrustfully. Eric floundered for a response for a moment before William let out a sigh.

"It's okay Eric. I know you're worried about my fight. You can tell me. I won't be offended," said William blushing slightly. Eric let out a deep breath, tracing William's train of thought. It was better than the truth. William would never sleep beside him if he knew how the monster had been tormenting him, but Eric needed to watch over him. He needed to keep William safe. He needed to keep everybody safe. Before Eric could respond, there was suddenly an urgent knock on their door that startled both of the boys.

William hopped up and unlatched the door. Immediately he was taken aback by the large collection of individuals standing in the hallway. Among the group were the three knights, each wearing an expression of concern, even Ivar. He and Azalea were also notably carrying their full armaments with them. Among them was also Kane, who was standing further down the hallway looking as tired and angsty as always. Maud was there too, with Gerald's arm over her shoulder, reassuring her. At the very front of the door there was a tall, pale man with black hair in a pompous well-groomed bob. He was adorned with extremely fancy burgundy robes and an extravagant hat. Beside him was the man that William recognized as the chancellor of the college from the exam day.

"Is this him?!" asked the chancellor, looking William up and down before turning to the knights curiously. Azalea nodded her head.

"He's perfect!" exclaimed the tall man, clasping his hands together excitedly. Eric looked out of the window of their room. It looked like it was barely sunrise. What were all of these people doing here? The chancellor suddenly cleared his throat.

"William Lakhdorian, we are here to escort you to your combat trial," announced the chancellor. The slender man also cleared his throat.

"Yes. Quite," he agreed, unnecessarily. William gawked blankly at the crowd of important individuals before him.

"What?" he blurted. Eric approached William's side, placing a supportive hand on his shoulder.

"Talk of the town has been that the arena preparations have only just begun," said Eric, looking distrustfully at the crowd before him.

"Begone meddlesome boy. This is none of your concern," shooed the tall man to Eric. The chancellor raised an eyebrow at him.

"Well, Mister *Rothmane*," began the chancellor, turning with a sly grin on his face as he watched the slender man's face drop suddenly as he realized who Eric was.

"The situation has changed. By royal decree, the event is to be held tonight. The rector may be correct that this is not your business, however, given the circumstances, I think it should be fine for you to accompany young William for the journey if you see it necessary," suggested the chancellor, turning to the rest of his party who all nodded in agreement. Eric stared at the rector in stunned silence for a moment.

"I'm ready," said William. Eric turned to him in surprise.

"William, are you sure about this?" asked Eric. William let out a shaky breath.

"It's about time. Look how worried you are. How worried Maud is. It's time to get this over with. What choice do I have anyway?" asked William. Eric wanted to reassure him, but there was little he could really say. William was right. Whether the fight was today, or next week, it didn't make much of a difference. He let out a sigh, patting William on the shoulder.

"Aye. Let's do this," he agreed.

"May we please adorn our robes?" asked Eric to the chancellor. He nodded understandingly.

"I'll allow it," inserted the rector.

And with that, the day of the trial began. As William and Eric hurriedly donned their college robes, anxiety and panic began to fill Eric's chest. Was William really ready for this? Was it really going to be okay? Had Sir August's training really been enough?

***

As their carriage trundled down the familiar bumpy road, William stared in awe at the arena, still in the process of being erected.

"Is that really going to be ready by tonight?" asked Eric as he too stared out the window, captivated by the scene which was abuzz with builders and planners hurrying about in every direction.

"Of course it will be," assured the rector. William shot Eric a concerned glance. Both of them had helped out with enough construction work to see how shoddy the workmanship on the arena was. It actually gave William a little bit of hope that perhaps they were expecting the monster to put up as little of a fight as Sir August had suggested it would. The carriage suddenly drew to a halt as they arrived at the outer edge of the arena.

"I'm afraid this is where the three of us will be disembarking. Security and performers only beyond this point," said the chancellor standing up from his seat. William looked around in confusion, half standing up from his chair, as he was unsure of exactly what this meant.

"You're a performer," said the rector dryly, seeing William's confusion.

"I can stay with him though, right?" asked Eric. The chancellor shook his head.

"I'm afraid not. This is as far as you come," he explained, beckoning for Eric to follow him out of the carriage. Eric turned back to William, casting him a concerned glance. William gave him a confident smile and nodded his head reassuringly.

"It's alright. I'll be okay," said William. Eric shook his head, his face plastered with worry.

"Listen, remember everything that Sir August taught you. Keep your guard up, react according to its fighting style. He said that it's best if these things are kept on the defensive-" said Eric. William held his hand up, interrupting him.

"Aye. I'll remember," said William with a smile.

"Hurry now Rothmane," said the rector from outside the carriage. Eric looked back at Will, catching him in a tight hug. William laughed, reciprocating the melodramatic show of affection from Eric. When he caught sight of Kane sitting in the corner of the carriage, staring judgmentally, he immediately broke the hug.

"Just be careful, alright?" implored Eric. William nodded understandingly as Eric began to back away out of the carriage.

"Eric…" said William suddenly, stopping him in his tracks.

"If this is the last time I see you-" he began.

"It won't be," interrupted Eric assuredly. William smiled and nodded his head.

"Aye. But thanks for everything," said William earnestly. Eric stayed silent and simply nodded his head in response before turning away and disappearing out of the carriage. For a moment William had drifted off into thought, remembering the trials and tribulations the two boys had been through, before he suddenly made eye contact with Kane again and cleared his throat nervously.

"So, the lion's been training you?" asked Kane curiously. William nodded awkwardly.

"Yes sir," confirmed William. Kane seemed to ponder this as their carriage started moving again.

"Get it over with quickly then," he said after a few moments of silence. William looked at him in surprise, watching as the black knight continued to stare out of the window silently. Did Kane really think that the small amount of training that he'd gotten from Sir August was enough to tip the fight so much in his favor? Just how weak was this monster? A little confidence suddenly found its way into William's heart. The one thing that had previously given him doubt had been Kane's words in the Blue Lantern. With that put to rest there was nothing left holding him back from being focused and ready for the fight. He took a deep breath, looking out of his window as they slowly rolled towards their destination. This was it. Today was the day. Before the night ended, either him or that monster were going to be left standing alone in that arena. All he had to do was make sure that it was him.

***

Eric watched the scene as it became busier and busier. How had he managed to get himself included in such a cohort? He was surrounded by important people, all in a hectic rush to ensure that preparations would be made by tonight. He sat with a pewter cup of juice in his hand, the only person in the scene who was still stationary.

"Where is Terrowin?!" demanded the rector furiously.

"He still hasn't arrived sir," answered one of his aides.

"What could he possibly have going on that's more important than this?!" asked the rector, looking around at his aides expectantly. They all stared back blankly, wanting to provide an answer but having none.

As he shuffled awkwardly on his seat, Eric suddenly realized that he could feel a weight in his robe pocket. He reached in, feeling for whatever he'd accidentally brought along when he'd hurriedly put on his robes this morning. After a moment he found the culprit, pulling out his great grandfather's trinket and inspecting it curiously. It had a dull warmth to it, feeling more like it had been sitting in the sun than simply being in his pocket. He ran his thumb along its intricate design as he tried to take his mind off of worrying about the fight. They wouldn't let him past the barricades to see William, but even if they would, what more could he say? Eric was suddenly pulled from his thoughts when he felt a hand on his shoulder.

"What have you got there?" asked Azalea with a warm smile. She sat down at the chair next to him, sipping at a pewter cup of juice of her own. Eric let out a sigh, looking back down at his great grandfather's trinket.

"Just a family heirloom," said Eric without looking up. Azalea nodded absent mindedly, looking over the bustling preparation area and taking a sip from her cup.

"Listen Rothmane, I've been meaning to talk with you. I looked into your exam results and order offers like we'd discussed, and it seems that your results were exceptional to say the least. Perhaps the highest score I've ever seen actually! Very well done!" said Azalea.

"Thank you," replied Eric quietly, his mind a million miles away.

"So uh, you've probably received an offer from pretty much every order we've got. Heck, I sent you an offer from the order of the fox myself! I spoke with the chancellor, and he told me that there's been a complication with your offers, but that they will come through eventually. So just keep holding out for now, yeah?" asked Azalea. Eric nodded his head. With William on the cusp of his battle, little else mattered to him right now. What would it matter which order he got into if William was dead? Azalea looked at him silently with an expression of concern for a moment.

"Look Rothmane, I never had a chance to talk to you about this, but... August told us about what happened to your friend," said Azalea. Eric felt a sudden sense of dread come over him. He was used to William getting his hackles up when Annemarie was discussed. At this point he'd been conditioned to feel defensive simply by hearing her mentioned.

"Annemarie," replied Eric with a sigh, putting the trinket back in his pocket.

"Yes. Annemarie," said Azalea, looking away and taking a sip from her cup.

"I was taken with her the moment I set eyes on her. She was such a sweet girl. Brave too. Nobody else in that village had the gall to approach us, except for you two of course," said Azalea with a smile. Eric closed his eyes and nodded.

"Aye. She was brave," he agreed quietly.

"Good through and through too. And such a hard worker. She was always willing to lend a helping hand. Always smiling..." thought Eric aloud, sinking deep into bittersweet reflection on the girl whose memory the monster had been working hard to tarnish.

Azalea suddenly placed her hand on his knee, sending a jolt of surprise through him and pulling his mind back to the present. He looked up to meet her eyes, seeing a face wracked with emotion.

"Listen... I never thought he'd touch her," said Azalea, blushing slightly. Eric didn't know how to respond.

"We'd been traveling with him for a week before we arrived in Lakhdorian. The man barely had the energy to even stand on his own. We just never imagined that she was in any danger with him..." reasoned Azalea. Eric shook his head.

"It's no excuse," replied Eric. For a moment Azalea seemed to want to protest, but then caught herself and nodded in agreement.

"Yes. I suppose you're right," she agreed quietly.

"Look, I just wanted to say that I'm-" began Azalea. Eric held his hand up.

"It's no excuse for me either. I was there. I left her alone with him too. I'm not the one you need to be apologizing to," said Eric, nodding towards the sealed doors leading to the performer's area where William was housed. Azalea nodded understandingly, following his gaze.

A ruckus suddenly broke out as a middle-aged man with a goatee and fancy mustache burst onto the scene.

"Viscount Terrowin!" exclaimed the rector, garnering the attention of the many individuals around the waiting area who all hurried over towards the newly arrived Viscount. Seeing the avalanche of responsibility coming his way, the Viscount immediately began making a hasty retreat.

"Where have you been?!" interrogated the rector angrily to Terrowin as he backed away. He let out an exasperated sigh.

"There have been more cattle deaths, I needed to investigate it myself," answered the Viscount, straightening up and continuing to try to catch his breath as he was swarmed by people wanting his attention.

"How could that possibly take precedence over this event?!" asked the rector, struggling to be heard over the sea of people asking questions of their own.

"Because this time they were my bloody cows!" cried the Viscount furiously as he was swept away by the crowd. The rector sucked his teeth and turned around, seeing that Eric was staring at him.

"Mind your business Rothmane," said the rector spitefully. Eric was about to acquiesce, before suddenly a thought occurred to him.

"Sir, may I please ask you a question?" asked Eric suddenly, taking the rector by surprise.

"What? Do you have some kind of ancient footnote to a bylaw that dictates I must stand on one foot while addressing a Viscount? Hmm?!" asked the rector, clearly still spiteful that Eric had essentially choreographed this entire combat trial by himself. Azalea giggled, but caught herself, bringing her pewter cup back up to her mouth and averting her eyes.

"N... No sir. I have a question about the gateway creatures," said Eric, catching the rector off guard. The rector cleared his throat and stood upright, clearly proud to be addressed as an authority on this secret information.

"Fear not. I've heard of the plan to keep your little friend alive. I wouldn't worry too much about the creature," said the rector, surprisingly earnestly. Eric was taken aback to hear that the rector was aware of the plan of not letting William actually die, but he did suppose that having a child die on their watch would likely be just as bad of an image for the college as if William actually won.

"Actually sir, my question is about the language written on the gateway," said Eric. Immediately Azalea choked on her juice, erupting into a coughing fit. The rector looked shocked beyond belief.

"How in the world do you know about that?!" asked the rector, flabbergasted by Eric's question.

"I was just wondering whether the knights of old had used that language for some reason, and if so, whether I might be allowed to research it in your library?" asked Eric, swallowing nervously as he realized how awfully close he was treading to likely asking about forbidden knowledge. The rector stared open mouthed at Eric for a moment before closing his eyes and shaking his head to gather himself. Azalea managed to finally stop coughing, now joining the rector in staring at Eric in disbelief.

"Boy, if your family has kept forbidden materials from the dark ages, then I-" began the rector. Eric immediately shook his head.

"No sir, I was told of this by a traveling gypsy," said Eric, remembering back to what William had told him about his conversation with the old gypsy man. The rector shared an uneasy glance with Azalea.

"Listen boy, forget the nonsense that gypsy told you. It's just gypsy trickery," said the rector, looking away from Eric and straightening his robes.

"But sir I-" began Eric.

"Enough! I want to go the rest of my days without hearing any more of your old-world nonsense, do you understand me?!" asked the rector furiously. Eric nodded.

"Yes sir," replied Eric politely. The rector looked satisfied with his response.

"If you have any other questions pertaining to your curriculum, I suggest you chase them up with your chancellor. Now if you'll excuse me, I have business to attend to," said the rector, spinning around and trotting off with his chin raised haughtily. Eric let out a defeated sigh. He sat in thought for a moment before he felt a punch to his shoulder.

"That was an incredibly dangerous thing to do!" said Azalea seriously. Eric nodded his head understandingly.

"I know..." said Eric, looking down into his juice, deep in thought.

"Did you really hear about that from a gypsy?!" asked Azalea. Eric looked up and realized she was staring at him with an expression of utmost concern.

"Do you know something about it?" parried Eric, catching Azalea off guard. She averted her gaze, her cheeks flushing red.

"Dame Azalea, please. Is there anything you can tell me about that language?" asked Eric. Azalea shook her head, a pained expression appearing on her face.

"There is nothing more dangerous in this world Rothmane. Never mention that language ever again. Not to a soul. Of all the forbidden knowledge, that language is the most forbidden that there is. The only reason I know anything about it at all is because I've been to the gateway myself and I-" she suddenly caught herself, sucking her teeth in frustration that she'd overshared. Eric stared at her intently, captivated by her words.

"So it is written on the gateway..." thought Eric aloud, intrigued. Azalea stood up and shook her head.

"I told you to drop it, Rothmane! This isn't a game! To think that you'd ask the rector himself!" said Azalea incredulously, letting out a dumbfounded laugh at his audacity.

"Listen, there's a reason this knowledge is forbidden. Trust me. Don't mention it to anyone ever again. Not even to me," warned Azalea, before turning around and beginning to leave. Eric leaned back in his chair, once again withdrawing his great grandfather's trinket and inspecting it closely. He looked at the strange sigil beneath the Rothmane crest. What could it mean? It sounded as though he might be holding something incredibly dangerous, but even so, could it also hold the secret to discovering how to get that monster out of William?

CHAPTER THIRTY-ONE

The Trial of Lakhdorian

William watched as the Zarubian performers prepared for their dance, lighting the ends of their staves while some of the others donned their animal skin drums. Lakhdorian never had many visitors from other countries, except those from the northern kingdoms traveling down to Oxgate. Even then, most travelers would skip Lakhdorian. It wasn't until he'd come to Oxgate that he'd realized how multicultural their country actually was. He was suddenly pulled from his thoughts by Kane kicking his chair.

"Eat," said Kane, nodding towards William's now extremely tepid bowl of porridge. William let out a sigh.

"I'm not hungry, I just-" began William.

"Eat," repeated Kane. William nodded obediently and began force feeding himself the porridge. He'd barely eaten anything all day. His nerves were beginning to get the better of him and food was the last thing on his mind. Kane was becoming increasingly irritable throughout the day too. Apparently having to sit around making sure that William didn't run away was not his idea of a fun assignment. His team of black riders had recently arrived too, in merrier spirits than Kane to say the least. They were in charge of making sure that the beast was safely released into the arena with

William. After this, Kane and his troops duties would be fulfilled and they'd be able to go off frolicking in whore houses and whatever else the viper squad got up to for fun.

The audience erupted into applause shortly before the dwarf comedian playwrights returned from the arena. They wore proud smiles, and were abuzz with excitement as they discussed amongst themselves how well their performance had gone. William took a deep breath to try to steady his nerves. With every one of these performances William was one step closer to having to go out there himself. The Zarubian dance troop would be the final act before William's trial. As both performances required the sun to be down, with dusk falling, these were to be the finale of the show.

"Prince Alexander is here!" exclaimed the playwrights to the dance troop excitedly.

"And the King?!" asked the dancers eagerly. The dwarves shook their heads. William supposed a crudely erected arena out in the Bleaklands was probably not quite regal enough of a setting for a king. He was surprised to hear that the Prince was even here. As he watched the dance troop preparing to step out into the arena, he suddenly felt a hand slap roughly down on his shoulder.

"How are we doing?!" asked August haughtily, having a hand on both William and Kane's shoulders. Neither of them said a word, simply staring up at Sir August, William with surprise and Kane with disdain.

"That good huh?" asked August, letting out a sigh. He pulled a seat up next to William.

"So, they've appointed you to guard him while I release the thing, is that right?" asked Kane.

"Yes, exactly," August nodded affirmatively. Kane let out a sigh.

"Needless. The kid isn't going anywhere. They've made all the other knights turn up here with their weapons anyway. They could've appointed anyone. Why does it need to be us?" asked Kane despondently.

"Oh come now, the others aren't really on duty. They're just here to make the college look more impressive. I'm here with the boy because I volunteered to be! You needed to be here for the un-boxing of the beast anyway," reasoned August. He turned to William.

"How are you holding up?" he asked. William shrugged, as he couldn't find the words to express how panicked he was feeling.

"Well it's good to see that you've eaten something. Fighting on an empty stomach is a bad idea," said August. William realized at this moment that beneath it all, Kane might actually have his best interests at heart too.

"We have an hour before dusk becomes dark enough for that beast to come out," said Sir August, looking at the crate sitting silently in the corner, still covered with a canvas. William raised an eyebrow.

"Why does it have to be so dark?" asked William.

"They can't be out in the sunlight. They hate it," replied Kane.

"What does it matter if it hates the sunlight or not?" asked William. Kane let out a sigh.

"Listen kid, your fight is going to be easy enough as it is. Quit your whining," he said, standing from his chair and walking over towards the refreshments table.

"You've nothing to worry about William. Just remember to breathe and use what I've taught you," said August. William nodded, hoping that he could actually pull off the techniques that August had taught him. As the dancers got into the crux of their performance, William let out a deep sigh. It was almost time. This was it. He was finally going to have to fight that thing. Would he have what it takes, or was August going to have to run in there and save him after all?

***

Eric tapped his foot nervously as he watched the dancers twirling their staves around and breathing fire in the air. Ordinarily, this event would have captivated him, but the knowledge that William would come out next was the only thing on his mind. He played idly with the trinket in his pocket which still somehow felt like it was getting hotter. Was it just because he couldn't stop touching it?

"Eric!" called out a voice suddenly. Eric looked down the stands to see Maud and Gerald sidling their way towards him. He shifted to his left, making room for them to come and join him. Once they'd managed to edge their way past the disgruntled crowd, Maud caught Eric with a hug and gave him a kiss on the cheek.

"How are you holding up son?" asked Gerald. Eric let out a deep shaky breath but nodded his head.

"I'm doing okay. These dancers are almost finished, then William's up next..." said Eric, closing his eyes and shaking his head.

"I'm sure he'll be fine! He's a strong lad!" said Maud, holding Eric's hand. Eric nodded his head and smiled at her appreciatively. He'd never seen the two of them in their fanciest garb before. He'd never even seen them out of the clothes that they worked in.

"Who's watching over the Inn?" asked Eric, suddenly realizing that with both of them here there wasn't anyone there to keep the place running.

"Closed for the night," said Gerald distractedly, watching the fire dancers in awe.

"First time since we've owned the place..." said Maud with a smile, watching the amazing performance in front of them. Eric felt a warmth spread through his chest as he watched these two people who he'd come to adore. He and William really hadn't been in Oxgate for very long, but they'd already somehow found a family here. He looked back down at the arena and immediately felt worry churning in his gut again. William had to do this. If he didn't, there was not going to be anywhere for him to stay in Oxgate. Eric would still be enrolled in the college, but William would have nowhere to go. He couldn't rely on Sir Ivar's charity forever. The second that he won or lost this fight, Ivar would be settling his bond with the Blue Lantern Inn; that was for sure. It wouldn't be fair to ask Maud and Gerald to let him stay for free. William had no home to return to. His whole life rested on this battle. He had to win. He just had to. He didn't have a choice.

With an amazing finale involving backflips and calisthenics, the dancers sprayed an enormous fan of fire out of their mouths, earning themselves a standing ovation. Eric barely even had it in him to applaud. As he watched the dancers taking their leave, he knew that this meant it was time. William was finally going to be facing off against the monster.

Kane and the viper squad suddenly appeared at the side of the arena, wheeling out the enormous crate from backstage as they prepared for William's trial. A rack with a selection of sharp, high quality looking weapons was assembled on the opposite side of the arena as the monster was wheeled into place. Eric stared intently at the crate. Just what would this creature look like? Sir August had not been able to give them a description due to it being forbidden knowledge. It wouldn't be forbidden for long. After tonight everybody would be talking about what the monster looked like.

"Ouch!" said Maud suddenly, pulling her hand back from him and rubbing it. Eric turned and looked at her quizzically.

"What have you got in your pocket love, hot coal?!" asked Maud. The pocket of his loose robes had been dangling over the seat and Maud had touched the trinket within. He reached down and placed a finger on it, immediately pulling back when he realized that it was hot to the touch. What did it mean, and why was it happening now?

***

With the torches around the sides of the arena being lit, William knew this meant that in mere moments he would be locked inside that cage.

"Come on, it's time," said August, handing William his chain-mail coif. William nodded, accepting the coif, reluctantly standing from his seat and taking a shaky step towards the gate of the arena. Sir August looked at him and raised an eyebrow before placing a hand on William's shoulder.

"Breathe son. This is just like our training. What you're feeling now will pass. You need to calm yourself down so that you can hold your sword strong. Think of your family and friends. Let them give you strength," said Sir August, holding his other hand in a fist. Surprisingly, his words actually did strike some courage into William. Immediately an image of his father flashed before his eyes, hammering away at a horseshoe on his anvil back at home. He had managed to stay strong and brave right down until his final breath. He'd died trying to keep his family safe. If he'd had to fight this thing, there's no way he'd have had the shakes like William did right now. He took a deep breath, nodding understandingly at Sir August.

"Lakhdorian!" called out one of the organizers, signaling that it was time for him to enter the arena. William looked up at August who nodded, removing his hand from William's shoulder. This was it. Show time.

**

The second that they saw young William walking onto the stage beside the lion himself, the crowd subdued into a quiet whispered chatter. Next to the giant knight, William looked positively tiny.

"Oh…" said Maud, putting her hands over her mouth when she saw William.

"That must be awfully heavy…" said Gerald, shaking his head as he looked at William's chain mail armor and coif. They watched on as the young boy was led to the opposite end of the arena to the giant box. Eric couldn't think of a word to say. He could immediately see in William's gait that he was struggling under the cumbersome mail, but he also noticed his lack of confidence. Eric wished that he could jump into that arena and help him fight the thing, but the giant metal bars around the arena would prevent him from making entry even if he were of smaller stature. When William and August came to a stop, August put his hands on William's shoulders and said something to him that they couldn't hear. William seemed to be nodding along and breathing heavily, not being able to keep his eyes off of the giant crate on the other side of the arena.

"Shouldn't Sir August be wearing armor himself?" asked Eric, noticing that Sir August was wearing a fancy tunic.

"Maybe that's a good sign," said Gerald. Eric looked at him searchingly.

"Maybe it means that the monster isn't really that tough…" he elaborated, narrowing his eyes as he looked at the box which still sat silently on its side of the arena. Eric nodded, taking one last shaky breath himself as Sir August slapped William on the shoulders encouragingly, before taking his leave back to the waiting area on the other side of the gate. Eric couldn't take it anymore. He grabbed Maud's hand and held it tight. She squeezed his hand back, both of them looking down on William in the arena with worry gripping their hearts. As the gates dropped, leaving but William and the crate in the arena, this was it. There was no turning back now.

**

William could barely take his eyes off of that terrifying crate on the other side of the arena. There were ropes attached to its lid which, when pulled from the other side of the gate, would allow the crate to collapse, revealing whatever lay inside it. As he saw the gate on the far side of the arena being closed, he realized that this was it. There was truly no escape. After a few moments he heard a sudden whistle. He turned his head and saw one of the event organizers on the other side of the bars.

"Choose a weapon! Hurry up!" he urged, looking up at the lavish box of seats at the top of the stands, housing the aristocrats. William nodded, realizing that everybody was waiting for him. When he approached the weapon rack, he noticed that he actually had quite an assortment of fancy looking equipment to choose from. Swords, spears, hammers, there was even a halberd. William took the longsword, as this was the only weapon he'd had even the remotest practice with. It was considerably heavier than his wooden training sword, but August had made him practice swinging the real thing around enough that it didn't surprise him too much. After coming to terms with its weight, he took one final deep breath. He looked back at the event organizer and slowly nodded his head. He was as ready as he'd ever be.

As the organizer gave the signal to Kane and his troop, William bent his knees, getting into a defensive position. He had no idea what was about to be revealed in that box, but whatever it was could possibly launch itself at him the moment it was revealed.

Suddenly, the ropes were yanked back with a giant heave from the viper squad. Just like that, the lid of the crate suddenly flew open, with the walls falling down around it. What William saw revealed inside immediately sent a wave of shock and confusion spreading through his stomach. There, scuttling around on the spot, panicking at its newly exposed surroundings, was a moorcrawler.

CHAPTER THIRTY-TWO
No Way Out

The second that the creature was revealed, the crowd gasped in horror at what they beheld. Some screamed, others cried out in shock, some simply sat in silence, struggling to fathom what they were beholding. Eric stared down at the moorcrawler with his mouth agape. The moorcrawlers were gateway monsters?! How could that be possible?! How could there have been gateway creatures wandering around his farm all this time without the kingdom knowing?!

Maud suddenly clutched onto his hand even tighter than before. It was her first time seeing a moorcrawler, so Eric empathized with how scary it must look. He wasn't sure whether to feel relieved or even more scared. After seeing what those creatures were capable of in that gypsy camp, his gut was filled with unease. Despite this, memories of cutting them into pieces and feeding them to his pigs flooded back into his mind, rendering his fears slightly abated.

"Why does it look so..." began Maud.

"Human?" finished Gerald.

The moorcrawler seemed to be in its default sheepish state that Eric was more familiar with. It scuttled about a little, turning every which way as it looked for an exit and slowly fathomed that it was trapped. People had come here expecting a monster which would immediately launch itself at William, ripping and tearing at him with unheard of speed and strength. What they got instead was a terrified moorcrawler, tearing up fistfuls of grass as it prepared to dig itself into the ground in fear of the crowd. Eric was the only one here who wasn't still in shock from its initial appearances. How long would it be until the rest of the crowd noticed how pathetic it truly was?

***

Memories of watching the gypsies being torn to shreds were flooding back into William's mind. He couldn't underestimate this thing, but still he felt a dull feeling of relief flowing into his chest. They were dangerous foes, yes, but they were also familiar to him. It was beginning to dig into the ground, throwing tufts of grass and dirt over its back as it hurriedly tried to hide from the crowd. It still wore that dull, empty expressionless look on its face. That was a good sign. He just needed to strike it before it managed to undergo whatever transformation it had undergone at the gypsy camp. He raised his longsword and began to march determinedly towards it, staying in stance like August had taught him. He could hear the crowd beginning to erupt into concerned murmurs. It wouldn't be long before they realized how short of a fight this might actually be. William didn't care. All he cared about was ending this as quickly as he could, and now was the perfect time to strike.

William tentatively pressed his offensive march. After a few strides, the beast finally seemed to take notice of him, stopping its digging, and freezing in place while its giant black empty eye sockets looked up at him inquisitively. It seemed tensed up, ready to retreat at any moment. William took a deep breath, continuing to press forward towards the monster. It tilted its head, leaning forward towards William and inspecting him curiously. Suddenly William felt a strange vibration and warmth in his chest. He had no idea what he was feeling, but it made him pause on the spot. He wanted to look down and inspect whatever was happening in his body, but he couldn't take his eyes off of the creature which was now taking curious small steps towards him.

"Hey!" exclaimed William defensively, trying to startle the creature to start backing away from him again, which seemed to work for a moment, as it drew to a halt. It was only for a brief moment though, as it immediately began crawling towards him again, its face fixated on him.

"Hey!" exclaimed William again, more loudly this time, taking half a step backwards as panic began to creep into his heart. This time the crawler was unfazed.

"That's right..." whispered Annemarie in William's ear suddenly. The crowd was beginning to erupt into louder murmurs as the creature continued walking towards William, catching him in a steady retreat.

As the moorcrawler continued its approach, William began swinging his sword out in front of him every now and then, trying to make the beast flinch. As the blade came closer to it, the crawler would lean back slightly, but it never stopped its approach. William's fear suddenly escalated as he realized that he was being backed into a corner.

"That's right..." whispered Annemarie again. William swiped out at the moorcrawler, yelling as he did so, but it was no use. As his fear heightened, he suddenly tripped over the uneven Bleakland's earth, falling backwards into the grass. He cried out in fear, the crowd joining him, releasing a surprised choir of screams as he fell. He immediately tried to right himself, but the moorcrawler didn't hesitate for a second. It jumped forward, reaching out and grabbing his leg with one of its front arms, that horrible strong grip that had left wounds in Eric's sides dug into William's leg. He screamed out in pain and fear, swiping down with his longsword at the creature's hand. He managed to connect with its forearm, slashing it shallowly. It wasn't a major wound, but it was enough to make it release his leg, buying him just enough time to pull back and try to get up onto his feet. The moorcrawler screeched in pain, its face beginning to twitch away from the dull vacant expression. William had to end this now. He couldn't let whatever had happened at that gypsy camp happen again. He leaped forward, taking a strong high cut down towards the creature from above his head. The moorcrawler reared backwards defensively. It was fast, but not fast enough. William's strike plowed down into its torso. It screeched, scuttling backwards away from William. The crowd cheered jubilantly as William made his first real progress towards defeating this thing. He finally let a little courage flow back into his heart. Maybe he could do this after all.

"That's enough," whispered Annemarie suddenly. William instantly felt that heat in his chest erupt once again. His grip on his sword weakened as he put his other hand up to his chest, trying to feel what was happening. The crowd began to murmur as they realized that something was wrong with William. He dropped down to one knee, resting on his sword with his right hand while his left clutched at his chest. Pain was beginning to flow from his chest and down into his limbs with every heartbeat. The moorcrawler seemed to suddenly take intense interest in William. Rather than backing away, it simply froze on the spot, its head tilting curiously as the heat in William's chest intensified. His vision began to blur, fading to white as a migraine started pounding in his head. Visions of his room back in Lakhdorian suddenly started flashing before his eyes.

"What are you doing to me?!" cried out William, shaking his head to try to bring himself back to the present. Every time that the present flashed back before his eyes, he could see the moorcrawler drawing closer, that curious face with its tilting head drawing nearer and nearer.

"William," said Annemarie from the end of his bed.

"No!" yelled William, trying to stave off the vision which was being thrust upon him at the worst possible moment. As the white-hot pressure in his chest reached its peak, he suddenly realized that his left arm was moving on its own. It was rising up, open palmed towards the moorcrawler. No matter how hard William tried, he couldn't pull it back down. The moorcrawler seemed to be twitching its entire body uncomfortably. Its brows started furrowing, its dull eye sockets darkened, and its face began to twitch sporadically. Its expression twisted into that countenance of pure hatred that they'd been wearing that night in the gypsy camp. It began releasing a disgusting throaty growl as its body pulsated as though energized by something. All William could do was watch on in horror as his own arm continued to stretch out towards the moorcrawler, seemingly inciting this transformation. He needed to get a grip. He needed to overpower this dark force and take control of the battle. He needed to end this, and fast.

William cried out at the top of his lungs with exertion, trying his absolute hardest to stand up. As he did, he dropped his sword from his right arm, reaching over towards his left and pulling it down as hard as he could. As he struggled, he could feel the pain in his chest and his head lessening. He slowly felt control returning to his left arm as he pulled it down. It was working. With one final cry, William pulled down with all his might, finally managing to regain control of his entire body; but it was too late. When he looked up at the moorcrawler in front of him, he beheld that familiar terrifying visage of pure wrath and hatred. William gulped in fear, hearing its guttural growling as it stared at him with absolute malice. Would he have time to reach down for his sword? He had to; it was the only way he could get out of this alive.

He took a deep breath before slowly lowering down towards his sword. The very moment that he began to move however, the moorcrawler let out a howling shriek, galloping towards him at a blistering speed far faster than it would have been capable of mustering previously. It leapt at him with its arms outstretched, still releasing its guttural cry. William dropped down onto his hands and knees, sending the moorcrawler flying over his head. He reached down towards the hilt of his sword, but immediately felt a pressure on his head. The moorcrawler had grabbed the back of his mail coif with its furthest back arms as it sailed over his head. Still holding on as it fell, it yanked William backwards down onto the ground with it, his coif being pulled from his head in the process. It quickly turned back around to face him with superhuman speed. William had no time to react, as one of the creature's other arms immediately came crashing down, grabbing towards William's face. He rolled quickly to the side, narrowly avoiding the hand which futilely tore a great fistful of grass from where his head had just been. He managed to get onto his hands and knees, launching himself backwards just in time to dodge another mighty attack from the moorcrawler that came crashing down where he'd just been sitting moments ago. With the moorcrawler now on top of his dropped sword, and the weapon rack behind the creature, William suddenly realized how much trouble he was in. He had no weapon, his coif was gone and the monster was in the same terrifying state that it had been in at the gypsy camp. What was he possibly going to be able to do here?!

***

Kane jumped up from his chair, joining Sir August who was pressed up against the arena bars, watching in shock at the scene which was unfolding before them.

"I've never seen them behave like this before…" said Sir August, reaching instinctively for the sword at his hilt.

"Nor have I…" said Kane, a dark expression appearing on his face.

"I've got to go in there. This is too much," said Sir August, turning to run towards the gate. Kane grabbed him by the arm, stopping him in his tracks.

"What are you doing?!" asked Sir August, looking between Kane and the scene unfolding in the arena.

"You'd dishonor the boy," said Kane, his dark expression deepening as he watched the terrifying scene before them. Sir August gritted his teeth.

"Look at him!" shouted Sir August. William was backing away towards the remains of the crate that had previously been holding the moorcrawler, narrowly dodging attacks by the skin of his teeth.

"He's unarmed!" exclaimed Sir August, pulling his arm back from Kane.

"Give him a chance," said Kane without looking away from the fight. August took a deep breath, looking at Kane's serious expression. He turned back towards the fight and watched on with his hand on his sword. He'd give William one last chance to prove himself against this mysteriously invigorated foe. At the first sign that things were escalating, August was going in there.

***

William jumped to the right as the moorcrawler launched itself at him, narrowly missing him once more. For once William's small stature and strong muscles were coming in handy. He was exceptionally fast. Fast enough that even when faced with this superhuman beast he was managing to stay alive somehow. He suddenly felt something beneath his foot. He looked down and saw the remains of the crate. He didn't waste a second, picking up a large piece of crate to use as a shield. It was just in time, as the moorcrawler came leaping out directly towards him at that exact moment. William managed to heave the enormous piece of wood up at the beast, blocking its attack and deflecting it off to his right side. The moorcrawler quickly righted itself, spinning around to face him and lunging towards his shield. It smashed straight through the piece of wooden crate, cracking it into two pieces and out of William's hands. William cried out in fear, stumbling for a moment to steady himself on his feet. He noticed that now he'd managed to rotate the fight, he might be able to make a mad dash for his sword. He didn't have a second to waste, immediately breaking into the most ferocious sprint of his life. The moorcrawler let out another guttural cry, scurrying after him with terrifying haste.

William grunted in frustration at the heavy mail that he was wearing. He could see his sword just out of his reach. If he had been unarmored, he'd have been able to make it on time, but as he glanced over his shoulder, he immediately saw that the moorcrawler was upon him. He leapt forward reaching for the sword, but just as he did the moorcrawler grabbed his legs, pulling him back in midair and sending him crashing roughly to the ground. William screamed in horror, kicking as hard as he could against the giant hands that were wrapped around his legs, but it was no use. As he kicked and screamed, William could feel himself being pulled closer and closer to the monster. He reached out desperately for his sword, grabbing handfuls of mud and grass as he was pulled further and further away from it. Now that it had pulled him underneath it, the moor crawler grabbed him and flipped him over so that he was face up. It released a disgusting shriek down over William's face. William wailed in fear as he struggled feebly against the moorcrawler, but it was useless. Against such a monstrosity he stood no chance. As William watched the creature rearing up, he knew that it was over.

***

"That's enough!" bellowed Sir August, pulling out his sword and charging over towards the gate. The moment that he grabbed it however; he knew that something was wrong. As he pulled against it, he suddenly noticed a bundle of thick chains with a padlock wrapped around the gate.

"Who put this here?!" shouted August, looking around searchingly.

"I did," said the rector, stepping out from the shadows. August's face dropped in shock.

"What is the meaning of this?!" cried out August, looking between the rector and William who was by now entirely beneath the moorcrawler as it released its cry.

"They must see the true horror of the gateway. Only then will they understand why we need the knights," said the rector, a dark expression covering his face as he watched William in his final moments. August couldn't believe that this was happening. William was going to die, and there was nothing he could do about it.

CHAPTER THIRTY-THREE
Survivor's Guilt

The moorcrawler reared up, lifting its front arms up above its head. This was it. This was how he died. It had grabbed his legs with its back set of arms, and pinned his arms down against the ground with its middle set. He was completely defenseless. The moment that the moorcrawler released its first strike down on William's torso, he immediately felt his ribs break beneath the mail armor he was wearing. Searing pain shot through his entire body as the devastating blows collided with him. He let out a squeaking cry as his ribs were smashed in, blood erupting from his mouth as his chest cavity was punctured. Before he even had a chance to reel from the first attack, the moorcrawler continued. It released a hail of blows against William's chest and body, breaking bones and spilling blood even through the mail. William gargled through a mouthful of blood, as fear and pain overwhelmed him while he looked up helplessly at the creature on top of him. The crowd screamed with horror as they watched young William becoming more and more disheveled with every blow. With one final shriek, the moorcrawler raised its right arm up and released a heavy blow across William's cheek, taking a chunk of his face off in the process. With this final strike, William's world faded to black.

***

"William!" screamed Eric, looking down helplessly as William was torn to shreds by the monster. It was like his world was in slow motion. This couldn't really be happening. It couldn't. Maud held him back as he tried to climb over the barrier and into the arena. There was nothing he could do. William was gone.

***

Sir August watched on in horror as William was being demolished by the moorcrawler.

"Let me in!" demanded August, slamming the gate in anger.

"I'm sorry, but I can't do that," said the rector. Sir August reached out, grabbing the rector by the throat and pinning him up against the bars behind him.

"Let. Me. In!" demanded Sir August. As the rector gasped for breath, a pair of guards started pulling at Sir August's shoulders to make him release the man. August ignored them, easily overpowering them and slamming the rector up against the bars even harder.

"Where is the key?!" bellowed August.

"M... m... my p-pocket!" croaked the rector, feebly reaching for the key in his pocket as he was choked by the giant knight. August grabbed the key from the rector's hand, throwing him down to the ground and turning back to the padlock on the gate. When he looked up, he knew it was already too late. William lay on the ground completely motionless, the moorcrawler staring down over him curiously like a cat with a mouse. August's shoulders slumped in defeat. With the key halfway into the lock, he felt goosebumps run down his arms. He released a cry of fury and frustration, punching the gate roughly as the reality dawned on him. It was over. He'd failed.

***

Ash danced in the air as the world crumbled around them. The walls collapsed in the storm as only the final, fundamental pieces of him remained. William lay in his bed, coughing up mouthfuls of blood which spilled down into his sheets, leaving them a slick, crimson mess beneath him as he twisted and churned in agony. Annemarie placed a hand on his cheek and looked down over him with a deafeningly blank expression on her beautiful face. William tried to speak, but all that came out was a mouthful of blood, erupting from his mouth and down his chin.

"You're dying," said Annemarie quietly, still with her hand on his cheek as she sat on the side of his deathbed. He watched as she lifted her gaze to the window, her empty stare falling on the storm raging outside. She held up her hand and watched as it too, began to be blown away, just like everything else. Her skin was falling away into motes of dust, blown into the storm.

"You're dying too…" coughed William, a wry smile appearing on his face as he watched her looking down at her hand. Without moving her head, her gaze shifted up to stare him in the eyes.

"Am I?" she asked, looking over at the wardrobe which despite showing signs of degradation was still standing strong. William continued to cough through his broken ribs, staring up at her pretty face.

"If I die, you die with me…" murmured William. Annemarie sat up straight and let out a sigh. She shrugged.

"Who knows?" she asked flatly, standing up and walking over to the window, gazing out of it with her hands held casually behind her back.

"We'll soon find out," gargled William, coughing another mouthful of blood down over his chest.

"What about your friends? Your family?" asked Annemarie, not looking away from the window. William's expression darkened as he thought back to Eric. Even his family back home in Lakhdorian flashed before his eyes. Aunt Genevieve, digging away in her garden. Uncle Wilton, churning away at his green cheese. Little Sasha, with her nose buried deep in a book. Even Maud and Gerald made an appearance. Sir August too. William let out a dull sigh.

"They're better off without me," he said earnestly.

"Are you sure?" asked Annemarie cryptically. William snapped his head back up to look at her as a sick feeling erupted in his stomach.

"What do you mean?" he asked, trying his best to sit more upright in his bed, but immediately having the pain from his chest erupt over his body and send him back down.

"Can't you feel them?" asked Annemarie, slowly walking back over to his bed and sitting beside him.

"Look," she said, placing a hand over his eyes, encouraging him to close them. For a moment, all William saw was darkness, but then he felt it. He was connected to something. It was like he was connected to a hive mind. He could feel moorcrawlers. There must've been thirty of them. They were encroaching on the arena, unseen in the dead of night as all eyes were on William gargling his final breaths. They were being drawn to something that was glowing like a beacon within Eric's very own pocket.

"No..." murmured William.

"They were some of his first creations. So rudimentary," said Annemarie.

Suddenly another vision filled William's mind. He was in some kind of butchering room. Meat hung on all of the walls, dangling from hooks, and hanging on racks. The floor was covered with blood, entrails, and meat too. A cacophony of moans, wails and screams filled William's ears. As he looked around the grotesque scene, he suddenly realized what was actually happening here. The meat was people. They hung from hooks, some dead, others not. Most were missing limbs, others sat entirely, or half vivisected, organs partially removed or missing as they bled out, their innards mixing with the steadily growing carpet lining the floor of the room.

"It began with a simple idea," echoed Annemarie's voice. Suddenly the door of the dungeon crashed open, and what William beheld entering through it earned from him a whimper of horror. The creature that entered seemed to be made entirely of exposed flesh and bones. It had a disgusting tangled web of nonsensical appendages that it used to struggle its way into the room. It looked eight feet tall at least, and its fleshy mass of a body could barely be squeezed through the door. Grotesque tumorous pustules across its body burst as it forced itself through the narrow passageway. Kicking and screaming within some of its more hand-like appendages were two beaten and bloodied men. What remained of their outfits seemed to bear the sigils of knightly orders.

William gasped in horror as he watched them flailing about feebly within the vile appendages of the horrendous monster that was holding them.

"What if we could create more of ourselves?" asked Annemarie's voice.

The creature threw the two men down on the butcher's table, pressing them up against one another roughly and comparing the lengths of their limbs. The two men were of quite similar dimensions. The monster seemed pleased. One of its bonier appendages was suddenly brandished above the men. Before they could even react, it had begun hacking and sawing roughly away at their extremities. As the two men shrieked in agony, William covered his eyes and ears, curling up into a ball in the corner next to another half alive victim of the disgusting monstrosity.

"It didn't work of course, but what he did create was something new. Neither human, nor us," said Annemarie as the vision faded back to black, and William was once again being shown the moorcrawlers as they stalked through the night, encroaching ever closer to the arena.

"Stop!" cried out William desperately. The vision ended and he was brought back to reality, lying in his deathbed with Annemarie looking down over him. What little remained of the room would be blown away like the rest of this world in mere moments.

"Stop? I can't stop them. They've been waiting here for their master to return for all these years. They've been drawn out of hiding by a power that was stolen from him and sealed within a certain stone..." said Annemarie, unable to hide a smile that appeared on her face as William realized that she was talking about the Rothmane trinket that Eric had in his very pocket.

"Please, you have to stop them!" begged William desperately as he fathomed the mortal peril Eric was mere moments away from facing. Annemarie let out a sigh.

"These simple creatures may have mistaken me for him, but alas, I have no control over them," said Annemarie nonchalantly, patting William on the cheek.

"Please, stop them," said William, tears rolling from his eyes as he envisioned Eric being torn apart by those horrendous monsters.

"How am I to stop them if I'm stuck out here? You won't let me in," explained Annemarie, gesturing around at the ever-diminishing world around them. William closed his eyes, trying to hold back his tears of defeat. She'd done it. She'd won. He couldn't take it. The idea of Eric still being plagued by the remnants of William's presence even after his death. He couldn't die knowing that Eric was mere minutes away from suffering the same fate as him.

"Fine," said William dejectedly. Annemarie tilted her head, looking down at him searchingly.

"Say it properly," she said, her expression darkening, the glee of being able to twist this memorable quote of Annemarie's to its evil bidding evident on her face.

"I'll let you in, but you have to promise to save them. Save them all," said William. Annemarie beamed with joy as she began to assume her terrifying monstrous form. Once again, it was as though she was formed entirely of shadow. Her hair turned black, and her foot long dark claws extended out menacingly. Her eyes glowed that familiar deep red as a tangled web of shadowy tendrils extended all around her like wings.

"Oh, but I have so much to accomplish," she said, beginning to float menacingly over William's limp body.

"I'll only let you in if you promise to kill them. Every last one," said William as he began to lose consciousness.

"Nothing would bring me more joy," said Annemarie, beginning to slowly float down onto William. As his world faded to black, the last thing he saw was that horrendous, bastardized rendition of Annemarie's beautiful face as it lowered down on top of him with a twisted, evil grin.

***

"Have this man arrested!" demanded the rector, pointing at Sir August. The guards looked between the two of them for a moment, not sure of exactly what to do.

"It looked like the rector tripped to me," said Kane suddenly, from behind Sir August. The rector gaped his mouth silently, trying to find the words to protest what Kane was saying.

"Wouldn't you agree, boys?" asked Kane. The guards exchanged a glance, looking at the two enormous knights of legend standing before them. They both nodded in agreement, stepping away from the rector.

"What?! This is preposterous! An outrage! An assault has been committed!" spluttered the rector.

"Wait..." said Sir August suddenly. He was looking through the bars at William. Kane had seen it too. William had moved. He was still alive. Kane joined August by his side, as he stood looking through the bars his expression darkened.

"Hurry now, lion," said Kane quietly. August suddenly snapped back to reality, fumbling for the key and inserting it into the padlock hurriedly. Hope wasn't lost. Not yet.

***

As Eric sobbed uncontrollably, holding onto the bars and staring down at his dear dead friend, Maud and Gerald tried their best to console him. The audience was abuzz with concerned chatter, all moved by what they'd just witnessed.

"He didn't deserve this! He didn't deserve any of it!" cried Eric, tears streaming down his face as he stared at William's maimed corpse. Maud was crying too much herself to be able to effectively console him, continuing to simply rub his back comfortingly.

"We know sweetheart. We know," she managed to stammer. The moorcrawler lingered over him, staring down at his face curiously, tilting its head like a fox listening for a rodent under the snow.

Suddenly, inexplicably, the strong smell of tansies mixed with some kind of rancid odor erupted over the entire arena. Eric stopped crying, his memories of the last time he smelled this concoction flooding back into his mind.

William's eyes snapped back open, and his head tilted up to look at the moorcrawler. Before it had a chance to react, with its grip on his arms now released, William reached straight up into its face, inserting his fingers deep into its eye sockets. The moorcrawler let out a gut churning shriek as William tightened his grip, pulling down the creature's face with brutal force and throwing it down into the mud. As he slid his legs out from under the beast, he lifted his other hand and pressed down on the back of its head, pressing its face down into the ground as he got up onto his feet. The audience watched on in a stunned silence, nobody knowing quite what they were witnessing. Once on his feet, William stamped down hard on the back of the moorcrawler's head, again plunging its face roughly down into the dirt and breaking its jaw. It let out a garbled shriek as its limbs flailed around desperately.

"What is he... how is he..." stammered Eric. William took a step back from the moorcrawler, giving it a chance to ready itself for a counterattack. With another shriek, it launched itself straight at him. William ducked down, picking up the longsword from the ground and readying it in anticipation. With extraordinary speed he raised the sword up directly towards the moorcrawler, which was still in midair from its leap. It was unable to adjust its course, barreling straight down into the blade and releasing a shriek of pain.

"He's... he's doing it!" exclaimed Gerald excitedly. The crowd was beginning to erupt into a dull applause as they witnessed what William was somehow managing to pull off. He followed through the attack, charging forwards with the moorcrawler impaled on his blade, carrying the monster toppling over backwards with his momentum and planting its back on the floor. William shoved down hard on the blade, impaling the monster to the ground. It shrieked and flailed about like a bug on its back, its many hands reaching for the sword impaling it into the ground, but not being able to reach it.

***

As August and Kane burst into the arena, August immediately went to run to William's aid, but Kane grabbed him by the arm, holding him back.

"The battle isn't over yet," warned Kane, looking at the scene before them.

William's head snapped up to look at them. His eyes looked to be a deep black, with a dull crimson depth to them. The eye on the damaged half of his face was so bloodied that it was hard to see, but he was clearly staring straight at the two knights menacingly. An insidious grin appeared on William's broken face as he stared at them. August held out a hand.

"Okay, you've done it. It's over… just… try to relax now…" he said, feeling that same darkness in William that he'd seen during their first sparring match. William turned away from the moorcrawler which was flailing its limbs pathetically on the floor, still impaled to the spot. He looked over the weapons rack, tilting his head curiously as he surveyed each of the weapons on it. August looked around at the crowd who were going wild, cheering for William. They clearly hadn't sensed it yet. They weren't feeling that churning in their gut like he was.

"Keep your guard up," said Kane suddenly, now having his own sword drawn and at the ready. August nodded, realizing that Kane had sensed it too. Something wasn't right. There was a feeling in the air that August couldn't quite put his finger on. It was a subtle feeling of dread creeping into his heart, but it didn't feel like it was because of the monster. William picked up a spear from the weapon rack, holding it out in one hand and assessing it with a tilted head as he slowly made his way back over towards the impaled creature. August felt relief flow through him as he watched William preparing to end this. So why was it, with the battle all but won, that he could still not shake this uneasy feeling?

William slowly lowered the spear down onto the moorcrawler's exposed belly. The crowd was going wild, waiting for him to make his final blow to finish the fight. He dragged the spear lightly across the creature's belly until suddenly he started to dig into its flesh, twisting his spear as it entered into its abdomen. The monster squirmed and writhed on the ground as the spear penetrated deeper into its body. The crowd erupted, cheering for William as he finally ended the battle, but he wasn't done yet. He pulled the spear out, running it down its belly again before piercing once again into its abdomen, creating a fresh wound to torment the moorcrawler. It continued to writhe helplessly in agony on the floor at the mercy of William. Some of the cheers from the crowd were beginning to die down a little as they began to realize what they were actually watching.

"Come on William. It's time to end this," yelled August uneasily, looking around at the crowd.

William suddenly pulled the spear up, slashing it down across the wrist of one of the moorcrawler's arms, chopping its hand clean off. He didn't register August's words at all, continuing to walk around the moorcrawler, watching it struggle and squirm. He suddenly slashed out again, chopping off an arm this time. The creature squealed as it was slowly disassembled. William continued around the monster like this, making minor cuts and lacerations, slowly cutting off more and more of its appendages as his expression grew darker and darker.

"William…" said August, looking around at the crowd who were by now growing mostly silent. William suddenly squatted down by its head, putting his own face up against it and staring it in the eyes. He stared into its black eye sockets, watching as it squirmed and moaned from its torture. It was only now that the crowd drew entirely silent. As the monster's limbs continued to bleed out, the writhing finally began to cease. As William stood up, August raised his eyebrows with surprise. The expression on William's face was not one of excitement, or sadistic glee. He looked disappointed. With one final brutal slash from his spear, he beheaded the monster. As sporadic applause slowly began to break out again, there was largely silence over the arena as everybody came to terms with the sadistic display that they'd just been witness to. Despite the creature being a monster from the gateway, most of the crowd didn't seem sure whether to applaud or not. Sir August let out a sigh, wanting to lower his sword, yet an instinct incited him to keep it readied. The fight was over. William had won. So why was it that he still couldn't shake that feeling in his gut that something wasn't quite right?

CHAPTER THIRTY-FOUR

The Bleaklands Massacre

William was looking down at his arms, tensing his muscles and flexing his hands, staring down curiously as though assessing his own body for the first time. He could feel the power of the monster coursing through his chest, healing him and repairing his body into a state that it could better puppeteer.

"Well... you've done it... but you need to get those wounds looked at," said August. William snapped his head up and tilted it, looking at August and Kane curiously. He pulled his sword out of the moorcrawler with his right hand before walking directly towards them, now holding two weapons.

"William..." said August, readying his sword, once more feeling that animalistic killing intent from the boy. William ignored him, continuing closer, his expression darkening back to that sadistic visage of war that August had seen behind his eyes before.

"Hey!" exclaimed August, watching as William continued to close the gap between them, his pace growing by the moment. Kane looked between William and August searchingly, clearly not sure of why William was suddenly turning on them.

"Well, ahem!" said the rector suddenly from behind the two knights, entering the arena to address the crowd.

"The boy has done it! He's successfully defeated the monster! But as you can see, he's-" began the rector.

William suddenly leaped forwards towards the two knights with his spear raised in the air above him. Both Kane and August jumped backwards, narrowly avoiding William's spear as it penetrated the ground beneath them.

"What are you-?!" August began to yell, before suddenly he heard it. A screech erupted from under the ground beneath William's spear and the earth began to churn. A moorcrawler had been burrowing beneath their feet, and it had been mere inches away from reaching them. As William's spear pierced down through the ground and into the creature's back it screamed, hurriedly bursting out of the ground and up into the arena. The rector cried out in horror, falling over backwards as he beheld the new threat that had appeared. The two knights readied themselves, standing defensively between the rector and the monster. William seemed to be assessing himself again, completely ignoring the moorcrawler, appearing to have considered this a simple test of his own strength.

"Run!" exclaimed August without taking his eyes off of the new monster. The crowd seemed unsure of what to do, uncertain of whether this was all part of the show or not. The rector tried to scramble to his feet, but suddenly a hand erupted from under the ground, grabbing a hold of his ankle.

"Richard!" shouted August.

"On it," said Kane, turning and dashing to the rector's aid. As the monster in front of August prepared to charge, William suddenly dived at it preemptively, slashing down at it with his longsword and pulling his spear from its back at the same time. August watched on in confusion as the boy with half of his face missing and several clearly broken ribs continued fighting as though he was unscathed. Suddenly screams began to erupt from the audience as more moorcrawlers began to burst up from the ground in the arena. Just where could they possibly be coming from, and how many would there be?!

***

Eric stood with his face pressed up against the bars, staring down at the scene unfolding in the arena. Multiple moorcrawlers were beginning to emerge from the ground. He could tell by a single glance at William that he'd lost his internal battle with Annemarie. If the smell of the tansies weren't enough on its own, the sadistic display had said it all.

"Come on Eric! We have to leave, it's not safe here!" exclaimed Maud, reaching an arm out from within Gerald's protective grasp and pulling at Eric's robes.

"But William is-" began Eric, before suddenly one of the moorcrawlers from down in the arena launched itself directly at him up in the stands. The second that it collided with the arena bars, they immediately came loose, toppling aside and leaving a clear opening between Eric and the moorcrawler. Eric fell backwards in surprise, and the audience began screaming, realizing that the crudely erected bars had never actually been keeping them safe at all. Despite scrambling for a moment as the bars fell away, the moorcrawler continued its attack, grabbing onto the edge of the stands and leaping straight at Eric's face with its arms outstretched. Suddenly, out of nowhere, Azalea dove between Eric and the monster, holding her shield up to knock it back before stabbing straight over the top and into its face, her bastard sword entering through the beast's mouth and exploding out of the back of its skull. With a gargled shriek it fell back down into the arena.

"Get up Rothmane!" yelled Azalea commandingly. Immediately two more moorcrawlers jumped up towards the gap in the bars from down in the arena, clinging onto the side of the stands and leaping up towards Azalea.

"Dame Aza-" began Eric, getting to his feet.

"Run!" she exclaimed, crouching down to defend an attack from one of the crawlers which crunched loudly against her shield. As Azalea stabbed back at the monsters, Eric heard screams erupt from behind him in the stands. He turned to look back, his mouth dropping with shock when he did.

"Look out!" cried Eric, seeing a moorcrawler hurrying over the stands, throwing people aside as it scrambled directly towards him. Eric grabbed Maud and Gerald, roughly pulling them back behind him as the moorcrawler dove straight over the stands towards him. A crossbow bolt suddenly shot straight through the side of the moorcrawler's head, interrupting its motion and causing it to be knocked down into the seats. The knight who had fired the bolt dropped her crossbow, pulled out a dagger and dived onto the flailing monster, driving her dagger straight through the side of its skull.

"What's going on?!" screamed Maud as she and Gerald tried to get back up onto their feet. Eric looked around at the scene surrounding them, his stomach dropping as realization set in. They were surrounded. The monsters weren't only coming from inside the arena, but outside too. Every single angle of the arena seemed to have moorcrawlers clambering over it, tearing people apart and engaging in brutal battles with knights scattered throughout the stands. It was a massacre. There was bloodshed and battle in all directions as audience members were torn to shreds while the knights desperately tried to defend them. The terrified crowd had no safe direction to flee, trampling over one another in their attempts to find a safe place to run to, making things even worse. How had this happened, and what was he supposed to do here?!

Without warning, the battle that Azalea was locked in suddenly escalated as yet another moorcrawler burst up through the poorly constructed bars, sending them crashing down all around. One of the stray bars came barreling straight down towards Maud and Gerald. Gerald pulled Maud beneath him, taking the full brunt of the blow straight to his head. He immediately collapsed straight down onto the floor, completely unconscious.

***

The monster dived at August, but he charged back at it defensively, holding his longsword above his head and slicing down as he slid under the monster, his blade slicing cleanly through the skull and even deep into the torso of the beast. He didn't have a moment to waste however, as another moorcrawler grabbed at his leg from the side. He continued his swipe downwards, slicing through the arm of the new moorcrawler which shrieked, jumping up at him with its remaining limbs outstretched aggressively. He spun around to face it, swiping back upwards in time to slice cleanly through the neck of his new attacker.

"Behind!" yelled Kane, still locked in his own battle with multiple moorcrawlers. August, still squatting down at this point, spun around, falling down onto his back and holding his sword upwards as yet another moorcrawler dove at him from behind. As his sword pierced straight into its belly, he rolled over, pulling his sword out through the side of the monster's torso in the process. Now lying face down, a hand suddenly erupted from the ground beneath him, grabbing him by his neck and pulling him down into the earth. There was no angle for him to be able to reach the hand with his sword, so he let go of his blade, hurriedly reaching down for the dagger in his boot. The second that he managed to find its hilt, he brought it up to his throat and drew it straight through the wrist of the monster. There was a shriek from underground and the grip around his neck immediately loosened. August reared back up onto his knees, throwing the hand aside and looking up as he gasped for breath. He suddenly saw that William was standing above him, staring down over him. Without breaking eye contact with August, William suddenly spun his spear around, placing it under his armpit and bracing himself so that the point of the spear extended up into the air behind his back. At that very moment a moorcrawler came flying at him, being struck in the face by the spear and shrieking in pain, tumbling off to William's side. William spun the spear back around and shoved it directly into the creature's neck, causing it to gargle blood which erupted from its mouth. How was this boy fighting these creatures without even looking at them? How did he seem to know where they were before August did?

Kane suddenly came flying down between the two of them, locked in a melee with a moorcrawler. He'd lost his sword at some point during the fight and now fought unarmed against the monster. As he landed beneath the moorcrawler, he reached up and grabbed it by the throat, squeezing tightly. With brute strength, he dug his fingers straight through a wound in the monster's flesh and clutched its esophagus, tearing it out through its throat and showering himself in blood. He threw the moorcrawler's body aside as August too, got to his feet, extending a hand to help Kane up. Kane accepted his hand, suddenly looking over August's shoulder and launching straight back into action. He dove straight towards a moorcrawler which was encroaching on August from behind, punching it hard across the face, dislocating its jaw and sending it toppling down sideways. He immediately jumped on the creature, closing an arm around its neck and twisting abruptly, breaking its neck with an audible crunch. August cast his gaze to William, who was now standing in the middle of the arena with his eyes closed. He had a smile on his face as he breathed in deeply, seemingly drinking in the atmosphere. The moorcrawlers were avoiding him entirely now. As they scurried about, they kept a wide berth around him and never dared tread close. Just what was the darkness that lingered within that boy, and what kind of threat might it actually pose?

***

William opened his eyes, looking around at the world of darkness that surrounded him. Where was he? At first he thought that he was completely shrouded by darkness, but then he noticed a single thin keyhole shaped beam of light. He pressed his eye up against it, peering through. He immediately felt goosebumps run down his arms at what he saw. Through the keyhole he could see his bedroom, but something was different. The entire room was covered in enormous, vein-like black tendrils which spiraled and spread their way over the floor, ceiling and every wall of the room. Between them extended a thick red glowing skin-like membrane that pulsated and crept over every inch of the room. Suddenly, an eyeball appeared in the keyhole, looking back through at him. William jumped back in shock.

"You're locked in here with me now..." whispered that disgusting, distorted voice that had been echoing in his mind when Annemarie had been sick.

"Let me out," demanded William, banging on the wardrobe door. He suddenly felt something slick and tendril-like wrap around his throat in the darkness. He reached for it, trying to pull away at it, but it was far too strong. Tendrils rubbed over every inch of his body in the darkness, tightening and binding around him firmly.

"Let me out!" screamed William.

"You will watch…" whispered the voice, as the tendrils pressed his face back up against the keyhole. The room through the keyhole began to swirl and change, now revealing the arena in the real world. It was in utter chaos. Knights fought with moorcrawlers in all directions, as terrified townsfolk tried to flee, being torn apart by moorcrawlers and trampling one another in their futile efforts to escape. Each knight was outnumbered, trying their best to fight off the monsters but being unable to save everybody, while the moorcrawlers ripped apart the defenseless townsfolk.

"Look…" whispered the voice in William's ear. The view suddenly turned to look down at August and Kane who were desperately trying to fight off three moorcrawlers each, as both men began to run out of stamina.

"Help them!" begged William.

"No," whispered back the voice, continuing to stand still as it watched the carnage escalating in the arena. One of the moorcrawlers suddenly got the better of Sir August, managing to grab one of his legs and pull it hard, bringing the knight crashing down onto the floor.

"You told me that you'd kill them! You have to kill them!" screamed William desperately.

"I've changed my mind," whispered back the voice, this time chuckling slightly with glee. Kane dove onto the back of the moorcrawler that had a hold on Sir August. He pulled a dagger out from his belt and began rapidly stabbing into the side of the throat of the moorcrawler, causing it to release its grip on Sir August as it began to gargle blood.

"You said that you'd help them!" screamed William again, watching as a moorcrawler jumped on Kane's back, pulling him away from Sir August.

"I already tried that. It was boring. Their suffering is far too shallow. This is so much more fun..." whispered back the voice. Before William could respond, the view suddenly tilted back up and around to face Eric. Through his monstrous eyes, William could see a moorcrawler creeping up the side of the arena beside Eric. All of the nearby knights were too distracted with their battles to have noticed it.

"Stop it!" begged William desperately. The voice simply began to laugh as the moorcrawler drew closer.

"You have to stop it!" yelled William, pounding his forehead against the door of the wardrobe feebly. All he could do was look helplessly at Eric, who had his back to William, huddled around something that he couldn't see. Why wasn't he running? Why was he just sitting there like a lamb to the slaughter?

***

"Gerald!" cried Eric, shaking him to try and wake him up.

"Oh no, please no..." stammered Maud, staring into her husband's unconscious eyes.

"I think he's just..." Eric stopped mid-sentence, suddenly hearing something behind him. He looked over his shoulder just in time to see the moorcrawler descending on him.

"Quick! Get down!" cried Eric, pulling Maud on top of Gerald and covering both of them with his body. Instantly he felt a searing pain down his back as the moorcrawler slashed down at him with its inhuman strength, its fingers digging a gash across his back. He cried out in pain but kept his guard over Maud and Gerald.

"Eric!" screamed Maud. Eric shook his head and stayed where he was. He wasn't going to move. He needed to protect them no matter what.

***

William watched the brutal slash across Eric's back and screamed out in horror.

"Stop! Please, stop!" screamed William desperately as he watched the moorcrawler preparing for another attack while the nearby knights were all too distracted to run to Eric's aid. The dark voice laughed, delighting in William's despair. What was Eric doing?! Why was he just sitting there like that?! The moorcrawler suddenly released another brutal slash with both of its front hands down on Eric, leaving enormous streaks of red exposed flesh down his back. Eric reeled back from the attack, being pulled up momentarily by the impact, and screaming in pain, but that's when William noticed it. There, curled up beneath Eric, were Maud and Gerald. It was like William's world stopped for a moment, as he stared open mouthed at the scene, a whirlpool of emotions churning in his chest. Why were they here? Despite how much they worried about him and didn't want him to be in this stupid fight, they'd come anyway. They'd come all this way, for William. They'd come here to support him, and they were going to die for it. Just like his parents had. Just like the gypsies had, and just like Eric was about to. Everybody who tried to support him died, and there was nothing he could do to stop it. The tendrils tightened once more, pressing his face hard up against the keyhole while its grotesque voice continued to chuckle at him. William felt his muscles beginning to tense up with fury. He couldn't let this happen. Not again.

"This is my body..." said William, closing his eyes as rage swelled in his chest.

"This is my life…" he continued, balling his fists up in the darkness of the wardrobe.

"And I'm sick of watching you destroy it…" continued William, his anger boiling over more and more as the faces of everybody this monster had hurt flashed before his eyes. Annemarie's laughing stopped, and she began breathing heavily. She ducked down, placing her eye up to the keyhole, looking in at him.

"You let me in! I am in control now! You've lost!" said the monster furiously.

"If I really let you in, then why is the key still in my pocket?" asked William, suddenly unleashing all of his might to break free of the tendrils in the darkness. Immediately the creature in the dark released a bloodcurdling shriek as William felt it flailing around behind him. He had to retake control. He had to. This was his body. This was his life, and it was time for him to take it back.

He grabbed the key out of his pocket and began lifting it towards the keyhole. As the tendrils in the darkness once again began to wrap around him, he cried out with exertion, trying his hardest to raise his arm up. The monster continued squealing, while Annemarie paced back and forth outside the wardrobe furiously.

William let out one final burst of rage and exertion, finally managing to rip his arm free of the tendrils. He slotted the key into the keyhole from the inside, twisting it roughly and feeling the telltale clack of the door unlatching. As soon as it did, he pressed up against it with all of his might, tumbling out and falling onto his corrupted bedroom floor. Annemarie immediately released an ear-piercing shriek, flying down towards him with her claws outstretched. William hurriedly got up onto his feet, reaching out and grabbing her by the neck preemptively. With another deafening shriek, she pierced all of her claws up through William's torso. The pain shot through every inch of his ethereal body, but he held on tight, grimacing through the agony as he managed to tighten his grip around her neck. As the two of them wrestled against one another, that familiar red mist started oozing back out of the wardrobe.

"You fool! You've opened the door! Now you can never win!" screamed Annemarie in William's face, cackling maniacally as she gained strength from the red liquid-like smoke that was escaping the wardrobe and flowing into her. She used the invigoration to push William back, pressing him up against the far wall of his bedroom. He grunted with exertion, focusing with all of his might to keep his hands wrapped around her neck.

"You're just a filthy parasite! This isn't your body! This isn't your life!" screamed William, managing to push himself off from the wall and get some more ground, edging Annemarie back towards the wardrobe.

"I won't let them die! I'll save them, no matter what it takes!" cried William, continuing to press his position against the ever-growing strength of the monster before him.

"Without me you're dead! You only still breathe due to my power!" screeched Annemarie, pressing back against William.

"You think you're the one in control here?! You think that you're the one keeping me alive?!" asked William, pressing back against her with all of his might.

"This is my body, and if I die, you die too. That makes you, my prisoner," yelled William, finally managing to push Annemarie all the way back against the wardrobe, slamming the doors shut behind her as he pressed her up against them. She shrieked, and so too did the red mist which was sealed back inside. It smashed against the inside of the wardrobe, banging and pounding furiously from within as William pressed Annemarie up against its doors, continuing to tighten his grip on her throat.

"How?!" she gasped, his grip now tight enough to be asphyxiating her. He slowly pressed her down until she was gagging for breath on the floor of his bedroom. He loomed over her staring down hatefully into her eyes.

"As long as you are in my body, you are my slave. Now, you're going to help me save them, or I'll make sure we both die here together," said William with absolute conviction, as he stared down into the monster's red eyes which for the first time, were filled with fear.

***

"Rothmane!" screamed Azalea, wanting to run to his aid but having a moorcrawler jump onto her back viciously at just that moment. She screamed with exertion, jumping backwards into the stands and crushing the creature against the chairs. As its grip faltered, she spun around, releasing a deft swipe from her sword, slicing its head clean off.

As she once again started running towards Eric, another moorcrawler dove at her from the seats above her in the stands. She deflected it with her shield, turning around and following its trajectory down into a row of seats, stabbing down into its neck with her sword. She didn't waste a moment, continuing her momentum to spin back around to face Eric. She once again charged towards him, before a moorcrawler which had climbed its way up from the arena suddenly dove towards her, catching her by surprise and sending her crashing into the stands beside her. As the creature growled in her face, she managed to twist her blade up, screaming with exertion as she slid it up into the creature's belly. It shrieked in agony, releasing a hail of panicked blows down on her as it found itself impaled on her blade. She yelled out with exertion again, pulling the blade all the way up to its throat, gutting the beast above her and showering herself in its entrails. Its motionless body collapsed down over her, pinning her to the floor. She struggled as best she could beneath the creature, but it was too heavy for her to move. She looked through the carnage over at Eric desperately, just in time to see the moorcrawler rearing up for one final blow. Eric was already barely conscious, losing huge amounts of blood down his back. There was no way that he would survive this next strike. He was doomed.

Just as the moorcrawler was beginning its swipe down for its last attack, a spear suddenly flew up at an incredible speed, piercing straight through the back of the creature's head and exploding out the other side. Azalea looked down into the arena, seeing William standing there, somehow still conscious with half of his face missing and blood pooling on his chest. Despite all of this he'd somehow managed to throw that spear in time to save Eric. The moorcrawler was dead before it hit the floor, collapsing down behind Eric as he too finally lost consciousness, still protecting Maud and Gerald beneath him. The crossbow wielding knight from earlier suddenly appeared beside Azalea, helping her to flip the moorcrawler off of her and extending a hand to help her up.

"Thank you, Maggie!" exclaimed Azalea, accepting the helping hand before readying her shield and sword and looking around for the next moorcrawler.

"I think that's the last of them up here for now!" replied Dame Margaret, also looking around to see if there was anybody else left to save. Azalea cast her gaze down to the arena and her jaw dropped at what she saw. Kane and August were standing within a ring of bodies and carnage with the rector cowering between them.

They were both still locked in combat with one final moorcrawler each. The two legendary knights had clearly lived up to their reputations, but they both looked utterly exhausted. Azalea noticed a third and final moorcrawler rearing up for an attack from behind August that he'd clearly not noticed.

"August!" she yelled out desperately. Suddenly William, who had just picked up a longsword from the ground, swung it up from a weary fool's guard stance, over-exerting himself and screaming with pain as his broken ribs were clearly crushed by the exertion. His blade just managed to pierce through the moorcrawler's torso enough to interrupt its attack. August spun around, stabbing down into the moorcrawler to finish it off before looking at William who was beginning to stumble. The boy looked around, clearly searching for any more targets, and upon seeing none, collapsed roughly towards the ground. August just managed to catch him in time, lowering him down gently to rest.

Azalea looked around the stands, searching for any remaining moorcrawlers. Up in the aristocrat's section, it looked like Sir Ivar and Prince Alexander had managed to keep everybody safe, watching as Alexander beheaded the final moorcrawler that remained up there. All over the rest of the stands, knights were scattered throughout, having fought valiantly to protect as many of the audience members as they could. They were all still holding guard, searching for threats. A strange silence suddenly fell over the arena. For just a moment, there was no screaming, no crying and no sounds of combat. There was just an eerie silence as everybody collectively began to fathom that the battle was finally over. The silence remained for mere moments however, as suddenly the survivors of the massacre collectively let their guards down, exploding with the pain and emotion of having faced such a harrowing situation.

And with that, the combat trial concluded, as the knights began surveying the arena, searching through the survivors for the injured and making sure that there were no remaining threats.

CHAPTER THIRTY-FIVE
The Great Decision

"The King is furious..." said the Duke, shaking his head as he looked out the window.

"What am I to tell these people?" he asked, gesturing at the mob that had formed outside, awaiting the news from this important meeting. He looked around the room expectantly at the various knights and aristocrats who were gathered in the hall.

"After seeing the performance of the knights, support for the college has never been greater, your Grace..." piped up the chancellor, filling the awkward silence that had formed after the Duke's question. The Duke looked at him quizzically.

"How does that help?! They want answers! Are you really telling me that none of you have even the slightest clue how this happened?!" asked the Duke angrily, looking around at all of the highly ranked individuals who had played a part in the organization of the event.

"What say you Kane? You're supposed to be an expert on these creatures! How could you have let this happen?!" asked the Duke, raising his eyebrows at Kane. The intimidating behemoth of a knight stared back at him darkly, the fresh wounds on his face making him look even more imposing than usual. The Duke swallowed nervously, clearly too intimidated by the man to continue this line of questioning. One of the viper knights suddenly spoke up.

"We know that they couldn't have followed us here from the desert. These creatures are too afraid of sunlight to travel out in the open for all that way. They'd have never been able to keep up with us traveling only by night," they reported earnestly.

"Oh please, where else could they have possibly come from?!" asked the Duke. Somebody cleared their throats from the audience of aristocrats.

"Perhaps I can shed some light on that, your Grace," said Viscount Terrowin, standing up.

"For the past month we in the Bleaklands have been suffering from cattle mutilations," he began, looking around the crowd.

"After seeing the wounds inflicted by those monsters during the Bleaklands massacre, we believe that it was in fact these very same creatures that have been attacking our cattle," explained the Viscount.

"How could you have not come to me about this?!" asked the Duke angrily.

"I did your Grace! You told me that a few dead cows were not worthy of your attention!" defended the Viscount desperately.

"Pah!" the Duke waved away the Viscount's claim without providing any counter evidence.

"Ahem, there is a rather important matter to attend to. One to which the crowd outside are quite invested..." said the rector, standing up. The Duke let out a sigh.

"Yes, indeed. The boy," he said, sinking deep into thought.

"Considering the way that he behaved in that arena, I don't think that it would be appropriate for him to have a place in the college..." said the rector earnestly.

"The way he behaved?! You mean saving lives?! Slaying monsters?! What part of that doesn't sound knightly to you?!" asked Dame Azalea, standing to her feet to defend William.

"Now, now!" said the Duke, holding out a hand to restore order as the crowd began to murmur amongst themselves.

"The lady knight here does have a point. He has become somewhat of a hero to the survivors of the massacre. They all saw his inappropriate behavior during his trial, yes, but they also saw him slaying those monsters and saving lives. This is quite the divisive matter, and thus we must approach it delicately," explained the Duke.

"Who here has reason to speak against the boy becoming a squire?" asked the Duke, looking around the room. A few hands were raised.

"Beneath it all he's still a commoner! A stableboy, no less!" exclaimed an angry aristocrat from the crowd, garnering some hums of agreement. Azalea elbowed Ivar expectantly. The lazy knight let out a sigh and rolled his eyes before standing up.

"Forgive me, but I thought the point of this trial in the first place was to decide whether he had a place in the college? Has that not already been decided by the result of the battle? He survived, the monster did not. As per the rules, that makes him a squire, does it not?" asked Ivar, looking around expectantly.

"First of all..." began the Duke, looking down at Ivar.

"The King sends his regards for keeping his son safe. Your service will be rewarded duly," said the Duke, giving Sir Ivar a wry smile.

"A similar sentiment must be said for all of the knights who proved themselves worthy of their titles that night. You have proven why you are valuable, both to the crown, and to the people of

Oxgate," said the Duke, looking around at the knights who had valiantly fought against the monsters. Azalea and Ivar exchanged a triumphant glance with one another. At the very least, it seemed like the necessity for the college's taxes would no longer be under question.

"But Sir Ivar, surely you see how the boy being a commoner complicates matters. Even if we say yes, what then? Are we to hold this event again for every gong farmer and chimney sweep from here to Castellia?!" asked the Duke incredulously. The rector nodded his head in agreement with the Duke.

"It goes without saying that this event cannot be held again! Speaking on behalf of the great library, I can tell you that we still don't even know what caused those monsters to rise up, or how long they've even been here! We don't know how many more there are, or whether they will attack again! All we know is that the trial itself somehow seemed to spur on this massacre. The timing and location are too aligned for it to be a mere coincidence. On those grounds alone it must be abolished!" exclaimed the rector. The crowd broke into a murmur of approving chatter.

"We all seem to be in agreement about this at the very least. Rector, please see that it be added to the college constitution that these trials may never be held again!" decreed the Duke. The rector nodded in agreement, gesturing towards one of his aides who ran out of the room quickly to do as he was told.

"So then, what of the boy? If he were to enter the college what order would accept him? I have been told that the only order who even considered sending him an invitation after the written exam was the order of the destrier," said the Duke, looking around the crowd searchingly. A knight stood up, bowing slightly as he entered the spotlight.

"On behalf of the order of the destrier, we hereby rescind any offer which may have been presented to William Lakhdorian. After recent events, we do not believe that he would be a good fit for our order," said the knight, bowing his head again before hurriedly backing into the crowd once more. Azalea sucked her teeth and rolled her eyes in response. The Duke looked down at her quizzically.

"Do you have something to say? Would you like to extend him an offer yourself? Do you believe that he would be a suitable fit for the order of the fox?" asked the Duke, raising an eyebrow. Azalea went to respond, but then sank deep into thought before letting out a defeated sigh.

"Your Grace, I must admit that William Lakhdorian would be... ill suited... for my order," said Azalea, looking down at the ground. The Duke nodded understandingly.

"How about you Sir August? As I understand it you fought side by side with the boy. From what I've heard he may even have saved your life. He's demonstrated quite some prowess for combat, by far the most important factor for recruitment into your order. What say you?" asked the Duke, turning his attention to Sir August. The giant knight was uncharacteristically quiet, a dark expression plastering his face as he thought deeply about the question. He stood up, looking at the ground.

"I..." he began. He seemed to be struggling with his response. After a few moments he let out a defeated sigh of his own.

"On behalf of the order of the lion, I too hereby decline an invitation to William Lakhdorian. A talented fighter he may be, but he does not embody the qualities of our order," he finished, looking down regretfully. The Duke closed his eyes and nodded.

"Very well then. It would appear that even if we were to allow the boy enrollment into the college, a place for him does not exist. His atrocious exam scores exclude him from the majority of the more specialized orders, and he obviously lacks the lineage to enter the order of the drake," said the Duke, gesturing towards Sir Ivar.

"We could never send him to represent us in Castellia as a swan, nor does he have the specific skills to join the order of the wasp, or the lyre," said the Duke, looking over the room which was plunged into silence. He shrugged.

"Very well then! If there are no more objections, the boy will be denied a place within the college. He will not become a squire, nor will he-" began the Duke.

"We'll take him," said a gruff voice suddenly, earning a surprised murmur from the crowd. The Duke scoured the room and raised his eyebrows when he saw who it had come from. Kane stood from his chair, raising his chin up to stare intently at the Duke.

"My boy will keep an eye on him. He'll keep him in line," said Kane assuredly. The Duke recoiled slightly in surprise for a moment before narrowing his eyes.

"Are you sure about this?" asked the Duke. Kane nodded his head decisively in response. The Duke let out a sigh.

"Are there any objections?" asked the Duke, looking around the room of disgruntled aristocrats. Despite the disapproving chatter that had broken out in the crowd, no one dared raise their hands against Kane's offer.

"Very well then! The boy will be extended an offer to join the order of the goat! Chancellor, see to it that he receives it!" said the Duke, looking at the chancellor expectantly. The chancellor bowed his head obediently, hurriedly whispering to his aide.

"Then it has been decided. The boy will join the order of the goat!" finished the Duke, looking around the room which had erupted into divisive murmurs as the controversial order of the goat was brought into the limelight. Azalea and August gave each other a victorious glance, both thankful that William had found a place in the college, yet both filled with unease. Would it really be okay for him to be a squire? He had a lot of darkness in him, but also a lot of light. What kind of knight he became would depend entirely on the next few years of his life and how his talents were cultivated. Was the notorious order of the goat really the best place for him, or would they lead him even further astray? As the Duke continued on with the meeting, two questions lingered on everybody's minds: what kind of knight would William become, and would the goat make him, or would it break him?

***

As the sound of a songbird chirping pulled him out of the depths of his slumber, William wearily tried to open his eyes, finding that only one would open. Panic spread through his body as he remembered where he was. He tried to sit up to look around the arena, immediately feeling searing pain spreading through his chest. He moaned in pain but felt relief flow through him when he took in his surroundings. Rather than the arena, he was in some kind of hospital suite, the peaceful midday sun shining through his window as the shadows of the treetops outside danced around serenely on the windowsill. At the sound of a gasp from beside him, he craned his neck around to see who it had come from, feeling joy and relief spread through his entire body when he saw who it was.

"You're awake!" exclaimed Eric from his bed on the other side of the room. He struggled to sit up, grimacing in pain as he did.

"Hey, slow down!" croaked William, groaning slightly in pain himself from overexerting his broken ribs. The two boys chuckled at one another, both groaning with pain like old men. Eric sat up in his bed and slid his legs out from under the covers, standing up and beginning to make his way over towards William.

"Hey, stay there! Your back is hurt!" whispered William, remembering the horrendous attack the moorcrawler had unleashed on his friend.

"It's nothing compared to what you've been through!" said Eric, walking his way carefully over to William and sitting on the chair beside his bed.

"How on Earth are you even still alive?" asked Eric earnestly, casting his gaze over William's bandaged face and chest. William let out a sigh.

"I think she somehow saved me. Or... at least saved herself..." said William, placing a concerned hand over his chest as he remembered the strange feeling that had come over him when he'd lost control. Eric suddenly raised a hand expectantly over him. William looked up at Eric with his one unbandaged eye and slowly raised his hand up to match Eric's before clasping it victoriously.

"Hey," said Eric, looking down at him with a smile on his face.

"It doesn't matter how, all that matters is that somehow we did it," he said earnestly, squeezing his hand and raising his eyebrows. William looked up at him quizzically, not sure of what exactly he meant.

"Oh!" said Eric, suddenly reaching into the pocket of his hospital robes and withdrawing a scroll.

"Sorry... it came for you, but I couldn't resist..." said Eric, handing the parchment to William, who held it up and tried to read it with his one uncovered eye.

"The order of the goat?!" asked William, putting the parchment down and looking at Eric quizzically. Eric nodded his head excitedly.

"William, we're squires," said Eric excitedly. William lay back in his bed, speechless as the shock set in. They'd actually done it. Somehow, they were squires. It had been a long and painful journey, but they'd actually done it. Suddenly something occurred to him. He craned his neck back around to look at Eric.

"Where's yours?" asked William. Eric let out a sigh and shook his head.

"It's complicated…" said Eric, looking down at the ground.

"Surely you didn't actually fail that exam… did you?!" asked William.

"No! Of course I didn't! It's just… I didn't get into the order of the owl," said Eric, avoiding William's gaze.

"Well? Don't tell me you're in the order of the goat too? Whatever that is…" croaked William, grimacing in pain from talking too much. Eric laughed and shook his head.

"No brother… I'm… I'm in the order of the drake…" he said with a despondent sigh. William's head snapped back up to look at his friend in shock.

"You mean that order that you said was only for the fanciest nobles?!" asked William in surprise. Eric nodded, before letting out another sigh and slumping his shoulders.

"That's amazing!" gasped William, before groaning with pain again.

"Just relax!" said Eric, looking over William with concern.

"I just… I hope I can get the answers we need. I don't know much about this order…" said Eric, drifting off into thought.

"Hey," said William, bringing Eric's gaze back to him.

"We're squires," he said, with a beaming smile. Eric grinned in response, nodding in agreement.

"We did it," said Eric.

"We did it," agreed William. A look of concern suddenly came across Eric's face.

"And what about… you know… Annemarie?" asked Eric, his expression darkening. William closed his eyes and shook his head.

"She's gone," said William. Eric opened his eyes wide in surprise.

"Gone?!" asked Eric.

"Without a trace," confirmed William, groaning with pain. A mixture of emotions came across Eric's face before he suddenly stood from his chair.

"Sorry Will, I shouldn't be making you talk so much. Try to get some more rest and heal up fast. We've got a lot of work to do. We're squires now after all," said Eric with a wink, heading back over towards his bed. William smiled, before turning away and staring at the far corner of the room where Annemarie stood, looking back at him from the shadows.

"You lied to him," she said, with a spiteful grin. William closed his eyes and tried to ignore her. Whether he liked it or not, he was stuck with her for now. All that mattered was that Eric was safe, and not only that, but they'd succeeded in their mission. The two simple farm boys had actually managed to become squires. Would they ever actually find the answers that they were seeking? Would they find out where these monsters had come from, and what their insidious plan was with William? Would he ever manage to rid himself of his dark passenger? Their adventure was only just beginning, but as the sun shone its peaceful midday light through their hospital ward window, the boys relished in their victory so far, as short lived as it may be.

TO BE CONTINUED...

Acknowledgements

Thank you to all of the friends and family who have supported me throughout the process of writing this book. I could never have achieved the things I have without your consistent encouragement and enthusiasm.

Thank you to everybody who read my early drafts and provided me with valuable feedback all the way throughout the writing of this story. This would've been half the adventure it was without your help.

Thank you to all of the amazing musicians and artists who unwittingly provided the soundtrack and painted the scenes of this story. Your art will forever be a part of me and you inspire me to keep creating, no matter what.

ABOUT THE AUTHOR

Born in the German settlement of Hahndorf, nestled in the Adelaide hills of South Australia, Travis Kowlessar lived a childhood on the road. He and his family travelled all around the Australian continent on a wild adventure that culminated in the Daintree rainforest of far north Queensland. It was here, living in a caravan on the beach by the Daintree River, that Travis truly explored his creativity. Be it the music he passionately composed, the games he designed in his spare time, or the short films he created with his friends, Travis was obsessed with his creative endeavors. When it came time to enter University, he elected to study a bachelor's degree in game design with the vision of creating fantasy worlds and sharing them with others to explore. After graduating, he moved on to study filmmaking, and a master's degree with a thesis focused on immersion and engagement in digital games. No matter which creative outlet he explored, nothing gave him quite the same sense of creative liberty as story writing. The unfettered freedom to watch characters grow, create living worlds, and explore philosophies and emotions captivates him to this day. He dreams of a long career of sharing his stories with the world, and he greatly appreciates that you have chosen to explore them.

www.ingramcontent.com/pod-product-compliance
Lightning Source LLC
Chambersburg PA
CBHW030617250626
47154CB00006B/1822